I0819226

THE ARCANE ARTS

THE ARCANE ARTS

S. D. COVERLY

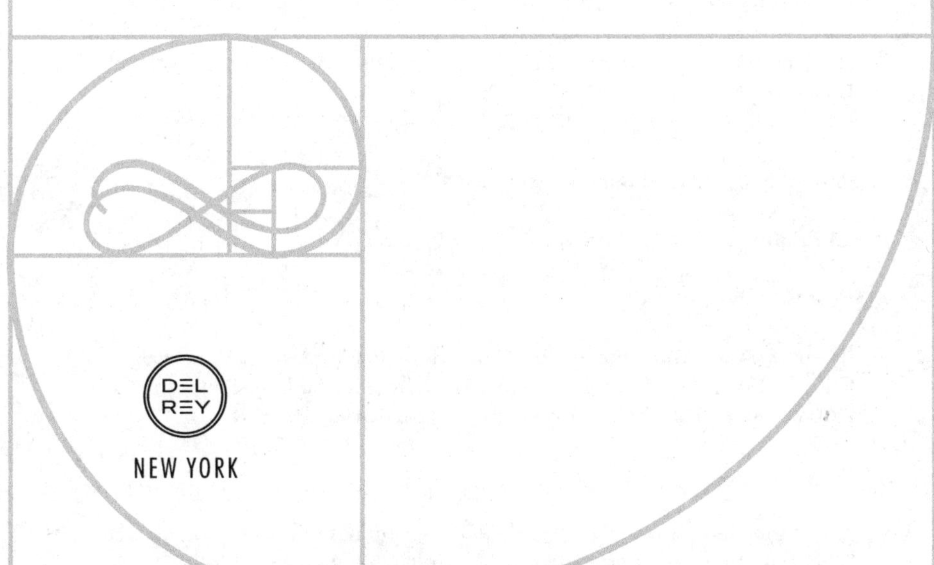

NEW YORK

Del Rey
An imprint of Random House
A division of Penguin Random House LLC
1745 Broadway, New York, NY 10019
randomhousebooks.com
penguinrandomhouse.com

Hardcover ISBN 978-0-593-97422-3
Ebook ISBN 978-0-593-97423-0
International edition ISBN 979-8-217-37466-3

Printed in the United States of America

1st Printing

First Edition

BOOK TEAM: Production editor: Cindy Berman | Managing editor: Paul Gilbert | Production manager: Angela McNally | Copy editor: Laura Jorstad | Proofreaders: Pam Rehm, Kristin Jones, Judy Kiviat

Book design by Alexis Flynn

The authorized representative in the EU for product safety and compliance is Penguin Random House Ireland, Morrison Chambers, 32 Nassau Street, Dublin D02 YH68, Ireland. https://eu-contact.penguin.ie.

"Where love rules, there is no will to power; and where power predominates, there love is lacking. The one is the shadow of the other."

—Carl Gustav Jung

THE ARCANE ARTS

PROLOGUE

Behind his white mask, the Magister frowned.

The ritual was proceeding to plan. The eight new Initiates stood around the edge of the mosaic circle on the floor with hooded black robes concealing their faces. They chanted with practiced precision, perfectly intoning the ancient syllables: "*Ex infortunio, potenter benedic nobis.*"

The male voices echoed pleasantly through the underground chamber, reverberating through air thick with the scents of incense and myrrh.

Within the mosaic circle, the elementals of the ritual were evenly spaced, each given a specific position corresponding to a Fibonacci spiral. The gold ingots had melted into a liquid that was bubbling happily, the powdered bones were swirling in fractal patterns, and the horsehair figurines sizzled before bursting into flame.

But the fourth elemental—the most important part of the induction, positioned at the crux of the Fibonacci spiral—wasn't behaving properly. It wriggled and grunted and cursed, refusing to cooperate. Which was why the Magister was not pleased.

The girl was bound and gagged. The cuffs had a practical purpose: to keep her in the correct spot, the mathematical center of the room, where she would act as a focal point for the energies unleashed by the ritual. But the *manner* in which her hands were tied to her feet, painfully bending and contorting her body, had the added benefit of heightening her terror and discomfort. That was important.

The Magister was not a cruel man. Or rather, his cruelty was practical. The power of the ceremony was contingent upon the emotional state of the sacrifice; they would only extract fortune for their own lives in proportion to what she surrendered in this moment. Which meant that they needed pain. Fear. *Despair.*

The problem was, the girl remained defiant.

She was scared, of course, and the dark streaks of mascara down her cheeks served as testament to her terror. But she was also *angry.* And fury kept her afloat. Normally, by this point in the ritual, the sacrifice would have soiled herself, weeping in pure and utter dejection. But this girl held out some irrational hope. Perhaps of escape. Perhaps even violent retribution.

The Magister wondered if they had chosen poorly. But it was too late to go back now. This girl had already been plucked neatly from her life. One death was always easy enough to hide, but two in the same year would arouse suspicion.

"Ex passione, potenter benedic nob—"

Brrreeet—the chanting was interrupted by the chipper ring of a cellphone echoing through the subterranean chamber.

The Magister glowered at the Initiates through the slits of his mask, furious at the ceremony being undermined. These young men had no idea how privileged they were to be in the rarefied echelon that would ever witness, much less benefit from, a ritual as forbidden as this.

The boys all shifted uncomfortably, glancing around the circle. *Brrreeet*. The sound continued.

One of the Initiates—Collins? Davis? Or was it the boyfriend? It was impossible to make out who it was beneath the cloak in the dim—abruptly broke from formation and went to the corner of the room. The girl's clothes were wadded up in a pile where they had been cut from her body and discarded. He fished in a small tan purse and pulled out the offending device as it gave one final noisy ring, no longer muffled. *Brrreeet!*

Despite the interruption, the elementals in the circle had continued their reactions. The ritual was still proceeding, and with a nod of his head, the Magister signaled the Initiates to resume the next line of chanting.

"Ex tenebris, potenter benedic nobis."

The Magister beckoned to the boy with the cellphone. Its home screen showed a single missed call. The Magister contemplated the device until, as he'd hoped, the phone beeped, signaling a new voicemail.

The Magister stepped across the ritual circle. The Initiates continued their chanting, louder now, excited. The Magister raised a hand, signaling them to pause. He approached the girl in the center of the circle and held the phone before her. Even with the gag stretching her cheeks, it recognized her face and opened with a happy chirp. The girl thrashed and grunted, trying to shout something at him, but her words were unintelligible.

The Magister clicked up the volume on the phone and pressed PLAY on the voicemail.

A young woman's voice, pleasantly husky, issued from the phone's speaker and echoed through the space, audible to all:

"Hey, sorry for calling so late, I know it's . . . what, almost midnight there? Just thought I might catch you before bed if you were studying."

The Initiates leaned in, beginning to understand now. The girl whimpered loudly, as though hoping the recorded voice might hear her and come to her aid.

"I'm up ungodly early here. Big day today. Wanted to hear your voice before I went in. But if I don't, wish me luck."

A muffled shriek issued from behind the gag, and the girl fought her bonds with such ferocity she practically convulsed. But it was useless. The ropes held. The message continued, a tremor of emotion creeping into the voice on the other line.

"Anyway, I know you're busy, but . . . I miss you. I'm gonna try to come home and visit soon. And . . . I hope you're doing great. Love you."

The message ended—and at last, the girl broke. Her bitter defiance was replaced by abject defeat, as she understood, finally and truly, that she would never see her loved ones again. Her short life would end alone and naked in this room, leaving those who knew her to mourn in pain and confusion.

Only the abyss was waiting.

A keening wail escaped the girl's throat.

The Magister beckoned to the Initiates. They all approached, closing in on the center of the circle. Long knives gleaming in the candlelight.

"Ex morte, potenter benedic nobis."

She screamed as the Initiates lowered their blades, and the Magister held out a chalice to collect the bounty her body would yield. It would be a good harvest. A successful ritual.

Behind his white mask, the Magister smiled.

ELLSBETH

Ellsbeth tried to blend in among the throng of undergraduates waiting outside the lecture hall for the locked doors to open. It was a few minutes before seven in the morning—the single class that Professor Rawlins offered to undergraduates was set, seemingly purposefully, punishingly early, and still, Introduction to the Principles of Arcane Mechanicals was the most sought-after class on Newlyn's campus. You could practically hear the frantic clicking through the freshman dorms when the online registration system opened, the frenetic attempts to claim one of the sixty seats. Rawlins did not permit students to audit the class, and there was no waitlist.

It was well understood that T. M. Rawlins believed a lecture for freshmen to be a waste of his time. He was a professor at Newlyn, of course, because of its famous graduate program in the arcane arts, with its handpicked cohort of eight students. Ellsbeth imagined that Rawlins only taught the one undergraduate lecture he *did* because it was some contractual obligation of his tenure, or else the dean of the College of the Arcane Arts had some blackmail on him.

The September morning was cold enough that her breath was visible, and Ellsbeth stepped out of the shadow of a red-brick building to try to claim whatever faint warmth she could from the watery sunlight. She pulsed her hands into fists in her pockets to try to get the blood flowing as she eyed the undergraduates around her. They were happily chattering in groups of twos and threes, their voices too high from excitement and the falseness of trying to impress people they were just meeting for the first time. Some wore new peacoats and too much perfume, and full faces of makeup masking teenage acne; others were studiedly casual, in filthy sneakers and baseball hats and the same backpack they'd used in high school slung over one shoulder, daring the world to believe that even for a moment they cared what anyone else thought. They were all halfway caught between arrogance and insecurity, still energized by the promise of an imagined reinvention upon matriculating to college—the chance to shed their insufferably suburban high school identities—and still buoyed by their good luck at having managed to secure a spot in Rawlins's coveted lecture and at being eighteen, and being at Newlyn, and knowing everything.

Ellsbeth was twenty-four years old and she had never felt so old as she did then, standing among a horde of college freshmen. She was not registered for Introduction to the Principles of Arcane Mechanicals. In fact, she was not a student at Newlyn University at all.

One of the peacoat girls standing nearby was holding a copy of *The Arcane and the Ordinary* clutched against her chest, as if she was going to ask Professor Rawlins to sign it for her after class. His author photo took up almost the entire back cover, and Ellsbeth found herself staring at it.

Rawlins was young in the picture—probably, infuriatingly, in his twenties—with a swoop of brown hair. Even in the black and white, Ellsbeth could make out blue eyes. He wasn't smiling. Perhaps he had thought that was too casual for a dense book of nonfiction, a work (as *The New York Times Book Review* promised in large letters) "of tremendous importance to the field." Instead, this black-and-white Rawlins was tilting his head back, gazing out at the viewer down his nose. Ellsbeth imagined him practicing the expression in the mirror, hoping to look serious, imperious even. Instead, something about the pose made her smile. He looked like a little boy playing grown-up in an Oxford shirt.

Just as the bell in the tower struck the hour, the heavy mechanical sounds of a lock being undone were audible from the outside, and a TA swung the heavy doors of Hale Hall open. The eager bodies pressed forward in a flood, Ellsbeth among them.

THE COLLEGE OF THE ARCANE Arts at Newlyn was almost its own university within the university, with a cluster of buildings on the west side of campus curled around a grassy courtyard like a dragon around its hoard. Hale Hall took up nearly one entire side of the quad, a stately granite-and-brownstone structure with a striped roof that peaked in a gothic point and tall, narrow windows.

The Practicum, for graduate students, was across the way, behind a small thicket of heritage elm trees. It had no windows at all.

Though Newlyn University had a respectable reputation as an undergraduate school, it was home to one of the most elite graduate programs for arcane arts in the world—certainly the best program in the United States, next to Yale.

Bertie had been trying to convince Ellsbeth of that when they were back home for Thanksgiving last year. It was after Ellsbeth had graduated from St. Andrews, but she had decided to stay in the UK for another year to study for her Arcanus. Bertie had recently begun her first semester as an undergraduate at Newlyn and they were both back in New Jersey to spend a week half-heartedly forking at their mother's latest attempt at a fat-free turkey loaf and watching network television with their dad before he fell asleep on the couch.

"You'd love the trees on campus," Bertie had said, flopping onto Ellsbeth's childhood bed. "The red and orange leaves. It's like something out of a J. Crew catalog. So *Vermont-y.* Makes you want to drink maple syrup."

"I'm not getting my DAA in arcane mechanicals because I want to look at trees," Ellsbeth said.

"Well, *obviously,*" Bertie shot back, grinning. "But if you went to Newlyn next year, we could room together. They let sophomores live off-campus. You and I could get an apartment!" That did appeal to Ellsbeth. While she left for St. Andrews in Scotland, she found she didn't miss her mother or father nearly as much as she missed her younger sister. Every time she visited home again, Bertie shocked her anew with just how much of a *person* she had become since she last saw her. No longer a child, the little sibling made anonymous by the four years in between them, but an actual *person* full of wit and passion and opinions and a surprisingly sharp sense of humor.

The idea of living in an apartment tucked on a tree-lined street near Newlyn with Bertie, boiling water for tea together and studying side by side on the couch, made Ellsbeth smile. "It's a thought," she said. Bertie rolled her eyes. Both of them knew that Ellsbeth was planning on getting her DAA in arcane mechanicals at Cambridge. Her undergraduate adviser had already reached out to the dean of Trinity College, a friend of his, and informed him that Ellsbeth was the most promising arcanist he had ever taught. Her slot in the program was a foregone conclusion, merely waiting on Ellsbeth taking the Arcanus.

Because you were only permitted to sit for the Arcanus once, most students, like Ellsbeth, took a few months off after graduation to study before taking the test in January. Cambridge required at least a fifty-five out of seventy-one on the Arcanus for admission to its DAA program; Ellsbeth had taken three practice tests so far, and received a perfect score every time.

Bertie reached over to pull Ellsbeth's old paperback copy of *The Arcane and the Ordinary* off her bedside table. "The guy who wrote this teaches at Newlyn."

"How do you know? Last I heard, you're studying French. And *dance*."

"He's famous," Bertie said, thumbing through the book. "Or he was. They brag about it in the school brochures and stuff. Come on. It's cool that he's at Newlyn."

"I mean, sure," Ellsbeth said. "But I'm pretty sure he *went* to Cambridge." Bertie flipped to the back of the book for an About the Author section that she read silently, then scowled and threw the book down onto the bed beside her.

Had Bertie been so insistent on getting Ellsbeth to join her at Newlyn because she was lonely? Because she needed her sister? There were so many moments that Ellsbeth replayed in her mind, trying to make sense of what happened. It was like trying to complete a puzzle, but the pieces were soggy and torn and dissolving in her hands.

In the end, Ellsbeth had not gone to Cambridge. Ellsbeth had sat for her one and only Arcanus that winter, and she had failed, destroying any possible future she would ever have as an arcanist, the only thing she had ever wanted to be. And when she flew home to New Jersey the next time, Bertie wasn't there. Her clothes were sealed in vacuum-packed plastic and her bedroom door remained shut.

"DO YOU THINK WE'RE ACTUALLY going to, like, do arcane mechanicals?" A girl in expensive leggings and a ponytail so tight it pulled at her temples was practically vibrating with excitement as the mass of students slowly pressed forward into the lecture hall itself.

Ellsbeth snorted. She couldn't help herself. The girl shot her a look. "This is a freshman lecture," Ellsbeth said. "You'll be lucky if they pass around a piece of compounding clay at the end of the semester just so you can feel it in your hands. This is going to be all theory and basic math."

The Ponytail Girl continued glaring at Ellsbeth, and now her friend beside her was glaring, too. "How do *you* know?"

"I mean, it's kind of obvious. What? You're really expecting T. M. Rawlins to let a bunch of eighteen-year-olds start doing bone-bindings?"

"Okayyyyy," the girl's friend said. "You don't have to be such a bitch about it." The two of them, muttering and shooting further dark glances back at Ellsbeth, found seats near the front of the room.

The lecture hall echoed with chatter and the shuffling of books and feet as Ellsbeth slipped into an open seat on the right side of the room, six rows back. It was an older classroom, with its front wall lined with green chalkboards from the floor to the ceiling (and another layer of chalkboards hidden behind the first, accessible via a system of ropes and pulleys). The students sat in ascending rows, forced to squeeze into uncomfortably small wooden chairs with attached desks.

Ellsbeth absently wished she had worn a less conspicuous sweater. Surely Rawlins wouldn't be able to count visually and see that there was an additional student in the lecture hall, but it seemed unwise to have chosen a red wool jumper. There was no need to draw any additional attention to herself; she was already irrationally certain that there was something indelible about her that made it obvious she didn't belong here. Her age, yes, but also her sadness. She had lived what felt like a thousand lives in the months since Bertie died. The students around her felt like children.

And then, as if cued by a conductor, the chatter in the hall stopped in an instant. From a small door behind the podium, Rawlins had appeared, and the room was silent.

The handsome boy from the photo in his book was still visible, but he was graying at the temples of his hairline, which was receding into a deep widow's peak that suited him perfectly. Fine lines spiderwebbed from the corners of his eyes, which were bleary from too much caffeine or too little sleep or both.

"Welcome," Rawlins said. His voice was lower than Ellsbeth had expected. "This is Introduction to the Principles of Arcane Mechanicals. If you're looking for British Literature 101, that's on the North Quad." There were a few polite chuckles. Rawlins had delivered his half joke flatly, unsmiling; Ellsbeth was certain he opened the lecture the same way every single year.

Before he said another word, he pulled an iron ingot from his pocket, snapped it in two, and let the dust settle on his desk. Using his finger, he traced a circle in the iron filaments. The lecture hall gasped and then burst into applause. Rawlins allowed himself a small smile without looking up. The chalkboard behind him had instantly become covered with messy scrawling handwriting—important dates in the history of the arcane arts, along with basic equations. "Have to do something to impress you all on our first day," he said. "After all, I know how competitive registration can be. Those of you who managed to enroll in this class are part of a lucky group."

And at that moment, he looked up, directly at Ellsbeth.

She felt her underarms prickle with sweat and her heart tighten in her chest. He was holding her gaze, his eyes locked on hers. They flicked down to her sweater, and then away, toward the papers he was keeping in a stack on the lectern.

Ellsbeth held her breath, exhaling only once he began talking about Norman contributions to thaumaturgy and she was fairly confident he wouldn't interrupt the lecture to publicly shame her as an interloper.

The content of the introductory class was basic, information that Ellsbeth had studied back when she was in high school, reading books that made the librarians at the local branch raise their eyebrows. But from the way Rawlins spoke, she understood immediately why his class always had a waiting list. He was clear without being dull, reverential without veering into the poetic. He talked about the science of augury like he was telling a story.

He was brilliant. But more important, Ellsbeth realized, he was *bored.* He was reciting the same lecture he had been giving on the first day of class for years, probably verbatim.

When Rawlins glanced back in her direction toward the end of the lecture, she was smiling at him. The truth was, Ellsbeth hadn't snuck onto campus simply to attend a single undergraduate lecture. She had come to Newlyn for her sister, and she had come here for Professor Rawlins.

From: Storer.Ellsbeth
To: Rawlins DAA
Subject: Your Arcane Mechanicals course

Hi Professor,

First, let me apologize for writing an email to you at all given that I'm sure with classes just starting, you're incredibly busy. And I'm also sorry for beginning said email with "Hi" when you might find that incredibly overly familiar and unprofessional. Please be assured that I went through several drafts of initial salutations. (*Dear* felt informal and strained; *To,* robotic to the point of rudeness. And so I'm left with *hi.*) Hi.

A bit about me: I graduated from St. Andrews, First Class Honors, with an independent study in augury under Professor Arthur Binder that received the Flint-Marxcy Prize for undergraduate achievement. I spent the fall of last year living in London while studying for the Arcanus, planning on applying to graduate programs in the spring. Unfortunately, my plans were derailed by life circumstances that I would be happy to discuss more in person, but suffice it to say, with an incomplete Arcanus score, I was well aware that I would not have merited any significant consideration had I sent in a formal application to the graduate program for admission this term. Which is why I am writing to you now—in the hope that a personal appeal might be the best way forward.

Please be sure, I am well aware of how competitive the DAA program at Newlyn is, with only a small group of hand-selected students each year. But I know I would be an asset to the department and, as I said, I would be happy to offer an explanation of the extenuating circumstances around my Arcanus and convince you why that result is not at all reflective of my passion or my natural predisposition for mechanicals.

Here is where I should offer another apology: I snuck into your introductory lecture yesterday morning (and borrowed your email address off the syllabus). If you happened to notice a twenty-something girl in a red sweater a few sizes too big looking like a child on Christmas morning, that was me.

I've never seen anyone talk about arcane mechanicals the way you did—in the past when I heard teachers discuss conservation of matter and the rudimentary mechanicals, they made it sound so sterile. You made it sound like we were conductors in a symphony, like the strings of reality are ours to be teased out at will and played in harmony. (That is not to say I don't appreciate the incredibly rigorous mathematics required to study arcane mechanicals, because I do (I'm attaching my transcript below, in case you're curious, and in case this email hasn't already wasted enough of your time, and if you find yourself curious, please be sure to check my undergraduate coursework in Differential Equations and Multivariables. Top of the class in both)).

I know traditionally you wouldn't accept students into your program once the semester has already begun, and I realize this is an incredibly unorthodox request, but seeing as I don't have access to a genie, time travel, or a *Fortunatis Favori* ritual, there's only one course of action left to me: you.

If there were ever a chance you could make an exception, I can promise you will never teach a student more willing to work hard than me.

I've already taken up too much of your time, and so, I'm sorry (again).

Best (how is that?),
Ellsbeth Storer

P.S. When I was sixteen, my parents gave me a copy of *The Arcane and the Ordinary* and I practically memorized it. I think I slept with it under my pillow for a few months. Seeing you in person in the lecture yesterday was surreal after only seeing the photo of you from the back cover.

From: Rawlins DAA
To: Storer.Ellsbeth
Subject: Re: Your Arcane Mechanicals course

Ms. Stoller,

Assuming your undergraduate education afforded you some familiarity with the history of persuasive writing, perhaps you can point me to the precedent of a rhetorician who convinced his audience primarily through the use of *apology*—or indeed, numerous apologies piled upon one another to the point of stupefaction. Or did you expect to be the first to win over a skeptic through a cacophony of "sorry"?

It matters not. The system of selection that we have developed at the CotAA has been honed across generations. Other fields, perhaps, can afford the luxury of exceptions based on such dubious virtues as diligence and presumptuousness. But a cursory overview of the history of the arcane will reveal the danger of entrusting magical knowledge in the hands of those who have not been properly vetted and prepared.

More important, my own experience with students not suited to the study has shown that the costs can be grave. The crucible is not merely a tool of our trade, it is a fitting metaphor for the field itself, which reveals any impurity in the heart of the practitioner.

Many a young applicant has felt improperly represented by her Arcanus score, but often that indignation arises from a misunderstanding of the test itself. The exam does not seek only to measure intellectual capability, but is an instrument intended to assess holistic fitness for the rigors of this study and the responsibilities of its practice. If the face I vaguely recall connected to that unfortunate red sweater is any indication, you are quite young, and as such, you may lack the self-awareness to soberly judge your own shortcomings. Worry not; life will reveal them to you, ruthlessly and relentlessly.

Even if I wanted to admit you, the decision is not mine to make; Dean Lennox oversees the admissions process, and we already have a full cohort of capable students who followed the guidelines and submitted their applications six months ago.

A final thought: I'm sure you intended for me to be flattered by extolling the quality of my first book, but I can hardly take the compliment. While I stand by every word in that text, its author—represented handsomely by that author photo—is a different man than I am. Barely older than you are now, and, while better versed than you in the arcane, no less naïve and foolhardy. It would hardly even be appropriate for me to autograph your copy, since I am so far removed from him, and the intervening years have taken such a toll on my body and soul.

Evidently, I am in a procrastinatory mood and avoiding the quizzes piled upon my desktop, because many words have now been written, when perhaps one would suffice.

No.

Best of luck with your studies,
T. M. Rawlins, DAA

From: Storer.Ellsbeth
To: Rawlins DAA
Subject: Re: Re: Your Arcane Mechanicals course

Hi again Professor Rawlins,

"To be a student of the Arcane is to subject oneself, again and again, to the study of Humility. In fact, it is Humility and a willingness to prostrate oneself before the unknown Mechanikal operations that will ultimately predict one's success within the Field."

I admit, it feels silly to quote the *Mythikum Mythicarum* to you (I believe you actually wrote the introduction to Dawes's new translation several years ago?). But I was thinking about your email, and I decided to consult the original Latin text. While most translators (Dawes, quoted above, included) land on the word "Humility," in the original Latin text from 1402, the word used is *paenitere.* The root word for "penitent." Repenting. Apologetic. And so, I think we should reevaluate my "cacophony" of apologies as evidence NOT of my being star-struck and intimidated by any communication with you, but instead of my inherent proclivity for arcane mechanicals.

And here is where *you* get a chance to apologize: My name is Ms. Storer, not "Stoller."

Yesterday (before I went down a rabbit hole of Latin translation) I had messaged Dean Lennox and explained the unusual circumstances surrounding my incomplete Arcanus score. I mentioned that you had communicated that any decision regarding a late admission to the arcane mechanicals course would be entirely up to her judgment, which came as somewhat of a surprise to her. Dean Lennox seemed to be under the impression that *you* are the one with the power to admit a student outside the conventional channels if you were willing to independently supervise their thesis and account for their progress.

I will offer no more apologies, but I will offer you a proposition: tea, over which I can tell you the story of what happened to me on the day I took the Arcanus. I promise to buy if you agree to sign my copy of *The Arcane and the Ordinary.* (I would have asked you to also sign my copy of Dawes's translation of the *Mythikum*, but when I revisited the translation again this morning I found it so infuriatingly lacking that I . . . threw it out the window.)

I am not someone accustomed to asking for favors, nor am I someone who relishes being granted any special treatment. But as you're aware, the Arcanus can only be taken once, and I fear that if I don't get the chance to explain to you what happened on that day last January, you won't have a full understanding of who I am as a student and what I'll be capable of in the arcane mechanicals.

I'll be at The Puddle Jumper from 9 to 11 a.m. this Friday if you're willing to submit yourself to a hot beverage and a good story. I'll try to find a less unfortunate sweater to wear.

Best,
Ellsbeth

P.S. I am, in fact, vaguely aware of the Maxwell Keene situation, but I am not Maxwell Keene. For one thing, I would never attempt a thaumaturgy ritual alone or without a rune circle. Also: I'm a little better looking.

RAWLINS

Rawlins slept poorly.

This was true as a general statement, stretching back to his earliest memories of childhood, but it was particularly true that first week of the new semester.

There were all manner of suitable causes to which he might accredit his insomnia. The obscene workload he had taken on—three (!) graduate students he was advising, in addition to the advanced studies seminars he taught. His needlessly time-consuming undergraduate lecture. Pressure from Lennox to draft the wholesale order of ritual elementals for the Practicum. His failure to get his editor a draft of his manuscript over the summer break (and his knowledge that he had hardly begun).

Yet when he woke on Friday at 4 a.m., after falling asleep past midnight, the first name on his mind, against all odds, was not that of the chancellor or the dean or his publisher. It was *Ellsbeth Storer.*

He had noticed Ellsbeth Storer, of course, in his introductory class the other day, sitting off to the right—a girl with long brown hair in an oversized sweater. The animal part of his brain had immediately been alerted to her presence in his lecture hall, as though instinctively registering a threat. Upon scrutiny, of course, the notion that a twenty-something pseudointellectual posed any sort of danger to him was laughable.

But now, he realized, his intuition had been reasonable: She *was* a threat. To his serenity, certainly, and to the *sanctity* of the subject of arcane mechanicals. If youthful entitlement and "passion" were sufficient to force oneself into a life of magical study, the field would be overrun with power-hungry dilettantes. There was nothing more dangerous than a young mind that felt it was *owed* knowledge and power. That was a lesson Rawlins had learned the hard way, and he would not repeat the mistake. Not with Ellsbeth Storer or anyone else.

Still in bed, he reread her last email several times. The invitation to meet her could be construed as casual, but he knew better. She was *assuming* he would be there. Counting on his curiosity about her misfortune to drive him there . . . and counting on his *guilt* to prevent him from standing her up. But he saw right through her. He imagined her sitting there, brown hair still damp from a recent shower, waiting to drink a cooling cup of tea while glancing for him at the door, and felt irritated with himself for feeling bad at all. She did not deserve his guilt, or even his pity. She had presumptuously thrust this situation upon herself.

Yet he kept returning to her in his mind. Something about the girl's name felt familiar to him, though he was certain they had never met. The image of her face, for reasons he could not articulate, kept projecting intrusively upon his closed eyelids when he tried to sleep. It was preposterous; of all the things to lose sleep over, another arrogant student to whom he owed nothing. Ellsbeth Storer was just another among the handful of usually young, usually pretty women who emailed him about their admiration for his long-ago book, idealizing a life of *magic,* with no appetite for the rigorous dedication it demanded. (And, he allowed himself to think, idealizing a version of *him,* the decades-ago boy with bright-blue eyes and a knowing smile. A boy that no longer existed in the man now past forty.)

Rawlins pondered his options for getting back to sleep. In the past, he had occasional success with Winograd's *Soporificum*—but it was forty-five minutes of work and required several expensive elementals. Far simpler to take a sleeping pill, and he had a medicine cabinet full of options—but at this hour, they would leave him foggy for the entire morning, and he'd rather be bleary-eyed but sharp.

So Rawlins surrendered to the day. He pulled back the sheets and stepped out of bed, the floorboards creaking loudly as though mocking his defeat.

Rawlins often had the impression that his house was a living being—and if so, it was a real asshole. It was nearly two centuries old, a quasi-gothic two-story that hugged the side of the hill, showing its age but nonetheless commanding in its perch over the town. The arched windows resembled half-lidded eyes, perpetually passing judgment on the campus below.

The house had come up at auction five years earlier, when Rawlins had recently gotten tenure and was thus (barely) in a position to afford it. Most of the other residents of the town found its grandiose eeriness off-putting, but Rawlins was instantly drawn. It was more house than he needed, and even at auction a stretch for his budget, but he'd dipped into the reservoir of savings from his book sales to afford it.

He grumbled about the decision nearly every day, especially as the perpetual need for repairs ate into his limited free time. Every burst pipe or leaky roof tile felt like a taunt from the house, as though it knew he would resent the intrusion and took pleasure in mocking his scholarly fastidiousness by forcing him to learn more about replacing copper pipes and repairing drywall than he ever wanted to know. If he were ever fired from the university, he was confident he could now make ends meet as a handyman, thanks to the litany of complaints the house had demanded he correct.

The stairs squeaked on his descent as his hand skimmed across the well-worn wood of the banister, finding his way in the dark; at the bottom, he navigated around boxes of books that were still awaiting a home on a shelf. Rawlins's book collection had long since overflowed the library, and he had added more shelves whenever possible, packing them with volumes of arcane study and items collected on his scholarly travels: a ritual mask from Fiji, a pewter cauldron from ancient Mesopotamia. Even though the house was immense, every room and nook and hallway felt *full*.

Dean Lennox, on a visit last summer to discuss the curriculum, had remarked on the indiscriminate expansiveness of his collection, then asked pointedly, "You afraid that if there's any space, someone else will try to move in?" Rawlins had frowned at the question. Not because she was wrong, but because it revealed an assumption that he *should* want to share his house, his life, with someone else. That there was something *wrong* with his commitment to a life of the mind.

He wasn't a recluse, or even antisocial, by any means—he spent hours every week teaching and interacting with his colleagues. He wasn't immune to the pleasures of sex, either—just careful to set expectations and keep it separate from any lasting entanglements.

Why did Lennox, and everyone else, seem to find something morally wrong with him knowing his priorities and keeping his life orderly? Why did people assume that being alone meant he had to be *lonely*?

Rawlins didn't begrudge anyone else their relationship, he just didn't see what was to be gained by romantic partnership. Inviting someone into his home and his life would allow them to make demands upon his decor, his space, his time. In exchange for what? *Company?* It struck him as little to gain relative to the immense cost.

Lennox, of all people, ought to understand why he felt that way.

The espresso machine hummed as it warmed up; he packed grounds into the tray, loaded it, and while he watched it fill, his thoughts returned to Ellsbeth Storer. Sitting in that café, waiting for him. He *did* want to know why a girl whose entire life seemed to revolve around arcane mechanicals would fail to even complete her exam. Perhaps he could stop by and see her, just to get the answer. Just to show her that her sob-story would still not compel him.

But no. He would not give her the satisfaction of arriving on her terms. He sipped his espresso, preparing to face the day and attempting to banish her from his mind.

THE GRADUATE COHORT WAS WAITING for him in the Practicum when he entered, all straight-backed and eager. He had been instrumental in selecting the group, and he could not have hoped for a more impressive and well-heeled collection of students, carrying eager minds and impressive résumés; they were a credit to Newlyn. Neither he nor the institution would ever be *embarrassed* by a single one of them.

Yet as he surveyed the group, searching their eyes, he could not help but wonder: Would any one of them *push* the field further? Would any one of them make a genuinely new discovery or challenge a long-held assumption?

It shouldn't matter. The goal of his instruction was not to revolutionize the field of arcane arts; it was to produce responsible stewards, practitioners, and instructors. That was enough.

And yet.

The Practicum was an airy but windowless chamber with a gleaming black-and-white-tile floor. Down one wall, neatly labeled cabinets and drawers contained a bewildering array of materials, from the prosaic (table salt) to the volatile (mercury, hareheart). On the opposite side, glass cabinets displayed a variety of vessels (beakers, vials, cauldrons) and tools (mortar and pestle, droppers, tongs). The center of the room was dominated by a twenty-by-twenty platform with a chalkboard floor.

Rawlins sat on the edge of the platform, and the students gathered round. Once the pleasantries were out of the way, he began the speech he had delivered at the start of the term for more than a decade already. "We will have sixteen weekly sessions of this Practicum, along with two exams, midterm and final. Each Practicum will be devoted to a different advanced ritual."

Rawlins paused. He knew the next words of his script by heart, but he was struck by the immediate realization that if he continued, the rest of the semester—and by extension, the rest of his career—would be utterly predictable. Predictability had been the goal for a long time . . . but suddenly it felt like death. He had been rendered a passenger on the ride of his own life.

He blinked and looked out at his students. "Today," he said, "we'll be starting with chronomancy."

A ripple of interest coursed through the cohort. For years, his first Practicum of the semester had always been a sneaky little bit of numerology—fairly simple, but still impressive enough in its demonstration to leave the students excited for the semester. But today would be different.

He continued on, as though oblivious to his students' murmurs and confused glances among themselves. "Manipulating time is considered an advanced practice but is in fact one of the more mathematically straightforward applications of arcane mechanicals. As long as your variables are carefully defined, the outcomes could not be more predictable. Now . . ." He opened the textbook to a lengthy treatise on the ritual of dilation. "Who will serve as our first Initiator?"

There was a long silence and an exchange of glances. Rawlins shook his head, irritated: "You'll all go first eventually, so one of you might as well get it over with."

In response to his prodding, Gracie Fitzwilliams raised her hand. She was exactly the sort of student the graduate program attracted: ambitious and competitive and eager to prove herself. Perfectly suited to a life in academia.

Rawlins nodded and invited Gracie to step up onto the platform with him, entering the ritual circle. "Time dilation is the localized acceleration or deceleration of the passage of time," he said. "We will narrowly define the casting radius so that the effects remain limited to the object we target." At the center of the platform, Rawlins placed a Newton's cradle. "What are our other variables?"

"Degree of dilation," Gracie answered. "How fast or slow we want time to go." Rawlins nodded and looked to the rest of the class.

"Duration, obviously," said Victor Hamada. "I think that's it."

"One more," Rawlins prompted, raising an eyebrow and drawing blank stares; when it was clear no one had the answer, he gave it: "*Direction.* It's often ignored, and it usually *can* be ignored, because we default to using positive values. But it's important to ensure that time is moving *forward* at the speed in question."

"So it's possible to reverse it?" Gracie asked, clearly skeptical.

"In theory," Rawlins answered. "But if the anecdotal reports are to be believed, it's a disaster. So—let's get started. The floor is yours."

Gracie presided over the preparation for the ritual, taking charge of the class. She consulted the textbook and told her fellow students which elementals to fetch, in what quantities, and calculated their placement on the ritual circle. A rope protractor was used to draw concentric circles, then Gracie calculated the divisions she would need—eventually subdividing the circle into sixty-four sections. Rawlins didn't correct her, though it was possible to achieve the ritual with only sixteen, if you knew what you were doing. A whiteboard was used for the trigonometric calculations, which Rawlins noted she handled easily.

After ninety minutes, Gracie was ready to initiate. Rawlins pulled back one ball of the Newton's cradle and started it *clack-clack-clacking.* He dimmed the lights. Even if near-darkness was not technically necessary for the reactions to unfold, Rawlins enjoyed the theatricality of it.

Gracie chanted the incantation, her voice rising and falling in perfect time—like a computer-generated approximation of music. Perfect pitch, no melody. Then she lit the fuse, touching a match to the catalyst. The sulfur sizzled, and in a chain reaction, other elementals throughout the ritual circle started to react. Eight vials of lamp oil, evenly spaced, began to bubble; rolls of vellum paper burst into flame and the smoke wafted upward, quickly pulled away by the ventilation ducts overhead; geometrically cut pieces of jade and amethyst glowed. A low, vibrating humming expanded through the hall, a sign that the ritual was working. The sound, barely audible but still perceptible, wasn't the direct result of any part of the ritual itself. So much of the arcane could be explained, but the humming simply existed.

The students all scribbled notes furiously; Rawlins, irritated, wondered if any of them were watching.

As the ritual took effect, the air at the center of the ritual circle subtly distorted, like a mirage appearing midair, and the *clack-clack-clack* diminished to a *clack . . . clack . . . clack* as the Newton's cradle slowed. It was beautiful to watch the way the silvery orbs arced through the air like they were swimming through amber, seemingly in defiance of gravity, though in fact defying only time. Twenty-four years since he had first seen this demonstration and Rawlins was still enchanted by it.

Gracie had calculated for a sixty-second duration, and Rawlins intended the class to watch the full minute in silent appreciation. But the reverie was broken thirty seconds in by a question from Curt Ladove, a handsome Connecticut prep-schooler who had gone straight from Newlyn undergrad into the graduate program and was now wearing a polo shirt that tightly hugged his biceps: "Professor, what are the practical applications of dilation?"

Rawlins sighed. "Contraction is often used in conjunction with the sciences. We can help study chemical reactions by slowing them down to a fraction of their speed. Acceleration has applications in botany and farming in particular—we can speed up a growth cycle for a given plant. Of course, it's a lot of effort and energy, certainly not going to happen on any industrial scale, but for small quantities. You know, if you just planted your crop and found yourself very, very hungry." He looked to his students, none of whom found his comment funny.

As the sixty-second duration ended, they measured the change in speed and calculated that it had gone from one collision per second to one every eight, exactly to specification.

After that, Rawlins had each of the students lead a variation on the experiment, speeding or slowing the cradle by different degrees, trying out various durations, occasionally altering the radius. Each fresh instance required a recalculation of quantities and distances, but the procedure was essentially the same. Their errors were minor and easily corrected, and they finished all the rituals he had planned with fifteen minutes to spare. The students shifted, clearly waiting to see if they would be dismissed early.

But Rawlins, perhaps due to his sleeplessness, was feeling ornery. The Practicum had gone well. *Too* well. His students were going to leave the hall thoroughly untransformed, unchallenged, unawed.

On another day, he might not have been bothered by that; he would've been satisfied with their competence. But even *that* bothered him today—his own complacency, and theirs.

In that moment, his thoughts leapt to Maxwell Keene—to the young man's excitement, his *rapture,* at the wonders of arcane mechanicals. Rawlins wondered if a single one of these graduate students was even *capable* of such passion. He could teach them everything he knew and they could memorize it easily, but how could he ever awaken a sense of boundless curiosity?

Well, at least he could try. Rawlins cleared his throat. "Seems we have time for one more ritual," he said, his voice unnaturally loud in his ears. "Would anyone like to try being the *object* of the time dilation?"

The cohort froze, stupefied by the proposition. Rawlins went on, noticing the sweat prickling unpleasantly in his underarms: "I'll lead it myself. All you have to do is stand at the center. We've seen it work numerous times on the cradle, without a major error."

Rawlins's gaze scanned the cohort, seeking to lock eyes with one who would accept his challenge. "Come on. Aren't you curious what it would feel like? For time to crawl, or race by?"

The students all exchanged looks—simultaneously eager to answer correctly and not entirely certain what was happening. Gracie was the one who broke the silence. "It's illegal," she said. "Time-dilation spells have been limited to non-human objects since the Hagia Sophia Accords were ratified."

All eyes went to Rawlins, anxious for his reaction. A line had been drawn in the sand. For Rawlins to continue insisting on a volunteer, he would now have to do so with acknowledgment that it was forbidden. Part of him, the prickly part, wanted to do just that—to defy Lennox and an entire generation of overcautious orthodoxy, and enlist these students in his quiet rebellion. To make them *feel* the power of arcane mechanicals.

But then, again, he thought of Maxwell. And this time, the images were much darker. Blue flame consuming a tower.

Three charred bodies, draped in sheets, wheeled into ambulances.

And Maxwell's face, eyes wide in shock and terror as he was taken away by the police, leaving Rawlins alone with the guilt and shame of what he had wrought.

"Professor?" Gracie chirped, breaking Rawlins's reverie, and he snapped to attention, forcing his mouth into what he hoped was a pleasant smile.

"Very good, Ms. Fitzwilliams. The final test of the day, and you have admirably demonstrated yourself to be a conscientious practitioner of arcane mechanicals."

The students exhaled, and a few laughed nervously; all were relieved not to have volunteered, and a few seemed irritated that *they* had not been the first to offer the correct response to the professor's eccentric test.

Rawlins surveyed the students in the cohort. They would all make diligent and capable scholars, and for that, he should feel grateful, even relieved. He could teach their lessons and grade their papers and write their recommendations without fear of any catastrophe like the one Max had caused.

And yet . . . there was something he missed, even if rationally he knew better. Rawlins had always been fascinated by the mysteries of the arcane. His first attempts were simple levitation rituals undertaken surreptitiously in his childhood bedroom, and ever since, his investigations in the field had been shot through with a current of illicit excitement.

As he grew older and built a career as a scholar, he had tried to accept the limitations that academic institutions and the culture at large had placed on that study. But on some deep level, he could not. Some corner of his mind still yearned for arcane practice that felt *dangerous.* For a ritual that might surprise him, and a student who was not merely a pupil but a protégé. Someone who could challenge him, who had a curiosity and an intellect that matched Rawlins's own. Someone who could make magic feel *magical* once again.

For a time, he had found exactly what he was looking for in Max. The boy had arrived on campus when Rawlins was still in the bloom of his idealism about teaching. Max was a cocky freshman, but Rawlins soon found that Max's talent and intelligence exceeded even his considerable ambition. For a few glorious months, Rawlins had provided academic counsel that evolved into private tutoring, far beyond the reaches of whatever would have been permissible to teach an undergraduate; he delighted at the discovery that Max would read books as quickly as Rawlins could recommend them, memorizing passages and reciting rituals as if they were nursery rhymes. Rawlins encouraged him—more than encouraged him; he pushed him, thrilled by Max's accelerating progress—without ever pausing to consider the potential consequences.

Even after everything that happened, as he looked at his graduate cohort, Rawlins couldn't help but feel a guilty twinge of disappointment. That none of them would ever ask questions with the same impatient, carnivorous hunger for knowledge. None of them would ever possess the arrogance needed to challenge dogma and revolutionize the field.

But he tried to remind himself: *That is a good thing.* Because none of them was likely to cause the death of three other students. None of them would ever end up in the back of a police car, staring out at Rawlins with terrified, hopeless eyes. None of them would break down in tears when they were sentenced to spending the rest of their lives in prison. And none of them would haunt his dreams for years to come.

From: Rawlins DAA
To: Dean Lennox
Subject: Max

Maggie,

Hope you're well.

I'm writing to remind you that Tuesday is Max's birthday. While I'm sure that the date is not one you're likely to forget, I suspect you may need some encouragement to actually make an effort to reach out. A card at least, or even a visit, would go a long way.

I understand that you feel the need to protect your status as dean, and you might be fearful of keeping him in your life. Might even convince yourself that he doesn't want to hear from you. But he needs to know that he has not been forgotten. We owe that to him, at the very least.

Sincerely,
Tad

From: Dean Lennox
To: Rawlins DAA
Subject: Re: Max

Thaddeus,

What a cruel and unnecessary email. Benjamin and I do not need a reminder of the birthday of our son.

I'm sure it helps alleviate your guilt to take a position of moral superiority toward me and the whole situation; perhaps casting me as a cold, uncaring mother allows you to feel less guilty for the direct role you played in the disaster seven years ago.

I do empathize, and so I will forgive your unsettlingly casual tone, writing as though Maxwell were an undergraduate organization I had forgotten I had agreed to chaperone. I greatly value both our friendship and the important role you play at the university. If you do the same, this will be the last time you mention Maxwell to me.

I hope your arcane cohort is as promising in person as they are on paper. I look forward to getting to know them more at our department's autumn dinner.

M

ELLSBETH

She had waited at The Puddle Jumper for three hours total, or the duration of two milky mugs of tea and one and a half slices of slightly dry lemon loaf. The Puddle Jumper was a cozy café, with vintage bicycles strung up on the ceiling and bulletin boards plastered with a decade of advertisements for piano lessons and Latin tutors. Ellsbeth had brought a book—*The Letters of Madame de Staël*—but she found herself too distracted to offer it much focus. She would skim a paragraph and glance up at the door to see if Professor Rawlins had arrived, look back down at the book and realize she hadn't retained a single thing she read. It took her forty minutes to get through a single page.

The café buzzed with the September energy of students excited to be back at school, undergraduates with faces still pimpled from their teenage hormones. She listened in on the way they talked to one another in proud declarative statements—convinced their every opinion was brilliant and every obvious, self-evident observation was a philosophical breakthrough. It should have made her smile, the ability granted by a few short years to float above their harmless youthful arrogance. But instead, Ellsbeth realized she was grinding her teeth. She hated them—the rosy-cheeked strangers in new sweaters, peeling plastic off their textbooks and playing grown-up with their newly cigarette-stained fingers. She *hated* them. What did they know of life, of pain, of loss?

Ellsbeth had never visited her sister back when Bertie had been an undergraduate here at Newlyn, but she still felt her presence lingering like smoke from a cheap candle in a small room. Had Bertie sat in this very café? Had she ordered coffee during those lonely months, waiting for a friend or professor to sit across from her and ask if she was all right? Waiting for Ellsbeth to call? Students and faculty members bustled through The Puddle Jumper, clutching their coffees in to-go cups. Any one of them might have known Bertie last year, might have passed by her, might have guessed she was suffering and done nothing. Ellsbeth knew what happened wasn't their fault, but still, she hated them all the same.

Ellsbeth was well practiced in the art of self-flagellation, of resurrecting memories of her sister that became weapons of masochism. She forced herself to turn her attention back to her book. *One must, in one's life, make a choice between boredom and suffering,* Madame de Staël wrote. Ellsbeth wished she could be the type of person who might be satisfied with boredom. With *contentment.* Instead, she was here at Newlyn, torturing herself with the memory of her sister and the pursuit of a professor who was not showing up for tea.

Ellsbeth checked the time again on her phone. It was certain now that Rawlins wouldn't be coming. He was probably across campus, already beginning his next graduate seminar. She sighed and returned Madame de Staël to her backpack, brushing a handful of crumbs into her palm to throw away before a trio of infuriatingly perky students in matching a cappella group sweatshirts swooped in to claim the table.

STRICTLY SPEAKING, THE PRACTICUM WAS off limits to all but the graduate students of the College of the Arcane Arts. But the entryway, an airy rotunda inlaid with mosaic tiles, was open to the public—it was a frequent stop on tours of wide-eyed high school students applying to the university, easily awed by the centuries-old architecture designed as a celebration of Greek and Roman philosophical ideals.

Still, as Ellsbeth stood there, chilled by the marble, she felt conscious of her intrusion. She could hear voices from inside: a chronomancy ritual, she guessed, based on the rhythmic chanting of one of the students, who, even muffled by the door, Ellsbeth could tell was pronouncing the phrases with an accent so exaggeratedly perfect it verged on smug.

Ellsbeth waited. The Practicum would end soon enough, and she would get her chance to talk to Professor Rawlins face-to-face. She straightened her sweater and flattened the back of her hair with her hand. She reapplied her lip gloss. And then she waited some more, pacing the tiled floor and reading and rereading the motto carved into the marble in the archway above the door to the Practicum: *HIC, FIDES ET RATIO AMBO VINCUNT.* HERE, BOTH FAITH AND REASON PREVAIL.

Finally, she heard the energy in the room let out: the sound of books being gathered, bags being zipped. But then she heard Rawlins's voice, and Ellsbeth pressed her ear to the seam of the wooden door to try to make out his words: "Would anyone like to try being the *object* of the ritual?"

Ellsbeth almost had to stifle a laugh. It was illegal—everyone who had taken a middle school arcane mechanicals class knew that. She heard Professor Rawlins commend whichever of the cohort students pointed that out, but Ellsbeth identified something unmistakable in his tone: disappointment. He *wanted* to try the induction. But more than that: He wanted someone who was willing to try the induction with him. She was right about him.

A few seconds later, Ellsbeth pulled away from the door just before it swung open and the graduate students filed out from beneath the archway. A few of them shot Ellsbeth sidelong glances as they passed. She straightened her back and tightened her grip on the two cups of tea she held in her hands, steam still inexplicably pulling itself from the narrow openings in their lids. Finally, when all of the students had exited, Professor Rawlins emerged from the Practicum, closing the heavy wooden doors behind him and locking them with a large metal key.

"Professor," Ellsbeth said before he finished turning around. "I'm Ellsbeth Storer. I emailed. You missed our appointment to meet for tea, and so I brought some to you. I have Earl Grey and jasmine. Whichever you prefer."

He was taller than Ellsbeth had realized, with lean shoulders hunched beneath a well-fitted blazer and long, aristocratic legs. He turned, and Ellsbeth saw, for the first time, just how startling the blue of his eyes was.

Rawlins blinked. "Ms. Storer." He eyed the cups as if they might be poisoned. "Seeing as we had not formally agreed to meet, this is less of an accommodation and more of an ambush." He deposited the Practicum's metal key snugly into the pocket of his blazer. "And I dislike tea."

Without hesitating, Ellsbeth took a sip from one of the cups.

Rawlins inhaled through his nose: "The Practicum is restricted except to those admitted to the program." Ellsbeth thought she heard his voice catch with a mocking lilt on the word "admitted." His eyes narrowed slightly. "Were you listening in at the door?"

"No," Ellsbeth said. "Of course not."

He took a step closer to her and allowed his height to loom. He was close enough for Ellsbeth to smell his aftershave, woodsy and tannic. "Auditing an undergraduate lecture is one thing. The content of a graduate-level Practicum, that is . . ."

"I'm not here to eavesdrop," Ellsbeth said. "I'm here because I want to do meaningful research. And because this is where I *belong*."

"Your Arcanus score—or rather, the lack thereof—tells a different story," he replied, and he strode past Ellsbeth, out of the entryway rotunda.

Ellsbeth followed through the breezeway and onto the green, trying to match the pace Rawlins managed with his long legs. His speed increased as he approached the department building; Ellsbeth sensed he was looking forward to sealing himself behind his office door. "I'd like to *tell you what happened*," she said, to his back. "If you'll just *listen*. If you're not so *closed-minded* that you can't consider the possibility that—"

"That what?" Rawlins said, stopping suddenly in front of the bronze statue of Gregory Hale, a railroad magnate who donated enough in the nineteenth century to fund half the buildings in the College of the Arcane Arts. "That your *feelings* about what you *deserve* are more important than the *rules* of this institution?"

"No," Ellsbeth said. "No, that's not it at all. If we could maybe go to your office—"

Rawlins shifted his weight slightly. Perhaps he sensed that indulging Ellsbeth might be less trouble than the alternative. "If you have something you feel the need to say to me," he said stiffly, "you may do so here."

"Fine," Ellsbeth said. "It's about my sister."

Though she had planned exactly what she wanted to say to him for weeks, thought about the words and how they would feel in her mouth, now that she was standing in front of him, Ellsbeth felt shockingly naked, exposed, and vulnerable. She sat on a bench and cleared her throat, inviting Rawlins to sit beside her. Mercifully, he did. She placed the two cups of tea at her side.

"Okay," she said. "It was January twelfth. My Arcanus. Obviously, I had prepared, and it was going—forgive me—very, very well. But—" She paused and sucked in, trying to pull courage out of the air. "Then came the augury portion. It was—"

"Scrying," he said. It was a ritual in which an arcanist could conjure an image in a shallow basin of water. Though theoretical arcanists had proven that foretelling the future should be mathematically possible, it had yet to ever actually be achieved in practice. That the ritual was still called scrying was a quirk of academic convention; the image was always, stubbornly, a scene happening somewhere concurrently, in the present.

"I've always been very good at scrying. And the ritual worked. I saw my sister." Ellsbeth looked at her skirt then. "She was . . . in the bathtub. And there was so much *blood.*" Ellsbeth could feel Rawlins stiffen next to her, but she tried to continue on, forcing out the words. "My younger sister. She was still breathing—I thought she was, at least. I had to go tell someone. I had to call someone. I had to try and save her."

Finally, Ellsbeth allowed her eyes to meet his. Light blue and unblinking, narrowed with something that might be concern or pity as he nodded absently. Ellsbeth knew that expression well. It was the one that happened when she gave an account of Bertie's death that rang a bell in someone's memory—that poor girl who killed herself, the tragedy whose details they had forgotten. But Rawlins didn't say anything, so Ellsbeth kept talking. "It was a choice between my future . . . and my sister's life. I had been selfish enough. I went to school overseas. Left her alone. She was a student here, actually. Undergraduate. She had just finished her first semester. It was there—" She tilted her head toward the south end of campus. "In the Perkins bathroom. Her name was Bertie. Roberta, but I always called her Bertie. She didn't make it. Suicide." She wiped at her nose with the back of her hand. "Or they said it was suicide, I guess."

When Rawlins finally spoke, his voice was low and neutral. "I am sorry," he said. "I understand that must have been difficult to see." He cleared his throat, ineffectually, unnecessarily. "But it sounds like you made your choice. And personal tragedy is not a qualifier for admission into a graduate studies program."

It took Ellsbeth a moment to register what he was saying. She felt her eyes prickle with tears, and for a moment she was afraid she was going to begin crying. But then fury rose to the surface in the form of a tiny laugh of disbelief. "I'm not asking to be let into the program out of pity. Look at my records. Look at my examination scores. Test me! Try me! Ask me a question—any ritual, any initiation." She rose to her feet. Rawlins remained sitting. "I belong in this department and I would have been here—or at Cambridge, or at Yale, or at Persky—if I had finished my Arcanus."

Rawlins didn't remove his gaze from the patch of grass between his feet.

"The graduate student cohort was selected months ago," he said. "I don't allow late admissions." His voice sounded very far away.

"So you won't even consider allowing me into the program," she said. A statement not a question.

He didn't respond.

Ellsbeth turned to walk away, but she spun back on her heels before she could stop herself. "I have one more thing to ask you," Ellsbeth said, relieved that there was no quiver in her voice. "It wasn't really a test, was it? Back in the Practicum, when you asked for someone to stand in for the time-dilation ritual . . . you played it off, but you would've gone through with it."

"I thought you weren't listening," Rawlins said. "But if you were, you would have heard what Miss Fitzwilliams said. It's illegal."

Ellsbeth twisted her lips into a bitter smile. "I just want you to know, I would've volunteered. They're scared. But I'm not."

She held Rawlins's gaze for as long as she could manage before she turned away again to begin her walk back toward her apartment on Governor Street, the shame and disappointment in her stomach slowly souring into something closer to heartbreak. Rawlins called her name as she was walking, but Ellsbeth didn't turn around. She would not let him see her cry.

From: Rawlins DAA
To: Storer.Ellsbeth
Subject: On Second Thought

Ms. Storer,

After our last encounter, I had not planned on emailing you, or (to be frank) even thinking about you, ever again. But since I have been compelled to do the latter, I find myself doing the former. As such, let the record show, I have at least gotten your name right this time, and can assure you that the error will not be repeated. You are many things—impolitic, insistent, and infuriating come to mind—but *forgettable* you are not. For better or worse.

The story you shared regarding the events of your Arcanus exam are indeed rather singular, and I am sorry the scrying you undertook revealed such devastating personal news. Arcane mechanical practice is often frustrating in its limitations; while it is incredible to be able to see at such a distance, what is the point, if you cannot avert the events you witness? When someone in my life was endangered (not a sister, but a person equally dear), I learned of the tragedy as most do—when it was too late to do anything. As a diviner of fortunes, I tormented myself for years wondering what I might have done to save him, if only I had been practicing the right ritual at the right time.

Alas, one arena in which the arcane holds no sway is upon the past. And the past, indeed, is where my mind has gone, ironically, as I've pondered your future. The downside of age is that memories—particularly the painful ones we keep at bay—accumulate like water behind a dam. It can be dangerous to open the floodgate even a little, for the deluge may prove unstoppable. Last night, while struggling to focus on the *Herbanicum Journal* editorial work I foolishly agreed to, I found myself distracted by thoughts of your situation, and stepped out onto the veranda to enjoy my last taboo pleasure (tobacco, gloriously perfected in its cheapest form, the cigarette).

From my home on Partridge Hill, the entire town is visible,

and in the wee hours of Saturday morning it hums with the festivities of undergraduates, as they set aside their studies and lose themselves in the restless pursuit of excitement and human collision. I am normally energized by proximity to that natural force. But lately I have felt estranged from it, and alienated from the thrum of human vitality. Perhaps it is middle age; perhaps the silence of the home I now occupy alone; perhaps the weight of those damn memories.

When I review the last few years of students I have taught, and the diminished state of our field—increasingly regarded as an Ivory Tower relic, with limited innovation to offer the world—I am compelled to consider that I may, in my tenure, have become a rusty cog in a creaky machine. The invigoration of that device may require not only the same grease we've put to it for ages, but new parts with clever design. And as your emails and your academic record have made abundantly clear, you are nothing if not clever.

Thus it is with some trepidation that I am willing to reverse my earlier course, and offer a different, albeit qualified, response to your request:

Yes, with provisions, for now.

Your syllabi, course schedule, and reading lists are attached. I expect you to be fully caught up by the time class starts on Monday.

Do not make me regret this.

Sincerely,
T. M. Rawlins, DAA

From: Storer.Ellsbeth
To: Rawlins DAA
Subject: Re: On Second Thought

Dear Professor,

My apartment is on Governor, down the street from Banestooth Club. The neighborhood is nowhere near as charming as Partridge Hill, but it does have its occasional perks. Such as: Last night, the Banestooth boys were having one of their many raucous parties, and if it had not been for the thumping bass, loud enough to vibrate my windowpanes, then all of my neighbors would have heard me yelp out loud when I got your email.

Thank you. Thank you. Thank you.

I recognize that taking on a new arcane student even a few weeks after the start of the semester, especially one without the qualifications of the Arcanus, is an incredibly rare concession and I do not intend to waste your faith in me. I assure you, the assurances in our earlier communication with regard to my discipline and the work I intend to put into this course were not made frivolously. (Would you believe me if I told you I had managed to procure an old syllabus and already did all of the required reading? I suppose it doesn't matter what you believe, but do feel free to quiz me in detail in class on Howland's Principles.)

Again, thank you. Looking forward to Monday. I will wear my best sweater.

Best,
Ellsbeth

From: Rawlins DAA
To: Storer.Ellsbeth
Subject: Re: Re: On Second Thought

Ms. Storer,

Before you pop the proverbial champagne, let me dispel any cause for celebration with a bracing dose of reality. To start the program now, without the months of preparation afforded to your classmates, will be exceedingly difficult, and accommodations cannot be made. Your admission will be deemed provisional and probationary, with quarterly evaluation of your fitness to proceed. You must immediately familiarize yourself with the Ritual Procedure Manual, as you cannot participate in next week's Practicum until you've passed your safety certification.

But none of those compare to the greatest challenge you will face here. The Doctorate of Arcane Arts is directed toward a thesis, and this is not a program that affords funded students years to languish and "explore their interests." I instructed your peers who applied through the proper channels to begin sending me their ideas over the summer, since the criteria are so stringent, and the process of homing in on a topic invariably requires extensive dialogue. So in this important area, you are already months behind. You need to propose a *novel* arena of study, the investigation of which will meaningfully contribute to the arcane corpus. Yet the scope of your scholarship must be narrow enough to investigate and analyze during your time here.

Moreover, I cannot hold your hand through the process. When I studied under Dr. Lennox, she gave me an analogy that I have embraced: An adviser is a student's *opponent* more than her ally. I will challenge your ideas, damage your confidence, and reject your proposals when they do not meet the most rigorous academic criteria. (Come to think of it, I suspect you may have steered clear of seeking out Lennox as an adviser due to her reputation for toughness, but I can assure you that you'll find my own standards every bit as exacting.)

You are already months behind your peers. Mr. Hamada, for

example, has an entire distinguished medical career that led him to his topic on the potentially detrimental longevity effects of transmutation rituals. Ms. Josten has already been through seven iterations of her proposed topic, homing in on a particular subset of conjuration rituals for which practical applications have not been discovered, knowing full well she may merely be closing the door on them forever.

Your thesis will not be a book that will make your name. I sense in you a capacity for self-dramatizing grandiosity that I wish to nip in the bud. We begin our careers in arcane mechanicals as humble cultivators of knowledge, and most end that way as well.

I do not intend to be discouraging, only to emphatically communicate the challenges you face. So bring me a topic. Do so quickly. Make it interesting. Focus its scope. And perhaps, with an appropriate dose of *paenitere,* we may yet sculpt you into a scholar.

Cordially,
T. M. Rawlins, DAA

From: Storer.Ellsbeth
To: Rawlins DAA
Subject: Re: Re: Re: On Second Thought

Dear Professor Rawlins,

Yes. Absolutely. Of course. I do not underestimate the difficulty of the program, and I am confident the probationary nature of my admission will not be a problem.

With regard to my thesis, this is actually a matter to which I have already given a considerable amount of thought. I have several ideas for topics that I know would be perfectly adequate, the types of projects that Dean Lennox and the university would approve without a second glance. For example: "Using Augury as a Tool for Understanding Decreasing Rainfall in the Western United States." Gathering data would be simple enough, the runework is more or less accessible in the archives, and if I tied the subject to a broader social issue (climate change, human interference with the weather), I know I could give the subject just enough polish to make it publishable in a reputable journal before it would be quickly forgotten in the continuously flowing stream of myopic academia.

A project like that would be (forgive me) easy. It would allow me to graduate perfectly on schedule and would allow you to not need to afford me any additional attention.

But adequacy doesn't interest me. I have a thesis idea that I recognize is slightly controversial, but one that I feel is far more worthwhile than the typical theses that I feel (as perhaps you also do) are emblematic of the "Ivory Tower relic" mentality. Detached from the real world, knowledge for the sake of self-congratulations, bloodless and dispassionate.

The idea that I'm actually interested in pursuing is writ magic.

Of course, my work would be *entirely theoretical.* Since the statute was passed in 1949, there has been almost no new literature on writ magic, even in an academic context. In fact, by my estimation, the most recent fully published book about the subject is Cavendish-Grey's pamphlet from 1909. Again, I want to assure you (as you will no doubt need to assure the rest of the thesis committee if you accept my proposal) that I intend to explore writ magic from an *academic perspective only.* But we are academics! And the statute (instituted for more than worthy reasons, of course) should not be an entirely paralyzing force on the pursuit of knowledge.

(I am, let's say, slightly embarrassed about proposing such a . . . controversial topic when you've already granted me the tremendous indulgence of joining the program at all, but not embarrassed enough not to want to focus on the area that truly interests me. An area in which, forgive me, based on your own academic history, I think you'll be uniquely suited to mentoring me. Because though Cavendish-Grey might be the last time someone published a full book on writ magic, I did come across a few-decades-old journal article from a certain familiar name. *The New England Journal of Mechanicals* does not include author photos, heartbreakingly, so now I will never know if you had an "unfortunate undergraduate facial hair" phase.)

I have a few thoughts on the proper scope and way to approach the topic that I think would be best to discuss in person. You mentioned you live on Partridge Hill? Do you know The Frayed Page? It's a used bookstore and café on Providence Street with below-average fiction offerings but above-average lemon muffins. Are you free anytime to meet there to chat?

Best,
Ellsbeth

P.S. Surely now, you can address your emails to me as "Ellsbeth"?

From: Rawlins DAA
To: Storer.Ellsbeth
Subject: Re: Re: Re: Re: On Second Thought

Ms. Storer,

I'm not sure if your proposal is intended as a joke, or perhaps a ploy so that I will be more amenable to whatever you suggest next, but it sounds like we should indeed discuss the matter; please come with a list of backup topics (that is, ones that are even remotely feasible). And while I cannot comprehend your apparent allergy to my office hours, yes, having lived on Partridge Hill for over a decade, I am well acquainted with The Frayed Page, and am typically there on Thursday afternoon around 4 p.m. What it lacks in selection, it generally makes up for in quiet, so please don't make a habit of intruding upon my time there.

Sincerely,
Rawlins

RAWLINS

The Frayed Page was a sleepy bookstore with a quaint coffee shop attached, far enough from the campus that it was rarely a hangout for undergraduates. It generally attracted an older crowd, mostly local eccentrics and retirees, the sort with free time on a Thursday afternoon. The proprietors, a couple in their seventies, were generally content to let "customers" pick up books off the shelf and read them for hours without spending a cent. Rawlins often wondered how the place stayed in business.

He had adopted The Frayed Page as a refuge, and made a weekly practice of coming there for a few hours of reading whatever battered paperback caught his eye, ideally something entirely unrelated to his field of study. But now, his sanctuary was being violated by, of course, Ellsbeth Storer. She not only had invited herself into the shop in his neighborhood but had again shown up unbidden in his mind. He had hoped that admitting her to the program would silence the thoughts, but instead, she had promptly sent him a proposal for a topic that was so flagrantly absurd, he could not understand what she was playing at.

Writ magic? The subset of the arcane arts that enabled a practitioner to control and manipulate others had been banned for decades, and with good reason; yet Ellsbeth Storer—presumptuous, arrogant, infuriating—seemed to think it the ideal topic of study.

What was the girl playing at? And why had she insisted on coming to speak on the matter in person? *Paenitere* indeed. Perhaps he should simply rescind the offer of admission. No doubt she would kick up a fuss, but the paperwork hadn't cleared yet. It would be messy. It would be humiliating for her. Good.

But Rawlins couldn't help but be intrigued by Ellsbeth's—there was no other word for it—*gumption*. Why in God's name would she be so driven to study writ magic of all things? Was it simply her ambition to make an impact on the field? If so, it was daring to the point of unwise. Was she intrinsically disagreeable? So intellectually restless that only the most taboo knowledge would satisfy her? So obsessed with being *unique* that she would spite her own prospects to set herself apart?

These thoughts and more churned through Rawlins's mind as he collected his espresso and fig scone from the counter and took a seat in the corner of the café, where he had a view of the entire bookstore. He opened his laptop, half intending to get back into his past-due manuscript, but instead, he found himself opening a webpage and typing the name "Ellsbeth Storer" into the search bar.

Her social media presence was robust; it seemed that, for years, she had maintained a deliberate and calculated cultivation of her public persona, attempting to present herself as a sophisticated iconoclast. She had studied in Scotland as an undergrad, no doubt imagining that this afforded her some measure of gravitas, and her posts featured not debauched parties but literary events, classical music, and visits to historic castles.

There were the requisite selfies, of course, but even when she smiled, it was with lips sealed, head tilted, as if showing genuine happiness would be embarrassing. Even in the pictures with friends, she seemed to float apart from the group, alone in a crowd, distancing herself from her peers. It was laughable, how clearly she wanted to be taken seriously.

He studied her face, looking for clues. She was not the sort of natural beauty who would have been praised for her looks since youth, but he conceded that she wasn't unattractive. Her facial features had sharpened as she escaped puberty so that she emerged into adulthood with a look that was, at least, distinctive. At some point, she must have realized that her mouth was her most striking feature, with full lips and a cupid's-bow curve, and she had started to accentuate it with bold red lipstick and a coy smile. No doubt the grin was calculated to project the air of intellectual mystery she aspired to, but Rawlins had to admit that it was effective.

He stopped at a post in which she boasted of receiving an award for a paper she had submitted to a contest. He clicked the link, wondering if her writing might provide some clue to her mind.

The paper was an essay on the impact of the arcane on American history, and none of the ideas within were nearly as bold as the notion of studying writ magic. But he was impressed by the clarity of her prose, and paused on an illuminating phrase: *The arcane does not change us; it merely gives us the power to call forth that which we dream—thus revealing the dreams of the nation to itself.*

And what do *you* dream, Ellsbeth Storer? He found himself trying to imagine her as she had been writing those words years prior. Where had she been? In a grand library? In a dorm room in pajamas?

He drifted back to the post, which featured a photo of Ellsbeth with a hollow smile on her face as she accepted an award, posing with a tacky gold paperweight. She wore a too-large blazer and a too-short skirt, which, in a picture meant to commemorate her academic achievement, drew the eye inevitably to her thighs.

Rawlins glanced around the café, startled from his reverie, suddenly paranoid that someone might see his screen and wonder why he was poring over the social media of a student. Even worse, that Ellsbeth might arrive early and see him—and yes, he had to admit this is what he was doing—digitally stalking her; he suspected she would absolutely *love* that. He needed to get back to his actual work.

And yet he continued scrolling, and he started to see a change when he got to photographs of Ellsbeth and her sister, easily identified by their visible familial resemblance. The same round cheeks, the same brown eyes. Laughing together at a mini-golf course. Posing at an art museum in front of a Renaissance painting, making goofy faces in mockery of the serious expressions behind them. There was a *joy* there, a vitality, which disappeared in the procession toward the highly curated photos of the present day.

When Ellsbeth relayed the story of her sister's death during their conversation in the garden, it had clicked with Rawlins why the name *Storer* had sounded so familiar. But now, looking at the two sisters side by side, he felt a deeper appreciation for what a monumental event the loss had been, the sort that can divide a life into before and after eras. He was meeting her in the aftermath—a driven girl who had known sorrow on a nearly unfathomable scale.

The chime of the bell hanging over the door drew Rawlins's attention, and suddenly, she was there. In a sweater that did indeed fit her well, and another skirt that was shorter than it ought to be, and that red lipstick he recognized from her photos as the shade she wore when she wanted to be noticed.

Seeing her in person after nearly an hour of studying her online, he found himself uncomfortably nervous. He hastily closed his laptop and opened a book, pretending to be absorbed in the text.

Ellsbeth spotted him and approached the table, an infectious grin filling her face. "I love it here," she said. "It's a little far for me, but it's worth the trip every time."

Rawlins did not look up from the book, merely held up a finger to signal her to wait while he pretended to finish his chapter, before he finally marked the (random) page and indicated for her to sit.

The table was small, and as she took her seat, setting her backpack to the side, their legs briefly touched. A glancing brush against his knee, but he could not help but wonder if it was deliberate, and he could not help but hope it would come again.

"So. Your thesis topic," he said, his voice oddly low.

Ellsbeth had clearly hoped for a bit of small talk first, but seeing his demeanor, she switched gears for intellectual combat. "Writ magic," she said, elaborating no further than she had in her email.

He stared at her. His first question—*Are you serious?*—had been clearly answered by her defiant expression. The girl certainly didn't want for courage. Not fearlessness—he could tell that she was afraid, but she was steering her ship straight into the winds of her own terror.

Rawlins was intrigued. He had been fascinated by writ magic in his youth—find any arcane scholar who wasn't, even if they wouldn't admit it—and it remained an illicit fascination, though it was nothing he would dare speak about openly. And nothing he would even consider pursuing publicly.

Rawlins knew that whoever spoke next was ceding ground, and he would not give her the satisfaction. At last, Ellsbeth relented. "I'm aware that it's controversial, but—"

"Controversy is one thing," he said, cutting her off. "Writ magic is illegal."

"There are *statutory* bans," she corrected, and he snorted, interrupting her again, but this time Ellsbeth pressed on. "And whatever you want to call them, those bans were enacted in a very reactive political environment."

"By people *reacting* to the way writ magic was used," Rawlins said. "And *abused.*"

"I'm aware," Ellsbeth replied. "Of course I know that there have been certain . . . unfortunate uses of writ magic. But I'm interested in much more *subtle* uses, which might require entirely new avenues of research."

"Writ magic is not subtle."

"But maybe it *could* be," Ellsbeth said. "I'm just saying, the statutes have meant that our scholarly understanding of writ magic is *decades* behind that in other fields. Writ magic touches on the foundational questions of human behavior. Of motivation. Free will. I understand that when people actually *use* writ magic, there's the possibility of violence, but the magic itself—I mean, we're scholars. Don't we have a duty to try to understand the power of the natural world? Isn't that the role of an elite institution like Newlyn? To be willing to challenge the fear-based status quo and push the field of arcane mechanicals forward."

She was proud of her line of reasoning, he could tell, and Rawlins was impressed by her persuasive skills. In the short time he'd known Ellsbeth, he somehow kept underestimating her. It was irritating, as if the floor kept falling out beneath him, forcing him to recalibrate his expectations repeatedly.

"It is . . . a compelling approach," he conceded, finally, wishing he had a cigarette to distract his fingers. "But as disproportionate as the cultural resistance to writ magic may be—and I don't necessarily think it is—that resistance is deep-seated. The rest of the faculty certainly won't approve."

"Then we'll have to change their minds," she said simply. And she placed her hand on top of his, just for a moment, before she removed it.

Rawlins's heart caught in his chest in a way he didn't quite understand.

He looked away from her, trying to think about this rationally. His scalp was tingling. In lieu of a cigarette, Rawlins found himself tearing at the corner of a napkin. "Even if I do agree to advise a thesis on writ magic," he said slowly, deliberately not making eye contact, "we require our graduate students to actually perform the rituals they focus their studies on. And those remain illegal."

To his surprise, Ellsbeth didn't seem deterred. "I didn't expect the professor who pulled off the first exothermic reversal ritual in North America to be so bound by the rules."

"And I didn't expect such a bright young scholar to be so untethered from reality," he replied.

She shot back another infuriating half smile. "Oh, *reality.* Let's leave that to the philosophy department. We both know that in the arcane arts, reality is . . . flexible."

Her tone had turned playful; she was enjoying this exchange—and, he realized reluctantly, he was, too. They were practically *bantering.*

Unacceptable. He was her adviser, and she was badly in need of a bracing dose of reality. He leaned across the table, his tone growing serious as he lowered his voice. "You are quite young, so you may not understand the depth of the aversion people have to writ magic, because in your lifetime, there hasn't been a documented case of its use. But there are people alive today who remember the Stokely trial."

She took the hint, and matched his seriousness, her face becoming stony and inscrutable. "Of course. It's horrible. But people have done equally horrible things without magical influence."

"Have you seen the *interviews*?" he said. "Not just with the victims and their families—with Eleanor Stokely herself. Imagine being forced to do the things she did. And remembering all of it."

"I mean . . . she shouldn't really feel *guilty,*" Ellsbeth said. "We all understand it wasn't her choice, so—"

"Don't be a *child,*" Rawlins snapped. "Imagine yourself in her position. Imagine that *you* had done something like that, to someone you love. You think you wouldn't feel *guilty*?" Ellsbeth squirmed and Rawlins barreled onward, seeking to drive the point home and extinguish her foolish stubbornness once and for all. "Writ magic is a violation of our most fundamental sense of agency."

Ellsbeth looked directly into Rawlins's eyes then. "Whether or not people are using writ magic—and I'm not saying they should—the point remains that it exists as a power available in the arcane arts. And the fact that it hasn't been studied for decades doesn't undo that. In fact, I would argue that *not* studying it, not understanding it, does a profound disservice to our entire academic discipline. It *keeps* writ magic taboo. I don't think it's childish to imagine the possibility that some therapeutic, rehabilitating applications of writ magic are possible. Or in a legal context. Imagine law enforcement compelling people to tell the truth, to help find victims—"

"How old are you?" Rawlins interrupted.

"Twenty-four."

"You sound impossibly naïve," Rawlins said. "You're talking with the same elitist attitude as those who went on to abuse writ magic in the first place. You think you get to decide when it's actually *worthwhile* to have people under magical control." Ellsbeth tried to interject, but he continued speaking. "There is a reason that writ magic is banned. The autonomy of the mind and body is our most basic human right."

"But there are all *kinds* of ways that people are controlled," Ellsbeth continued, maddeningly undaunted by what should have been the concluding point in the matter. "Is using writ magic on someone more of an inherent violation of human rights than putting them in handcuffs? Of locking someone in prison? Or a system that forces them to live in poverty, in situations where they have to work twelve-hour days in inhuman conditions?"

Rawlins swallowed hard. "It's . . . a fair point. An interesting philosophical argument. But the existence of unjust forms of control in the world doesn't excuse adding another. And it's impossible to even conceive of an ethical application of writ magic without the full consent of its subject. And no one would consent to being controlled."

"Well, *that's* just not true," Ellsbeth said. "Now you sound naïve." Rawlins blinked, unsure for a moment exactly what they were debating.

Ellsbeth tilted her head in a peculiar, challenging way. The sound of laughter chirping at a nearby table startled Rawlins. The music playing in the shop was tinny and discordant; he realized he couldn't pull his eyes from Ellsbeth's face, her narrowed eyes and the curl at the corner of her mouth.

"Sometimes," Ellsbeth said carefully, "I like being told what to do."

The adrenaline and pace of the argument was a buoying force, and Rawlins felt his mouth open even before he had found his retort—but he paused when he realized a flush was rising in his cheeks. Ellsbeth finally broke their eye contact, glancing down at the napkin Rawlins had spun into a needle-thin line. "I mean, in certain contexts," she said. "I like being . . . ordered around. *Compelled,* even. To do what's best for me, or . . . things I wouldn't do otherwise. As long as it comes from someone I trust."

For an instant, her knee pressed against his. Then it was gone so fast that if it hadn't been for the lingering heat, he couldn't have been entirely certain he hadn't imagined it.

Rawlins's heart raced. He shifted in his seat and forced his fingers to abandon the shred of cotton that was becoming confetti on their table. He looked toward the window, hoping he appeared to be deep in thought, when in fact he was afraid that she would see in his eyes how thoroughly he was consumed by an effort to resist the inexplicable urge to reach across the table and brush his thumb across her lower lip.

Finally, he broke the silence, searching for a logical argument with which to find some handhold on this slippery conversation. "Even if your interest in writ magic is purely theoretical, this degree is not in theory, it is arcane *mechanicals.* For your dissertation, you need to compose a novel ritual that can be evaluated. And I can't see how you plan to do so, if you're writing up a ritual that you are legally barred from carrying out."

"There's precedent," Ellsbeth said. "Newlyn approved a thesis on energetic sublimation that was never put into practice. Pure theory."

"That was because the cost of the elementals would have been astronomical," Rawlins replied. "And that was, what, forty years ago?"

"Okay, well, Persky's arcane mechanicals department has approved a number of theses on theoretical topics, including one as recently as two years ago." Clearly, Ellsbeth had done her research and come in prepared for exactly this argument, which earned another notch of grudging respect from Rawlins.

"Persky has a reputation as an Ivory Tower with their collective head in the clouds," he said. "And most of those are topics in astronomy, on a scale that *couldn't* be tested. What you're talking about is a ritual that would either work or *not,* and without the ability to iterate, with data, you'll be flying blind. You won't know what you're missing unless you're able to test your ritual, and testing is illegal. Your work will go before the committee, and if they spot something you overlooked, you'll fail."

"I mean . . . I *could* test my work. Even if I couldn't necessarily include the results in my paper, I could conduct rituals independently to steer my progress, refine the writing."

Rawlins regarded her across the table. Her sweater, her backpack, her conservatively pinned-back hair—none of these suggested an iconoclast, much less a criminal. Yet here she was, casually hinting that she would engage in felonious arcane practice to develop her doctoral dissertation. Unsure if she even realized what she was saying, he pressed her: "To be clear: You're talking about simply flouting the law?"

"I'm talking about *privately* carrying out scholarly work, in a spirit of exploration, that might not strictly adhere to the letter of the law." Her words were not merely precise, they were also . . . playful. As if she was teasing him. "That's what arcane scholars have done since the earliest days of the field, when this work was viewed as demonic. I thought you, of all people, might see the value in genuinely *independent* study."

He felt himself being drawn in, his curiosity piqued—but he leaned back, working to maintain an air of objective detachment. "Even if I were to tacitly approve this course of action . . . which I'm not saying I do . . . any writ magic would require a test *subject.* And I can't imagine you'll find anyone in your cohort who will consent to being the target of an untested ritual to control their will."

He intended it as a challenge, half hoping she would back down and half hoping she would reluctantly accept. What he hadn't counted on was the way that a small smile curled the corner of her mouth. "I only need to *design* the ritual, right? Not be the one to actually perform it? Well, then I would be willing to be the subject. As long as someone whose skill I trusted entirely was conducting the ritual. Like you."

Rawlins realized at that moment he had lost the debate. Not only that; she had *played* him into this corner. And yet, even as he bristled at feeling manipulated . . . his heart was accelerating, his breath shallow and quick. He was *excited.* By the danger of it, yes, and by the intellectual audacity, but even more so—by *her.*

He leaned forward now, his face coming perilously close to hers. "If you proceed with this idea, and it goes badly—if it doesn't work, or your abstract is not approved—then your academic career will be finished. So if we are to proceed on this course, I need you to be absolutely *certain* of your decision."

Ellsbeth appeared unfazed by his warnings. "I'm aware."

His mind spun, unmoored. *This would be a disaster.* If he allowed himself to open the door to practicing writ magic, the consequences would be dire and lasting.

But then there was Ellsbeth. And the red slash of her lips. And her leg against his.

Rawlins had lines, very clear lines he had drawn early on in his career. Lines that he could never cross. It had been easy for him to bat away flirtations and confine fantasies to a few quiet moments alone in a shower before they were dismissed entirely. Something about Ellsbeth was different. She was drawing him in, down toward an abyss, and he knew as soon as he stepped forward, gravity would take over.

He suddenly had a vision of his life, his perfectly respectable career, the quiet existence he had built for himself, quivering like custard. Allowing himself to study writ magic again, and allowing himself to spend time alone with Ellsbeth Storer—they were both illogical choices, verging on foolishness. They were unnecessary and irresistible temptations, either of which could easily lead to complete catastrophe. He *knew* this. But Rawlins also knew something else, something deep in his soul: He wasn't going to stop.

"You—you're sure you want to do this?" he said.

Ellsbeth tried to suppress her smile and her eyes flashed. "Oh, I'm very clear about what *I* want, Professor Rawlins," she said. "Are you?"

ELLSBETH

When Ellsbeth was in her final year at the University of St. Andrews, she had an affair with the semi-acclaimed British novelist Amos Paul. Well, *she* thought of it as an affair. No doubt he viewed it as a brief, forgettable conquest, merely one more of the many young girls who threw themselves at him, hoping his talent or fame would be sexually transmittable. She understood that now.

Here is how it happened: Ellsbeth was in a ten-person seminar, under a professor who happened to have been classmates with Amos Paul at Harrow. So, when Amos Paul was touring Scotland to promote his latest book (a bleak novella called *Pallbearers*), Ellsbeth's professor invited him to stop by the university to speak to the class.

Ellsbeth was humiliated on behalf of her fellow students during the whole ordeal. Their questions ranged from the inane ("Where do you get your ideas?") to the cringe inducing ("Do you think your agent might be willing to read a manuscript from a new, up-and-coming writer straight out of uni?"). Ellsbeth restrained herself to one question that she hoped came across as mature and dignified, asking Paul which other writer had inspired him the most (Chekhov).

She decided she wanted to sleep with him about thirty minutes into the class. It wasn't because he was particularly handsome (although she liked his horn-rimmed glasses). It wasn't even because he was successful. If Ellsbeth was truly being honest with herself, the reason she decided to seduce Amos Paul was to see if she could. She was twenty-two at the time, and reasonably pretty. He was in his forties and unmarried according to his Wikipedia page and lack of wedding ring. The attempt at seduction was almost clinical in her mind, an experiment: What behavior could she input in order to achieve her desired outcome?

Amos Paul had left the seminar without lingering, and so Ellsbeth went to his reading at Waterstones the next day, wearing a short skirt and high boots. She sat in the second row and tried to make eye contact with him as often as possible, and when he happened to glance her way, she tried to give him a flirtatious smile. When his reading was over, she waited in line to have him sign her book.

"I was in Professor Miller's writing workshop," Ellsbeth said when she finally reached Amos Paul, who had already begun to robotically sign the book she slid in front of him (*Best, Amos Paul*). "You were so incredibly insightful."

"Thank you," he said, already looking past her at the older man in a sweater vest elbowing his way forward.

"What a rare opportunity it is," Ellsbeth said, "to get to see one of my favorite authors in such an intimate setting."

"Oh," Amos Paul said, giving Ellsbeth another glance. His eyes lingered for an instant on the strip of pale flesh between where her boots ended and her skirt began. "Well, thank you."

The old man in the sweater vest cleared his throat, but Ellsbeth refused to cede any ground at the signing table. She slipped the receipt out from her newly purchased hardcover and fished a pen from her purse. "I'm sure you've got plenty of friends in town, but if you want someone to show you where to get the good drinks around here—" She slid the receipt, with her full name and phone number written on it, toward Amos Paul, then left before she could see what he chose to do with it.

The first text came at ten thirty-five that night: so miss ellsbeth, good drinking places in town?

It was followed a moment later by another text: this is amos paul by the way.

Ellsbeth's heart was racing. She hadn't imagined it would be quite so easy. Hi there. Glad you texted. Consider me your local tour guide. What area are you staying in?

He gave the name of a hotel, and twenty minutes later, Ellsbeth was shivering in the back of an Uber wearing a cotton dress and lingerie that she had bought months ago but hadn't yet found the opportunity to wear. He was waiting in the hotel's lobby bar, wearing a sweater that pulled across his belly, and Ellsbeth ordered an Old-Fashioned, because that's what he ordered.

Was she attracted to him? She wasn't entirely sure. If she was, it was an attraction to the situation itself, the thrill of imagining herself as he saw her: the shamelessly flirtatious co-ed.

He was strangely stiff as they drank, talking about his book tour and his complaints about his recent publisher and the possibility of an adaptation in America that didn't seem to be progressing. Ellsbeth drank, and wondered if this was a mistake, if she had misread the cues, if she had spent forty pounds on a car to come here to say things like, "Oh, sure," and "That sounds so frustrating," and "Well, you're brilliant, that's why."

When Amos Paul finished his Old-Fashioned, he licked his lips and looked Ellsbeth square in the face: "Well, how about popping up to my room?"

They kissed in the elevator, a shockingly wet, full-contact kind of kiss during which Ellsbeth had to remind herself to keep her eyes closed.

The smell of his sweat became acrid as it chilled on his naked body, and as soon as he finished, he rolled across the bed into the bathroom, where he remained, with the light on and the door closed, for a considerable amount of time.

She called her own car to return to her place, and though Amos Paul would politely reply to her texts on occasion (ha ha), she never saw him again.

Ellsbeth was not ashamed for having sex with a man she desired; she was ashamed upon realizing that her ego had written a self-aggrandizing narrative in which she had dazzled the famous and talented Amos Paul and he had slept with her because of who she was as a person, not because she was merely young and available. It was whiplash, a sting to the ego more than to the heart.

The experience hardened her in a way she hadn't anticipated, reinforcing her unspoken beliefs that sex was transactional and mechanical, a mutually enjoyable endgame of a seduction well played. *He says X, I say Y.* Every possible response from a man had some corresponding response she could calculate in order to move the dance forward. It was more fun than chess; there were more possible variables, more improvisations she could tease out, and also occasionally at the end she had an orgasm.

Sex had not been the goal with Rawlins. She needed him to like her, because she needed him to study writ magic. If she had to perform the bubbly co-ed in order to achieve that, then so be it.

She had been thinking of Amos Paul when she was preparing to meet Rawlins at The Frayed Page, of her ability to say the correct things in order to achieve her desired outcome. She hadn't found any information on the internet about whether Rawlins was married or dating anyone (she couldn't resist searching), but that was no indication of anything really: There were mentions of his book, and citations of his many academic articles, but the closest Ellsbeth came to finding anything personal was his faculty page for Newlyn University. It featured a list of the classes he taught and a biography only a few sentences long: "Thaddeus M. Rawlins is a graduate of Yale University, where he also received his master's and PhD in ancient translations. He received his DAA from Cambridge University, where he also served as a distinguished lecturer. He is the author of seven books, including the international bestseller *The Arcane and the Ordinary*, which won the Keller Prize for excellence in academia and has been translated into twenty-four languages."

The photo was low-resolution and probably at least a decade old, a grainy shot of Rawlins offering the photographer a pained smile against a blank wall, probably somewhere on campus. Rawlins was an anomaly in the internet age—an unknown entity—but because she had read *The Arcane and the Ordinary* so many times, Ellsbeth had felt an unearned kinship with him, a sense of knowing him, or at least the rhythms of his voice.

If there was any arcanist alive capable of helping her learn writ magic, it was him. She knew it from seeing his name in the byline of an old article in *The New England Journal of Mechanicals*—an article that danced right up to the edge of what was publicly appropriate to say about writ magic. The lesson she had overheard in the Practicum the other day had only confirmed it. Rawlins was bored by rote, mundane applications of magic, and he would be willing to bend the rules for a brilliant student with vision. More than willing, Ellsbeth believed. He was *hungry* for it.

Her early flirting had been purposeful and planned; she hoped the guileless familiarity in her emails would jostle him off-balance enough to allow her to plead her case, to grant her more grace than he otherwise might in allowing her to join the program. She understood what was a shameful fact about men—that even the ones who believed themselves above flirtation were vulnerable to the biological response when faced with an *ingénue* deploying her charms correctly, the hero impulse.

And so her red lipstick and skirt that morning had been a tactical choice. It was the costume for the character she needed him to see her as: the alluring, impetuous young scholar. If he flattered himself with the notion that she had a crush on him, even better. Ellsbeth had no delusions about her own attractiveness—out of all of the lithe twenty-somethings Rawlins encountered, there was no reason to believe that he would be particularly dazzled by *her*. But if she charmed him, if she intrigued him . . . then she would be able to do what she came to Newlyn to do.

The battle plan was drawn up, the moves clear in her mind. Smile, flirt with plausible deniability, and get permission to study writ magic.

But when Ellsbeth saw Rawlins sitting at a small table at The Frayed Page, pretending to read a book, a jolt of something passed through her that she hadn't expected. She smiled without planning on it. His hair was rumpled, almost boyish; a flush was rising in his cheeks. She ran her hand through her own hair. She *wanted him.*

There was no tactical advantage to sleeping with him. An affair was out of the question. Ellsbeth reminded herself of that as the heat between them across the increasingly small table seemed to spark like an exposed electrical cable. Sleeping with her professor would be a disaster. It would be a distraction from finding the truth about Bertie. It would isolate her from her cohort and undermine her academic credibility. Rawlins would see her as a conquest, a disposable little girl, and not a colleague. And then when things went bad (as they almost certainly would), her precious position in the program would be put at risk.

She knew that she would never sleep with Professor Rawlins. It was a cliché. It was foolish. And Ellsbeth Storer was not foolish.

And yet.

Why had she moved her leg to slide against his? Why had she held his gaze when she told him she liked to be controlled? It was a mistake, she recognized that as soon as she was walking the long blocks back to her apartment on Governor Street, her backpack thudding against her hip. He had agreed. He would let her study writ magic, and now she needed to quiet the voice in the back of her brain that imagined the long lines of his arm muscles, that flat firm stomach. The voice that wondered whether his lips would be soft on hers, what he would taste like. They were irrational, buzzing thoughts, and Ellsbeth found that she was almost dizzy as she walked, lightheaded in a way that she had thought only happened to heroines in gauzy romance novels. She forced herself to laugh out loud. It could live as a fantasy—of course it was fantasy! Who wouldn't fantasize about their blue-eyed professor!—and be put neatly away into a box. And yet.

AFTER SHE OFFICIALLY ENROLLED, THE university had offered Ellsbeth an option for standard graduate student housing: a prison cell room in a Soviet Bloc complex designed in the neo-Brutalist period of the 1970s when they thought that the efficiency and discipline of poured concrete would serve as inspiration to the academic minds within. But Ellsbeth found the rooms sterile to the point of suffocation, and so she opted to pay nine hundred dollars a month to sublet the second story of a crumbling Victorian house on Governor Street.

The walls were custard yellow, and both the fridge and the stove (white, disconcertingly sticky) seemed too risky to rely on with any confidence, but the place had—what was that old-fashioned word?—*character.* A word that hair-sprayed realtors use to seduce insecure newlyweds into spending two hundred over asking on a ranch without a working electrical system. But there was no other word for it here.

There was the sense that this place had been lived in, that a hundred years of Newlyn students had occupied and then departed this very room. The smell of their anxiety and egotism and vomit had soaked into the walls like rum into a Christmas cake.

So: *character*. The wood of her bedroom window frame splintered upward like the spears of a Roman phalanx, and the floor tilted drunkenly, which meant the bathroom door left a scratch every time it closed and that Ellsbeth's dresser drawers habitually hung open. But those were the things she loved about the place. The house was from the 1800s, two blocks away from the campus of a college that was founded before the country. The settling creak of the floorboards and the way the wind whistled through the flue might have made someone else fear the place was haunted, but she found the house's noises comforting. Ellsbeth liked the thought that she was sharing the world with forces she couldn't see. Perhaps it was why she had always wanted to study arcane mechanicals.

Bertie had always been puzzled by Ellsbeth's fascination with the subject. "It's *magic*," Ellsbeth had said once, trying to explain. "It's the *poetry* of the universe given rules that *we can control*! Don't you see how extraordinary that is?" Bertie had sighed and stretched her tan legs on Ellsbeth's bed. She was lying backward, with her head carelessly dangling off the baseboard, but she was careful not to touch her bare feet to Ellsbeth's pillows. She must have been fifteen or so, watching on while Ellsbeth re-alphabetized her already impressive library of arcane books. Bertie's toenails were painted green, the color of industrial waste.

"I know that it's technically 'magic,'" she said, sighing. "But really, it's no more magical than chemistry, or . . . physics. And just as much math. And having to translate, like, ancient Assyrian or whatever. And for what? To move a stapler six inches to the left. You could do that just by picking it up, and then you wouldn't have to spend four hundred dollars on distilled mercury and take three hours drawing concentric circles."

Bertie wasn't wrong: The field of arcane mechanicals was, by and large, expensive and impractical, with results that were seldom worth the effort, especially considering that the consequences of a millimeter's miscalculation would be dire. There was a reason that, especially given the international legal restrictions on the arcane, it was pursued almost exclusively in academia or rarefied corporate laboratories—and occasionally, by children's entertainers applying basic transfiguratory devices to the delight of clapping toddlers. The twenty-first century had, somehow, restricted applications of arcane mechanicals to two distant, opposite realms: the most elite and esoteric, and the most inane.

But Ellsbeth didn't care. Bertie would never understand—she came to Newlyn University as an undergraduate in order to pursue subjects comfortably beyond the reach of any class that would require her to reckon with integrals or Mersenne prime numbers—but Ellsbeth would forever be the teenager reading and rereading *The Arcane and the Ordinary,* enthralled by the fact that the pulsing matter of human existence was something with hidden rules that, with enough study, she could master.

Ellsbeth was trying to remind herself of her childhood passion for the arcane while sitting on the South Green and struggling through a paragraph in Rawlins's assigned reading so dull that she found her eyelids drooping shut mid-sentence as if in protest. It was an academic treatise, published by the Oxford University Press several decades prior, centered on the debate over whether ancient Etruscans used pi in their rituals. To the best of Ellsbeth's understanding, the answer was maybe, but the author found it worth six thousand words and several lengthy tangents, usually embarked on mid-sentence, in order to get there. She needed to finish it before Rawlins's lecture.

"So it's true."

Ellsbeth shielded her eyes and looked up at the speaker. In a pair of high, clean riding boots and a silk blouse, Gracie Fitzwilliams stood over Ellsbeth, one of her perfectly manicured eyebrows raised. "They really let you into the program." She gestured with one of her boots toward the pages Ellsbeth was holding. "No one would be reading *The Etruscan Understanding of Irrational Numbers as Demonstrated Through Cultural and Physical Evidence: A Debate* for fun."

"Oh, no," Ellsbeth said, deadpan. "This is for my book club."

A thin smile expanded over Gracie's face in slow motion. "I'm Gracie Fitzwilliams."

"Ellsbeth Storer."

"Oh, I know," Gracie said. "We haven't been talking about anything else."

Ellsbeth folded the article back into her bag and pressed herself to her feet. She was several inches shorter than Gracie. "You've been talking about me?"

From the bright flickering in Gracie's eyes as they ran up and down Ellsbeth's person, Ellsbeth became aware that there was an evaluation happening in real time; Gracie had taken it upon herself to act as emissary for the other CotAA students, to scope out the interloper and report back. She imagined herself as Gracie must see her—grass stains on her jeans, unpolished and quick-bitten nails—and did her best to square her shoulders, to ensure, at least, that her posture matched her evaluator's.

"The girl who joined the arcane arts program two weeks in, without even taking the Arcanus? How could we not?" Gracie said. "The current bet is that you have some really good blackmail on Dean Lennox. Otherwise, why would they bother?"

"*Really* compromising photos," Ellsbeth said.

Gracie's smile was quicker this time, almost a smirk. "So is Rawlins your adviser? Or Gallway?"

"Rawlins."

"Well," Gracie said, tucking a glossy strand of blond hair behind her ear. "However you did it, I'm impressed. Though don't tell the others I said that. Priya Srinavasan—do you know her?—she's convinced you have a thing going with Curt Ladove, and I'm not sure she'll forgive you for that."

"Oh, she can have him," Ellsbeth said. There were so few graduate students in the arcane arts department that Ellsbeth found she could easily identify them on sight the way one might celebrities. They were lean, coltish types, with ink-stained fingers and round glasses. They strolled across the greens in pairs and trios, holding thick manuscripts and airs of self-satisfaction. Curt Ladove was tall and blond, favoring fleece vests and expensive shoes. They hadn't actually met, and so Ellsbeth wondered abstractly why Priya would have ever connected them. "That prep-school, my-daddy-bought-me-a-sailboat thing never did it for me."

"It's like you know him already," Gracie said. "You could give a grizzly bear a lacrosse stick and I swear Priya would blow him. So what's your thesis on? Our proposals were due last week, did you already send yours in? I don't see how you could have."

"I haven't decided yet," Ellsbeth lied. "And no, I think the department is giving me a few extra days to gather my thoughts."

"Sure," Gracie said. "You know, not everyone actually graduates. This program is incredibly competitive. I think most years, half the students end up dropping out before they actually get their DAA."

"I've heard."

Gracie gave Ellsbeth a frank, appraising look, as though Ellsbeth were a puzzle she wasn't certain was worth the energy of trying to crack. "I'm hosting a little get-together for the cohort this Thursday," she said finally. "We listen to a record all the way through and try to be the first to come up with a ritual that works with the rhythm of a song. Every time a ritual fails, you have to finish your drink. Of course, the drunker you get, the harder it is."

"You do rituals? Out of the Practicum?" The words were out before Ellsbeth realized how they made her sound—nervous and unsophisticated. Gracie's eyes rolled and Ellsbeth quickly amended her response. "I mean, yeah. Thank you. I'll be there."

"I'll text you the address," Gracie said, turning away as if she was already regretting extending the invitation. Ellsbeth resisted calling out after her that she had forgotten to ask for her number. If she was still invited to the party, Ellsbeth had no doubt in her mind that Gracie Fitzwilliams was the type of girl capable of finding a phone number.

It wasn't until Gracie was halfway across the green that Ellsbeth realized they were headed to the same place—Rawlins's lecture. And it only took a moment after that for Ellsbeth to realize that the class began in exactly three minutes, and if she was going to make it on time, she would need to race, undignified as a newborn giraffe, across the lawn. The conversation with Gracie had been unplanned and unexpectedly lengthy: Ellsbeth hadn't managed to finish the reading.

Ellsbeth slid into the wooden classroom seat just as the old-fashioned clock on the wall struck one, her forehead beaded with sweat and her ponytail sticking to her neck. The graduate symposiums took place in the turret of the red-brick department building, in a round room that looked like a Victorian surgical amphitheater in miniature. Rawlins stood onstage before a large, empty blackboard. He gave her an imperceptible glance, the tiniest raise of an eyebrow, before turning his attention to the class.

But he had barely managed the basic greetings before Gracie's manicured hand shot into the air.

"Professor? Obviously we have a new student in our cohort, and I had the pleasure of meeting her a little earlier. Ellsbeth?" Ellsbeth felt every pair of eyes in the room turn toward her.

"Very astute, Ms. Fitzwilliams," Rawlins said. "You are correct. Everyone, welcome Ms. Ellsbeth Storer, whom I know will be an asset to our scholarly pursuits." Ellsbeth gave an awkward half wave.

"I have *no doubt,*" Gracie continued, her voice a purr, "that she will be an asset. In fact, she and I were talking earlier, about the article you assigned? And Ellsbeth had some really brilliant thoughts on Etruscan numerology—you disagreed with the author's last paragraph, isn't that right?"

She knows. Gracie knows that I wasn't able to finish the article. A flush crawled up Ellsbeth's neck, and her mouth became sand. Rawlins's face was masklike and inscrutable.

"Uh, yes," Ellsbeth said. She muttered something nonsensical then, a string of words strung together in such a way as to say nothing at all. It was babbling; it was bullshit. Rawlins's face remained completely blank. When Ellsbeth finished speaking ("so, well, yeah"), he cleared his throat.

"Well," he said, "thank you for that insight, Ms. Storer, and Ms. Fitzwilliams, for your generous introduction." He turned toward the blackboard and drew a perfect hexagon with six confident strokes of the chalk. "Let's get started on the lesson, then, shall we?"

From: Rawlins DAA
To: {Graduate Cohort List}
Subject: Your Theses

Scholars,

I need revised thesis proposals from everyone by next Friday, including a preliminary bibliography and a precis on your research methods. The year is well under way, and some of your topics remain hazy. You will all need to submit for department approval, and you underestimate bureaucratic slowness at your own peril.

As testament to the value of doing good work ahead of schedule: Congratulations to Curt, who has just been named a MacGregor Fellow, with two years of funding for his research on energetic amplification rituals. There are still funding opportunities available to those who are able to get their proverbial shit together in a timely fashion.

Rawlins

From: Rawlins DAA
To: Storer.Ellsbeth
Subject: Re: Your Theses

Ms. Storer,

Sending you an addendum, since you are dreadfully behind the rest of the class, and I am already anticipating the blind alleys you will go down if left to your own devices; for my own sanity, if nothing else, I'd like to start by setting you on a more fruitful path.

Your topic, obviously, is outside the academic mainstream, and you will find little in the way of relevant recent publication. You may be tempted by the resurgence of literature on mentalism from the 1970s, but most of that work is pseudointellectual drivel masquerading as rigorous research. Steer clear.

Instead, consider early-20th-century pioneers who brought writ magic into the modern era: Bertram Gorky (start with his 1927 treatise "On the Magick of Mental Manipulation," progress to the 1931 doorstopper *The Mind's Eye*) and Rudolf Wentz (*Magickal Influence upon Cognition and Behavior* is the cornerstone). Citing these authors has become virtually verboten, but you will have to swallow your discomfort if you're to get anywhere.

As you're reading Wentz, try to track the source of his innovations; he is woefully lax in his citations, so I will point you toward the main texts he is referencing: *Arcanus Mentis* (1647), *The Diviner's Touch* (1598), and of course the seminal but inscrutable ur-text of this subfield: *Writ Magic* (1511). Those Renaissance-era accounts include little practical advice on the rituals you will eventually need to design, but they constitute the theoretical framework you will be working from.

Texts on this topic may of course be difficult to find; none of them are in common circulation, but the Bowles Annex has some on hand (I imagine you will be spending considerable time there). Let me know if you're coming up empty, as I have several of the texts in my personal collection, and may be willing to lend with the proper assurances.

Obviously, you will need to expand the scope of your research beyond this initial list, but hopefully this lands you on firm ground from which to explore. I am taking a more prescriptive approach here than usual, but I'm told some people rather enjoy being told what to do.

Rawlins

RAWLINS

Rawlins always did his best thinking on his morning walks to campus. It was a thirty-minute trip that he did not have time for every day, but whenever possible, it was well worthwhile. Navigating the familiar route—down Beacon Hill Drive, past a business district full of quaint shops, through the housing block favored by undergrads—opened his mind, still buzzing from his morning coffee, to chew through topics.

That particular Thursday, he thought he might be able to solve the problem of his overdue manuscript and either home in on a workable thesis that might move him forward, or at least come up with a better excuse for the book's years-long delay. But instead, his thoughts turned—not to Ellsbeth Storer, thank god, not directly at least, but to the complication she had introduced into his professional life.

A thesis on writ magic.

He had agreed to let her undertake the topic, knowing full well the challenges it entailed.

Rawlins was confident that he could justify her research as strictly academic and navigate the bureaucratic hurdles. The part that made it both interesting and dangerous was the fact that Ellsbeth intended to actually carry out *tests*—and that he had tacitly consented to help her. If they were caught, they would be imprisoned; engaging in such rituals privately and willingly might diminish their sentencing, but especially after what had happened with Max, the DA would aggressively prosecute any such case. Rawlins was not about to spend his next decade in jail and see his academic reputation permanently ruined.

That meant their undertaking would need to remain clandestine. Personally, Rawlins had no qualms keeping a secret. They were his specialty; ever since childhood, he had been enlisted to keep them on his parents' behalf. The very fact of his alcoholically chaotic home life was a secret he had learned to keep from the outside world. A prying question from a teacher, or worse, a visit from a concerned social-services bureaucrat, was a crisis.

On those occasions, Rawlins had watched his father turn on the charm, play the part of the responsible adult, and easily dispense with the concerned authority figure before shutting the door and turning his newly inflamed rage on the traitors who had betrayed him: his wife and children. Rawlins had learned that the consequences of showing your dysfunction to the world were only terror and pain.

All of which contributed to his gift for . . . well, it was not necessarily *deception* so much as *compartmentalization.* The sorting of facts and truths into different buckets, airtight and hermetically sealed.

The challenge was the question of whether *Ellsbeth* could keep a secret. There was no basis for trust between them, and he had no reason to assume she had any gift for guile. Her attempts to maneuver him through flirtation when they had met at The Frayed Page had been utterly transparent, hardly suggesting a temperament suited to subterfuge.

Of course, he had to concede that those clumsy efforts had elicited a certain . . . *reaction.* A flare-up of desire that caught him quite off guard. But it was not something *she* was in control of. His attraction to Ellsbeth was primal, but it was also something he could easily suppress and ignore, and he was confident that it would blow over soon.

THE BUILDING THAT HOUSED THE faculty offices for the College of the Arcane Arts had been grand when it was constructed in the 1890s. At that time, Gilded Age money flowed freely into the department; the arcane was viewed then as a helpful ally to the burgeoning industrial economy, which had not yet supplanted it for virtually all commercial purposes.

But what had seemed grand a century ago—arched entryways, thick-paned windows, heavy-beamed ceilings, dark wood everywhere—now only enhanced the sense that the building was a relic of another era.

Rawlins entered the Penrose Conference Room, joining the meeting ten minutes after it had begun. His tardiness, while unintentional, was hardly uncommon. Among the perks he enjoyed, as a result of his fame in the field of the arcane arts, were certain indulgences; Lennox shot him an irritated look at the interruption, but did not comment.

The conference table was crowded already with the College of the Arcane Arts' eleven professors—four tenured, the rest adjunct—all in attendance at the meeting. Fortunately, Paul Gallway, the blandly handsome alchemy professor, slid down a seat, making room for Rawlins. "Late night?" Gallway whispered with a knowing cock of his eyebrow, no doubt implying that a hangover was to blame for Rawlins's late arrival rather than hours of troubled rumination about the study of illegal magic. Rawlins merely shrugged. He found Gallway's guys-like-us camaraderie grating, but the path of least resistance was to blithely go along with it.

Dean Lennox led the meeting from a seat in the middle of the table. No doubt she eschewed the position at the head in an effort to ingratiate herself with the faculty, to signal that she was not a hierarchical leader so much as a fellow scholar who happened to be charged with governing them all. But in conjunction with the clipped, efficient way in which she made her way through her agenda, she came off more as a beleaguered bureaucrat.

Lennox had become a middle manager for magical education. Rawlins was almost unable to believe how highly he had once esteemed her. "Tonight's the opening dinner of the Denton Colloquium," she said, "and many of our donors will be present, so please, help the department out? Dress to impress, share some funny anecdotes, flatter appropriately, et cetera."

She looked around the room, seeking nods of support. But many of the senior faculty members frowned in irritation; Babbs Tran scratched at her notebook and offered a sotto voce retort: "The colloquium *used to be* an academic affair."

"It still is and always will be," said Lennox. "But we won't be able to do *any* of this without funding. Undergraduate enrollment is down by ten percent, and the number of freshmen declaring as majors has dropped even more. While we are told that our funding is untethered from such factors, this coincides with a roughly commensurate cut in our budget, so I'd like to juice our numbers before next semester."

"I would be happy to help grease the wheels of funding with the administration," said Gallway, scratching at his nose. "But I'm not sure there's much we can do about a generational indifference to the arcane arts."

"I'm only suggesting we try to appeal to our students on a more personal level," Lennox replied. "We're firming up the course list for next year, and it would be nice to list a couple of new courses that might have more general interest. Nothing gimmicky, of course. I'm merely offering the opportunity for any of you to step up and help the department. It would certainly be noticed."

Rawlins watched the adjunct faculty sit up straighter at the tacit offer of tenure consideration in exchange for coming up with a more popular course. He smirked, grateful to be free from such concerns—but then Lennox turned to him. "*The Arcane and the Ordinary* was quite popular in its day. I'm sure plenty of prospective students would still love to study it."

Rawlins felt his neck prickle with irritation. For years, he had taught an undergraduate course named for and based on his career-founding book. It had been exceedingly popular, drawing students from every major at the university and burnishing his reputation as a charismatic teacher. But he had gradually become aware that while students loved the course, other academics quietly sneered at anyone who taught their own work; at a conference, one speaker joked about "professors who sell their books by making them required texts," and though Rawlins's students were a drop in the bucket of his book sales, he had taken the remark personally. As soon as his tenure was granted, he abandoned the class.

"My introductory class is full every year," Rawlins said. "I assume that suffices for my undergraduate responsibilities."

"Most tenured faculty teach *two* undergraduate courses, Thaddeus," Lennox said. He could feel the glares of the other faculty, who made less money than he did while teaching more courses.

"I'll think about it," Rawlins said, looking down. He could sense Lennox was letting it go for now, but he knew she would press him on the matter later.

Across the table, Dr. Gaines gently waved her hand, signaling a desire to speak.

Lennox nodded to her, and she leaned forward over the table, drumming her fingers on a notebook as though playing chords on a piano. "I'm wondering how we should handle things with our students, in terms of Roberta Storer?"

Rawlins tensed up at the mention of Ellsbeth's sister, suddenly self-conscious, as though everyone were looking at him for his reaction. But no, of course no one knew of his new student's connection to the tragedy; it was merely a major event that had occurred on campus.

"I'm just not sure what you mean," Lennox said. "I mean, it's tragic, of course, but it's been . . ."

Gaines's voice rose, a manic edge creeping in. "The students are still *quite* upset. I've had two students request delays in their first assignments because they're still processing their grief. It was a trauma!"

Rawlins felt his chest tighten; he could tell that Gaines, for all her faux-outrage, was secretly delighted by having a bloody scandal on campus. Her prurient enjoyment rankled him, sending his mind back to the weeks following the Maxwell Keene incident. The ubiquitous, public outpourings of grief from people who had never even heard the names of the victims until they were dead. The *rage* Rawlins had experienced years ago at witnessing all that performative mourning came bubbling back up as Gaines carried on. "It happened in Perkins! Some of my students lived in that hall! It's no wonder they're still traumatized. And we have a responsibility to try to understand what they're going through."

Rawlins spoke up before he was even aware he intended to: "You think her parents would want that? For you to still be rubbernecking at the tragedy of their dead daughter *months* later—you think that's the responsible thing to do?"

Gaines opened her mouth as if to debate Rawlins, and then shut it again. Lennox broke the tense silence with a more tactful addition: "It's a sensitive matter, and if students need to discuss what happened, please refer them to the school's mental-health resources."

From the opposite end of the table, Michael Portnoy, a long-tenured and liver-spotted professor desperately holding on to his job and his corner office, piped in unhelpfully: "I heard the girl was sleeping with one of her TAs. A *female* TA, matter of fact."

Rawlins cleared his throat, his indignation growing. "Are we honestly going to *gossip* about this?"

"I heard that, too!" Gaines said, ignoring Rawlins. "And it was when the TA ended things that Roberta . . . you know."

"It wasn't a female TA," Babbs Tran said. "It was a boy. Another student. I remember seeing them together." She glanced at Rawlins, apologetic, and shrugged.

Lennox sighed. "This is all wildly unnecessary speculation. I'd ask that we remain focused on the items of today's meeting." And then she paused. "But please, obviously, try to keep relationships with all of your students supportive and professional."

From the corners of her eyes, Lennox allowed her gaze to flicker to Rawlins before quickly looking away. *He* had never indulged in an *unprofessional* relationship with a student in his entire career. Not while one was *still* a student, at least.

But he knew that was not what Lennox was thinking. He knew exactly what was on her mind and resented her for it bitterly.

WHEN RAWLINS WAS FOURTEEN YEARS old, he had shown up for his first day at Middlewaite Preparatory Academy without a blazer, unaware that it was required by the school's dress code. His family lived nearly an hour from the campus, so it was rare for them to cross paths with students from the prep school. When they did, it was always after hours, when the students invariably removed their jackets as they gathered in diners and clustered outside the movie theater. It was thus an innocent mistake that led Rawlins's mother to assume that a blazer was optional, and as such, to skip out on purchasing one, aiming to save up enough money to get one before the winter.

Thus Rawlins found himself, on his first day, compelled to wear an oversized blazer provided by the school emblazoned with its logo. For another freshman who had come to Middlewaite from one of its feeder schools and already had a group of friends, this might not have been a social death sentence. But for Rawlins, who knew exactly no one, and was desperate to hide the fact that he was there on scholarship, they might as well have stamped his forehead with the words POOR KID.

All day long, he watched people clock the jacket, knowing exactly what it meant. His cheeks burned with shame. At lunchtime, he retreated behind the dumpsters to eat his sandwich like a stray dog.

After that, Rawlins vowed to never let himself be viewed with such pity again. He convinced his mother to lend him her credit card and scoured every secondhand store the bus could take him to, searching out clothes that were up to the standards of his wealthy peers.

His transformation didn't stop there. He made a habit of studying accents, seeking to drop his raised-in-the-hollers twang and instead match the posh tones of the kids who grew up in the city. He forced himself to learn all the country-club sports. And he showed up for *every* school event dressed at the upper end of what might be considered appropriate.

Gradually, aided by newfound income, he developed his own sense of taste, opting for a color palette that complemented his dark hair and light eyes. He became well acquainted with designer suits and vintage watches, and built a relationship with a tailor.

It was not so much that he took aesthetic joy in the intricacies of fashion; rather, he viewed social life as an endless battle, and clothes were his armor, insurance that he would never be subjected to the pity that had spoiled his first day of high school.

Thus it was that he arrived at the opening dinner of the Denton Colloquium wearing a perfectly pressed black tuxedo. He patted his breast pocket, making sure he had the note cards for his speech before his Uber drove off, leaving him in the heart of the Newlyn Civic Center. The colloquium's scholarly functions would mainly be hosted on campus, but the opening-night gala was held in the grand ballroom of the Newlyn Country Club, which sat across the way from the town's city hall.

Rawlins took a breath, steeling himself to join the throng of scholars and donors striding up toward the entrance of the building, when he was interrupted by a familiar voice. "Professor Rawlins!"

He turned, and the sight of Ellsbeth walking up the sidewalk toward him felt surreal; she had been on his mind so much lately, it was as though his thoughts had summoned her. "Ms. Storer. Fancy running into you here."

"You're the *fancy* one," she said, indicating his tux. "What are you all dressed up for? Wedding? Funeral?"

"A tuxedo at a funeral would be in exceptionally poor taste," he said dryly. "But this should be about as much fun as one. It's the opening dinner for the colloquium."

"Ohhh, very glamorous," she said, her gaze turning toward the academics heading inside, looking for a face she might recognize. "So this is what I have to look forward to when I make it big as a scholar?"

"Exactly. Four-hour dinners sucking up to donors is about as glamorous as it gets. The trick is to get yourself something nice to wear that you can wear for years to come."

"They don't make it that easy for women," Ellsbeth replied. "Styles change, and recycled dresses get noticed. Very unfair; a terrible double standard. I bet you've been wearing this tux for . . . what, a decade?"

"Nearly two, and it still fits like a glove," he said, surprising himself by the playful tone in his voice.

"Hmmm," Ellsbeth said, flicking her finger across his lapel. "I think this double-breasted situation is a little out of vogue." Her finger lingered there a moment longer than necessary, sliding against the fabric, and Rawlins felt himself subtly incline himself forward, leaning into her touch.

"Classic never goes out of style," he replied.

His eyes met hers, and her hand retreated from his chest. "Well, I hope you have a fun night. Or as fun as these things can go. I bet wine helps."

"And the same to you," he said. "A fun night." And then he looked around at the downtown square, far from campus. "Where are you off to, anyway?" He tried to make his voice sound casual, as if he didn't actually care.

"Oh, I'm actually going to a party tonight, too," Ellsbeth said. "Fraternizing with my fellow students, if you can believe it. I'm sure the wine won't be as good."

"Glad you're making friends," he said, then checked his watch. "Though things must have changed since my day, when student parties did not typically start before dinnertime."

"Oh, yeah, of course that's later," she said, letting out a nervous laugh. "Right now I'm just . . . passing through this area, doing . . . an errand. Just . . . there's a place I have to go. To do something . . ." Her vague non-explanation fizzled out with an awkward shrug.

"Yes, I suppose that is the definition of an errand," he said lightly.

She twisted her mouth into something like a half smile. "Nice running into you, Professor."

"And you as well, Ms. Storer," he said.

They nodded their farewells, and Rawlins headed up toward the dinner, the interaction looping on repeat in his mind as he tried to make sense of it. She had flirted with him, undeniably, and he had flirted right back, and it was *fun.* The rapport they shared was somehow both charged and effortless; there was an *ease* to talking with Ellsbeth that disarmed him.

But at the end of the conversation, something had shifted. Ellsbeth had *lied.* Or at the very least, she had deliberately concealed the truth. It may have been for any perfectly innocent reason—she was on her way to a medical appointment, perhaps, and didn't want to get into her health conditions, or say the word *gynecologist* to her teacher. And he certainly didn't have the right to surveil her whereabouts. Still, something in her avoidance left him feeling empty, uneasy. He could not imagine why, but he was certain: *She was hiding something.*

ELLSBETH

The police department smelled like ammonia and new carpeting. Ellsbeth waited at the reception desk for several minutes while the woman behind a computer finished talking on the phone.

"Hi, *sorry,*" the receptionist finally exhaled. She turned her attention to Ellsbeth. "Can I help you?"

"I'm here to see Officer Marcos."

"He's out right now."

"Really? When I called, they said he'd be here at the end of the day."

"Sorry, he's out."

Ellsbeth sighed. "I can wait."

The receptionist blinked eyelids heavy with mascara. According to a plaque slotted into the bulletproof glass, her name was Rosa. "You've been here before, right?"

"Yeah, last spring. A few times."

"You're the one with the sister?"

Ellsbeth nodded.

Rosa sighed and scribbled something on a Post-it note. "Look, I'll tell him you came by, but I don't know if it's going to be much help." She gave Ellsbeth a pitying glance, then returned her attention to her computer screen, waiting for Ellsbeth to leave.

∞

A MONTH AFTER BERTIE'S FUNERAL, Ellsbeth had driven alone from New Jersey to Newlyn in order to speak to a police officer who had handled Bertie's case. She knew she couldn't explain on the phone, and she had spent the entire eight-hour car ride rehearsing exactly what she would say when she finally was in front of someone. What *could* she say that wouldn't sound insane, or like she hadn't gone mad with grief? *My sister, Bertie Storer, committed suicide here on campus, do you remember her? Well, you said she committed suicide. I was taking the Arcanus—do you know about the Arcanus?—and I did a scrying ritual. It's probably not worth getting into what that is. But I saw her bleeding. And it looked strange to me. It didn't look like a suicide.* There were plenty of people in the general public who viewed arcane mechanicals as sinister and off-putting, especially after the Maxwell Keene disaster. Ellsbeth certainly couldn't expect the police officers to give her words any weight, but maybe if she could see Bertie's file herself, the anguish and uncertainty that had been with Ellsbeth since that day might be put to rest.

It didn't look like a suicide. That thought had repeated on an endless loop in her brain since the Arcanus, like a thumping heartbeat in Ellsbeth's head, a constant companion that burned her from the inside. Sometimes with rage, sometimes with shame, sometimes as a taunt, but always there.

She had tried to explain to her parents what she saw during the scrying ritual, but they had met her with blank faces and confusion. They were broken and deep in mourning. Ellsbeth felt cruel, asking them to trust her amateur ritual enough to unravel their daughter's death, forcing them to wade through the grotesque details when they needed to find a way to move forward and make peace.

But Ellsbeth had seen the image in the basin with her own eyes and she couldn't get it out of her head.

It didn't look like a suicide.

Bertie had been in a bathtub somewhere, a clawfoot tub with white linoleum stained pink with her blood. Her body was contorted and unnatural—a foot hanging over the edge of the tub, her waist twisted, and her arm thrown over her head. There was violence to the scene. The way it looked to Ellsbeth, someone had put her there.

In the weeks since, there were moments when she had half convinced herself that her memory was lying to her. Maybe grief and trauma had distorted her recollection of the scrying image. Had Bertie's legs really stuck out at that terrible angle? Was the blood really splattered across the room? The memory of what she had seen became distorted and grotesque in Ellsbeth's dreams. It burned itself onto her brain like a ghost image on a fuzzing cathode-ray television. If she could see Bertie's file, make sense of it slowly, perhaps the nightmarish uncertainty would diminish.

When Ellsbeth finally arrived at the Newlyn police station that day, her breath stale and knees tight from the drive, they hadn't made her wait long. Officer Marcos had been kind and sympathetic, leading her to sit in his office and offering Ellsbeth a small Styrofoam cup of coffee. When she told him that she was Bertie's sister, his face sagged with genuine empathy.

"I was hoping to see her file myself," Ellsbeth said.

Officer Marcos's mouth tightened as he tried to gauge exactly how much trouble this mourning family member would be. "I can get you the file," he said. He pulled his hand through his thinning hair. "But I'm telling you, I've seen this before. People looking for big answers where there aren't any. Conspiracy theories. Foul play. Young suicide is . . . it's unthinkable. It's hard for anyone to accept."

"I would like to just see her file, please," Ellsbeth said.

Officer Marcos sighed, the first indication of impatience, and left the room. When he returned, it was with a thin manila folder with a single piece of paper inside.

"This is it?" Ellsbeth said. She turned the paper over in disbelief, as if it could have been hiding a ream of detailed reporting underneath. "This is one page."

"Some cases don't require much investigation. This is a standard report."

"*Nineteen-year-old female. Found in bed. Lacerations consistent with suicide.* That's *it*? That's everything you have on her?" Ellsbeth was aware that she was raising her voice, that other officers in the precinct were turning their heads, but she couldn't help herself. "This was a *person. This was my sister.* And she didn't die in bed! She was in a bathtub."

Officer Marcos stared at her. He had a gap between his front teeth, and when he sucked in air, it made a small whistling sound. "And why would you think that?"

Ellsbeth's stomach dropped. She would need to try to explain. "I—saw it in a scrying ritual. It's an arcane mechanicals ritual to—"

"I'm aware what a scrying ritual is, Miss Storer."

"Okay, well, then. Yeah. I saw her. In a bathtub. You need to reopen this case. I have information that can help! I remember what I saw."

Agent Marcos plucked the file—was it even a *file*?—from Ellsbeth's hands and stood. "I would advise against you giving too much credence to a little magic spell."

"It's not a spell. It's a scrying ritual. And I know what I saw."

"Maybe you made a mistake," Marcos said gently. "Arcane stuff is complicated, right? It's hard even for professionals."

Ellsbeth could feel her cheeks burning. "I didn't make a mistake." She watched as Officer Marcos sighed and stood, smoothing at a pleat in his khakis. "Please," Ellsbeth said, making her voice as gentle as possible. "There has to be more to her file. Some sort of investigation. Surely the college makes you do more. Aren't there notes from the officer who found her? Interviews he did with people who knew her? Where did those reports go? If I could just see them myself . . ."

Officer Marcos was done with her, Ellsbeth understood that very well. His face had closed off; any pity he had felt was replaced with exasperation.

"There are no more files," he said, his voice filed to a sharp edge.

And Ellsbeth realized something: He was lying.

"There *are,*" she said. "Of *course* there are. How could there possibly be *one sheet of paper* for the death of a teenage girl? Is it Newlyn? Did they put you up to this? Do they prefer that these things are kept quiet and covered up? I get that maybe a suicide is more palatable than—"

"If you'll excuse me." Officer Marcos stood, scratching at the pink spots visible on his scalp, and left Ellsbeth sitting alone with her Styrofoam cup of coffee turning cold and bitter in her hand, her mind already working a thousand new ways she could get the answers she needed. She had returned to the police station a few more times, but she was met with increasingly curt dismissals.

The university had been even less helpful throughout the spring.

There were the polite expressions of sympathy, but then Ellsbeth's emails had been shuttled from the dean of the college to the administrator student coordinator. One day, Ellsbeth waited on hold for an hour before her call was connected to someone who turned out to be the campus therapist specializing in trauma. "I don't *need* a therapist!" Ellsbeth had spat in exasperation when she realized who she was talking with. "I just need someone to say something other than, 'We're so sorry for your loss.'"

"I understand," the therapist had said in a tone dripping with condescension. "And I'm so sorry for your loss."

Their reticence to reopen Bertie's case was obvious—it had been a tragic suicide, but that was it. There was nothing more to investigate, and she, Ellsbeth, was clearly distraught with grief, attempting to cause problems where there weren't any. "It's a common phenomenon when a loved one takes their own life," the therapist had told her. "There's the grief, of course, and then sometimes an element of self-blame—*Is there something I might have done differently?* And then there's what you seem to be experiencing, which is very, very common. Looking for an external answer even where one doesn't exist."

The university wanted to let the past rest. Why couldn't Ellsbeth?

There were moments in the months since Bertie's death that Ellsbeth found herself so exhausted by the bureaucratic walls and tormented by her own doubts that the thought of simply accepting what she had been told seemed tantalizingly appealing. Wouldn't that be easier? Maybe she could convince herself that she had made a mistake in the scrying incantation, or that she hadn't seen anything terrible at all: The image that played in her nightmares was just her mind playing tricks on her. Maybe she could believe that the pressure had just been too much for Bertie, that Bertie had been lonely, and heartbroken from a bad boyfriend.

But then the vision of the bathtub came back to her, as real in her memory as the moment she had conjured it in the basin. Her little sister, broken and bloody. Ellsbeth hadn't been mistaken. That image would stay with her until she got the answers she needed.

There was a way to get people to do what you wanted, to make condescending university administrators or bored sheriffs open file cabinets, to tell you the truth, even if they didn't want to. There were areas of study within the field of the arcane that were obscure and verboten, ways of controlling people's bodies and people's minds. The months since seeing Bertie's death had changed Ellsbeth, made her hard and angry and on-edge. She spent her days adrenalized, new ideas for formulas and incantations causing her fingertips to twitch.

She was here, at Newlyn, where someone knew the truth. The pieces of her plan were forming day by day. Whether he knew it or not, Professor Rawlins was the key to Ellsbeth getting what she needed.

RAWLINS

Standing behind the podium at the dais on the north end of the room, Rawlins endeavored to muster the enthusiasm of his words: "The duty we have is not only to educate the young minds that pass through our classrooms, but to imbue them with the necessary sense of gravitas to become responsible and conscientious practitioners of the arcane mechanicals."

He glanced out at the sea of faces, lit with a soft amber glow summoned by an *Illuminatis* ritual. Such magic was rarely employed, given that electricity had long since provided a vastly easier alternative, but for symbolic occasions such as this, it offered an attractive display of flattering light with no discernible source.

His colleagues all watched him respectfully but with evident disinterest. Some picked at their salmon; others signaled waiters to refill their wine. At the closest banquet table, he saw Lennox, ignoring his speech and laughing quietly with one of the school's boosters. Her complacency irritated him, and when his eyes returned to his speech, he found he had momentarily lost his place.

His mind stalled, going blank, and the emptiness was filled, as it always was these days, by Ellsbeth. He thought of seeing her outside before he entered—of how badly she wanted to be the sort of person who would be invited to take a seat in this room . . . and how disappointed she would be to see the blasé indifference and complacency on display. As he considered what she would think, Rawlins abandoned his prepared speech entirely.

"Let's not pretend here, shall we? The study of magic, many would say . . . is a dying art." A ripple of surprise coursed through the ballroom at his heresy, and Lennox's expression darkened. But Rawlins went on, off the cuff. "Our place in the culture is marginalized. The range of what can be accomplished is shrinking. And what is the reason for the decline? In a word: *fear.*"

Around the room, he heard the rustle of fabric as people sat up in their chairs. Enjoying his power over the crowd, Rawlins let the silence hang for a moment before he continued.

"At some point, the world became fearful of what we could do . . . and so did we. We internalized their fear. Turned on one another. We've witnessed witch hunts in our field, purity tests, all ensuring against any ideas that could be construed as *dangerous.* But fear drives out curiosity. It does not serve scholarship, much less innovation."

With the crowd now in his palm, he sought to wrap up his talk on an inspiring note. "Spaces like this colloquium and the universities we all represent—they need to be forums for free thought and exploration. For what is our field . . . if not the study of what is possible? Thank you."

The applause was robust as Rawlins stepped down from the stage. But he was not satisfied; he knew the speech was giving voice to something that was still only dimly forming inside him, and he had a long way to go.

THE REST OF THE NIGHT, he moved through the ballroom as if he were navigating a minefield, avoiding ambush at every turn.

Academic conferences were the place where Rawlins's star of celebrity shone most brightly. Out in the larger world, he was occasionally recognized, but he could mostly move unaccosted through the world. In the company of arcanists, however, his name and face were ubiquitously familiar, and he could feel the weight of his reputation upon each interaction. Every visiting professor who came to an event at Newlyn would inevitably want to return home with a story about the conversation they'd had with the author of *The Arcane and the Ordinary*. Which made him the target both of fawning sycophants eager to praise his contribution to the field and of Ivory Tower skeptics who sought to embarrass him. The former had once brought him pleasure, but whatever nourishment his self-esteem used to get from the praise of strangers, that well had long since run dry.

As soon as Rawlins had gotten himself a drink, Paul Gallway appeared out of nowhere and put an arm on his shoulder, steering him over to meet a pair of "fascinating" visiting lecturers from Cambridge who turned out to be anything but. Gallway acted like he and Rawlins were the best of old pals, evidently eager to show off his closeness with Newlyn's most well-known professor. After a few minutes of Gallway's complaining about academic publishers, Rawlins announced that he needed a breath of fresh air and headed outside.

Fresh air, of course, meant a cigarette, which he hoped to bum from some other beleaguered smoker—but he found the balcony empty and leaned against the balustrade, breathing in the crisp night air.

"Settle for a cigar?" He turned to find Lennox approaching. Even with her pushing sixty-five, he had to concede that she looked great in a dress with a slit up the thigh. She carried two cigars, offering him one along with a lighter. "The talk was great, by the way. When you first gave it—what was that, three years ago, in Stockholm?"

"I play the hits," he said with a shrug. "But I added a new riff to the end. How'd it work?"

"Very . . . *vive la révolution,*" she said dryly.

"Seemed to get the crowd going," he offered. "Isn't that what the donors want to hear?"

Lennox shook her head, exasperated. "I'm just wondering if I need to be worried about some kind of midlife crisis. Going off script . . . and taking on that pretty young Storer girl, despite an incomplete on the Arcanus. Out of character for you."

Rawlins lit his cigar, puffing thoughtfully. "I thought you wanted me to take her on."

"I wanted her out of my office, and for you to take responsibility for your choices," Lennox replied. "And that's exactly what I need you to do now that you've let her in. Proceed with caution."

Rawlins didn't appreciate her tone, or her insinuation, and replied bluntly, "Maggie. *I* don't fuck my students."

Lennox winced; it was a low blow and they both knew it, but she did not dignify the implicit accusation with a response. "I couldn't care less about your sex life, Thaddeus. Not as long as you keep it private and don't embarrass the university. But I do care a great deal about maintaining a safe learning environment for our students. And in that regard, you do not have a pristine track record."

Rawlins's lip curled instinctively, his anger starting to rise. "You really want to bring up Max with me right now? I thought I was told not to mention him to you if I valued my position and our friendship."

"All I'm saying," Lennox replied, "is that you were the one who tutored him. Beyond the curriculum. Beyond what he was capable of . . . managing. You *pushed* him. And I want to ensure that none of our arcane students are ever in a position to . . . do what he did."

Rawlins knew that he should back off, to leave things be and walk away. But a numbness spread from his scalp down his neck. His field of vision narrowed, swimming black at the edges. She had opened the door, and Rawlins found himself unable to resist saying the words he had been trying not to say for so many years.

"You know, Max might not have been so lost if *his mother* had just paid him a little attention." Rawlins could see Lennox's mouth opening in protest, but he barreled on. "And he might not have been convicted at all if you had been willing to stick your neck out and speak up on his behalf. Cared a little less about your reputation, and damage control for the fucking university, and a little more about your own *son*."

Her left eye twitched, a small clump of mascara spidering at its corner. Rawlins knew that he had poked at a deep wound, and it was not entirely fair.

Lennox, of course, cared immensely about Max, as any mother would; the whole affair had nearly unraveled her. While Max had begun at Newlyn, the relationship between him and the school's dean was not even widely known, since Lennox had never taken the last name of her husband, Benjamin Keene. But within days, the press learned the truth, and the already sensational story leapt into the stratosphere, as it was reported that the young man responsible for innocent deaths at Newlyn was the son of the dean of the College of the Arcane Arts.

Lennox had cited that prurient interest as her reason not to testify on Max's behalf; she would never be viewed favorably by a jury, she said, when the press had already tarnished her so viciously. Surely her position of power within the university had been the reason Maxwell had been granted special treatment, why he had been granted permission to study rituals that never should have been accessed by a teenager. Rawlins suspected her refusal to testify had been more out of craven self-interest, protecting her own reputation and her position at the university. Likely, her motives involved some indecipherable combination of both reasons.

In public, Lennox had maintained a stoic façade, commenting on the "tragedy" involving her son only as proof of the necessity of a responsible approach to teaching arcane mechanicals, and requesting privacy with regard to her personal life. Still, Rawlins knew that in private, she had been beside herself, and was still traumatized by the whole affair.

So it was not without a twinge of guilt that he now impugned how much she cared about her child. But he was spoiling for a fight, and Lennox was always a worthy opponent; he expected her to lambaste him just as sharply, as she certainly had good reason to do.

Instead, she looked away wistfully and shook her head, as though she were more disappointed than angered. But Rawlins knew that look: It was cold-fusion fury, controlled and powerful. Without another word, Lennox stubbed out her cigar on the balustrade and headed inside, leaving Rawlins to consider his error.

Lennox had not been a friend in any meaningful sense for quite some time, but they hadn't been adversaries, either. Considering that she was his boss, and that he was planning on undertaking a secret and illegal course of study with Ellsbeth Storer, it was very unfortunate timing for him to have just made Lennox his enemy.

ELLSBETH

Gracie lived in a loft with a wall of windows with glass so thick it warped the view down to the ink-dark river. After years of living in dormitories, among particleboard bookshelves and chipped IKEA consoles, Ellsbeth found Gracie's place astonishing in its adultness, its *completeness.* Her furniture wasn't accumulated from a rotation of latchkey roommates who left behind an end table, a dresser, a fraying couch with Rorschach-test stains. Gracie's coffee table wasn't cluttered with crumbs or unread magazines; it was vast and shining, mirror-clean beneath a few arcane journals and a ceramic, architectural ashtray. Her couch was black leather and low to the ground—Curt Ladove at one end, one arm casually thrown across the back of it, while Sora Burns smoked across from him, her eyes barely visible beneath her long bangs.

Ellsbeth hadn't brought a hostess gift for Gracie, but as soon as she saw her loft, like something out of an *Architectural Digest* spread, she was relieved. Anything she might have brought—a lemon loaf, a candle—would have been humiliatingly out of place, a reminder that Gracie was privy to an adult world of money and careful curation that Ellsbeth could inexpertly only play at.

"Ellsbeth," Gracie purred as soon as she entered. Gracie embraced Ellsbeth in a half hug, enveloping Ellsbeth more in her scent (something musky and complex) than in her arms. "I'm so glad you made it. Have you met everyone yet?"

Ellsbeth knew the cohort by name, but Gracie pointed them out one by one: Curt and Sora, over on the couch. Priya Srinavasan, dark hair blown out in perfect waves, making herself a gin and tonic. Valentine Pall-Thomas and Victor Hamada were playing chess on a set that looked as though it might be made of carved ivory, both boys too deep in concentration to offer more than a raised hand of acknowledgment when Gracie said their names.

Mary-Abigail Pinkney thrust a cup into Ellsbeth's hand. "Drink," she said in her southern drawl, and when Ellsbeth took a sip, Mary-Abigail nodded in approval. "Good girl." Ellsbeth tried to recall what Mary-Abigail was focused on. Translations? She knew she'd done a master's already, at Vanderbilt.

"What is it?"

"Don't worry," Mary-Abigail said, her straight white teeth Day-Glo bright in the dim evening light. "It's just a whiskey Coke."

The drink was stronger than Ellsbeth had anticipated. Before her glass was half empty she and Mary-Abigail were both on the couch with Curt, listening to his faux-modesty about his recent fellowship.

"Really, it's just a publication game," he said. "My essay on energy amplification got into *Cambridge Review,* and the MacGregor people eat that shit up."

Sora blew a thin cloud of smoke from between her red lips. "As if you needed the funding. Didn't your dad, like, donate a building here when you were an undergraduate? And you were in the Banestooth Club, right? I heard that to join they make you buy a first-class ticket to Paris and then burn it just to show you don't need money."

Curt rolled his eyes. "That's a rumor. And the building was a tax break. And don't pretend you're here representing the proletariat when your dad owns half of Seoul."

"Stepdad."

"Oh, my sincerest apologies."

"Wait," Ellsbeth said. "You went to undergrad here? At Newlyn?"

Curt turned to her, his beer half raised. "Yeah, why?"

Sora smirked. "Didn't you know he was punched by the Banestooth Club? He only talks about it constantly?"

Of course he was, Ellsbeth thought. She often saw those undergraduate boys congratulating one another on their existence as they entered and exited the three-story brick clubhouse at the end of her street. The most exclusive fraternity on campus, which boasted as alumni a handful of senators, a president, and half the subjects of any given issue of *Fortune*.

"How old are you? Did you take time off to study for the Arcanus?" Ellsbeth asked.

Curt smiled at Ellsbeth then, all charm, and from the other side of the room, Ellsbeth could sense Priya clocking it, eyeing them both from the kitchen island. "I'm twenty-two," he said. "Took the Arcanus my senior year." He grinned. "Too young for you? Too old?"

"No," Ellsbeth said, trying to prevent the flush crawling up her neck. She wasn't attracted to Curt, with his perfectly combed blond hair and polo shirt layered under a quarter-zip sweatshirt. But even as there was something in his energy that made her feel as though his attention on her was a prank, that a vat of pig's blood was bound to spill from the ceiling at any moment, there was also something undeniable about his fundamental attractiveness in the abstract, the masculine contours of his low, prominent brows and square jaw. "I was wondering if you maybe knew my sister. She was only here for one semester, though, and you were probably already a senior."

"Oh," Curt said, already losing interest, his eyes circling back toward Sora and the black tattoos that crawled up her arm. "What's her name?"

"Bertie—uh, Roberta Storer."

"Sorry," Curt said. He shrugged absently. "Doesn't ring a bell."

Sora extinguished her cigarette in the ashtray, and Ellsbeth realized from the smell that there was something more than tobacco rolled into it. "Why did she only go here for a semester?" she asked. Ellsbeth was surprised that she had been listening at all.

"Oh," Ellsbeth said. "She died."

That unleashed a deep, sympathetic moan from Mary-Abigail, whose southern manners manifested in comforting gestures of condolences, as if Ellsbeth had lost her sister mere moments ago.

The change in energy summoned Gracie, a cigarette and a champagne flute both balanced in one hand. "So how'd she die?" She dropped down next to Curt and wrapped an arm around his neck. "Sorry, is that rude?"

"No, it's fine. She . . ." Ellsbeth paused here, and let the simplest version of the story come out. "Committed suicide."

Gracie deposited her cigarette neatly between her lips. "Jesus Christ," she said, and then she faced Curt. "And you didn't hear about that when you were here?"

"Oh, shit," Curt said. "Yeah, that does sort of sound familiar. I didn't realize that was your sister. Fuck. I'm sorry."

Ellsbeth felt the room's eyes on her, the combination of pity and the prurient, vampiric fascination that surrounded tragedy. "It's okay," she said quickly, hoping to get off the subject. "My parents didn't want to make it a big story. It wasn't really a scandal or anything."

"God, yeah," Gracie said. "I guess if it's not the dean's son burning down half of Pembroke dorm and killing his entire suite, it's not a real Newlyn scandal."

Ellsbeth sat forward. "Do you mean Maxwell Keene? He was *Dean Lennox's* son?"

"Uh, yeah," Gracie said, "You didn't know that? But obviously he died and killed, like, a bunch of kids by accident, so no wonder she doesn't like to talk about it. Probably because she gave him special treatment. Otherwise why would an undergraduate have been actually *doing* arcane mechanicals in the first place?"

"He didn't die," Valentine called out from his chess game without looking up from the board. "Just went to prison forever." He took Victor Hamada's queen. "And checkmate."

Gracie gasped, and her unlit cigarette leapt in her mouth. "That's what we're doing tonight. Thaumaturgy. Conjuring fire. Rules are the same as always. Everyone makes the protective circle, and if you fail you take a shot." She looked at Ellsbeth like a snake sizing up a mouse to determine if it could swallow it in a single go. "How about you go first?"

Ellsbeth laughed, but no one else did. "Is this the hazing ritual? A prank? Asking me to do the thaumaturgy that caused half of Pembroke to burn down?"

"And killed three people," Sora added.

Gracie rolled her eyes. "It's fine if you're scared, Ellsbeth. You don't *have* to do it."

From across the room, Priya shifted her weight between her legs.

"Maybe she's right, Sisi," she said quietly. "We've already been drinking."

"Don't be boring, Priya," Gracie spat back.

"Wait. Priya's right," Curt said, and for a second, Priya's face beamed with the glow of his approval. But then his face twisted into a smirk and he swigged his beer, a ring of condensation left on the coffee table. "We all know rituals should only be performed by completely sober professionals. Hamada, come help me move the couch."

The couch was pushed back, and the group of them gathered in a circle: Ellsbeth, Priya, Valentine, Curt, Gracie, Victor, Mary-Abigail, Sora, and two more students whom Ellsbeth hadn't met yet—a short boy with a mop of messy curls and a girl with cornrows braided like a swirling galaxy across her head.

Valentine cleared his throat and stepped forward to begin the ritual, pulling a gold ring off his own finger and placing it in the center of the circle. "All right, all?" he asked. He was a few drinks in, swaying slightly, his posh English accent coming out stronger than normal.

"Step a little to the left," Ellsbeth whispered to Priya, who shot a venomous sideways glance at Ellsbeth before realizing she was correct and obeying.

Valentine swaggered up to Sora and extended his hand. She placed an unlit cigarette into his palm, and he thanked her with a wet smack of a kiss on the cheek. "Gross," she said. "You smell like booze."

"Don't pretend you don't love it, darling." Still swaying slightly, he raised the cigarette to eye level.

"Hold on." It was the short boy who was speaking, with the curly hair. "He's *actually* drunk. I don't want him to burn Gracie's loft down."

"God, what is it with all of you tonight? He's lighting a *cigarette,* Ari," Gracie said.

"Go on, Val," Curt said. "But if you can't do it on the first try, you're taking a shot."

Valentine *was* drunk, Ellsbeth could tell, but she was still impressed by the focus in his eyes and the skill of his pronunciations when he began chanting.

At least, she was impressed until his wool vest caught on fire.

"Fuck!" Valentine tore the vest off before the flames began to lick at his skin and threw it down to the floor. He stomped at it until the fire transformed into smoldering embers. "Bollocks," he said. "That was Loro Piana."

Curt was already pouring him a shot.

"That isn't fair," Val protested. "I did make a fire. Technically, the ritual worked."

Gracie shook her head. "Ritual isn't just wielding the correct power; it's wielding it in the correct application. That's Arcane 101. Drink up."

Valentine took the shot while Gracie looked around the circle. "Who's up next?"

Ellsbeth had been drinking on an empty stomach, and the booze was making a pleasant buzz in her brain and warming the tips of her fingers. "I'll do it," she said.

No one challenged her, but Gracie did raise an eyebrow. Ellsbeth glanced at Valentine's gold signet ring, still sitting undisturbed in the middle of the circle. "Mind if I use your ring? I didn't bring one." Valentine just shrugged. Before she entered the circle, Ellsbeth pulled an unlit taper from the candelabra on the dining room table.

She adjusted their standing positions slightly—Gracie was still standing too close to Curt, and the ratio wasn't correct. "And you—Valentine, you're swaying. Get out of the circle, I'd prefer fewer focal points as long as they're standing still." Valentine took a step back, happy to obey and take the chance to pour himself another drink.

Ellsbeth closed her eyes. She tried to see the ritual the way it would be written out on the page. She hadn't practiced the incantation, of course, but she knew how it should go. She kept her eyes closed, shut out the world, and began the chant.

Her fist clenched around the taper, her palm sweating. She could feel their gazes on her, feel their anticipation and impatience.

And then the electricity in the room went out. Someone—Mary-Abigail?—shrieked.

But it was dark only for a split second. Not even long enough for Gracie to make a snide comment about Ellsbeth failing. After just a moment, a yellow glow reflected back on the faces of the students in the circle. The taper in Ellsbeth's hand was lit, but so was every candle in the apartment. The loft was lit like a Catholic mass, and for a moment, the entire cohort held their breath, in surprise and something like reverence. Then came a low, monotonous buzz and the electricity vibrated back to life and the magnificent light of the candles diminished like stars disappearing in a daytime sky.

"Jesus fuckin' Christ," Curt muttered.

"She definitely doesn't have to take a shot," Sora said.

"I'm bored," Gracie said. "Someone put on some music."

From: Storer.Ellsbeth
To: Rawlins DAA
Subject: my thesis Proposal

Hi Professor,

It is probably not a good thing that I am writing this email at 2:36 in the morning, but I have just returned home from a party at our friend Gracie's house and I have had more than one drink and so I can't help myself. I figure now is as good a time as any because I'm probably already behind on my thesis work, aren't I?

So, my idea. Writ magic. I know the first step is writing/creating the procedure for a successful ritual, seeing as most of the historical rituals have been destroyed under the statute. But once I'm there, I think the questions I'll focus my thesis on are more biological: Does the writ magic bypass the central nervous system and cause a reaction entirely in the peripheral nervous system? If I can come up with an answer to that, we'd be well on our way to potentially groundbreaking developments in advancement of the treatment of paralysis patients.

But I'm getting ahead of myself. First, a successful ritual. I was able to find the Gorky readings online, and strangely, also the full text of *Arcanus Mentis* online for free. But I couldn't find *Diviner's Touch* or *Writ Magic* OR any Wentz—online OR in the library. If you had those, I would love to borrow them (or read them at your house, if you were wary of lending out centuries-old books to a random graduate student).

I would be more nervous about the fact that I just invited myself over to your house if I hadn't had multiple whiskey Cokes with nothing but half a travel pack of almonds for dinner. I also don't feel nervous about telling you that I may or may not have successfully performed a fire thaumaturgy on the overpriced candles in Gracie's loft without having ever practiced the incantation before. Of course, because doing any rituals outside the supervision of the Practicum is illegal, that's only something I might have done hypothetically. Definitely not on my first try, creating a field so dense that it lit all of the candles in a five-yard radius almost instantaneously.

I'm rambling. It's late. I'm possibly drunk. I probably shouldn't send this email but I'm going to anyway, and I probably shouldn't tell you that I wore a short skirt that time we met at the coffee shop on purpose because I wanted to see what you would do if I put my bare leg against yours. Turns out, nothing. Shame. It's boring having a crush on a professor when he's well behaved. At least you're willing to do writ magic with me. That's something.

x
Ellsbeth

From: Rawlins.T.M.
To: Storer.Ellsbeth
Subject: Re: my thesis Proposal

Ms. Storer,

As you see, I have taken the liberty of switching to my personal email account to safeguard against the unwanted reading of what should be a private correspondence. For future reference: The contents of any university email account are wholly available to the administration. Hopefully in the course of your academic career, you will learn a measure of discretion. And I would point you toward a vital resource, available on any email platform: the "Save Draft" function. With this incredible tool, you can pour your heart out at any absurd hour of the night, then return to your rambling thoughts in the clear light of day to revise or, even better, delete entirely.

Of course, proper utilization requires some measure of self-control, which, it is increasingly apparent, is not your strong suit.

But in the spirit of generosity and letting you (slightly) off the proverbial hook, I will confide that this knowledge was hard-won on my part, as I have sent no shortage of ill-advised middle-of-the-night missives myself, for reasons both professional and personal. Just ask Dean Lennox. (Actually, for both our sakes, please don't.)

I'll turn now to the academic context of your email, which is not only coherent but fairly cogent, given the circumstances of its writing. Taking a biological approach to the study of writ magic is not entirely groundbreaking, but it is a potentially powerful direction, provided that you are willing to expand your horizons; there are decades of medical research you can draw upon, which have been incorporated into other arcane fields, but not this one, since it has sat so long untouched.

My challenge to you would be this: to design a ritual that can test and tease out the biological effects of writ magic upon the nervous system of its subject. For this purpose, you will find Wentz indispensable; while his notions of neuroscience were primitive, his thoughts on the mind-body connection were far ahead of their time. I'm certain that we can find an occasion for you to come borrow a volume from my personal collection, and given your proclivity for drunken fire-summoning, probably best that you read it here so I can ensure that you take proper care of the manuscript.

On that note: I have been called many pejoratives by members of this department, students and faculty alike, but "well behaved" has never been one of them. I suspect, in time, you will find that it is hardly appropriate to my character, and my conduct in The Frayed Page owed nothing to conventions of propriety. I was quite aware of and not displeased by the length of your skirt and the movement of your leg; but I was also aware, as you've admitted, that you merely wanted to see what would happen—and I am not particularly keen on being *tested.* Save your tests for your research.

A word of advice, for both life and arcane mechanicals: Proceed with the courage of your convictions, or not at all.

Sincerely,
Rawlins

From: Storer.Ellsbeth
To: Rawlins.T.M.
Subject: Re: Re: my thesis Proposal

Dear Professor Rawlins,

Thank you for the generosity of your reply to my . . . slightly uncentered email, and the generosity of your offer to read Wentz in your private collection. I would love to take you up on that. Are you free Friday evening, after your symposium?

I spent the day reading through Gorky and the texts I could find online that cited him—strangely, one of the most fruitful sources turned out to be a 15,000-word story in an issue of *The New Yorker* from 1981 discussing the mentalists who might have actually been using a subsidiary of writ magic to perform tricks on late-night television shows in the 1970s. The author makes the case that the famous "floating zombie" trick that "Frederico Federico" performed on Johnny Carson—which looks like a simple illusion of levitation that any hack magician on a cruise ship could perform—was *actually* done using arcane mechanicals. The theory is that Federico performed an immobilization writ backstage on a pre-selected subject so that they would remain "stiff as a board" when he lifted them in the air. The author also posits that a number of stage hypnotists in the late 1970s might have also been using writ magic, but the evidence is understandably shaky.

"Federico" (a walking polyester vest of a man—real name Connor Parsons, from New Jersey) died in 2001, so no one can actually ask him whether he did utilize tricky and illegal magic when the same effect could have been achieved with simple illusion. (You should absolutely read the article—I linked it in case you're curious—if only for the hilarious reference to Federico's abandoned plan for a free-love compound in upstate New York, in which, to quote the article here, "a bevy of buxom co-eds and brawny hippie-types, all hypnotized into a perpetual state of readiness, might live together in a utopia of sexual enlightenment that would only resemble a cult to those unwilling to cast off the chains of their bourgeois mentality.")

All of that fun aside, the idea of an immobilization writ struck me as the ideal first ritual to write a procedure for: something simple, with limited mitigating risk factors, with the added benefit of serving as an effective means of testing my hypothesis on the interaction between the central and peripheral nervous systems when a subject is compelled. Thoughts? I haven't found any texts that offer any guidance on the actual orchestration of the ritual (naturally), but I have a few guesses for how it might be done, and I'm hoping Wentz will offer more clues. Let me know if Friday works. I am not accustomed to being behind in my schoolwork and I would like to remedy that as soon as possible with at least a draft of my ritual procedure written by the end of the month.

A side note: Since you and I are going to be working closely together studying magic that would be illegal to actually perform, it seems like a good idea we actually get to know each other. And though I'm sure any . . . flirtation between graduate students and thesis advisers is frowned upon by the administration, I haven't been able to find any evidence that it's actually against the rules.

Still, for the sake of propriety, let's pretend it's merely in the spirit of cultivating a friendship when I ask: Are you married? You don't wear a ring, but since precious metals disrupt rituals, I know many arcanists simply do away with rings in and out of the Practicum (or worse, wear those terrible siliconized plastic "man bands" marketed toward husbands who find jewelry of any kind to be an insurmountable concession toward, gasp, femininity).

Here's something I'll tell you so you can get to know me: I'm an impatient and selfish person, and I don't like the feeling of wanting things I can't have.

x
Ellsbeth

From: Rawlins.T.M.
To: Storer.Ellsbeth
Subject: Re: Re: Re: my thesis Proposal

Ellsbeth,

Your impatience may prove to be an impediment to your success, as the gears of the academy turn slowly. But your selfishness, owned and acknowledged, will be a great asset; whatever drivel you hear about the selfless nobility of teaching, the pursuit of novel arcane knowledge demands relentless, singular focus.

On that note: No, I am not married, by choice. You probably are not either, given your age, but is there anyone in your life who would take exception to your leg-brushing and drunken emailing? I hope not, for the sake of your academic future: The focused study of arcane mechanicals does not allow for the sacrifices that romantic partnerships invariably demand. You may be tempted to imagine partnership with a fellow scholar, one you can respect as an equal, but such pleasures are invariably short-lived. Our department's own Babbs Tran, a brilliant transmutation professor, briefly enjoyed a passionate and enviable marriage to her colleague Paula Veldt—until they were both up for the same fellowship. I'll spare you the details, but they involved an undergraduate lover, the thaumaturgical obliteration of all Veldt's possessions, and a restraining order.

Perhaps a more pragmatic approach to matrimony is that of Dean Lennox, who has been stably wedded for decades to a man outside our field entirely—but he is so agreeably dull, he resembles a suitcase dragged through her life, ceaselessly oppressed by her moods and whims. I would prefer occasional loneliness to such *settling.* Don't worry, I'm not advocating monastic self-denial; the carnal appetites just have to be indulged without messy entanglements, in order for the mind to preserve the autonomy it needs.

I am telling you all this for your own good, and mine. Your character as an academic will reflect on me for years to come. Toward that end, I would draw your attention to a trait of yours that you'll need to work on before you present at any reputable conference: your rambling digressiveness. But I will also point toward, underlying it, something worth preserving: your curiosity. You see the merit in subjects (like stage magic) that most would ignore to their detriment. And I do wonder (my own curiosity) at where the trait came from, in someone such as yourself—if it was natural or learned, if it was cultivated deliberately, and what discoveries and difficulties it may have led you to in the past? I know from experience that a restless mind can be both a blessing and a curse.

Regardless of its origins, curiosity will serve you, especially when it leads to ideas at the margins and dark corners of our field—which is exactly where you will have to look in your study of writ magic. But such notions need to be approached with caution. Are you familiar with the work of Ariana Greyburn? In 2015, she published a well-received paper on arcane practices with medical benefits for prostate function. But the article does little to explain the theoretical basis of the ritual she developed; she certainly does not cite Martin Perl's controversial 2011 field study on ritual practices in Berlin's underground "sex magick" clubs, even though a close look reveals that Greyburn's innovation is only a minor revision of one of the rituals Perl describes.

While Perl was pilloried as a pervert, the academic who built on his work (without attribution) has gone on to great acclaim and (pardon my pun) bottomless funding. Innovative ideas may be found in the disreputable gutters of our field, but they must be shined up with a veneer of respectability before they can find public acceptance. I'll not bother with clichés about curiosity and cats, but I urge caution as you undertake the study you have in mind—for what you propose carries the threat of academic exile (and also, if you happen to get caught performing such rituals, federal prison).

As for Friday night, shouldn't you, as a not unattractive young woman with a new cohort of colleagues, have some sort of social plans? I do. But since we've established your impatience and how far behind you are, you can come by while I'm out (1022 N. Bernwick Lane); I'll leave a key in the birdhouse on the elm out front. My Wentz volumes will be on the coffee table in the study. Everything you need should be downstairs, so please, mitigate your curiosity with a modicum of self-control.

I will be back around nine to verify that you are not making a mess of my books, evaluate the appropriateness of your attire, and answer your questions—about Wentz and whatever else you wish to know. I am, after all, holistically responsible for your education, and knowledgeable on a good many things beyond century-old arcane theory. And perhaps it is because you have proven so headstrong, but I confess to a certain Pygmalion pleasure at the prospect of shaping you into a perfect pupil.

Sincerely,
Rawlins

From: Storer.Ellsbeth
To: Rawlins.T.M.
Subject: Re: Re: Re: Re: my thesis Proposal

Dear Professor,

Friday is great. Thank you so much for your hospitality. I promise to restrict my curiosity to just the contents of the Wentz volumes (and your fridge, closets, medicine cabinet, etc.).

Having pored through all of the Gorky material I could find online, I'm already feeling incredibly optimistic about the possibility of crafting a successful writ magic ritual (she wrote, cue dramatic irony). Obviously, Gorky didn't detail the actual steps, but I do feel as though I have a basic grasp of the core principles behind the actual mechanics of writ magic. It seems to me the trickiest part is whether—in a technical sense—to treat the biological matter of the subject as a solid or a liquid. *Arcanus Mentis* was unhelpfully written back when they thought that writ magic was the biological control of the "humours," but given that the human body is approximately 60 percent water, it does seem possible the 17th-century arcanists stumbled upon a correct approach with incorrect logic. I'm hoping Wentz will help me sort out my thoughts on this, and I think it's possible I'll have a successfully written ritual in the next week or so.

Of course, since actually performing the ritual would be illegal, perhaps it's better to discuss whether or not it might be tested . . . not in writing, personal email accounts or not. I'd give you my cellphone number but seeing as I've already (a) explicitly flirted and (b) asked about your marital status, I feel like giving you my number here would be going past "charmingly forward" and landing squarely somewhere around "pathetic." I think the best course of action is probably to see how far I get with the ritual on Friday and then talk in person.

As for my social life, there is a medical student who shares the same running route as me (well, he runs. I listen to a podcast and trot arrhythmically while sweating through my T-shirt). He seems nice enough, with very little to indicate that he's planning on stealing my organs, and so I said yes to seeing a movie with him Saturday, but I can say with some authority that I do not think he will be a distraction to my scholarship.

I guess that leads into my answer to your next question, my apparently far-reaching curiosity. I'm almost embarrassed to tell you how devoted I've been to arcane mechanicals my entire life. I've loved the arcane since I was a kid. It was the subject of the children's books I asked for and then the not-so-childish books I read throughout high school, usually under my desk during home economics classes. I think I might have mentioned this in an earlier email to you, but I got a copy of *The Arcane and the Ordinary* for my 16th birthday. I was *that* type of kid. And I went to study at St. Andrews because I knew they had the best undergraduate program in runes and ancient mathematics (and yes, also because they filmed some of the exteriors of the *Golden Seeker* series at the castles there). I walked into my Arcanus completely confident that I was taking the next step in my life's clear path; I left the exam completely undone.

Transparently, it was an incredibly rough few months. I was mourning the death of my little sister, who had been my best friend since she was born, and I was also mourning the career trajectory I had planned on for almost as long. I believed my career in arcane mechanicals to be completely over. I am an impatient person, as we've established, someone who relies on forward motion and accomplishment as a way to stave off feelings of boredom, inadequacy, doubt, fear. At the same time I lost Bertie, I also lost what would have been my most effective way of dealing with the grief—namely, an ability to throw myself into my work. And so I spent months lost and miserable—my mind spinning and gnawing at itself like a confused animal—unsure which of my impulses were productive and which were self-sabotage.

I apologize that this email became something of a diary entry as I struggled to answer your question appropriately. I'll ask you one in return (feel free to answer in person when I see you Friday): Was it ever enough? When you were the wunderkind of the arcane world, the guest of honor at banquets; when your book went into its fifth, sixth, seventh printing—did you ever feel as though you *made* it? From the outside, you're the most successful and popular arcanist since Hewlitt Hudson; it certainly *seems* as though you've made it, as though you've reached a point of critical and commercial success such that no more satisfaction could possibly be asked for. I'm actually realizing now as I write that my real question is a much simpler one: Are you happy? Maybe the truth of my impatience is that I'm convinced when I amass a certain level of accomplishments, my answer will be yes, and I would rather reach that point as quickly as possible.

Thank you again for your generosity in allowing me access to your Wentz volumes and your home. I promise to treat both with respect and minimal BBQ / chocolate pudding / coffee / mustard stains.

See you tomorrow night,
Ellsbeth

From: Rawlins.T.M.
To: Storer.Ellsbeth
Subject: Good Morning

Ellsbeth,

Your impatience must be rubbing off on me, because it has been only 36 hours since you left my house on Friday night, yet I woke this morning hoping to find a writ magic ritual—and accompanying email from you—in my inbox. I guess a bright young woman *might* have better things to do with a crisp autumn Saturday than spend sixteen hours in a research library typing out arcane ritual instructions. (How was your movie, by the way, and your runner?)

Don't worry, I did not email you just to check on your progress on your thesis. I wanted to let you know that it was nice having you over, and I look forward to the next time we can continue your education in the art of fine wine; if you are to make your way in this world, to secure funding and court the support of wealthy benefactors, you will need to demonstrate an ability to select a decent bottle, or at least fake convincing appreciation. (Just remember "notes of cherry," works every time.)

I don't usually share much in the way of personal information with students, but you were open with me, and your candor deserved to be met. Keep in mind, I have worked hard to cultivate an air of opaque mystery, and it would be scuttled quickly if you started sharing details of my past, or my present grudges and resentments. So hopefully I don't need to email you merely to encourage you to keep my secrets, as I will keep yours.

I've been thinking more about the happiness question. I was honest with you on Friday, but on reflection, that was not the whole story. The truth is, I don't believe that happiness was ever available to me. There is something in my nature that does not allow for it, not unlike your inability to stand still. As a younger man, I aspired to happiness, thinking it might accompany great achievement, but every accolade and triumph provided little in the way of lasting contentment, only revealing new challenges to be tackled next. *San neomeo san,* goes the Korean proverb: mountains after mountains. With each peak that you summit, another reveals itself. The task of climbing may seem Sisyphean, but it is all we have.

In other words: No, I'm not happy, but I no longer aim to be, so much as I want to be engaged in meaningful work. The end is not my goal, only to be on the road toward it. I cringe at the grandiosity of the comparison, but I have felt like the Ulysses of Tennyson's poem, an "idle king" of this department, perhaps this entire field of study; "Made weak by time and fate, but strong in will / To strive, to seek, to find and not to yield."

It is not lost on me that this rediscovery of a sense of purpose has coincided with your arrival in my life. Your curiosity and ambition have been refreshing and invigorating, and I thought you might be heartened to know that you have, even accidentally, stirred something in me. But that is not the reason for my email to you, either.

Why, then, am I using the free hours of my Sunday morning to send this message? Simple: to let you know that you left your jacket here. And as we established last night, it clashes with my decor, so for the sake of my study's appearance if nothing else, I should get it back to you soon.

But I do find myself wondering how you managed, on a cold evening, to depart without your outer layer? Were you so thoroughly flummoxed by the moment we shared before you left that you did not even think of it? Or perhaps, recalling the way your face flushed, I wonder if you were warmed by the rush of blood to your cheeks so much that you made it halfway home before the chill set in? Or (more interesting) did you leave it on purpose? Hoping that I would see it and recall the moment you shrugged it off when you came and sat beside me on the sofa? Imagining that I might remember the way its removal revealed the delicacy of your neck? Or perhaps you thought you might stop by to pick it up this afternoon, and the restraint I exhibited at the moment of your departure would evaporate at the sight of you on my doorstep?

Alas, I will be out for the rest of the day. I'll drop the coat off tomorrow morning in the graduate TA office, discreetly so that other members of the cohort don't gossip. And as much as my home will be aesthetically improved by its departure, I might miss having a piece of you in my possession.

Sincerely,
Rawlins

From: Storer.Ellsbeth
To: Rawlins.T.M.
Subject: The Ritual

Happy Monday.

I hope this makes all of your waiting worth it: a functional writ magic ritual (attached below). At least, I think there's a pretty good chance it *might* be a functional magic ritual.

I think I was too flustered when I saw you Friday night and then slightly too buzzed on the very good wine to have actually let you know that the ostensible reason I came to your house—studying Wentz—proved incredibly useful. I did not go on my Saturday date with the runner (his name, for the record, is Oscar) because I had hit that perfect, enviable state when work feels easy and even words from dusty, centuries-old texts make perfect sense and I wasn't able to pull myself away. We postponed; next weekend.

And so, here it is. I will say now that I am more than a little sleep-deprived, and so the ritual might be much less coherent than I think it is, but the way it makes sense to me, this is a ritual that could (hypothetically) be performed with only two individuals—the binder and the subject—and with relatively inexpensive materials: a chalk circle, fully charred ash from cedarwood to draw the actual writ (diagram 1c in the PDF), and a piece of thread to tie the knot (diagram 2a).

Maybe success is an endless slog on the hedonic treadmill, and every victory will eventually become pat and pointless. But I have to admit that even writing a first draft of this ritual felt good. If you had time in the next week or so, I would love your thoughts on whether my analysis was sound, and whether you think the ritual would actually work. If I was completely delusional in my reasoning at any point, please go easy on me.

I think part of the reason I was so productive this weekend is because I was willing myself not to think about you. If I was translating Aramaic and Italian, then maybe my brain would be too occupied to dwell on the way your smile reveals your ever-so-slightly crooked teeth, or how good you smell. Even I know that it's not smart to be thinking this much about how good your thesis adviser smells.

I spent my life wanting to become a scholar of arcane mechanicals; it was my singular focus, and after the disaster of my Arcanus, I thought that dream was over. Now that I've been granted this rare second chance, an invaluable opportunity, I *know* I should avoid *anything* at all that might risk my future. And yet . . .

How do I best put this? Have you ever been driving along a coastal highway and imagined how easy it would be to jerk the steering wheel and disappear into oblivion? It's not that you *want* to die—it's almost as if your brain is taunting you with how fine the line between chaos and order truly is. It's a fairly common psychological phenomenon. They call it *L'appel du Vide.* The Call of the Void.

All of that is to say, I should be focused entirely on protecting my precious academic career, but it's taking everything in me to stop thinking about that moment by the door, when we stood so close I could feel your breath on my skin. When you almost kissed me. That was what almost happened, wasn't it? I can't stop thinking about you, and I can't stop thinking about the possibility of you and I performing an illegal ritual together. Two equally dangerous prospects.

I admit, with other boys I've pulled the classic "leaving my coat" trick in order to guarantee a second encounter and I should probably preserve the fiction here that I am a cool femme fatale, the vixen who knows exactly what she's doing. But we're getting to know each other. We're supposed to trust each other. And so I will be honest with you here: I left my coat only because that moment with you left me lightheaded and a little senseless. I didn't even notice it was missing until you emailed yesterday.

x

RAWLINS

It was an unseasonably warm night, fragrant with autumn decay. Rawlins sat on his back deck, ignoring the expansive view of Newlyn, his attention fully engrossed in his laptop. He was oblivious to the creak of his wooden chair, to the clink of the single ice cube in his highball glass as he swirled it back and forth. The glowing screen periodically attracted bugs; he shooed away a moth as he scrolled back up to the top of the PDF for the third time, trying to understand what he was looking at.

As soon as he opened it, he found the organization of Ellsbeth's ritual annoying and slightly pretentious; she was employing the two-column structure popularized by European scholars in the nineteenth century, which required the reader to ping-pong between elemental activations and diagrams. The style was probably thanks to the time she had spent reading Wentz; he found it stuffy and counterintuitive.

As was typically the case with nearly any first-year grad student's work, it was unnecessarily long; the third and fourth steps could be easily combined, and Rawlins found several other inelegant repetitions. He also noted a handful of typos and an obvious but crucial mistake she had made with the abbreviation of an elemental.

Even with these mistakes and imperfections, he was struck, upon reading it, with a singular, certain conclusion: It was brilliant.

It would work.

A written ritual was somewhere between a baking recipe and a mathematical proof; it had an insular logic, combining scientific principles of biology and physics with the energetic forces of arcane mechanics. Devising a new ritual was thus a complex undertaking, one that inevitably required endless rounds of iteration, a search for the delicate balance of forces that would yield the desired result. When it was completed, it always needed to be tested—but Rawlins had developed a nearly infallible sense for when a ritual as written would actually *work.* His ability to spot it on the page was honed by his own trial and error, his years of grading graduate theses, and the tedious hours of peer-review journal work he contributed.

Somehow, Ellsbeth had—in a weekend, with little input beyond what she could glean from some antiquated volumes—constructed an original written ritual from the ground up. For a banned magical practice. That, in itself, was a miracle.

In a sense, she had actually found a very clever way to reconstruct a very old ritual. Ellsbeth had determined the ritual's function by combining a vague allusion in Wentz (*a binding useful for restraint of the accused*) with a document on sixteenth-century courtroom procedure, which dictated that a defendant's wrists ought to be tied and their legs immobilized. Ellsbeth had then extrapolated the forces necessary to achieve such a binding through arcane mechanical forces by cross-referencing a wide array of related effects.

It was an astonishingly impressive feat of scholarship. Rawlins would be tempted to think the work was plagiarized if not for the fact that he couldn't even imagine where one might find a source to copy from.

Perhaps she had gotten lucky? Not likely, given the density of ideas needed to populate a ritual of this complexity. Layers of new thoughts and extrapolations. Connections that couldn't be looked up in the back of any book or searched for on the internet. Perhaps she had been helped by someone else? That seemed even less likely, given the foolishness of involving a stranger in her banned topic.

Or perhaps she was truly, prodigiously *gifted* at the study of arcane mechanicals. Perhaps she had arrived at his door with her vast ability completely obscured by the unique circumstances of her aborted attempt at the Arcanus exam. Perhaps she was a singular mind with the potential to revolutionize his field of study.

That was the possibility that troubled Rawlins most of all.

He closed his laptop, and gray spots appeared in his vision as his eyes adjusted to the night. The view of Newlyn at dusk swam into clarity—the valley below him, the river that cut through town, the red-brick buildings of campus hugging its curves.

Amid the familiar buildings, his gaze found the Pembroke dorm. Rebuilt and renovated years ago, but he could still see, in his mind's eye, the blue flame that had once consumed its top two floors.

ON TUESDAY AFTERNOON, RAWLINS ATE lunch alone in the faculty dining hall while flipping through a dull paper on thaumaturgy for one of the conferences he chaired, when he was interrupted by a familiar voice.

"Afternoon, Tad," said Paul Gallway as he slid uninvited into an empty chair. "Wanted to chat about something. Cone of silence." He clearly expected that would get Rawlins's attention; Gallway always loved to invoke an air of collegial secrecy, but Rawlins saw through the transparent strategy and found it grating. "It's about the Taylor Prize," Gallway added when Rawlins didn't reply.

The Taylor Prize was the most prestigious student award in the field of the arcane arts; the winner was always a graduate student from one of the most elite universities, and the schools all bragged about the number of Taylor Prize winners that had matriculated from their programs. Newlyn had had its share, but it had been half a decade since the last one.

"You're nominating someone?" Rawlins asked, thinking about the students whose thesis committees were chaired by Gallway. "Victor Hamada?"

Gallway shook his head. "Actually, I'm hoping *you'll* nominate someone. And certainly not Hamada. I was thinking Curt. He won the MacGregor Fellowship already. He has a legitimate shot!"

Rawlins squinted. Curt becoming a MacGregor Fellow was impressive, but also, to Rawlins, utterly baffling for such an ordinary scholar. He suspected there may have been a late disqualification, or that Curt had family connections pulling strings on the committee that granted it. Probably both.

"Curt is a fine student," Rawlins said. "But he's not exactly a genius."

"Come on, Tad. This isn't a field for geniuses anymore. And honestly, that's a good thing. We're not going to find a place within the culture by pioneering esoteric use cases. It's about practical applications that have social benefit and commercial value. Curt's work might not seem intellectually exciting to you, but it *is* the future of the arcane arts."

"So why don't *you* nominate him?" Rawlins asked.

"Because I want him to win the damn thing. I'm his adviser, and it reflects better on both of us if someone else puts him forward. Plus," Gallway added, "your name still has a certain . . . cachet. Fame, you know. The bestseller. Don't be modest. Your endorsement would give him a leg up."

Rawlins was not entirely immune to flattery, but Gallway's attempt had backfired; the subtext of the word "still" spoke volumes, implying a *despite* that went unspoken. Despite the fact that you haven't published a new book in several years. Despite the fact that your contributions to the field are effectively finished.

"So you want *me* to do the work of nominating him, while *you* accrue the benefit," Rawlins said. It was true that nominating a student was not a simple matter of writing a letter; to limit the number of applicants, they had made the process laborious and time-consuming.

"Oh, don't worry about any of that." Gallway put a hand on Rawlins's shoulder and shook it playfully. "I'll take care of all the work. I just need you to personalize the letter and then sign off on it all."

"Sorry," Rawlins said. "I just don't view him as the caliber of scholar that the award is meant for."

"Come on now. You know it would be good for our program," Gallway said. "And it's not like there's anyone else in this cohort who's better qualified for it."

Rawlins checked his watch. "Maybe," he murmured, then picked up his bag. "I've got a class to teach. And if he's qualified for the prize, I'm sure the nomination of his own adviser will mean more than mine."

While Rawlins was teaching his Tuesday lecture section, he discovered that he now had two different Ellsbeth problems, which were distinct but not wholly unrelated.

The first was the question of how to handle a particularly gifted student. His approach with Max had been unrestrained encouragement, and that had ended disastrously. He could not help but wonder if his praise had stoked the boy's ego, convinced him of his own power and entitlement, when what he had needed were boundaries that would have kept him safe.

There was a simple lesson Rawlins took from that tragedy: Among students, effort should be more valuable to him than talent. He praised discipline now, not potential.

So he forced himself, with difficulty, to give Ellsbeth no special treatment. The girl had already admitted her own impatience, he didn't need her walking around convinced of her own genius.

But after reading her ritual, treating her like any other student wasn't easy. He was excited by her insights and opinions: When he asked the class a challenging question about the theoretical basis for performing a thermomantic ritual on a liquid-state substance, Ellsbeth's hand rose immediately, and Rawlins found himself genuinely curious to hear her reply. For a moment, he wished they weren't in class at all, that he was sitting across from her in a restaurant, discussing rituals over dinner.

That was the second Ellsbeth problem: For the first time in his professional career, he was fiercely attracted to one of his students. Plenty of pretty girls had come through the program, and he'd entertained idle fantasies, but this was different. His mind was constantly pulled toward Ellsbeth, the same way his gaze was pulled toward her in class. He would turn away from the blackboard, and suddenly their eyes would meet, and he would experience a thrill—a tingle on his scalp as he wondered what she was thinking—followed by a rush of nervousness, as though surely the moment of eye contact had given away the connection between them. Ellsbeth would look down at her notebook, and he would see the ghost of a coy smile on her lips. He would lose his place and need to vamp, grateful that he had done this lecture a dozen times, and even his rambling had the weight and cadence of importance.

It wasn't merely a physical attraction; Ellsbeth lingered in his mind like a wine stain. He *liked* her. Her humor, her flirtatiousness, her brazenness. Their email exchanges left him charged, energized as if he had just downed several small cups of espresso.

It was intoxicating—which only added to the problem. The force of his desire left him unmoored, but it also made him distrustful—of his own thoughts, yes, but of her motivations as well. Wanting like this did not simply *happen;* it was cultivated, it was caused. And while it seemed paranoid to view this bookish girl as some sort of femme fatale, it was true that she had pursued him, from the very beginning, with an agenda. To get into the program, to study a forbidden discipline. Which was more likely: that she might have happened to fall for him *while* getting what she wanted, or that the two were connected?

He thought of the day he had seen her downtown at the civic center, when she had concealed something from him. A student telling him a white lie was generally no cause for alarm—but when he was *falling* like this, finding himself wanting to know her inside and out and *trust* her—it was a bracing reminder that he was on shaky ground.

He needed to proceed with caution. To keep his libido in check. To make sure their delightfully provocative email exchanges, toeing the line of propriety, did not escalate into something more serious, which could have grave potential consequences. Even if he *wanted* it to, so badly he could taste it, he had to confine his longings to the plausible-deniability realm of a few overly flirtatious emails. That was his only hope of maintaining his equilibrium and whatever measure of power he had in this situation.

When he wrapped up his graduate lecture about Galvani's insights on thermomantism, it was a relief to reach the end of the discussion that day and dismiss the students. He reminded them of their assigned reading before Practicum and avoided eye contact as he added, in a voice of practiced casualness, "Anyone who sent me work this weekend, stick around for a minute."

The students filed out, and Rawlins rifled through his bag, as though he couldn't remember which cohort member, or how many, had turned in a paper for him to hand back. He looked up, feigning surprise, to find that only Ellsbeth remained in the room.

"Ms. Storer. That's right. Your rough draft." He handed over a printout of Ellsbeth's ritual, marked up in red pen. Shockingly little red pen, for how complex the ritual was.

She didn't simply take the paper and leave; she hovered, looking through his comments.

She saw the error she had made with an abbreviation and winced. "Ugh, sorry about that."

"A careless mistake," he said.

"Maybe I was a little distracted," she said. "Thinking about something else this weekend."

"You'll have to learn focus, then. Discipline." His heart raced. God, was he *blushing*?

Ellsbeth finished scanning his notes, then lowered the page and studied his expression. "Thank you for the feedback. This all feels very manageable. But I'm just wondering . . . I mean. What do you think? Will it work?"

Rawlins felt his mouth go dry, and reminded himself: *Be professional*. "Do the revision, and then we can talk about that."

"Okay," Ellsbeth said. "But these are mostly typos. The ritual itself is going to be the same in the next draft. What do you think? Of the work?"

"What *I* think," Rawlins said, "is that you should focus on addressing the notes."

"Whatever you say, Professor." She headed out the door, glancing back as she left to see if he was watching her go. He was, of course, and their gaze lingered for a full second. She was the one who smiled and turned away first.

THE REVISION WAS IN HIS inbox when he woke the next morning; from the timestamp, he could see that she had stayed up most of the night reworking it, abandoning the two-column approach. She hadn't merely corrected the errors; she had actually *understood* his feedback regarding the unnecessary complication and had found a more streamlined approach to the entire thing.

It was common for grad students to spend an entire semester perfecting a written ritual of this level of complexity—yet Ellsbeth, with her second draft, only four days after she had begun, had given him a draft that was worthy of testing—and likely of publication.

There was no way to reply without praising her. And if he praised her, he would be making his feelings obvious. And so, Rawlins blinked and closed his computer. He would figure out how to respond later. He told himself that if she weren't working on such controversial magic, he would find her another adviser to work with, but he was aware even as he had the thought, silent and internal, that it was a lie.

When Ellsbeth arrived at his office hours the next week, he realized he had been anticipating her. He had worn his favorite green sweater that day hoping she would come. "I never got your thoughts back on my second draft," Ellsbeth said, sitting in the chair across from his desk.

Rawlins had the presence of mind to pretend to be busy for a few seconds. "I didn't have a chance to look at it," he said, hoping his voice sounded convincing. It didn't. He tried again. "I mean, I didn't get a chance to get my thoughts together."

"But what did you think?" Ellsbeth said. "Just looking at it."

"It's . . ." He tried to choose the word carefully. "Solid."

Ellsbeth picked at her cuticles. He tried to read her expression, but he couldn't. "I was hoping for a little bit more feedback," she said. "I want to grow as a scholar. You haven't even told me if the ritual is any good."

"Ellsbeth, it doesn't matter if I think your ritual is any good or not," he said.

"Actually, it does," she said. "You're my adviser."

At that, Rawlins laughed. He couldn't help himself, and Ellsbeth, too, relaxed slightly, almost smiling. "Yes," he said finally, quietly. "It's very, very good. Is that what you wanted me to say? Did you want to know if you impressed me? You did. Do I think you're special? I do." His heart was pounding now. He could see the downy hair that softened her cheek; he fought the urge to reach out and touch it. "But that doesn't matter. All that matters is whether the ritual will work."

He wished he had asked her to close the door. No; thank god she hadn't. He was grateful the door was open and Professor Langdon could be strolling down the hall at any moment after reheating her mug of tea in the faculty microwave. There was a desk between them, but Rawlins felt as though their bodies were connected by a taut, vibrating string. He couldn't look away from her, and he felt his breath quicken.

"Okay," Ellsbeth said. "Then let's test it."

His mind echoed with voices of concern: *It's dangerous. It's illegal. This is what she's wanted all along, she's maneuvered you into this position, and you don't even understand why . . .*

But before Rawlins had the chance to properly contemplate any of these concerns, some combination of curiosity and hunger shut down all his protests. "Let's test it," he said.

On Friday night, Rawlins walked to campus around nine in the evening. The night air was alive with the tumult of undergraduate carousing. Students pre-gaming in dorms and apartments, rowdy voices in packs coming down the streets and across the quads. Raucous laughter. "Professor Rawlins!" He lifted his hand in silent greeting to a gaggle of students who had taken his undergraduate lecture as he walked past, away from the dormitories and toward the academic buildings.

A cold front had moved in, driving back the earlier week's warmth and filling the night air with a chilly fog that swirled in the glow of the yellow lamps that lined the campus walkways. Ellsbeth stood waiting for him near the statue of Gregory Hale, wearing a long coat that, while appropriate to the weather, struck him as amusing—the type of thing a detective in a noir film would wear. He thought of her trying on various outfits, selecting the one most suited to a clandestine meetup . . . then tried to banish thoughts of her dressing and undressing.

Unhelpful.

"Shall we?" he said, and indicated for her to follow. She glanced up and down the walkway as she fell into step beside him toward the Practicum.

After hours, the buildings of the College of the Arcane Arts were locked. Rawlins swiped a card that opened the door to the Practicum with a satisfying click. Their entry would be recorded electronically, but it was not out of the ordinary for professors to come in after hours;

use of the Practicum required reservations and permissions, but as the one tasked with managing its supplies, he was confident no one would question his presence.

Their shoes clicked on the cold tile floors, echoing in the empty hallways. Ellsbeth stayed at his heels, and he could sense her nervous excitement while he tried to hide his own. She huddled close as he slid his key into the lock and opened it into the dark expanse.

Rawlins flipped a switch near the door but neglected the overhead lights, which would be visible through the high windows and might draw attention. The small tungsten lamp barely penetrated the darkness, leaving the platform of the ritual space obscured.

"Think you can manage?"

Ellsbeth nodded; if she was daunted, she hid it well.

In the cavernous space, every sound echoed, and she slipped off her shoes along with her coat. Underneath, she wore a light blouse and black pants.

Rawlins unlocked the cabinets, leaving them open one by one. "We'll need to make a record of everything we use."

"Thank you," she said. "For . . . you know."

"Risking my job?" He shrugged. "It's not the first time I've engaged in after-hours ritual practice."

"For trusting me," she said.

He blinked, startled into clarity. Her comment, even if it was intended as gratitude, sent a shiver of fear through his body, throwing into relief the actual weight of the choice he was making here. *Should* he trust her? He felt some natural inclination to, as if he'd known her in some past life. But his rational mind reminded him of a dozen reasons he should know better.

It was not too late to turn back. But that was not in his nature.

After lighting a ring of candles around the platform, Ellsbeth set her written procedure on a table for reference and began to prepare the ritual space. Rawlins let her take the lead, offering only occasional guidance—where to find the iridium, how best to hang the incense.

The ritual was mathematically advanced, but the elementals involved were relatively common—mostly precious metals, which would be activated but mercifully not consumed by the process. Gold, silver, and copper ingots were laid out in sequence on three intersecting lines, which converged on a focal point at the center.

The quantities needed were determined by the period of time for which they wanted to induce immobilization. "I'm calculating for a five-minute duration," Ellsbeth said, writing her math out neatly in her notebook.

"Make it two," Rawlins replied.

She looked up at him, conflicted. "Five is an easier divisor and gives us more time for observation."

"Two minutes," he said definitively.

She narrowed her eyes, clearly wanting to know why but able to see he had no desire to explain himself. She relented and went about calculating for a two-minute duration.

In truth, Rawlins was nervous about the possibility of an unintended effect. It was rare for him—for anyone—to perform a ritual that was untested, and in this case, one that was not even *related* to any other ritual he had previously performed. He had a solid grasp on the underlying principles, but there were risks, especially with magic that directly impacted a person as its subject. The human body and mind were notoriously tricky targets of arcane mechanical influence.

The ritual was meant to restrain only the wrists of the subject, but with an untested activation, it was always possible there could be spillover. If Ellsbeth's lungs were somehow immobilized, she wouldn't be able to breathe. He had a brief, awful vision of her collapsing to the floor, suffocating, which he tried to purge from his mind.

Two minutes might make her pass out; five would be lethal. But he didn't need her thinking about that while she did the preparations.

Ellsbeth moved confidently through the space, making careful measurements. Rawlins rechecked as she went without finding a single error. Once she finished laying out the last trail of metals, she wasted no time stepping into the circle at the center of the platform.

Rawlins was starting to feel conflicted; surely, she knew the risks, and she had no doubt read gory reports of what could happen to people subjected to untested rituals. If she was certain she wanted to do this, there was nothing to be gained by reminding her of the dangers now; he would only evoke fear and compromise the process. So he asked simply, to clear his conscience, "You're sure you're comfortable being the subject?"

She nodded. "I'm confident in my work. And in you to conduct it."

"All right, then." He picked up her written instructions and walked around the ritual circle, igniting the incense in four hanging burners, each suspended above a rune inscribed in chalk on the platform. The pungent smoke wafted across the space, already dim in the candle-light.

Rawlins stood at the edge of the ritual circle. He looked at Ellsbeth in the center; she was visibly self-conscious, arms at her sides, feet planted slightly apart. He could see her fear and, in proportion to it, her courage. Admiration swelled within him as he began chanting. "*Teneatur corpus. Animiat dormus.*"

Ellsbeth exhaled and rolled her shoulders as Rawlins continued, intoning the Latin that she had written. "*Teneatur corpus. Membra rigus.*"

The metals on the floor began to gleam. In the dim candlelight, the effect was subtle, but it became more pronounced as he continued the invocation. The faint hum he loved so much pierced the silence; the mysterious droning sound, with no discernible source, enveloped them.

He kept his voice steady and slow, even as his excitement grew line by line—and with it, his fear. It was undeniable that the ritual was working, but the final effect remained unknown. He hadn't experienced this thrill of discovery since early in his career, and the stakes were heightened vastly by the fact that the mysterious forces he summoned were not directed at some inanimate object. They were very much about to impact a person—one whose body and safety he had, in a short time, come to care about more than he ever expected to.

So he struggled to maintain his equanimity and the even pace of his voice as he pronounced the final line: "*Teneatur corpus. Manus ligatum.*"

The glow of the metals on the floor flared to a new level of brightness, and instantly a suffocated gasp escaped Ellsbeth's throat. Her entire body tightened, and her hands, which had previously been hanging at her sides, snapped together in front of her. Her eyes went wide, and Rawlins felt a moment of panic, fearing he had collapsed her windpipe or permanently altered some other internal system he could not reverse.

But he could see that she was still breathing. And there was excitement in her eyes.

"I'm okay," she said, reading his mind.

"Your hands?" he asked. She held them out in front of her, showing that they were pressed together at the wrists, as though bound by an invisible pair of cuffs. He watched her flex and intertwine her fingers, marveling at the unseen force that kept them together.

"Pull them apart," he said intently. "Try as hard as you can."

Her arms flexed with the strain, then went slack as she gave up. "*I can't.*"

Never had those two words been spoken with such joy and wonder, and Rawlins smiled at her delight. She deserved to celebrate. *They had done it.* The first instance of writ magic he had ever witnessed. It had *worked.*

"Incredible," he murmured. Her joy moved him, its effortless transparency, and he surrendered to the moment, in ways that again brought him back to his first days as a practitioner of arcane mechanicals.

And then both of their smiles melted, replaced by . . . something else. A current of electricity coursed between them, shifting the energy in the room.

Rawlins's mind moved off the fact of their accomplishment and instead was struck by Ellsbeth *herself.* Standing in front of him. Her wrists immobilized in this way, for . . . what? Another minute and a half? He felt a surge of excitement at her incapacitation—and was alarmed by his own reaction. It was a predatory instinct, stirred in some distant evolutionary remnant of his mind. The part of his genetic heritage that had once savored domination over prey. A corner of his libido that he had long since sought to civilize into submission.

He felt shame, for a moment, at discovering the thoughts—not even thoughts, the *impulses* that were stirred by her helplessness. He tried to suppress the instinct, to deny it. He shook his head and looked away, attempting to bring himself to his senses—but, again as though she could read his mind, she said simply, quietly, "It's okay."

Heat spread through his chest. Without even being aware of what he was doing, he stepped forward into the ritual circle. Approaching her.

The soft hum of the magic persisted, and the glow of the metals cast flickering golden light across her features, making her skin look ethereal. He pondered her face more closely than he ever had before, her expression a study in contradiction. There was joy at their success alongside terror at what they had done. There was pride in her work, and *power,* alongside the natural, inevitable fear response of being physically captive.

But there was something else that burned even more brightly. *Desire.* He could see it nakedly in her eyes, and he knew exactly what it was, unmistakably, because it was pitched in exact proportion to his own, which was growing by the second. He fought to keep his expression restrained, not to betray what was happening inside him, even as it felt like a tether connected her body to his and was reeling him in.

This was not the force of magic, but of . . . what? Biology and psychology and chemistry in some blend that could not be untangled, that had not had a hold on him like this since he was a much younger man. A more foolish one. He was not about to *abandon* himself, to lose his senses, to succumb.

Yet he could not bring himself to retreat, either. He enjoyed riding the edge of this feeling.

As he strode across the platform, he savored how every step that brought him closer to her intensified the connection between them. Was this what it felt like to genuinely *want* someone? Had it been so long he had simply forgotten? Or perhaps this was unique to the circumstances . . . unique to *her.*

He stepped directly in front of Ellsbeth. "Give me your hands." She lifted her arms and he grabbed her wrists, encircling them tightly, feeling the softness of her skin under his fingertips, the delicacy of her bones.

Then he pulled her wrists apart, forcefully, and her hands separated as he overpowered her. He held them a foot apart for a moment, and her arms *shook* with effort, resisting him involuntarily, fighting to press back into each other. The moment he stopped pulling, her wrists snapped back together. "Guess you're stronger than me," she said, and those few words flooded his brain with the primal urge to keep holding on to her wrists, to pull her closer to him.

But there was a lesson to teach. He let her wrists fall. "What did we just prove?"

"It's internal," she said, her voice hoarse. "The effect is on *me,* from within. As opposed to an external force pressing *against* me, from without."

"Most likely the ritual is affecting your nervous system," Rawlins said, keeping his voice level, acutely aware of their proximity, as he instructed her softly. "Your somatic nervous system. But you're blushing, Miss Storer, and your heart rate is increasing, which indicates?" His voice was low. He raised his eyebrows, waiting for her to answer.

"My sympathetic nervous system isn't affected," she said. Ellsbeth's eyes sought his, but he wouldn't quite meet her gaze, fighting to maintain some semblance of control, fearing what he would do otherwise.

"The other muscle groups? Still functioning correctly?" Rawlins asked.

In answer, Ellsbeth raised her arms, still bound at the wrist, and put them behind his head, her forearms resting on his shoulders, her fingertips grazing the back of his neck, as if they were slow dancing.

Rawlins struggled to breathe normally, but it suddenly felt like an effort to drag air raggedly through his throat. And he was so close he could feel the warmth from her lungs, grazing his chin, intermingling with his own breath in the charged space between them.

"You blushed," Rawlins said, and his finger brushed her cheek, where the skin was turning red, blood blossoming just below the surface. "Just like you are now." He felt the warmth of her flesh, and his finger trailed down, to her jawline, to her throat.

"Pesky sympathetic nervous system," she said.

He had no more academic points to prove. No more reasons to be standing so close to her, with her bound wrists around his neck pulling him even closer. He was suspended in this limbo, on an impossible precipice. Physically unable to retreat to safety, but not willing to leap forward. He *wanted* to grab her and pull her into him, press her body into his. But he fought the urge, because he didn't know where it would stop.

His hands found her waist, and Ellsbeth shivered under his touch as his thumbs tightened into the contours of her rib cage through the soft fabric of her blouse. Simultaneously holding her and holding her back, in sync with the warring impulses inside him.

Ellsbeth leaned forward, bridging the distance between them, her lips moving toward his.

He was so acutely inclined toward her, it was almost like he could *already* feel the sensation.

But his chest tightened as the guilt that he had been trying to keep down roared to the surface. She may not be helpless, he thought, she may want this as badly as he did, but she was his student. She was his *responsibility,* and the prospect of violating that trust was repulsive to him.

So his hand came up between them, and he put his thumb to her lower lip, stopping her. She froze, embarrassed and exposed in the middle of the act. He searched for the right words—to explain, to apologize, to soften this—but couldn't find them.

Instead, he pressed the pad of his thumb into the tenderness of her mouth, barely grazing her bottom teeth. He could feel her soft breath on his thumb.

His resistance began to collapse into itself, and he could feel his body begin to relax, ready to let go of the self-control he had been fighting to maintain.

But at that moment, the energy in the room shifted. The glow of the metals dimmed, and the hum of the ritual went silent. A tremble convulsed her body; her shoulders shook and her arms relaxed, her wrists separating as the effect of the ritual ended.

The spell was broken. Two minutes was up.

Even though it was darker than ever, it was as if the lights had been thrown on at the end of a high school dance, the music cut, and without thinking they both took a step back, separating, suddenly self-conscious.

Ellsbeth spoke first. "I'm sorry," she said, although she didn't look quite sure what she was sorry for.

Rawlins shook his head. "You have nothing to be sorry for. We were just . . . testing the effect. It worked. Congratulations."

She exhaled—*right, of course*—and hugged her sides. He could see that she was wounded by his denial, and felt torn by his empathy for her, uncertain how best to proceed. Tell her the truth? That he had seen her physically restrained and wanted to strip her naked and drag her to the floor and take her again and again, touching her and teasing her and pleasuring her until she forgot her own name? What he'd felt for her was dangerously excessive, and he didn't know how to let out only a little.

Ellsbeth glanced around at the elementals scattered across the ritual platform and said to the floor, "I should probably start getting this all put away before someone comes in and arrests us." She began to pick up ingots from the floor, but he stopped her, putting a hand on her shoulder. He desperately longed to explain himself. To tell her . . .

Yes, it works, like I knew it would.

And *Yes, I wanted to kiss you last Friday.*

And *Fucking hell, yes, I wanted to do more than that tonight.*

But his tongue was heavy and numb. Anything he said would change their relationship forever. Would only cause problems down the line. Would only weaken his resolve. "Yes," he said finally. "We should clean up."

He forced himself to lift his hand from her shoulder, and turned to take down the hanging incense. He felt impossibly idiotic, knowing he looked like an absolute fool—but at the same time, a strange realization: He was *hoping* she could see through him. That she could read his mind.

When he glanced back and watched her kneeling to pick up gold ingots, her face was partly turned away, but he was glad that by the glow of the streetlight reflecting through the high window of the Practicum, he could see her smiling.

ELLSBETH

For their date, Oscar took Ellsbeth to a trendy restaurant nestled inside an arcade meant for adults, a place where you had to raise your voice over the mechanical clanging of an aggressive game of pinball ten yards away in order to order a thirty-six-dollar deconstructed Caesar salad.

"Sorry," Oscar said as soon as they settled into their seats. "This place got amazing reviews. I didn't expect it to be so loud."

"Oh. No! It's fun," Ellsbeth said. "I've been meaning to try this place."

Oscar gave her a shaky smile, clearly grateful at her grace, and Ellsbeth settled into her seat, placing her napkin neatly on her lap.

Ellsbeth and Oscar had seen each other on jogs around campus for weeks. Eventually, when their faces became familiar, they would smile or wave as they passed, but their communication never ventured beyond a mouthed "hi" or "good morning" until one morning, Oscar had slowed up where Ellsbeth was stretching by a park bench and asked if she wanted to get a cup of coffee.

"I've been trying to build up the courage to talk to you," Oscar had confessed over oat milk flat whites. "But I didn't want to be that creepy guy who bothers a girl on her run, you know? Like, call campus security or whatever. A girl is allowed to work out in public without a guy making it all about him."

Ellsbeth found him to be endearing and sweet, if a little self-congratulatory in his campus-ready feminism. He was on the shorter side, with curly blond hair cropped close to his head. He was handsome in a way that made her think of country clubs, or dentists in commercials recommending toothpaste. When he had asked for Ellsbeth's phone number ("So I could ask to take you out to dinner on a night you're free"), it was with a tone of such polite, old-fashioned courtship that she half expected him to ask for her father's phone number, too, so that he might ask permission.

But of course, Oscar would never be that regressive. Sitting opposite her at the restaurant in the arcade was a boy twenty-four years old, well trained in consent, in intersectionality, in emotional labor, and in the importance of self-care. Ellsbeth had no doubt that at the end of their dinner, he would offer to pay but not feel threatened if she insisted on splitting the bill. He was the type, she knew, instantly, who would put his arm around her at dinner parties and kiss her cheek and call her his "partner."

Ellsbeth studied him after they both ordered their cocktails, how shockingly *non-neurotic* he seemed. It was easy for him to tell her about his mom, his dad, his older brother who'd gotten into trouble with the law but seemed to be straightening out now. He told her about his favorite movies without a shred of self-deprecation or irony. Here was a boy, Ellsbeth thought, who was happy with who he was. And it was nice, Ellsbeth realized, how visible his effort on the date was, how unashamed he was to reveal the fact that he liked her. He had looked up a fancy restaurant and made a reservation. He had picked Ellsbeth up outside her apartment in his used Honda and worn a button-down shirt.

"So," Oscar said, elbows perched on the table, gnawing on the toothpick that came in his drink, "what made you want to study arcane mechanicals?"

Ellsbeth's mind flashed back to the evening in the Practicum, holding her breath as she watched Professor Rawlins prepare to test the ritual she wrote. His mouth had been a tight straight line, and she could see a vein lifted in his forearm as he checked to make sure the ingots were the proper distance apart. Just that: The vein in his forearm, visible because he had rolled up the sleeve of his button-down shirt, had been enough to cause her heart to race and an uncomfortable warmth to spread between her legs. She was excited and impatient and eager to test the ritual, and there was the thrill of sneaking into the Practicum with the professor after hours, but there was something else: an urge she knew would only lead to trouble for both of them.

When the ritual had worked, the sensation had been like nothing she had ever experienced, nothing she could have prepared herself for. How much of the lightheaded thrill had been due to the success itself, her pride at getting firsthand evidence that her research and her instincts had led to this, a miracle of the arcane, in a single weekend? How much had been the effect of the ritual itself, the strange strangle on her nervous system paralyzing her limbs and leaving her muscles numb and heavy? And how much had been Professor Rawlins standing so close to her that she could smell his aftershave, see the texture on his skin, his long almost feminine eyelashes, and the way he was clenching his jaw?

I want to sleep with my professor. She was embarrassed even as she thought it. It was a cliché out of tawdry pornography, evoking too-short tartan skirts and too-tight button-down blouses over ample breasts. It was wrong, it was regressive, it was dangerous, and it was impossible: Professor Rawlins was not the type to risk his professional career for a brief dalliance, and even if he *was*, Ellsbeth was certain there was a younger, lither, glossier student that would have a hold on his attention.

And then there was the ritual itself, the tingling warmth that had come when he had been standing before her while her hands were bound. It was just a test, it was arcane mechanicals, there was nothing *kinky* about it. And yet in that moment, she understood why fuzzy handcuffs were a mainstay of cheap motel ephemera—what a *rush* to imagine that she could be standing there, helpless and bound, while someone like *him* wanted her. He had felt it, too. She knew he had. But it was impossible to talk about without incriminating them both, without risking the future of her thesis. *My thesis that now has a functional ritual.* She was so close to getting everything she needed. She had already unlocked writ magic. It would only be a matter of time before she would have the tools to get at the truth of what had happened to Bertie.

"Oh," Ellsbeth said after too long a pause. "It's sort of the only thing I ever loved. It's like . . . physics, if you added poetry. Arcane mechanicals has rules, like science, but it's sort of closer to cooking, if that makes sense. No matter how much you learn, there are still mysteries that you'll never fully be able to understand. There are infinite factors that can affect a ritual. I think that's why I like it. With most science, the goal is finding a concrete answer. With the arcane, you're always looking for new questions."

"Wow," Oscar laughed. "That's a really good answer. When people ask me why I want to be a doctor, I say it's because I passed orgo and it seemed like a good way to help people."

"Well, it is," Ellsbeth said. "The problem with arcane mechanicals is it's a pretty . . . dusty, isolated field these days. Being a doctor, you know you're actually doing good in the world. Making people's lives better."

"I guess," Oscar said. "Although I'm not looking forward to my loans coming due when med school is over."

"Do you know what kind of doctor you want to be?"

"I still have time to decide, obviously, but I think pediatric oncology."

"Oh, my god," Ellsbeth said just as their salads arrived. "So you're a saint. You're, like, actually just a very good person."

"No, god no," Oscar said. "I just want to do my best to help people through tough times."

"Do you foster amputee kittens, too? Volunteer at soup kitchens?"

"Well, yes to the soup kitchen, actually, but it's a program through the medical school. You should come sometime! We all go to the big church downtown on Saturdays. It's fun."

Ellsbeth fake-*tutted*. "But no kitten fostering. That's strike one, Oscar."

"I'm allergic."

"And that's strike two."

Oscar smiled, but Ellsbeth wasn't sure if it was because he was nervous or because he understood her sarcasm.

The conversation wasn't difficult—they chatted about the television show everyone was watching, and the movies coming out this summer they were looking forward to—but Ellsbeth found herself feeling as though she was playing a part, reciting lines in the role of "polite, winsome date." Did he feel it, too, the artifice in the way they said phrases like, "It's going to be nice on campus once the weather becomes a little cooler"? It was more than just tentative first-date banter; it was like they were aliens in an improv scene pretending to be normal human beings. Or maybe Ellsbeth was the alien, only able to relate to this perfectly nice, normal boy through a pane of glass. Maybe, Ellsbeth thought, some people are just *content.* Able to exist frictionlessly in a world that makes sense, cheerfully building a life one socially acceptable brick at a time.

OSCAR PARKED HIS CAR OUTSIDE her apartment to walk Ellsbeth to her door. "This was really nice," he said when they reached her stoop, slumping his shoulders to shield her from the wind. "I'm glad we did this."

"Me too," she said.

"Hey, maybe we could do it again sometime," Oscar said. "Catch a movie or something."

"Yeah, for sure," Ellsbeth said before she could think about the words.

"Definitely before I leave for Thanksgiving. I'm going back a few days early. My family always does a Turkey Trot the morning of. It's a whole thing."

"That's almost cartoonishly adorable."

"You should come to New Hampshire!" Oscar said. "I mean, obviously not this year, that's weird, we just went out. But if you wanted. My parents would be thrilled to have someone to weigh in on the pumpkin-versus-cherry-pie debate. It's been a dead heat for years."

"That's really, really nice," she said. "But I'm going to be in the throes of working on my thesis, so I'm just going to stay on campus. Bring some pie back for me."

Oscar cleared his throat and shimmied a hand into the pocket of his pants. He gazed at her, thoughtfully, through eyelashes so pale they were almost translucent. "I really want to kiss you right now," he said, and all Ellsbeth could think at that moment was *Why?* And perhaps an even harder question: *Why don't I want to kiss him?*

Ellsbeth could see herself through his eyes, how he must see her: a Newlyn graduate student who wears cardigans, the type of girl you can take to microbreweries and picnics before introducing her to his bread-with-the-crust-on New Hampshire family. But that wasn't who she was. She could play the part—maybe for years. She could be a girlfriend, a fiancée, even a wife eventually. She could see a frictionless future play in which she became the thing that Oscar imagined her to be, in which his sheer normalcy communicated something to the world about her because she existed in his orbit: She was chosen by him, and so she was normal, too. Not the broken girl whose sister had died, who had seen it in a ritual, who had spent the previous night with her hand between her legs under her duvet imagining her professor tying her hands behind her back.

Oscar leaned in to kiss her then, a kiss somehow both wet and with no tongue at all. It felt like nothing, a purely mechanical exercise, almost scientific. *Interesting,* Ellsbeth thought. She pulled away. "You are a great guy," she said. "I just think maybe I see you more as a friend."

Oscar rolled his eyes. "I *have* friends," he scoffed, wiping his lip with the back of his hand. It was the first time all night a sharpness had crept into his tone. "But yeah, sure. Fine."

They had split the dinner bill after all, but Ellsbeth still thanked him anyway before she turned the key in her lock, and listened to his car rev and drive down the street.

If Bertie were here, she would have thought Ellsbeth was crazy. "You went out with a cute *future doctor* who actually liked you and rejected him . . . why?" The urge to call Bertie was so strong it felt like a compulsion, and Ellsbeth found that she had pulled out her phone and opened it to where her sister's name still lingered on her short FAVORITE CONTACTS list. Right after Bertie had died, Ellsbeth called the number habitually, almost ritualistically. Bertie had not recorded an outgoing message, it was just mechanical instructions to leave a message at the tone, but still, Ellsbeth called and called again. Sometimes she left a message, pretending her sister was still alive, and that she would be listening to Ellsbeth's complaints about grad school applications or landlords who wouldn't fix leaky sinks. Sometimes Ellsbeth hung up as soon as the ringing stopped. She dreaded the thought that one day the phone line would be disconnected, or the number would be given to a stranger, and gradually the habit stopped, around the time Ellsbeth stopped instinctually expecting Bertie to pick up.

Her fingers hovered over Bertie's number. She wanted to talk about what happened tonight with *someone,* to talk out loud in order to make sense of her own thoughts. The date hadn't been *bad;* there had been nothing *wrong* with Oscar. But he had left her feeling removed and clinical. An evening out with Oscar making polite small talk had been a reminder of how much more she enjoyed her time spent with Rawlins, their knees just far enough apart that the static electricity of their skin made her hairs stand on end. She was herself with him, a better version of herself—smarter, funnier, quicker, able to make any joke, any reference, and know that he would understand. It was a strange and rare intimacy that she didn't know she had lacked until this moment: the peace you feel when you're able to be completely yourself with somebody else.

The only person she wanted to talk to was Rawlins. And so instead of dialing Bertie's number, she opened her email app and began clicking out a message to Professor Rawlins.

From: Storer.Ellsbeth
To: Rawlins.T.M.
Subject: (No Subject)

Are you home? Can I come over?

She hit SEND before the flood of adrenaline left her system, and she had a panicked moment of wondering if she'd made a mistake. But the reply was in her inbox as soon as she hit REFRESH.

From: Rawlins.T.M.
To: Storer.Ellsbeth
Subject: Re: (No Subject)

Come over.

She flew out her door. The cold air stung her cheeks—she hadn't grabbed a jacket—but she didn't slow her pace. She walked like a woman possessed, each step sure, each stride long. The campus had never seemed so expansive, each quad of inky-black grass somehow, impossibly, a football field now. She passed the late-night commissary on her left, the place where chicken fingers and quesadillas could be bought with a swipe of a student ID card after midnight, and managed to avoid a few drunken underclassmen calling out what might have been compliments in her direction. Ellsbeth kept her clip as her thighs burned until she was through campus and climbing the hill where Professor Rawlins's Victorian house sat perched.

Once she reached his house, the dreamlike quality of the entire situation began to fade. She was standing outside her professor's door, breathing heavily, with her sneakers and the hems of her jeans damp with mud. What would he say when he opened the door? There was a chance, Ellsbeth knew, that he would admonish her, send her home. Worse, that he wouldn't open the door at all. Had she imagined his email response? She almost reached into her pocket to check her phone when the door swung open.

Rawlins was wearing a T-shirt stretched low enough to expose his chest hair, and a pair of jeans. She had never seen him in jeans before. He was barefoot.

"I saw you out on the porch," he said. "Do you want to come in?" Ellsbeth didn't answer.

It was like gravity, then, a movement so fast and inevitable that it would be impossible to know who had started it, and how it had started. Ellsbeth had been standing on Rawlins's porch, and then she had taken a step forward through his door, and then they were entangled in each other, kissing harder and deeper than seemed possible. His arms wrapped around her, pulling her in closer and she felt her hands make their way behind his head, her fingers entangling themselves in his thick hair.

He pulled away quicker than she would have liked, and stared at her. "This is a bad idea," he said.

Ellsbeth didn't argue. She just leaned in to kiss him again.

They kissed as if they needed each other like air, their bodies pressing in to fill in all the empty space between them. Rawlins's arms were thin, but they were surprisingly strong, pulling Ellsbeth closer into his warm chest.

Her brain was on fire. There were no rational thoughts to be had. The only thing in her mind was *more.* More of his tongue in her mouth, more of his fist in her hair, more of his lips as they made their way down her neck. She was drunk on his touch, hungry for him in a way she didn't know was possible. Had this been what the movies and songs had always been about? Had everyone else been feeling *this* the entire time?

They were still standing in his foyer, Ellsbeth's hands running down Rawlins's chest, when he broke the kiss and pulled back.

"Ellsbeth," he said, and the way he said her name sounded like prayer. His eyes moved over her, studying her, like he was trying to memorize her. It was nothing like the meticulous way she had seen him study the pages of books or proposals. He was gazing at her with such an earnestness, she knew with abject certainty that the strange and inexplicable hunger gnawing at her from the inside out—the vise-grip like a clenched fist in the center of her chest—was something he felt, too.

"Your eyes look different in this light," she said. She had only ever been this close to him during the ritual, when her wrists were immobilized and her hands were around his neck. But now her hands trailed down his chest, feeling the ridges of his stomach muscles through his T-shirt. "They're a little green in the middle, did you know that?"

Rawlins kept staring at Ellsbeth, kept his hands touching her body like he was afraid if he broke contact with her she would disappear.

After a moment of silence, he inhaled a ragged breath. "Ellsbeth, I don't want to fuck any of this up. You're . . . You're brilliant. And your thesis is—" He swallowed. "Your work is so important. Your future is so important. If this is a mistake . . ." He trailed off, but she understood what he was trying to say, even if the words weren't coming out the way he wanted them to.

There was a threshold they were crossing here, a step into the unknown with consequences that might unravel them both.

"It's not against any rules," Ellsbeth said.

"It's against the *spirit* of the rules," he said, but he didn't remove his hands from her hips.

Ellsbeth leaned in to feel the rough shadow of his stubble against her cheek, nuzzling him like an animal, already addicted to his smell. "I'm twenty-four years old," she murmured into his ear. "I'm an adult. A *colleague.*"

Rawlins moaned and took a step back. "I'm finding you a new adviser tomorrow morning," he said.

"Don't you dare."

And then they were kissing again, frenetic with the energy of teenagers, hands and mouths and tongues and skin pressing against each other until somehow they fell onto Rawlins's overstuffed leather couch. Ellsbeth swung one leg over him, straddling him, pressing their foreheads together. She pulled off her shirt and then tugged at Rawlins's. He understood, ripping the shirt off with a single clean motion, revealing his chest hair and his toned stomach. She could feel his erection through his jeans, but he didn't seem to be in any hurry to take off more clothes. His arms stayed wrapped around Ellsbeth, holding her tight, and his gaze stayed locked on her.

She mussed his hair and bit his ear. She ran her teeth down his neck and then took his hand and kissed every one of his fingers. He closed his hand around hers and brought her hand up to his lips to kiss it like an old-fashioned beau. Something in her heart burst open then, a back cellar she hadn't even realized was boarded shut. His touch felt like yellow sunlight streaming through a clean window, and suddenly being here, touching him, was the only thing in the world that mattered. "Ellsbeth," he said quietly, "how is it possible I want you this much?"

She kissed him and couldn't stop the wide, spreading smile that caused their teeth to clink. She pulled away, wondering if her teenage thrill at touching him was visible on her face. "Do you have a condom?" she asked.

He blinked as her words registered. "Yes," he said, scrambling to his feet. "Somewhere. Don't move."

"You can always use writ magic on me," Ellsbeth said as he strode to the bathroom.

"Tempting," he called back from the bathroom.

She heard him rummaging through a medicine cabinet when the buzzing started from his phone, which had somehow landed on the floor halfway underneath the couch. She leaned forward to peek at the screen and saw it flashing with the name: MARGARET LENNOX. Ellsbeth stared, perplexed, wondering why the dean might possibly be calling him this late—but as she heard his footsteps, she shifted back where she could not see the phone.

Rawlins returned, his erection visibly pressing against the fabric of his jeans, holding up the foil square. "Found it."

"Your phone is ringing," Ellsbeth said. "It's on the floor."

Rawlins lowered himself onto the couch and pressed into Ellsbeth to kiss her again. "I could not care less about anything in the world right now."

Ellsbeth twisted her head away from him. "What if it's important? No one calls this late if it's not something important."

Rawlins's mouth tightened but he acquiesced, reaching down to pick up the violently vibrating phone. "Hello?"

He listened for a moment, his face growing tight. Ellsbeth could faintly hear the dean's voice on the other line, but she couldn't make out any of the words. Without looking at Ellsbeth, Rawlins walked into another room of his home and closed the door.

Ellsbeth had begun putting her shirt back on before Rawlins even hung up the phone. The real world had arrived at their evening together and shifted the temperature. "I'm sorry," Rawlins said. "It's something of an emergency. I have to go . . . handle something." He didn't offer any more of an explanation. Ellsbeth felt herself wanting to ask, but she stopped the question before it made it out. He clearly didn't want to tell her, whatever it was, and if she asked, he might lie. She had lied to him, hadn't she? When she had been going to the police station. There were things about her life that she wasn't willing to tell him, and she realized at that moment with a small chill that the same might certainly be true for him.

"You can stay if you want," Rawlins said, lacing his shoes. "I'm sure it won't be longer than a few hours."

It was an idle offer, not a request. It was bad enough to be the graduate student lusting after her professor. Ellsbeth's sense of internal shame and pity wouldn't let her be the girl hanging around a man's home if he didn't want her to. Ellsbeth shook her head. "I should get home. Try to actually get some sleep."

Rawlins looked as though he'd aged ten years in the span of a ten-minute phone call. His lips were tight and eyes bloodshot. They finished getting dressed together in silence, Ellsbeth wondering the entire time if she should say something, but unable to come up with a good answer for what that something might be.

Rawlins put on his shoes and grabbed his coat. "You didn't bring a jacket," he said.

"No."

"Please, borrow one of mine. I insist." He shrugged the heavy waxed coat off his shoulders and wrapped it around Ellsbeth. It was still warm from his body heat.

They stood by the door for an awkward moment, Ellsbeth feeling very small in his oversized jacket, unsure how to say goodbye. Rawlins leaned down then and kissed Ellsbeth square on the forehead. "Ellsbeth Storer," he said in an exhale. "You have no idea how much I wish I didn't have to go."

THE WALK BACK TO HER apartment seemed to take no time at all, and within an hour she had brushed her teeth and pulled herself into bed. Had that really happened? Had she really done that? She would have thought the entire thing was a dream, if it hadn't been for the coat that hung neatly on the hook behind her door, and hunger that still gnawed in the center of her chest, and the way that if she closed her eyes, she could feel his fingertips brushing her skin as vividly as if he were there in bed beside her.

RAWLINS

The car engine whined as Rawlins sped through the night, leaving Newlyn behind as he headed south. By day, the drive would have been scenic—lined with leafy trees turned gold and red by the arrival of fall. But in the night, his headlights illuminated only a shallow pool of asphalt and the menacing hint of branches stretching over the road while everything beyond vanished into inky abyss.

Occasionally the darkness ahead was pierced by another pair of headlights hurtling toward him before sliding past. But mostly the drive was solitary, leaving him alone with the panicky feeling in his chest and a mind that swirled with dark, chaotic thoughts.

His mind had already *been* chaotic before the call came. The entire evening had spun him on his axis, starting with Ellsbeth's email, and the reply he'd fired off without a thought. *Come over.* Like a reaction. Something he was doing before his rational brain could kick in and talk him out of it.

Rawlins could not explain the effect that Ellsbeth had on him. He wanted her in a way that short-circuited his defenses. She had not broken through his walls; she had simply passed through as if they didn't matter. He wasn't sure when that Rubicon had been crossed, but it frightened him to realize that after years of keeping everyone at bay, avoiding any emotional entanglement, he had let her in without even *deciding* to. It was not something he'd intended to pursue, it was what *she* wanted. Yet his suspicion that he had been played was not sufficient to overwhelm his desire to see her. To *have* her, at least once.

While he had waited for her to arrive, he busied himself nervously, straightening the books on his coffee table and smoothing his shirt and lighting a candle, all the while second-guessing himself: Was this real? Had she even seen his reply? Should he send another and tell her he'd changed his mind, he was foolish for being so rash, they shouldn't get carried away . . .

And then she was there. Standing at his front door, slightly out of breath, her skin flushed from hurrying through the cold night. In that moment, she came into sharp relief to him—not as a student, or a younger woman, not any concept or category, she was just . . . Ellsbeth. Shockingly *specific* in her beauty. Eyes alive with intelligence and verve and vulnerability all at once.

A frozen moment as he met her gaze. A split second of wondering. *Will we . . . Should we . . . Can we possibly, at this point, not?* Then *will* and *should* became irrelevant concepts as their lips met and their bodies collided, as he was lost in his passion for her. *Consumed* by desire, in a way he didn't know he was still capable of—a way he was not sure he had *ever* been capable of. A way that narrowed his world and broke his brain and realigned the cosmos around their mouths, hungry for each other, and their hands, craving and searching and pulling their bodies into each other, a straight line toward the thing he wanted more than anything and could not possibly be deterred from . . .

Until he was, by the ringing phone. The moment he glanced at the screen, Lennox's name had brought a dose of sobriety—which was followed by a stomach-dropping plunge into reality with the first words she spoke when he picked up:

"Max is in the hospital."

It was one of those jolts that felt like waking up, imbuing the moments preceding it with the hazy sheen of a half-forgotten dream.

The conversation on the phone with Lennox was brief and focused. Rawlins's mind fought to make rational sense of the information she communicated, even as he was puzzled by the lack of emotion that it evoked in him, until he realized he was simply numb from shock.

When he returned to the living room, he was almost surprised to find Ellsbeth there.

Every detail of her came into stark relief—her flushed cheeks, her delicate eyelashes, her slightly tousled hair, the flyaways catching the light. He fixated on her fingers, deftly refastening the buttons of her blouse. She looked so vulnerable even as she was closing herself off, retreating. A sorrow entered him at the loss of the intimacy that had been so effortless moments before. He wanted to stop her, to wrap her up in his arms and pull her against him. But when her eyes met his with an open, quizzical expression, seeking an explanation, he swallowed hard and looked away.

Part of him wanted to explain everything. Wanted to take her into his confidence. Trust her with his secrets. Hell, even get her counsel on how to handle this. It had been so long since there was anyone he could genuinely confide in, and Ellsbeth was smart and thoughtful and sensitive and . . .

No. He wouldn't know where to begin . . . and where to stop. Where to draw the line. So he wrapped her in his coat and kissed her good night and tried to say goodbye in a way that communicated some fraction of what he was feeling. He left his house with a visceral ache in his body. For her.

The rising whine of the engine cut through his thoughts and he checked the speedometer. On the dark, traffic-free road, he was accelerating dangerously, heedless of consequence. But the last thing he needed right now was an accident, and the way his attention had been hijacked, he knew it was a risk. He slowed down and set the cruise control at seventy-five, grateful to give over control to something else, even temporarily.

THE GREENE COUNTY HOSPITAL LOOKED like it had not been updated since the 1980s, with fluorescent lights that glinted on mint-green tile. He checked in at the front desk and, too impatient to wait for the elevator, took the stairs up to the ICU.

The waiting area was empty at this hour except for Lennox and her husband, Benjamin. It was strange to see the dean, who always dressed the part of an academic bureaucrat, wearing a pair of jeans. Benjamin was wearing gray sweatpants and a Newlyn sweatshirt that looked like it had been pulled from the floor.

Lennox rose when Rawlins approached. "You didn't have to come *tonight.*" She took him into a dry, perfunctory hug, punctuated by a pat on the back.

Benjamin stood to offer Rawlins a quick handshake, but he didn't make eye contact. Rawlins coughed. "How are you doing?"

"My son tried to kill himself, Thaddeus," Benjamin said tightly. "I'm a wreck. We both are." He put his arm around Lennox's shoulder, and Rawlins felt chastised for even asking.

Lennox sighed. "We appreciate you coming. Max won't really talk to either of us. We thought, given how close you two used to be . . ."

She trailed off and Rawlins nodded, memories flooding back from when Max had been his student. More than a student, really. Even before the tragedy, before his arrest, Max had stopped speaking with his parents, and Rawlins had been his only confidant. It emerged as a point of tension between Rawlins and Benjamin during the trial, and apparently was still a sore spot. But clearly Lennox, at least, saw the relationship between Max and Rawlins as an opportunity to get through to her son—though she may not have been aware of how Max had been refusing prison visits from Rawlins, too.

"How . . . I mean, what happened?" Rawlins asked.

"They found him in his cell during a bed-check," Lennox said. "He had slashed both of his arms with a pair of scissors. Children's safety scissors. Apparently he works in the library, and he might've snuck them out and sharpened them for weeks. Did it right after lights-out, and if they hadn't caught him, he would've been dead in the morning."

"But he's okay now," Rawlins said, hoping the certainty in his voice would make it true.

"He lost a lot of blood," Lennox said, trying to keep her voice even. "But they gave him a transfusion, plus the tetanus shot and antibiotics, and now he's . . . stable. They might discharge him tomorrow or the next day, but he'll be under observation for a week."

"Did he say . . . anything?" he asked.

Lennox pulled herself from beneath her husband's arms. "You know he won't say anything to me. He hates me."

"I'm sure he's just . . . upset."

His words were empty. They felt stiff and false even as he said them, the equivalent of hospital carnation flowers wrapped in cellophane.

"Do you want to see him?" Lennox asked. She didn't wait for an answer before she started down the linoleum hall, beckoning Rawlins to follow with a tilt of her head. Benjamin stayed behind in the waiting room.

Lennox led the way to a patient room at the back corner of the floor, and through the glass, he could see the correctional officer on duty, sitting in a chair, engrossed in his glowing phone screen. As they approached, the CO stood, blocking the way and eyeing Rawlins. "Sorry, visitation is family only."

"He's family," Lennox said decisively, a hint of warning in her voice.

The CO eyed Rawlins, then Lennox, and decided it wasn't worth the trouble; he stepped back, allowing Rawlins inside, though apparently he was not about to leave; he sat back down on his perch by the door as Rawlins stepped into the darkened room.

Six years had passed since he had seen the boy in person—and really, now that Max was twenty-five, it was hardly appropriate to think of him as "the boy" any longer, but even so, Rawlins could not help it. Max had never been large, but now he was even leaner, his body hardened by prison, his arms and neck ropy. His cheekbones were sharp, and his dark eyes seemed to have sunken deeper in his skull. His lashes had always been dark and long. He was still beautiful, in a more haunting way than ever.

Rawlins had prepared himself on the drive over for the sight of Max in a half-reclined hospital bed. He had pictured the EKG machine beeping, IV tubes hooked up. But there were details he hadn't prepared himself for. The boy's forearms were wrapped in gauze, with dark spots where blood had seeped through the sutures. His wrists were bound with cuffs, secured to the side rails. His eyes hardened into a coldly hateful glare when he saw Rawlins tentatively approaching the bed.

"*It's you,*" Max said. He lolled his head toward the CO. "Guess I've lost my right to choose my visitors."

"You want him out of here?" the CO asked.

Max considered for a moment, then shrugged, settling back into his pillows.

"It's good to see you, Max," Rawlins said, his throat dry. "Even under these circumstances, it's . . ." He coughed, trying to stay on track. "I know you're angry with me, about what happened . . ."

Before he could form an apology, Max cut in. "Oh, I don't worry about that anymore. I never should have trusted you in the first place. The *famous, extraordinary* teacher. Hah."

Rawlins lowered himself into a chair at Max's bedside, his eyes fixating on the bandages. "Do you like it?" Max said, limply lifting his wrists. "I thought I would try a new look for autumn. They say red is very in this year."

"I just . . . I don't understand," Rawlins said. "You're *weeks* out from your first parole hearing."

Max rolled his eyes. "From my parole *denial,* you mean."

"I'll do whatever I can to support your case," Rawlins said. "And your mother . . . I think I can get her to be a bit more helpful than she was during the trial."

Max snorted and turned away. "Good luck. It wouldn't matter anyway. Greywall and everyone like him . . . you know what they think about the arcane arts. That it's elitist and dangerous. That it should *all* be banned. And I get to be the poster child for that whole way of thinking. The perfect cautionary tale for everything they stand for. Am I wrong?"

He wasn't wrong. Max's case was still cited in nearly every political effort to curtail the scope of legal arcane practice, and nearly every time the government denied public funding for an expansion of education in arcane mechanicals.

"You're not wrong," Rawlins said, and then he straightened, trying to summon a tone of inspiration, even though he felt tapped out himself. "But you still have to *fight.* A parole review, even if the odds are against you the first time around, it's a chance to tell your story."

"You really want me to tell the *whole* story?" Max said, a threatening tone in his voice.

Rawlins's chest tightened; he knew that Max, during the investigation trial, had never fully disclosed just how much his teacher had recklessly taught him, and Rawlins was grateful for the boy's loyalty and discretion. But seeing him now, he could not bear the thought that he was being protected at the boy's expense. "If you think it will help, then yes, absolutely. I'll back up whatever you have to say."

Max snorted, skeptical. "Doesn't matter anyway. They've all made up their minds for a generation to come. I'm a monster, and nothing I say will change that."

"You're not a monster," Rawlins said quickly. "You were so young. It was a mistake."

"Yes, it was, and I'll suffer for it for the rest of my life," Max snapped, then nodded toward his wounds. "So excuse me for wanting that suffering to be shortened a bit."

Rawlins put a hand on Max's shoulder, so desperate to get through to the boy he nearly shook him. "You can't think like that . . . as long as there's a parole possibility, there's *hope,* at least."

"Hope is *cruel,*" Max said dismissively, shrugging away Rawlins's touch. He settled into his pillows, looking like a teenager again, so impossibly small that Rawlins had to clench his hands into fists to resist the urge to embrace him. "I'm not going to put myself through that again. And try to *justify* my existence. Get all dressed up so I can listen to people go on and on about how awful I am. All so I can get sent back into a hole and forgotten."

The intensity of Max's despair was like a blade driven into Rawlins's belly. He remembered the boy's eyes gleaming with excitement at the possibility of arcane study. Rawlins had been drawn to that light, had fed it more and more with each meeting and study session, offering texts and lessons, continually dangling the carrot of new knowledge to drive his pupil forward.

But now that light was gone. Replaced by the steely glare of a young man who knew he had been cosmically wronged.

It was not just the system that had wronged him. *It was Rawlins.* A teacher whom Max should have been able to trust. Rawlins had not only provided forbidden arcane knowledge but also stoked a dangerous fire inside the boy. Rawlins had sought to impart courage to challenge dogma, and conviction to overturn accepted norms—the traits of a great scholar. But in Max, a young man without life experience to dampen his ambition, the result had been disastrous. A belief that he could do anything, that the rules did not apply to him, that prohibitions on dangerous arcane practice were for lesser minds. Rawlins's own hubris had trickled down and infected the mind of his student.

If Max was a monster, as the state had decreed, Rawlins was his creator. And now Max was paying with his life, his very *soul,* for the recklessness of his teacher, who should have known better.

It was unfair. Unacceptable, in fact—Rawlins could not bring himself to accept it. He refused.

"Just try to hang in there for a little while longer," he told Max. "No matter what, we have a chance. Think about what you're going to tell the parole board." Max started to shake his head, but Rawlins continued. "Humility is the key. Try to apologize, even if it's not easy. I'll help you draft the statement if you'd like."

"Greywall is never going to change his mind," Max said. The boy's mouth drew into a hard line as he turned his eyes away from his former mentor. Rawlins reached out to hold Max's hand, but Max pulled away and looked past him toward the CO. "I'm done now."

The words were spoken with a cold finality that eviscerated Rawlins. He nodded and stood, forcing himself to look one last time at Max's bloody gauze wrappings before he turned and left him.

THE IMAGE OF MAX IN his hospital bed came back to Rawlins at strange times over the next few days. One moment Rawlins would be looking at his undergrad lecture students, eagerly taking notes—then suddenly, he would catch a glimpse of a freshman boy with shaggy shoulder-length hair, and Rawlins would be back in the hospital room, trying to break down the walls of a hardened, miserable young man who was desperate to end his own life.

He tried to set aside those troubling recollections—but they inevitably intertwined with the *other* memories from that night, leading him back to thoughts of Ellsbeth. He wanted to disentangle the two, but they bled into each other. His guilt about Max crossed over and intruded upon his desire for Ellsbeth, so the two feelings mixed darkly in his mind. The painful experience with Max cautioned him away from getting too involved with a student, while another voice answered, *This is different.* She *is different.*

No matter how much he tried to stop dwelling on her, Ellsbeth lingered at the periphery of every thought, every sensation, every moment—waiting for her turn to step onstage and fill his mind. Every time he checked his email, his brain skipped back to her unexpected message—to the image of her standing nervously at his front door—to the feeling of her body pressing against his. The memories taunted him. Their interrupted encounter could not have been more perfectly calibrated to stoke the embers of desire that had been smoldering all semester.

In idle moments, he would refresh his inbox, ignoring messages that actually needed a reply in the hope that something would land from Ellsbeth. After the way he had left, the onus to reach out was most certainly on him, but he wasn't sure what to say, so he kept hoping she would break the seal and let him off the hook.

He still hadn't heard from her, or figured out how to behave around her, when his graduate lecture rolled around. In previous classes, Ellsbeth had always been eager to take a seat near the front. This time, however, she sat off to one side and farther back, right on the aisle, as though she might need to get up and leave halfway through. She wore a checked skirt that fell just above her knees and crossed her legs as she settled into her seat. Was she daring him not to stare at the glimpse of her thigh that it afforded? Or was he reading too much into every detail, primed by hours of thoughts returning endlessly, obsessively, to her?

He met her gaze for a moment as she took her seat. She raised her eyebrows almost imperceptibly, but didn't give anything away in her expression. He watched as she settled into her seat with a deep breath—and though of course he couldn't hear her exhale from across the auditorium, he recalled with crisp clarity the sound of her breath in his ear, tinged with the shuddering charge of pleasure as she ground herself against him. He could practically feel the warmth of the air from her lungs, and he had to look away to break the spell.

It took everything in him to focus on his lecture, and still he repeatedly lost his place. If Ellsbeth was similarly distracted by their last encounter, she refused to show it; she answered questions confidently and intellectually sparred with her peers, appearing to *enjoy* herself in class.

It aggravated him. *She* should be the one with her stomach fluttering, not him—a professor renowned for his stoic rigor. Was she really so unbothered? Or was she merely hiding it remarkably well? If her performance of nonchalance was *intended* to get under his skin, to make him second-guess himself and wonder if he was losing his mind over a girl who had moved on and could not care less about him, then she was doing a remarkable job.

He was determined to find out. In the midst of discussion, he turned to her suddenly, pretending to remember something. "Ellsbeth, you emailed me a question this weekend, remind me—what was it?"

He intended to tease her, hoping to catch her flat-footed and make her stumble on her words, as he had repeatedly done throughout the class. But she didn't even hesitate, inventing an answer on the spot. "Oh, I was asking if you knew of any alternative layouts for longevity divination rituals. The ones in the textbook seem needlessly complex." Only her expression gave anything away, and it was the look of a worthy competitor, challenging him back, as she added, "But you never sent me a reply."

"I must've been distracted," he said. "But you have my full attention now." Then he turned back to the board, drawing a diagram to answer her question.

When he dismissed the class, Ellsbeth put her notebook into her bag and started heading for the door, which he knew would doom him to another two days of frustration, wondering when they'd speak again. "Ellsbeth, do you have a minute?" he said before he could stop himself.

While the other students filed out, she came down the steps to the lectern, hiking her bag up onto her shoulder and giving him an expectant look, requiring him to break the silence.

Once the room was cleared, he realized he lacked any plan for what he was going to say to her. "Hi." The single syllable was forced to bear the weight of all that went unspoken between them.

She raised her eyebrows—*That's it?* She was going to make him work for this. "I'm sorry about how I had to leave the other night," Rawlins said. "It was a difficult personal matter."

She nodded, apparently accepting his apology, and looked sincerely empathetic. "I hope everything's okay."

Again, Rawlins wanted to tell her the truth, but he could foresee only more damage from talking about Max, so he said simply, “I’m all right, thanks. And believe me, leaving like that was the last thing in the world I wanted to do. So . . . I hope you’ll email me again sometime.”

She smirked. “Well, don’t worry, you’ll have another email soon. About my *research.*”

“Fantastic,” he said. “That’s exactly what I meant. We need to figure out the next ritual for you to untangle.”

“I’ve already started working on one,” she said. “A more advanced binding.”

“And you didn’t think you should get my approval first?” he replied with mock-indignation. “I thought you might want my input.”

“I know what I want to study,” she said. “And I’m pretty sure you’ll approve when you see it.”

A genuine smile spread across his face. “Glad to see you’re finding your confidence.”

Ellsbeth shrugged. “Maybe you’re rubbing off on me.”

“All right, then. I look forward to discussing the next stage of your work.” He was enjoying their flirtation, their banter, but then looking at her, he was abruptly overcome with a sense of warmth and could not help himself. He blinked, and the words came out: “You have a remarkable mind, Ellsbeth. And you’re going to do great things.”

“Thank you, Professor,” she said.

Their conversation seemed to have reached a logical end point, but Ellsbeth didn’t budge. She seemed to be weighing something now, and he delighted in watching the wheels turn as she figured out how to broach whatever it was she *really* wanted to talk about. Rawlins’s chest clenched with desire—a visceral impulse that roared inside him, so he had to stop himself from crossing the charged distance between them and kissing her. He kept himself in check and asked, “Was there something else?”

“There was, actually,” Ellsbeth said, her voice light. “I’ve encountered something during my research. Not a topic I’d pursue as part of my thesis, but . . . something I’m curious to investigate further, and I’m hoping you could help.”

Rawlins leaned in. “Well, as your intellectual shepherd, I’ll certainly do what I can. What is it you want to learn about?”

She looked him in the eyes and answered: "Obscuration."

Instinctively, Rawlins's entire body tightened, and he glanced toward the door as though afraid her uttering that single word might be enough to get them both arrested.

Obscuration was the Holy Grail of writ magic practice, targeting not only the physical body but also the *mind,* and theoretically capable of doing so in such a way that the target would never even be aware. Undetected mental manipulation was both a coveted power and a complete taboo.

But like the Holy Grail, it had always remained a mythical notion. It occupied the same category as the *Chrono Vicissim* ritual for turning back time, or the *Fortunatis Favori* ritual for increasing one's luck. Such practices were documented in the literature of antiquity, but most modern academics viewed their possibility with intense skepticism.

Historical references to obscuration abounded, with pre-modern scholars citing various applications—princes compelled to fall in love, kings compelled to abdicate their thrones. But it was impossible to *prove* that any of those effects had been the result of an obscuration ritual. The very nature of obscuration meant that it would never be verifiable, since successfully carrying it out would leave the subject feeling they had never been influenced at all. Most in the field now regarded obscuration as a piece of medieval folklore, a relic of the days before arcane practice had become standardized and properly studied.

Rawlins tried to keep his voice level and his face impassive. "And what's your interest in the topic? Given that it's most likely apocryphal."

"Just curiosity," she said. "About history, certainly. It's an interesting frontier. There are a handful of respected scholars who have regarded it as worthy of study. I forget who, but one of the old dinosaurs of the field said that obscuration was worth investigating because it would represent 'a categorical advance in the scope of what the arcane mechanicals can achieve.'" She smiled slyly.

Rawlins couldn't help it; he grinned back like a teenager. "I wrote that back when I was a graduate student. And the essay that contained that sentence is undisciplined, to say the least. Practically *unhinged.*"

"Not your most sophisticated work," she said. "But I enjoyed it. I like seeing where your mind goes when you let it run wild."

Rawlins studied Ellsbeth and the coy smile that tugged at her lips. They both knew that her interest in obscuration would not be confined to interesting historical anecdotes. She wanted to see if it could be done. It was like she was inviting him to look through her, to see not only her true agenda, her plan to test out and use secret forbidden arcane rituals . . . but *her,* her unspoken desires and complications.

But at the same time, Rawlins could not help but wonder if this apparent transparency was itself a manipulation. Perhaps one that Ellsbeth was not even conscious of. She *knew* he would be excited by the tantalizing glimpse she offered; she *knew* he'd be drawn not only to the topic itself, but to *her,* a student daring enough to pursue it. She was baiting him. And though he was aware of it, he still could not resist.

"Even if it is possible, it's forbidden," he said, knowing very well that would not deter her in the least.

"*All* writ magic is forbidden," she said. "And you still seemed to enjoy the ritual we did last weekend. Or was I mistaken?"

His stomach somersaulted at the thought of her bound wrists around his neck, her face inches from his own. "I did," he conceded. "And I suppose . . . there's nothing wrong with a bit of scholarly investigation."

"Does that mean you'll help me? Obviously, never to actually practice. Just to . . . look into."

"I'm not sure I can say no to you." As soon as the words left his mouth, he regretted them; he couldn't let her know the power she had. He straightened and cleared his throat, looking away. "Why don't you come by my office? I have hours tomorrow from three to five."

"I know," she said. "I'll be there at three."

"Come at five. I don't mind staying late, and I don't want to be interrupted."

ELLSBETH

Ellsbeth waited outside Professor Rawlins's office at 4:58 p.m. His door was closed, and she could tell from the hum of voices on the other side that he was still meeting with a student. Ellsbeth had brought a new issue of a journal of arcane studies that she could read while waiting, but she was too nervous. She told herself again and again that nothing was going to happen, that their meeting would be strictly professional, and yet she had prepared for office hours like she was getting ready for a date. She washed and dried her hair, shaved every inch of her body using the good shaving cream she usually forgot she had, and then sprayed herself with perfume, once between her wrists, once on her neck, and once between her knees. She put on a matching set of lingerie and a silky top she knew she looked good in, pairing it with a skirt long enough that she hoped it made the entire effect look casual, just thrown together.

There was no other way to explain it: She had a *crush.* It was an unfamiliar feeling for Ellsbeth, who was more accustomed to viewing romantic prospects on their logical merits. And she knew, intellectually, that there was far more to lose from having sex with her arcane arts adviser than there was to gain. She was lucky enough to be in the program—it was a miracle, really, that he had overlooked her disastrous Arcanus. She had achieved what she had set out to do—to study here, among the best, and at the one place where she might get answers about what had happened the night that Bertie died. And Rawlins had agreed to help her study obscuration. He hadn't laughed in her face, kicked her out of the program, or called the university to put her on psychiatric watch—all of which would have been understandable reactions.

To risk everything she had already achieved, the impossibly fortunate position she had shockingly managed to secure for herself, for a moment of pleasure—it wasn't just foolish. It was self-sabotage. And it wasn't just the risk of the administration discovering their impropriety; men's feelings changed after sex. Ellsbeth knew that. That interrupting phone call had been a miraculous intervention. At least for now, Rawlins saw her as the charming, seductive *ingénue.* But if he actually *had* her, if he saw her naked and vulnerable, if he knew that her crush was more than a controlled titration, he would pull away. She could see the chess pieces as they moved: If they had sex, her flaws would no longer be disguised by his longing. He would see her, needy and pimpled, in the fluorescent light, and whatever power she had wielded as the pretty, precocious girl two decades younger than him would dissolve, replaced by Rawlins's guilt and shame at having slept with a student that he would sublimate into resentment for her. He would almost certainly be smart enough to know that he couldn't kick her out of the program, but he would probably foist her on a less prestigious adviser, citing a busy workload. His emails would become distant, less frequent, purposefully polite, as though he was preempting the possibility that they might be read by some scrupulous university administrator. He would certainly never help her with obscuration.

And so, even as Ellsbeth dotted her lashes with mascara and swiped gloss across her lips, she knew: She wasn't going to have sex with Rawlins. She would have to let the fizzing pleasure of a new crush be its own reward. Self-control was one of the most important tenets of being a good scholar of arcane mechanicals, and Ellsbeth was going to prove to herself that she deserved to be here at Newlyn, among the best.

It was Curt who had been in Professor Rawlins's office, and as he exited, he looked Ellsbeth up and down, as if noticing her for the first time. Under his gaze, Ellsbeth suddenly wished she had worn a shirt with a higher neckline.

"You can leave the door open, Curt," Rawlins called from his desk.

"Ellsbeth, come in." Ellsbeth closed the door behind her without being told. His office was small, and it looked even smaller because the walls and every flat surface seemed to be covered with books, some shelves stacked three- or four-deep. His desk was a mess of papers—it was a wonder how he found anything.

"Good meeting?" she asked.

"It's funny," Rawlins said, standing from his chair but not closing any of the distance between them. "I've been teaching at Newlyn for a very long time. And it's been a long time since a graduate student brought a thesis proposal to me that actually excited me."

"Curt's proposal was that good, huh?"

Rawlins eyed the closed door. "Fortunately Professor Gallway is Curt's adviser. Because I couldn't give less of a fuck about his proposal."

Ellsbeth smiled, and she noticed how strong Rawlins's hands looked, how the veins pressed against his skin and his fingers extended elegantly. She wondered if he played the piano.

"So of those *rare* proposals that excite you, how many of those advisees managed to pull off a fully functioning ritual already by this point in the year?" She wasn't supposed to be flirting, but she couldn't help it. With him, flirting felt like speaking in a mother tongue after being away from your home country for years, and only running into another native speaker by chance.

Rawlins smiled back at her then, but he kept his mouth closed, the crooked dog-teeth Ellsbeth fantasized about mercifully still hidden.

She eyed the bowl of black licorice on his desk and reached over to pop a few pieces into her mouth. "You know," Ellsbeth said, "professors who want students to come to their office hours put out candy that most people like. Chocolate, you know. M&M's or something. Most students don't like black licorice."

"But you do," he observed.

Ellsbeth ate another piece, chewing it slowly. "I'm not most students," she said after she'd swallowed. "I was serious, you know. Obscuration."

"Oh, I never had any doubt that you were serious. Whether it's *possible* is another matter entirely. And maybe I keep black licorice in my office because I don't *want* to make it too inviting."

She looked straight into his blue eyes. "You're telling me, you've never considered that there's actually a way to pull it off?"

He moved over toward his bookshelf, out from behind his desk but still no closer to Ellsbeth. He was standing six feet away from her, but Ellsbeth somehow felt as though her body was responding to the heat of his skin. "I don't know," he said, breaking eye contact and running his finger along the spines of the books stacked two-deep. "Maybe when I was younger and more foolish."

"I think the stigma against writ magic has made people scared to explore what might actually be possible. Think about all the new discoveries that have been made in modern neuroscience in the past five years alone. If we were methodical about it—combing through historical texts and applying modern scientific thought . . . Functionally, I *know* there's a way to do it, I just don't know how yet. That's why I need your help."

Rawlins's mouth was tight. "I suppose if—" He caught himself, shaking whatever thought he had out of his head. "No."

"What?"

"This is all academic, of course. It's not as though you would ever have any intention of *using* obscuration, even if you could—*and I'm not saying you could*—produce a functional ritual."

"No," Ellsbeth said quickly. "Of course not."

"Well then, *academically,* I might have a few ideas of where to start." Rawlins turned away from the bookshelf and took one step closer to Ellsbeth. "Give me a few days, and I'll pull some material for you on your . . . pet project." The word "pet" curled in his mouth as he said it, and Ellsbeth felt a shiver run from her belly button up to her chest.

"I suppose my pet project will wait until then. But don't take too long," Ellsbeth said. "I'm terrible at being patient."

"You are," Rawlins said. "I've noticed."

"It's too bad I haven't mastered obscuration yet. I could get you to give me those books right away."

"But then what would be the point? If you mastered obscuration, you could write the books yourself."

Ellsbeth smiled at that, and the familiar electric charge between them caused that buzzing sound in her brain again. On instinct she slipped past Rawlins and sat in his office chair. "Maybe I would just want the fun of bossing you around." She swiveled a few times in the chair experimentally. "Comfortable," she said.

"It's a small office," Rawlins said. "But it has its perks."

"Such as?"

"Such as . . . there are no other professors on this side of the floor, which affords me a level of quiet and privacy I find conducive to my work. When I'm not distracted."

"Have you been distracted lately?" Ellsbeth asked, spreading her legs slightly, and hoping he would notice. He did.

"Yes, Ellsbeth. I have been very distracted."

"Good." *This is strictly professional,* Ellsbeth reminded herself. It had to be. And yet she couldn't seem to help herself.

"Have you?" Rawlins said, and Ellsbeth was delighted to hear the lilt of longing in his voice. "Been . . . distracted?"

"No," Ellsbeth said matter-of-factly. "I haven't thought about you at all." She didn't let him break eye contact, and she let herself smile, just a little.

Rawlins groaned then and let his head loll on his neck. He leaned back onto his desk, and looked over at her. "This shouldn't be possible. I shouldn't be feeling the way I feel about you right now."

"What way is that?"

"Wanting you this badly."

Ellsbeth felt a pulse between her legs.

And then Rawlins leaned forward and bracketed her in the desk chair with his arms. He loomed over her and hovered there, waiting, like a ball caught in the moment of zero gravity at the top of its trajectory.

Ellsbeth let her eyes trace over Rawlins slowly, drinking him in—his thick brown hair only beginning to be streaked with gray, his strong arms in a dress shirt pushed up to reveal the sinews of his forearms, and his perfect blue eyes that were still looking directly at her.

There had probably been other girls in this office before, Ellsbeth knew. She wasn't a fool, and she wouldn't let herself become one. He probably slept with students every semester. Every pretty graduate student he advised for years had probably come here and melted under the power of his gaze. Girls probably threw themselves at him, hoping that his genius was sexually transferable, or that sex with him would make them more interesting or prove something about themselves that they didn't believe. Sex with her professor wasn't just a strategically terrible decision; it was a humiliation. It turned her into a cliché, a joke. It did seem like he cared about her—that he really wanted her—but that might be all part of his larger game: Show a girl your bleeding heart, pretend you're desperate for her, pretend she's unique so that she feels special.

As soon as his conquest was over, Rawlins could dismiss her thoughtlessly, leaving behind only the crumbled remnants of what had once been her dignity and his respect for her academic promise.

So why were her legs parting? Why did she feel herself take her right hand and move it up her thighs inside her skirt? Rawlins bit his lip—he *actually* bit his lip. Ellsbeth had never seen a man do that outside of the movies. "Should I close the blinds?" he said quietly.

Ellsbeth just nodded, and in a heartbeat Rawlins was up and across the room, adjusting the shades. Ellsbeth reached down to peel her underwear down her legs, still sitting in his desk chair.

In an instant, Rawlins was back at the chair and had lowered himself onto his knees, between her legs. He pushed her skirt up to her waistband. "I want to taste you," he said. And he looked up at her with an expression that she knew then would play on repeat in her mind for the rest of her life. His voice was low and soft. "But you're going to have to beg for it."

Now Ellsbeth groaned. She could feel the wetness between her legs, the hot, pulsing *want*. "I want you," she said.

"That's not begging."

Ellsbeth swallowed hard, and he ran his fingers along her inner thigh.

"Will you?" His finger drifted away, farther down her leg. "I said beg, Ellsbeth."

Ellsbeth pressed herself toward him. "*Please,*" she moaned. And in that instant, she was no longer thinking about whether she was being foolish or ruining any grand plans. All she could think about was his tongue inside her.

Rawlins needed no more encouragement. His arms braced against her thighs, and Ellsbeth bucked back against the chair as he swirled his tongue around her clit. She had told boys she dated in college that she wasn't a fan of oral sex—she found it awkward and stilted, a performance that she was required to applaud no matter how off-key the playing was. It turned out she just hadn't been with someone like Rawlins yet. He moved his mouth confidently, with an insatiable hunger that caused Ellsbeth to squirm. When she did, he just held her thighs firmer. Her hands raked through his hair. She needed more of him. She pulled him up, glistening and gasping, and brought his face to hers, kissing him hard.

"Stand up," Rawlins said when they finally separated. She did, enjoying the electric thrill of obeying him. She saw the outline of his thick erection pressing against his jeans and watched as he slowly unbuttoned himself and stepped out of his pants. He sat in his office chair and pulled a condom from the wallet sitting on his desk. He ripped the foil with his teeth and rolled it over his length.

Ellsbeth straddled him then, hovering a few inches above him, her knees balancing on either side of his thighs. She wanted him viscerally, in a way she hadn't known was even possible. It was a physical craving, and no amount of logic was going to override the gravity that was pulling her onto him. She lowered herself until she felt the tip of his cock. "I want you," she said. Rawlins wrapped his arms around her hips and thrust himself inside her.

She gasped then, so loudly that if he hadn't already promised the office was on a private wing of the department she would have panicked. It was unlike anything she had ever felt before. How had she gone so long not knowing that it could feel like *this*? It was a wholeness, a delicious stretching, pure pleasure with every thrust, and she just wanted more of him. Her hands were in his hair, and around his neck, and undoing the buttons from his shirt as quickly as she could so that she could feel his chest. Rawlins's breath was heavy; he sighed into her neck.

"*How does this feel so good?*" Ellsbeth whispered. "How are you doing this to me?"

"You're perfect," he said back into her hair. "God, Ellsbeth, you're perfect."

Her pace quickened instinctively with her excitement, hips bucking as she ground herself against him. But his hands found her waist and slowed her, insisting on a deliberate rhythm.

It was impossible to know how long they were there, intertwined in that office chair, pressing into each other and kissing every available inch of skin. Her orgasm rose up slowly and then hit again and again until her head was buzzing and balance seemed like a foreign concept. Eventually, Rawlins's self-control broke; his thrusts quickened, becoming jerky and forceful. He groaned and then collapsed in the chair. Ellsbeth lifted herself off him, and after a moment that felt like their souls returning to their bodies, Rawlins peeled the condom off and wrapped it neatly in a square of tissue paper before throwing it away.

Rawlins pulled his boxers back on and cocked his head, gesturing for Ellsbeth to come back. She curled on his lap, one arm around his neck, and kissed him deeply. The sex should have eased the wanting. It should have felt like a craving fulfilled. She should be satisfied. But no. A taste had only made her want him even more.

They were silent for a while, while the colors of the sunset through the slits of the window shades went from pink to red to navy blue. When Ellsbeth would go back to her own bed later that night, her mechanical, logical, list-making brain would remind her why she had just made a terrible mistake. But for the moment, the only thing that filled her mind was his smell, and how good his arms felt around her.

From: Rawlins.T.M
To: Storer.Ellsbeth
Subject: Obscuration

Ellsbeth,

It has been mere moments since you left my office, and already, embarrassingly, I am pulled away from work that is overdue and instead find myself writing to you. Some voice in my mind—pride, fear, common sense—tells me I ought to preserve dignity and wait until morning to send you a message, mild in its flirtation and measured in its tone. But other voices are louder, and there seems little point in denying what is patently obvious: *I want you.* To a degree I cannot explain or even understand.

So I will instead turn to the topic that supposedly brought you here this afternoon, which we somehow never quite got around to: obscuration. (Don't worry, I will come back around to the other subject.) To understand obscuration, you need to start with the most fundamental question. *What is it?* Mysterious, certainly. A manipulation of the subtle forces that guide human thought and behavior. The unconscious, as Freud would have called it. Science gives us tools to understand some of those forces—psychology, biology, sociology, and more. We know that every thought and feeling and choice arises from the complex interplay of countless factors.

Years ago, I came to believe that obscuration was effectively impossible. Because our fates are written by deterministic forces, and we don't even understand how those forces act upon *ourselves,* much less anyone else. Obscuration, therefore, is like trying to play a symphony without any sheet music, on an instrument you can't even see.

But today, I think otherwise. For two reasons. One is simply *you.* A force of nature, with the right combination of talent and intelligence and youthful audacity to unlock its secrets.

The second is because I am, at this moment, compelled to admit to the susceptibility and flexibility of the will. Whatever just happened between us demonstrates how the most staunch rational resistance can be melted away by ineffable forces we cannot explain, whether those are magical or merely what we call chemistry.

I certainly did not intend for any of this. Yet here I am, marveling at how desire can become a prism, perversely shifting my perception; the familiar office around me is warped through the lens of *want.* I will never again see my office chair without the glorious image of your thighs opening upon it, while every surface around me seems notable chiefly for the absence of you.

The desk is littered with books and papers, when the only thing that belongs there is your body, covered by nothing except my own. The bookshelf, strangely, looks like it was designed to press you up against it, to pin your wrists to the wood while I watch pain and pleasure intermingle in your eyes. The familiar floor beneath my feet suddenly seems made for you to kneel while I cup your chin and incline your face to look up at me.

Even my own fingers, at the moment, seem notable for the utter lack of your skin they are squeezing. They flex and tap the keyboard, wishing only to play, again, the instrument of your body, to trace a line from your lips down across the perfect terrain of your chest, and your belly, and beyond. To tease you to the breaking point and then conquer you with a fingertip.

Have I gone too far already? It is only a fraction of the depravity that springs to my mind now that you have burrowed under the skin and unleashed something inside me. I did not know this was possible at any age, least of all mine; I did not imagine anyone could feel this way, least of all me. Yet here we are. Proving, beyond a shadow of a doubt, the power of mysterious forces that sway the will, as my own bends powerfully toward you.

Yours,
Rawlins

From: Storer.Ellsbeth
To: Rawlins.T.M.
Subject: Re: Obscuration

Dear Professor,

Is it just me, or is there now something deliciously and terribly charged about me calling you "Professor"? It was nice to come home and see your email, but I confess you hadn't left my brain in the intervening time at all. I've half convinced myself that I'm misremembering, that it couldn't have felt *that* good, and then I read a few sentences of yours and I'm positive my memory is actually underplaying just how perfect your skin felt on mine.

What was I supposed to be talking about again? Oh. Yes. Obscuration. I'm aware that my certainty makes me sound a little naïve, but I genuinely *do* think it's possible for the basic principles of writ magic to be applied to human psychology and the brain cells that convince us we're in charge when we're making a decision. I've been reading a lot of Apogodric's work—his theories on whether writ magic could be applied to the self seem like they could be a helpful jumping-off point, because the purpose of his research was bypassing the decision-making portion of the brain, but I keep running into brick walls. Is it possible this is the wrong approach entirely? What do you think, Professor?

Professor. God. Now I'm distracted again, imagining you asking me to stay after class. Telling me to lift my skirt and spanking me with a ruler as punishment for going down this utterly useless Apogodric rabbit hole. Am I a bad feminist, do you think, for how much this co-ed cliché turns me on? The power dynamic of you being my adviser, of telling me what to do? Because . . . it does. I admit that when we were in the Practicum testing my writ magic ritual, there was a moment when my breath caught because I imagined all of the terrible things I wanted you to do to me while my wrists were bound. It feels like I might need to test a more powerful version of that ritual if my thesis is going to be as excellent as I want it to be. Maybe, just for the intellectual challenge, I'll write a ritual that binds one's wrists and ankles. I think it should probably last longer than two minutes, don't you?

x
Ellsbeth

From: Rawlins.T.M.
To: Storer.Ellsbeth
Subject: Re: Re: Obscuration

Ellsbeth,

I suspect that the rest of your thesis committee might wonder at the academic purpose of a ritual that binds your wrists and ankles to the four posts of a bed, splaying your body open for a time duration that would definitely exceed two minutes. So perhaps we ought not include it in your dissertation. But purely for the purposes of intellectual exploration, it sounds like a very good idea.

Your take on Apogodric is not entirely misguided, but it is not sufficient, either. His writing presupposes a straightforward cause-and-effect relationship between rational thought and human behavior. There is no singular decision-making portion of the brain to bypass; every choice is informed by a complex web of competing impulses. Whatever has passed between us demonstrates this; emotion and desire do not obey simplistic rules.

Successful obscuration will require changing someone's *feelings* so that the action you induce feels like their idea (otherwise you risk creating cognitive dissonance that can be damaging, or reveal your manipulation). Consider looking into the 14th-century writings of proto-arcane scholars of the Mandressi school. Setting aside the quasi-mysticism, their approach will be valuable for its embrace of the fullness and mystery of human behavior.

In other words, Apogodric is an avenue of inquiry for which you need not be reprimanded, only guided to go further—but should a bit of corporal punishment be required to motivate you, I am certainly up to the task. And if you are a terrible feminist for delighting in that prospect, consider how embarrassingly unprogressive it is for a middle-aged man to not only want a younger woman, but want to dominate her. How do I reconcile politics that incline me toward equality of the sexes with the base ways in which I crave you? How do I square my own clear moral opposition to ever taking advantage of a student with the way my mind races through depraved thoughts of my star pupil?

At least we are not alone in the retrograde "wrongness" of our desires. And I can assure you that whatever craven places your mind goes, mine will gladly follow, if it hasn't been there already.

Your Professor,
Rawlins

From: Storer.Ellsbeth
To: Rawlins.T.M.
Subject: (no subject)

I'm sorry, I have to know. Have you ever done this with a student before?

From: Rawlins.T.M.
To: Storer.Ellsbeth
Subject: Re: (no subject)

I'm sorry you have to ask, and given the hour of your email, I'm sorry it's troubled you. I understand. I promise.

No, I have not done this before. As a matter of principle, I have assiduously avoided entanglements with students, even former ones. In part, this is just professionally prudent. But the more important reason is that I have been in a relationship with an unbalanced power dynamic before. In the position of lower power. And I could not live with myself if I ever made someone else feel the way I was made to feel.

So I understand anything you need to do or think to protect yourself. But I assure you, the exception I've made is not out of any indifference to the whole range of potential consequences. It is for one reason only:

You are exceptional.

From: Storer.Ellsbeth
To: Rawlins.T.M.
Subject: Re: Re: (no subject)

Thank you for that. I'm sure I just got in my head a little bit.

Unrelated, one of the benefits of being awake for several hours in the middle of the night is that it offers one plenty of undistracted time to work. I put together a new ritual (single-column formatting, like you prefer, sigh) that will bind the hands and ankles for seven minutes. Even if the . . . specific applications of the ritual might not be fit for my thesis, I figure if it's successful (which I think it will be), the fact that one is able to apply writ magic to two distinct and isolated parts of the body at once will completely disprove A. R. Milton's theory of writ magic as a "solid orb of power."

That in and of itself seems worthy of publication eventually, don't you think? I can't believe Milton's articles *haven't* been disproven yet in the academic world (if you're ever bored, look up his 1952 article on whether women are able to cast while they're menstruating). It's astonishing, really, how little some men know about the human body and its potential.

Are you up for another ritual? I'm free Friday evening if you are.

x
Ellsbeth

P.S. Unfortunately the stigma against writ magic means that so many works aren't publicly available. Though the Hays Library has a copy of the Mandressi Compendium, students aren't allowed to check it out without faculty approval. Do you think you might be able to get the book for me? If you do, I won't even mind if you try to distract me while I'm reading it.

RAWLINS

Rawlins pulled his coat tight against the wind as he walked across campus after the last of the week's classes. He had no memory of the lecture he had just given, the way someone might arrive in their garage after a familiar commute having completely forgotten the drive to get there. While his mouth dutifully recited the same bullet points on Fritz theory and magnetism, his mind was entirely focused on Ellsbeth. On obscuration. On the rush, almost like drunkenness, that swept his body when he was near her.

His phone vibrated in his pocket, but it was only a text from Lennox, a polite but terse update that Max was being transferred out of the hospital and back to prison. Apparently the doctors had determined that he was no longer a suicide risk, which Rawlins found difficult to believe, but he knew that as soon as Max grew tired of being strapped to a bed, he would know what to tell them to get himself out of the hospital.

Of course, getting out of prison was another matter entirely, and no amount of knowing what to tell people would improve the boy's prospects for release.

Rawlins was determined to help in any way he could, so he had reached out to Max's lawyer, who was audibly annoyed to be receiving his call. Since she was paid by Lennox and her client was Max, she was clearly baffled by Rawlins's interest in the case, and actively discouraged his efforts to help. "You can write a letter on his behalf, but it's a waste of time." Rawlins had pressed her for strategies that might make an impact, but she had sighed heavily, eager to get off the phone. "From the state's perspective, paroling Max is a huge risk with no upside. Greywall was appointed to chair the parole board precisely because he's seen as tough, and his record on arcane mechanical offenses is consistent. You could have the most compelling argument in the world, but you're never going to change his mind."

The problem lingered in the back of Rawlins's thoughts all week as he pondered other ways that he might help—strings he could pull, favors he could call in. But the scope of his influence was limited to the academic world. So the days until Max's parole hearing ticked on, with Rawlins feeling increasingly hopeless.

Rawlins reached Trousdale's, a neighborhood market in the shopping plaza at the bottom of Beacon Hill, charming for its quasi-European decor, though he could not understand how it stayed open with so little business. He picked up groceries for dinner and a bottle of wine, and found himself in line behind a pair of undergrads, huddled close and trading smiles, apparently heading out on a date as the clerk rang up their wine and cheese. He looked at the girl—younger than Ellsbeth, but barely. And the boy, who was beautiful in a Byronic way, struck Rawlins as a *child.* They were sweet. Cute, even. But he couldn't help thinking that Ellsbeth ought to be pining for a boy like *that.*

For twenty years, Rawlins had maintained his resolution not to sleep with a student. There had been opportunities, certainly, but he had avoided them with relative ease. Young scholars eager for his attention were usually so transparent; they held no appeal.

But Ellsbeth was a *graduate* student. An adult, more than capable of making her own decisions. To his surprise, he had not been stricken with guilt after they slept together in his office. Perhaps it was because he regarded Ellsbeth as a colleague, despite the power imbalance inherent to their roles. She was an intellectual force to be reckoned with; he was impressed, even intimidated, by her talent.

Of course, being an intellectual prodigy did not mean that she was emotionally mature. She had never had her heart broken the way Rawlins had by her age. But she *had* experienced real loss. Ellsbeth did not often talk about the death of her sister, but Rawlins could see the way it colored her. The distance she maintained between herself and her peers. The way it somehow made her both emotionally guarded and a raw bundle of nerves. He felt some relief knowing that the heartbreak that would come, whenever this thing came to an end—and it had to end, eventually—would not be the worst thing that had happened to Ellsbeth. Not by a wide margin.

In that sense, she was actually more prepared for what was inevitably coming than Rawlins had been, when his own first great love affair had ended so disastrously.

At least, that's what he told himself, in an effort to make it all feel okay. And it *had to* feel okay. Because the way he wanted her, he could not possibly stop.

Her fantasies of submission struck a chord deep inside him, touching something he had been embarrassed and even frightened by. He had certainly never participated in any fetish subculture, and cringed at the thought of leather outfits and seedy sex dungeons. But he had occasionally, in past relationships, had experiences that revealed his own proclivities. An impulsive smack on the ass, a command obeyed that brought a rush of pleasure. But he had always been frightened by himself in those moments, fearful they would unleash some darkness that he could not contain.

With Ellsbeth, however, the desire for domination was more than an idle impulse. It was becoming an obsession. It had crept in gradually, starting as irritation with her claim on his thoughts; then admiration, respect, and affection all slowly took root, and colored his want, so his desire for her was strangely sharp and soft at the same time. He wanted to both punish and pleasure her, to hold her close and pin her down; the contradictions swirled in his mind and left him dizzy. At times it was almost *amusing*, to want with such intensity at his age, and pine for her like he was a lovesick adolescent.

But other times, he was more frightened than amused. His impulses felt wild and dangerously out of control, and he was not sure where they came from. He would replay the whole course of events in his mind—the headstrong girl marching into his life, conquering more and more of his mind every day—and sometimes it felt like a tale of kismet for two well-matched lovers. But other times, it played as the story of a girl who knew exactly how to get what she wanted. And she was getting it. Whether "it" was him, or his indulgence in her illicit project, or both.

That interpretation of events was ungenerous, to say the least. What was *certain* was that she had more and more power over him every day. It made him wonder if he should call the whole thing off . . . but even as he wondered, he knew with certainty that he wouldn't. Not with the twin pulls of curiosity and desire dragging him forward with more force than he could possibly resist.

Maybe another writ magic ritual was exactly what he needed. A remedy for his own sense of powerlessness. A way to indulge the passion he felt while clawing back the control he needed. If he could just get it out of his system, then he could take a step back and view the entire situation rationally once again, viewing himself and Ellsbeth with the logic and clarity he had once prided himself on.

Ellsbeth arrived at his house at six o'clock, punctual as ever, carrying a bottle of wine and, as always, a backpack slung over one shoulder, heavy with books. She wore, to his surprise, a cottony dress, loose and flowy but complementary to her figure, with three buttons at the top and a hem that brushed her knees. He understood the intention of her fashion choice, which was less uptight and professional than she tended to favor, leaning into the growing familiarity of their relationship. The dress promised a more fun, carefree Ellsbeth; seeing him appraise her outfit, she swished the bottom of it at him. "You like it?"

"It's cute," he said, stepping back to let her inside. The dress flattered her, but it also accentuated her youth in a way that stirred at his guilt.

He took her bag and hung it on the coatrack, beckoning her back to the kitchen. "I was thinking, since we're able to start earlier this time, we could get right to work and wait until later to make dinner."

"Dinner later would be lovely," she said. "And I'm happy to wait. We need to work up an appetite, right?"

Rawlins had feared sleeping together would create tension between them, but it seemed to put Ellsbeth more at ease, as though they had simply found the norm that should've existed between them all along.

"Sounds good," he said. "I planned to cook for two, but I didn't want to presume, in case you had other plans to scamper off to."

"You've got me all night," she told him, leaning across the kitchen counter.

"Good to know." Unable to help himself, he stepped toward her, closing the distance. Seeing her in his home filled him with an instinct to keep her there. Then he asked, despite himself, "So I get Friday, and the runner got Saturday?"

Ellsbeth cocked her head. "I'm sorry, was that . . . *jealousy*? Over me?" He shook his head at her teasing but she continued, clearly enjoying herself. "Out of all my academic achievements, I think that making Professor Thaddeus M. Rawlins *jealous* of a med student might just take the crown."

"I'm not jealous," he said. "Only curious about your life."

"There's no one else," she said, sincere now, and they shared a look that caught his breath in his chest.

He broke from her gaze and let out an exhale, trying to keep his head clear. "Our best bet, for your ritual, is upstairs."

As he led the way, Ellsbeth's gaze lingered on every detail of his decor. "So now I get to see the forbidden second story, huh?"

"If we're going to study forbidden rituals, we need to get you comfortable working outside of the Practicum," he said as he climbed the stairs, showing her down the second-story hallway.

"Oh, really? Is *that* the reason we're doing the ritual in your bedroom?"

He paused at the door and shot her a look. "It's not *my* bedroom, it's the guest room. Would you rather return to the Practicum? And for me to keep my conduct as professional as that would require?"

She shrugged. "You didn't seem to have a problem in your office."

"I'm the only one with a key to my office," he replied. He opened the door to the guest bedroom, which featured a four-poster mahogany bed with a carved headboard. Ellsbeth studied the inlaid design. "It's an antique, so try not to break it," he told her. "And I chose this space based on *your* ritual. You need four solid corners to secure the limbs of the subject. If you prefer, we can go outside and put down stakes in this configuration? Otherwise, give me a hand."

He stepped to the opposite corner of the bed, and they pulled it a few feet away from the wall, which would make it easier to mark off a circle that held the four corners entirely within its circumference.

Ellsbeth assessed the space, looking at the foot-high clearance under the bed. "This is perfect, actually. It provides an elevated platform, so I can place the activated elementals underneath, right?"

Rawlins nodded. "You need low candles, which can limit your durations in some cases, but for what you're doing tonight, this will be fine."

He showed her over to the roll-top desk in the corner, opening it to reveal a printed copy of the ritual she had emailed him, along with all the elementals it called for: various metal ingots, beakers holding liquids, candles, and incense.

"Thank you," she said. "For getting all of this. I mean, I know you said you would, but still . . . I appreciate it." Her genuine gratitude took him aback. Rawlins realized that Ellsbeth was not accustomed to feeling like she could count on anyone. It made sense, in a way; she was a smart, self-sufficient girl who had experienced tragic loss. She had moved mountains by the force of her will, and had been let down by life again and again in a thousand ways that made her feel small.

Rawlins's heart tightened in his chest, and the temperature of his feelings toward Ellsbeth somehow rose by yet another degree. He wanted to earn her trust as no one ever had. To show her that she could be supported and taken care of in a way she had never dared to ask for. But he feared the day would come, inevitably, when he disappointed her, and it would be very painful for them both.

"It's nothing," he said. "Shall we?"

Working off the instructions Ellsbeth had typed up, they began preparing the ritual space.

It was a double binding, or in a sense, quadruple. The previous writ magic ritual she crafted pulled the subject's wrists together, but that was a single effect, while this one would act on each of the limbs in a different direction. Ellsbeth had crafted a neat solution, so the new ritual was only slightly longer than the last.

"I was thinking: If this works, it will open up a range of possibilities," she said. "You could combine multiple effects and sequence them. Make someone do . . . whatever you want."

"In theory, yes," said Rawlins. "The limiting factor is complexity. The more specific the behavior, the more involved the instructions and the magic. Try actually writing the ritual—it'll make you appreciate how involved it is to do something as simple as make a sandwich."

"I don't want a *sandwich*," she said, brushing past him as she returned to the desk to check her calculations. The brief contact filled his nose with her scent, and he could not help but follow her to the desk.

"You have good instincts," he told her, tapping the paper she was writing on. "There are scholars working at high levels in our field who might be able to produce this effect, but never with this degree of elegance."

They worked together fluidly, their bodies negotiating the limited space as she took measurements and he set the elementals in place. The connection between them was electric, a palpable charge that quickened Rawlins's pulse every time Ellsbeth came closer and extended into yearning as she moved away from him.

He had conducted rituals at home, but never with anyone else present, and he was surprised by the ease he felt at seeing her move around his space. It was a dance they fell into seamlessly, both discovering that their bodies already knew the steps.

Only twenty minutes after they had begun, everything was set—and suddenly, Rawlins was confronted with the reality of what they were doing. Sex in his office had been spontaneous; they could feign ignorance to what was going to happen beforehand, and submit to the whims of the moment.

This was different. They were not just mixing work and pleasure; mixing magic and sex meant crossing a line he had never considered, and it raised concerns he had to broach both delicately and directly. "Before we start, I need you to tell me what you're comfortable with."

"Everything. Anything. I'm open," Ellsbeth said. "Whatever happens during the ritual is good with me."

But he shook his head, insistent. "We need some . . . boundaries, here. A safe word, at the very least. Just say it if you're uncomfortable at any point, and we'll stop. The ritual, and . . . whatever we're doing. All right?"

Ellsbeth shrugged. "If it'll make you feel better, fine. What's my word?"

He thought for a moment. "*Tangerine.*"

Ellsbeth smiled. "Okay then. That's fine. But I don't think I'm going to need it. I want . . . what you want."

He swallowed, both thrilled and frightened by her directness. "All right. Clear enough."

"What should I wear?" she asked, and the tone of her voice conveyed her willingness, eagerness even, to strip naked, to forget the ritual entirely if he asked her to. Rawlins was tempted to do just that.

But they were playing a game. And the game itself had become important in a way that surprised him. His passion for her had grown into a wild animal, unbroken, kicking out dangerously inside him, compelling him in directions he couldn't comprehend. He was frightened by where his desire might lead—and part of him resented her for eliciting that feeling.

The prospect of self-control felt impossible. But here, before him, was something else. The promise of control over *her.* With her permission, of course, and at the moment, with magic. Through some inexplicable sublimation, he imagined that control over her would deliver the respite he was looking for. It might tame his desire, or at least give him peace with how ungovernable it was.

So he shook his head, a notion forming in his mind for how he could indulge his yearning in the way he needed to. "Keep your clothes on." She looked disappointed but did not question him.

Ellsbeth did a final check on all the elementals and lit the candles. Rawlins turned off the lamp, and the room pulsated with the hazy orange glow of a dozen tiny flames. Ellsbeth climbed up onto the bed, and he guided her into position, her head at the top without a pillow so that her hair cascaded down over the edge.

"Should I put my hands out?" she asked, extending her arms toward the posts.

Rawlins shook his head. "The ritual will bind you to the posts once it takes effect. Try holding them at your sides. Legs straight. You'll be able to perceive the change more clearly."

He stood at the foot of the bed. Ellsbeth lay flat, her gaze fixed on the ceiling, her chest rising and falling with her breath. He stared at her, struck by the sheer vulnerability of her repose.

Rawlins began to chant the words she had written. "*Constringantur corpus, ligentur membra . . .*" The ritual was well designed; he was confident in its efficacy, but he felt a nervous flutter in his stomach. Not about what the magic would do, but about what *he* would do.

As the incantation progressed, the flames of the candles blazed more brightly, and the metals shone and hummed. The familiar droning sound gradually rose, filling the small space.

Ellsbeth remained perfectly still, and he could sense her apprehension, waiting to see if the effect she had designed was going to work.

It happened suddenly. Her arms, gripped by the invisible force of the ritual, were yanked across the sheets. Her legs were rapidly pulled apart, extended tightly toward the posts at the foot of the bed. Even though he had expected the change, Rawlins was startled by its suddenness.

The bed was large enough that Ellsbeth's wrists and ankles did not touch the posts, but he could see the effect of the magic, stretching her limbs and splaying her across the mattress.

"Does it hurt?" he asked. "I can stop if it's painful."

She squirmed, shifting her limbs as if she were tugging at invisible ropes tied impossibly taut. "No . . . it's strong, but it doesn't hurt."

"Good work," he said. "Your prize for this achievement in the field of the arcane arts is seven minutes of immobility." He started a timer on his phone to track the effect.

"I was hoping *you* might reward my scholarship," she said, slightly breathless, her chest visibly rising and falling beneath the cotton dress.

"We're not done working yet," he replied, leaving the foot of the bed and coming to the side. "We still have the physiological effects to observe."

He climbed onto the mattress on his knees, alongside her, looking down.

"Of course," Ellsbeth said. Her breath was quicker now. "We established last time, I can still blush."

"Does your breathing still feel entirely normal?" he asked, and his hand glided across her throat. With her head tilted back, his fingers traced the delicate shape of her windpipe, savoring the subtle vibration of her exhales.

"More or less," she said.

His hand climbed up to her mouth, and he ran a finger across her lower lip. She bit his first knuckle, and he grinned. "What was that for?"

She smirked up at him playfully.

"I'm just getting started," Rawlins said, "with our very important work." His hand descended now, gliding back over her throat to the top of her dress. He deftly unfastened the three buttons there with one hand and slid his palm across her chest. The fabric of her bralette was thin enough that he could feel her nipple straining against the material. He circled it with his finger and she arched her back, pushing against him. But his hand slipped away, pressing into her skin at the side of her neck with two fingers.

The thrum of her heartbeat became a drum pulsing through his veins as he fought to maintain control of himself. "Elevated heart rate," he murmured.

"You're killing me," she said.

"Only one more test to do," he told her. "And plenty of time for it."

His left hand moved up to her scalp, running through her hair, and she closed her eyes—until he tightened his hand into a fist, gripping her hair at the back of her head. It jolted her to attention and she met his gaze. "Focus."

She did, locking her eyes onto his as his other hand slid down her body to the hemline of her dress. With the effects of the ritual pulling her ankles toward the posts of the bed, the muscles of her thighs were taut, and her quadriceps quaked beneath his touch.

Rawlins could feel the pressure of desire building inside him. Yearning to kiss her, to tear off her clothes, to let go completely. But there was something to prove here. To her, and to himself.

His hand climbed the inside of her thigh deliberately, savoring the anticipation as he hiked her dress. When his fingers reached their target, he pressed one against her underwear, feeling her excitement. She shuddered.

"Arousal appears to be *quite* possible," he said. "Anything else we should test?"

He teased her through the fabric. With her entire body at his mercy, his attention was attuned to every detail of her reaction. The movement of her eyes, her lips, her hips. He had never felt so keenly fixated on another person's pleasure, so eager to elicit one reaction after another, to watch her excitement rise and fall in sync with his will. "I haven't encountered anything about orgasm in the literature on writ magic. Do you think it's possible?"

"Yes," she said, followed by an insistent, "*Please.*"

He thrilled at the desperation in her tone, but he kept his voice as measured as he could manage. "And when was the last time you came?" he asked, his fingers massaging her with delicate precision.

She squirmed at his question, barely able to move. "In your office?"

"Oh, I doubt that was the *last* time," he said. She let out a small laugh as if to say, *I can't believe you're doing this to me,* and his hand hesitated, hovering over her. Her hips rose off the mattress in frustration, and his fist tightened in her hair, pulling her head back. A reprimand, which elicited a moan that was not entirely one of pain. "If you lie, I'll stop."

"This morning," she blurted, and his hand descended, rubbing her through the fabric once again. "Before class."

"And what did you think about?"

She looked at him, her expression somehow both delighted and infuriated. Her limbs pulled uselessly at her invisible bonds while her neck tugged against his hand in her hair. "Is that really relevant?"

The defiance in her eyes only excited him further. But he asserted control by withdrawing, his fingers slipping off her. "If you don't like my approach, we can stop."

It was a test of wills. Ellsbeth bit her lip, and he could see that she was holding back a grin. He was, too, but he was better at it than her. Finally, she relented, leaning her head back.

"You," she said, her breathing fast and shallow. "Of course, you."

"More specific," he said. "I want to know exactly what you thought about this morning before coming to my class."

Surrendering to his request, she spoke dreamily to the ceiling. "Your garden."

"You get turned on by flowers?"

"I thought of interrupting you there," she said. "And being dragged down into the dirt."

The force of Ellsbeth's building desire was palpably exciting, and he felt himself harden. "That can be arranged." He pressed his fingers against her more firmly, and she shivered with pleasure as he asked, "Do you think about me every time?"

"Yes," she said quickly. "You think about me, too?"

"You don't get to ask the questions right now," he told her, and he slid his hand up to her belly, causing her to briefly buck with frustration—until his palm slipped down the front of her underwear, eliciting a shiver. "And how far back did that start, thinking about me?"

She hesitated again, and his hand retreated. "I'll stop if you don't cooperate. Since the start of the semester?"

"Even earlier," she said softly, avoiding his gaze. "I thought about what it would be like before I even met you."

He nodded, surprised and a little touched by the vulnerability of her admission. "An author photo and an idea of who I might be?" She nodded. "How do I compare to the fantasy?"

"Better in every way," she said without hesitation.

He rewarded her by pressing his middle finger into her, while his thumb rubbed circles around her clit. Her body strained ineffectually against the bonds that held her in place, as he maintained a controlled pace.

"And how long do you think it will be until you can think about anyone else?"

"I don't know," she said vaguely, closing her eyes. Her hips rocked slightly, willing him to speed up. Instead, he lifted himself off the bed completely. She looked at him with disappointment that verged on betrayal, fearful their game had ended. But her expression gave way to relief as he moved down to the foot of the bed, opening his jeans and tugging them down. He was eager to give her the release she wanted—but it was balanced by the urge, equally strong, to maintain control. Over her and, by extension, over himself.

"How long until you can come for anyone but me?" he asked. He opened a condom and rolled it onto his length. As he climbed back onto the bed between her open thighs, the impulse to take her was like a drumbeat inside him, deafening in its immediacy.

With Ellsbeth's legs magically bound and open, it was impossible to remove her underwear, so he simply grabbed the fabric, pulling it aside and stretching it beyond repair to expose her completely, positioning himself between her thighs.

Yet still, he held back, waiting for her reply. He wanted her to know he could wait forever, even though he was as hungry as she was. "How long? Until you want anyone else?"

"I don't know."

"How long?"

She pulled against the invisible bindings, pressing herself up and toward him, but he pulled away, not letting her reach him. She whimpered.

"Never," Ellsbeth finally whispered, her body immobilized and her gaze locked on his.

"Good," he said, and finally, he let go. He descended and sank into her, the force of his passion unleashed like a burst dam.

His timing was perfect. The effect of the ritual ended the moment he pressed into her, and Ellsbeth's limbs, suddenly freed, wrapped around him like a trap sprung. Her fingers dug into his back and her legs encircled his waist, compelling him deeper and faster.

He needed no encouragement, thrusting into her with abandon. She let out an involuntary yelp, some inchoate mixture of pleasure and pain. His own unguarded groan matched hers, guttural and savage. He fucked her ferociously, a starving man who'd spent hours at the window, finally let in to feast. He buried his face in her neck as he felt the deliberately delayed orgasm overtake her, radiating outward, as though every electric current of her pleasure flowed directly into him.

The façade of control he had maintained evaporated completely as he joined her in the primal, animalistic spasm, and they lost themselves in the time-stopping joy of each other.

LATER, RAWLINS SPRINKLED HERBS OVER a sizzling snapper fillet in a cast-iron skillet while turning stalks of lemony asparagus in the pan beside it.

Ellsbeth wore his button-down and a pair of his boxers while he stood in pants and no shirt—a single complete outfit divided evenly between them. She sat on a stool at the kitchen counter, swirling the wine in her glass, clearly pleased with herself as she looked around his well-appointed kitchen.

"When you get a lot of money, does someone come teach you how to be rich?" she asked. "I mean, is there some sort of class on all the fancy stuff you should buy?"

He chuckled. "If you have a modicum of taste, you figure it out as you go. But don't worry—if you're dead-set on an academic career, that won't be a problem."

"Maybe I'll just have to write my own bestselling book that revolutionizes the field."

"I wouldn't be shocked," he said as he plated her dinner, setting it on the counter. She dug in, ravenous and clearly enjoying the meal.

As he sat down with his own dinner, she asked, "Did you get a chance to pick up the Mandressi Compendium for me?"

Rawlins shook his head. "With the level of scrutiny this could attract, I don't want to leave a paper trail picking up university materials." Ellsbeth's face fell with visible disappointment, until he continued, "That's why I contacted a friend of mine in Leavenworth who collects rare arcane texts. He agreed to lend his copy, and I went and picked it up last night."

She brightened, and he saw gratitude in her eyes that made his two-hour round trip to get the book more than worth it. "Thank you."

"I'm happy to help with your studies, as long as you're cautious," he said. "But I do have to ask. Why obscuration?"

He watched her as she looked away, growing thoughtful. He already knew there were reasons for her study beyond the idle curiosity she had alluded to before, and now he could see her weighing whether or not to tell him the truth.

When she spoke, it was in a measured tone, weighing every word. "I've always wanted to push the limits of what's possible." She looked away but kept talking. "I know that the world's not fair. Life isn't fair. And that's fine, except that really, it's *people* that are unfair. And closed-minded. And sometimes . . . evil. So are we supposed to just accept that? When there might be a way to change things for the better?"

"Can you really make things better by *controlling* people?" Rawlins asked. "That's not persuasion—it's force."

"That's fair," she said, running the tines of her fork across her plate. "Well, in that case, let's go back to curiosity. I want to understand how the human mind works. Why we believe what we believe . . . and whether it's *possible* to change someone's mind, even if it is by force."

Rawlins sensed that she was speaking honestly, but that she also wasn't telling him the whole story. "Whose mind do you want to change?" he asked.

She looked up from her dinner, hesitating, as she appeared to weigh whether or not to say what she was thinking. But eventually, she merely shrugged, apparently deciding better of it. "I don't know, there are loads of people who won't listen to reason. I mean, isn't there anyone whose mind *you'd* want to change?"

He could tell that she was redirecting in order to dodge the question, and he was tempted to press her on it . . . to assure her that whatever she was thinking, it was better to tell him completely. But his mind went in another direction, as one phrase lodged in his mind sharply, drawing his memory back to his phone call with Max's lawyer. To her insistence that Rawlins would never persuade Greywall, never "change his mind."

Suddenly, it was like a chasm of possibility opened before him. The seeds of a plan began sprouting, even as he recognized how dangerous and possibly foolish it would be. But he could not yet speak it aloud, so he muttered simply, "I don't know . . . it's an interesting question."

"I'm glad you think so," Ellsbeth said, setting down her fork as she leaned forward. "I'd like to start reading tonight. I'm sure the material is dense, and it might be helpful to have you to bounce my thoughts off." She paused. Rawlins was staring into the distance as his thoughts wandered, and she apparently took his silence for a retreat, fearing she had overstepped. "Sorry, I don't mean to impose. You can let me know when you'd like me to leave."

He looked back at her and smiled in an attempt to reassure her. "No, I don't want you to leave." He cupped her face gently, leaned in, and kissed her softly. "Not tonight."

But it was a single word that came to Rawlins's mind when he contemplated the question of when he actually wanted her to leave. Unbidden and insane though it might be, it was the same word that he had thrilled at getting her to say earlier.

Never.

From: Storer.Ellsbeth
To: Rawlins.T.M.
Subject: Hello again

Perhaps you're just not very experienced when it comes to the world of arcane, brand-new, untested writ magic BDSM, but usually after you fuck someone like that, it's considered polite to message her the next day. Otherwise she'll just be left alone in her apartment playing the previous night in her head over and over and over again with nothing new to distract her.

x

From: Rawlins.T.M.
To: Storer.Ellsbeth
Subject: Re: Hello again

As the older and supposedly wiser one here, it's humbling to learn the etiquette, but I suppose I'll have to benefit from your extensive writ magic BDSM experience. Apologies for my faux pas. It arises, I assure you, from no shortage of thinking about you.

It was delightful to dine together, though the experience left me with more questions than answers. Was it really as delicious as I remember? How did I live so long, oblivious to such a hunger in myself? Can a single person be exactly what I've been starving for? What other flavors and dishes might we discover? How could I be so deeply sated, yet the next day, so consumed with wondering: How long until I can feast on you again?

From: Storer.Ellsbeth
To: Rawlins.T.M.
Subject: Re: Re: Hello again

I would offer to cook you dinner (that seems like the charmingly tit-for-tat thing one is supposed to do in this situation), but the best I would be able to offer you is a depressing pasta, boiled on a hot plate and strained in a shared kitchen sink (the miseries of graduate student apartment life). Before you get too big an ego, it's entirely possible my enjoyment of last night was partly because of how long it's been since I've had a genuinely good meal cooked in a real kitchen. Is it too risky to think maybe we can go out to dinner next weekend? There's a small Ethiopian place far enough down the hill and pricey enough that students rarely make the trek unless their parents are paying. Abyssinia, do you know it? Maybe we can ask for one of the quiet tables in their upstairs section, and if anyone affiliated with Newlyn walks in, immediately make it seem like you take all of your advisees out to a mid-semester meal to discuss their progress. I've only been there once before, but it seems like the type of food one wants to eat now that the weather has begun to turn. Food that warms one from the inside out.

On matters only slightly less important than food, I've been going through my notes on Mandressi and had a few thoughts I wanted to run past you. One of the more interesting patterns I've picked up on is that the language used to describe obscuration actually reads less like writ magic and more like valuation. Of course, valuation went out of modern use when the calculator was invented (no need to cast a full ritual to count how many coins you've amassed in your vaults or whatever when a computer is far more reliable for keeping track of that), but any undergraduate with a basic grasp of arcane mechanicals can manage a valuation ritual. Am I entirely misguided for seeing the way the language is similar? It's almost as if Mandressi is suggesting (consciously or not) that in order to accomplish an obscuration ritual, you need to "count" your target's brain first. Of course, it's not a literal instruction (a valuation ritual on any person's brain will always yield the same result: one. One brain. Well done, definitely worth the ingots and the setup time), but I feel like there might be something *behind* what he's implying.

That in order to achieve obscuration successfully, you need to be able to measure up your target uniquely, as an individual, something to account for the complexity of the human brain and the infinite ways individuals uniquely see the world. A numerical valuation ritual is useless, but maybe there's another type of ritual in the same field that will allow someone to understand something about someone else's mind. From there, one could begin to work a writ magic ritual, but I think without that first step—some sort of deeper mechanical understanding of the target, whether it's using the vocabulary of valuation or not—any attempts at obscuration would slip away like rain off plastic. We need to find the "stickiness" of the target first, so to speak.

Perhaps I'm rambling. I admit, I haven't slept as well as I nor mally do, distracted by thoughts of Mandressi and my professor's fingers inside me.

From: Rawlins.T.M.
To: Storer.Ellsbeth
Subject: Re: Re: Re: Hello again

The mind is a curious thing. The two thoughts that distract you, Mandressi and my fingers, are now linked in your brain. Perhaps someday you'll be lecturing at a prestigious conference when an attendee asks you a question about the Compendium, and you will instantly make the association. I hope that I am in the audience so I can be the only one present to recognize your brief delay in response for what it is; I hope that your eyes find mine, as you fumble for your words while being mentally transported back to the bed in my guest room, to memories of trembling anticipation and release.

I mention this mental phenomenon not only to linger on a pleasant recollection, but as a bridge to your thoughts on obscuration. The connections the mind makes are powerful, mysterious, and difficult to untangle. Your observation about the language of valuation surprised me (hardly the first time you've done that, Ms. Storer), and after rereading an obscuration text through that lens, I can see what you mean, and it makes perfect sense. The greatest challenge of obscuration has always been the incomprehensibility of consciousness and cognition. The neurons in the brain are virtually innumerable, and the number of *connections* is exponentially more. When you consider how those connections create the many factors that affect our behavior, it becomes apparent that a ritual could never adequately address it in any linear or algorithmic manner. To act on a human brain would be as complex as attempting to act on the entire ocean at once.

This got me thinking about the meteorological rituals developed in Europe during the Enlightenment. Have you read about Guillaume Poirier? He's mostly a historical footnote now, but Poirier constructed a system of arcane mechanicals that purported to influence weather patterns. It was ultimately abandoned for being unpredictable and impossible to verify, and of course the practice was later banned as overreaching. But there's a similar principle at work: a valuation, an accounting if you will, of the vast, complex atmosphere such that it could, in theory, be acted upon. (*Aconter* is the Old French word he uses, origin of the English *accounting,* which also meant "a reckoning.") Poirier's writing is worth a look, as I suspect you could employ his framework to create an *image* of the subject's brain. A representation, a simulacrum, a magical *understanding* that serves as a filter through which the desired effect could be applied.

Lots to consider, lots to discuss, and no better avenue than over dinner. I know Abyssinia well and have made a reservation a week from today at one of those discreet tables you mentioned. I'm sure waiting that long will test your impatience, but I'd like you to get a draft of a ritual completed before we dine, so we can discuss your work and, hopefully, celebrate your progress. I'm certainly not expecting something functional, but I'm hoping you'll be able to impress me. So let us say (as long as 8 that night works for you, and regardless of what other diners and eavesdroppers might perceive) . . .

It's a date.

ELLSBETH

Ellsbeth had stayed up all night reading before, but she had never done it previously with such singular focus, an attention that forewent the need for food or bathroom breaks, that meant she hadn't realized her laptop was running so hot and pressing so deep into her leg until she stood and saw the purple imprint it left on her thigh. She was working in bed, a habit she'd picked up as an undergrad when she needed to focus. Her usual daily routine was a commute to coffee shops and college libraries, where she could set up a workstation with a notebook and an overpriced latte. But there was a problem with that: She was always aware of an invisible observer, of a sense of "performing" being a graduate student while she was in public. Her facial expressions became more contemplative when she gazed off distracted mid-sentence; she sipped at her latte with quiet sighs; she nibbled at the end of her pen in a way that she would never do if she was alone.

When she was in her bed, her only focus was the work.

Rawlins had said he hoped she could impress him, and so that was exactly what she was going to do.

Someone had uploaded the pages of a translation of Poirier to an online library for free, and though the resolution was low, by zooming in and raising the brightness of her laptop screen, Ellsbeth didn't have too much trouble making out his sentences. The text itself was lengthy and dense; most of it involved storm systems and long-antiquated strategies for open sea navigation (rituals that would be no more helpful than a compass, and far *less* helpful than a working GPS), and Poirier was not a natural writer, prone to lengthy digressions and sentences that lost track of their own subject halfway through.

But sometime around two in the morning, when Ellsbeth reached a section on rituals to create rain, the hairs on her arm began to stand at attention. She wiped the sleep from her eyes and pulled a pillow behind her back so she could sit up straighter, and she opened an empty Word document to take notes. She read, and she wrote, for the next four hours straight. She was only half aware of the jovial celebratory sounds of whatever party the Banestooth Club was throwing down the street, and then the sound of the party ending and its participants dispersing a few hours later. She did not notice the sun begin to rise; it was only when a bird began chirping a mechanical trill startlingly close to her window that Ellsbeth blinked away from her computer screen and realized how long she had worked without moving.

Trying to develop a new arcane ritual sometimes felt to Ellsbeth like attempting to put a puzzle together when most of the puzzle pieces were swollen with damp and had lost their color from sitting in the sun for too long. She tried to hold as much of it in her mind at one time as she could, pulling at one thread and then another, and hoping the entire thing wouldn't fall apart. It was around 3 a.m. that she began to see the outlines of the ritual begin to take shape.

Rawlins was right; Poirier was the key to it all. People had attempted and quickly given up at attempts at obscuration because they assumed the answer was writ magic but stronger—hammering another's mind into obedience through brute force. But that approach was all wrong. It wasn't strength that obscuration required but finesse, an ability to *see* and understand another person's mind. Once that was accomplished, the path unfolded itself in front of Ellsbeth miraculously, as if she were in a car speeding down a darkened highway with headlights throwing light onto the road. One step at a time, one piece of the ritual feeding into the next. It came together. It became complete.

Maybe she was delusional with lack of sleep, but she almost wanted to burst out laughing.

It wasn't just *theoretically possible;* it was *doable.*

Ellsbeth began writing as quickly as she could, her handwriting a manic scrawl. When she finished, she attached it in a PDF to Rawlins, in an email without a subject line. Ellsbeth turned out the lamp by her bedside, but she didn't even bother to close the curtains to the sunlight of the already lightening dawn before she fell into a deep sleep.

RAWLINS

Rawlins sipped the bitter dregs of a Styrofoam cup of coffee as he sleepwalked his way through the CotAA Faculty Mixer, one of many in the endless stream of social obligations that academia foisted upon him. This event was held monthly, though this would be the last of the year taking place in the courtyard behind the department offices before the cold drove them inside; even now, in late October, they were pushing their luck. Glazed donuts and travel carriers of burnt coffee were set up on picnic tables while the professors "mingled" and "networked" with one another, a few colleagues from other schools, and university administrators. Attendance was mandatory, though the utility of the events was mainly reserved for the younger faculty, who were perpetually campaigning for tenure and funding.

Rawlins was buttonholed by Pierre Braier, a prematurely balding adjunct instructor at a nearby state school who had wanted to "pick his brain" (a phrase Rawlins despised) about how to tailor one's scholarship to maximize career prospects. Rawlins was tempted to tell the man that if people didn't seem interested in his work, perhaps his work simply wasn't all that interesting, but, fortunately or not, Braier seemed much more intent on unloading his frustrations than actually listening to feedback.

As Rawlins nodded absently, his eyes drifted. Across the garden, Professor Gallway was holding court, regaling some of the younger visiting faculty with stories of his travels. As if sensing Rawlins's gaze, he looked over, and Rawlins looked away, not wanting to invite another conversation after this one. He found himself contemplating an oak tree—and perversely imagining how Ellsbeth would look if she were bound to it, and what he might do to her there. He tried to shake off the thought; the last thing he needed was to get hard in the middle of a work function.

Braier was still talking at him, it seemed. Rawlins gave the man some pat advice about how to "play the game" and excused himself, stopping at the coffee table to refill his cup and checking his phone, mainly to discourage anyone else from coming up and talking to him. He swiped through notifications and paused on a new email without any subject line. From Ellsbeth. Intrigued, glancing around as though someone might look over his shoulder, he opened the message. The text was short—Look forward to your thoughts!—and he went straight for the PDF attachment.

Reading arcane mechanicals work on a phone screen was far from ideal, and Ellsbeth's obscuration ritual was particularly challenging—sixteen pages dense with written instructions and diagrams, so he had to zoom in and scroll with his finger to read it. As he scanned the work, at first he felt perplexed, wondering if Ellsbeth had veered off entirely in the wrong direction. But then he started to understand the strategy she was attempting—using Poirier's system to "account" for the mind of the subject, and then conducting the ritual in such a way that it could be rendered latent in the medium of a clay compound, to be used later by touching the target. Reading through the ritual was like watching someone move around puzzle pieces without clicking any two together, so it seemed like they were making no progress—until suddenly they were *all* in the right place and fit perfectly. There was not a single wasted step; Ellsbeth had apparently mastered his feedback and lost her tendency toward overcomplication. The ritual was stunning in its elegance. His heart rate quickened with a rush of excitement, not just at her achievement, but at the possibility of *trying it*. Of testing out this new form of arcane influence.

Then self-consciousness came upon him suddenly as he glanced up and realized he was standing to the side of the coffee table, hunched over his phone screen with an expression of delirious wonder. He probably looked psychotic, and he tried to adjust his face to appear more casual—worried his expression might somehow betray that he was reading a recipe for a highly illegal and dangerous strain of magic. He tried to calm himself, but he knew that simply by reading these words, he was taking another step down a dangerous path.

The faculty mixer suddenly felt oppressive; he needed to get out of there, to go back to his office and peruse the ritual on his computer, where he could take his time with it, understand it properly . . . and more important, figure out what to *do* here. He headed for the doors leading back inside the building, hoping he had stayed long enough that his attendance had been noted, but his absence would not be missed. But Lennox clocked his passage and broke from her conversational circle to intercept him on the steps.

"Tad, can I have a word?" she asked, her expression inscrutable. He felt a moment of panic, suddenly afraid that she might know what he had just read, but he simply gave her a tight smile and stepped aside to where they would not be overheard. "It's about Ellsbeth Storer," Lennox said flatly, then raised her eyebrows in a manner that felt accusatory.

Rawlins's stomach dropped; an adrenaline rush of fear flooded his veins. He fought to keep his expression neutral while his mind raced, wondering if they had been caught, and how had he been so foolish, and how had it happened? Had someone walked by and overheard them in his office? Stumbled upon them in the Practicum? Was this in response to rumor, which he could deny, or was there actual evidence that would get him fired? Was Lennox coming to him early so she could warn him to stop, or was he about to be publicly humiliated and ruined? Did she somehow know about the email he had received just minutes earlier?

The whirl of thoughts created a moment of deer-in-headlights silence, which Lennox mercifully broke. "You haven't submitted her thesis topic to the department. Those were due two weeks ago, and it's your responsibility, as her adviser, to keep her on track."

Relief washed over him, and his shoulders softened. He swallowed, finding his voice. "Right, sorry about that. I'll get on her about it."

He paused, awaiting a signal that there was nothing else to say, but Lennox evidently regarded his reply as exasperatingly vague. "Well, what *is* her topic?" Lennox asked.

"Sorry?"

"I understand if she's behind, with the late start and all, and I don't want to be insensitive about that business with her sister. But if I'm going to wait indefinitely for a précis to approve, at least *tell me* what to expect."

"Oh, well . . . she's been narrowing in on a topic," Rawlins said evasively. "We'll get you something once it's ready."

"Surely you can give me *some* sense of what you've been working on with her," Lennox insisted. "Or what she's deciding between? I might be able to weigh in, help steer the ship."

Rawlins should have been prepared for this inquiry, but he had been too caught up in the excitement of working with Ellsbeth—well, more than just *working*—to give much thought to the bureaucratic requirements of the university. His intention had been to get his arms around the problem and have a fully baked case to make before he went to Lennox and sought her approval for his student to write a thesis, even theoretically, about an illegal branch of magic. Now he was flat-footed, still reeling and trying to suss out how much Lennox knew or didn't.

"Give her a minute, Maggie. She's ambitious, and she knows what this means for her career, so it's been hard to pin her down," Rawlins said, wincing at his own choice of words.

"Surely you've made progress, in the many meetings you've had," Lennox said, an edge entering her tone. "Most of the cohort seem to think that she's your favorite student, so I know it's not an issue of *neglect.*"

There it was. The rumor. The *suspicion.* It was irritating to know he had been gossiped about, but also a relief in some ways, since a suspicion that ill formed and obliquely referenced meant that Lennox was in the dark about the extent of the relationship. But her hackles had been raised.

"Ellsbeth is a remarkably capable student," Rawlins said, trying to steer the conversation in another direction. "I think there's potential for her to do exceptional work, but that takes time . . ." He saw Lennox opening her mouth to speak, and added quickly, "I will impress upon her the importance of deadlines, and we'll have something for you to consider . . . soon."

Lennox frowned, but apparently thought better of pressing the matter further. "See that you do . . . I'm sure I don't need to remind you of the dangers of giving too long a leash to a gifted student."

Rawlins's eye twitched and his chest tightened; scathing replies crept up his throat, but he swallowed them down, knowing better than to provoke further conflict. "You certainly don't," he replied dryly, then headed back to his office.

He closed the door. The din of the gathering wafted up from down below, a murmur under the oppressive silence of his office. He could not help but try to tune his ear, attempting to overhear what was being said—as though every conversation down there were about him and Ellsbeth, and picking up on what was being said about them might somehow help him get ahead of the disaster they were hurtling toward.

Rawlins's mind raced with troubled thoughts, and he was gripped with a fever of anxiety. He hated that feeling; it was worse than fear. When you knew what a threat was, you could take action to address it. But this was only a vague, amorphous sense of potential danger, which left him hypervigilant, buzzing with uncertainty.

He opened Ellsbeth's email on his laptop and stared at the PDF. What had filled him with excitement ten minutes earlier . . . now only filled him with dread. He couldn't believe he had been so careless, had let this go so far.

Lennox was right, unfortunately. Infuriatingly. He had somehow forgotten the lesson he should have learned with Max. He had gotten himself into an even worse situation—not only a dangerous mentorship, but one entangled with desire and irrational affection. His entire relationship with Ellsbeth was like a sports car on an open road, accelerating dangerously; it was only a matter of time before they lost control and this ended very, very badly. Heartbreak was the least of his concerns; prison, or worse, was a very real possibility.

It was time to put a stop to this while he still could.

ELLSBETH

In the morning, Ellsbeth checked her email and saw that Rawlins hadn't replied to her ritual. She spent the day refreshing her inbox, waiting to see his name and the reply she expected—effusive with praise, possibly with an offer to help her be hired as a visiting professor at Newlyn immediately, completed degree be damned. But the email didn't come.

On Wednesday, she sat in the front row of Rawlins's graduate seminar. It was a lecture on numerology, the type of mind-numbing subject that surely didn't hold Rawlins's interest to the degree he was pretending it did. And yet his attention remained studiously fixed on his notes; he hardly looked at her once. Every time Ellsbeth tried to catch his eye, he seemed to purposefully avoid meeting her gaze. He didn't call on her even when her hand was raised, and rather than linger as he usually did after class, he mumbled something about a staff meeting and was out of the Practicum before any of the students had even risen from their seats.

She double- and then triple-checked to be sure that the email to him had actually gone through. It had. Still, nothing back from him even to acknowledge he had received it.

Ellsbeth drafted and deleted a dozen messages to Rawlins, cringing at herself at the neediness that came through even over text: *Just checking in to see if you read my ritual yet!?* No. *Hey, did you get my email?* Awful. She couldn't come up with anything that didn't sound nagging, petulant, inane. And so she put her phone away. If he were pulling away, demanding more of his attention would only make him pull further and faster. Moreover, he hadn't said anything to cancel their date that Saturday; it was possible he just hadn't had a chance to read it.

Ellsbeth reread the ritual, catching a typo but otherwise almost embarrassingly impressed with herself and the clarity of her writing. She was almost certain that it would work, but she wanted Rawlins to tell her as much.

Still, the longer he went without acknowledging her, the more impatient she became. Regardless of what she believed she had achieved, there was only one way to know for certain if she had actually written a ritual capable of obscuration.

On Saturday morning, Ellsbeth entered the coffee shop on the corner of Thayer Street, clay compound warming in her palm. Performing the ritual in her apartment earlier had taken an hour and a half—she might have been able to do it in half the time, but her hands had been shaking and she had to start over twice. The clay compound held the ritual in stasis until it was needed.

Ellsbeth picked up a protein bar she had no intention of eating and placed it down on the counter, slightly too close to her, which meant that the girl behind the counter had to reach forward to grab it, revealing a strip of skin at her wrist. As quickly as she could, Ellsbeth touched the red clay to the girl's wrist and in an instant felt the strange, delirious power take over when the ritual was a success. The girl's eyes went blank and glassy, and she made no move to pull her wrist back toward her.

Ellsbeth's heart began pumping so quickly she could feel the blood in her temples. She had *known* it was going to work, had been so confident in her gut about every single step in the ritual fitting together, inevitable and self-evident, mathematically certain. And yet seeing it actually work in practice was so shocking it was all Ellsbeth could do to remain upright.

"Small coffee, please," she said, and then Ellsbeth realized with a jolt that she hadn't actually planned for how she would test whether the obscuration worked properly or not. "You should charge me for a large," she said, her voice unnaturally loud in her ears.

The girl did, the higher number bleeping across the electronic screen.

Ellsbeth let out a crazed, barking laugh.

"What?" the girl said, oblivious. Ellsbeth pulled back the clay, and then asked for almond milk.

"That costs twenty-five cents extra," the barista said. The obscuration had worn off exactly as Ellsbeth had hoped, leaving only a faint pink mark on the girl's wrist that would hopefully wipe away without her ever having to wonder what had left it there.

Ellsbeth left a ten-dollar tip and walked down the street with nowhere to go, working off the giddy energy of what she had just done. The clay melted and rehardened under her nails. She kneaded at it in her palm while she walked and then stopped, panicked, in the middle of the sidewalk to shove it into her backpack, like she was disposing of evidence of a crime. Because she was.

What she had just done wasn't just wrong; it was *illegal,* and a violation of all of the most basic human principles of autonomy and decency. There *was* a part of her that knew that. And yet she had done it anyway. She had done it as soon as she was confident she understood the mechanics of the ritual. She had done it—invaded someone else's mind—without asking or needing Rawlins to double-check her work.

Ellsbeth had never thought of herself as a bad person before. An impulsive person, yes. Ambitious to a fault. But until now, she had never had the tangible evidence that she would, in fact, be willing to do bad things in order to achieve her goals. No one ever thinks they will, Ellsbeth realized, until they want something enough. The girl at the coffee shop had been fine, but as Ellsbeth walked away, she forced herself to reckon with the fact that it *could* have gone horribly wrong. She *could* have killed her, or left her brain-dead or permanently in a state of open suggestibility. She knew she should feel bad. But the truth was, she didn't.

She had accomplished something extraordinary: a functional *obscuration* ritual—and on her first try. She was euphoric with the miracle of it; everything about the day felt bright and shiny. Every store she passed was filled with delightful wares for her to browse, every restaurant and coffee shop quaint and charming, ready for her to enjoy. Ellsbeth's stride became confident and rhythmic as she walked through campus. Strangers sitting on the Main Green were so beautiful it almost made Ellsbeth want to cry from joy—there they were! Reading books! Laughing with friends! Curled up under the arms of lovers!

She had done it. It wasn't perfect, certainly—she would need to modify it for duration and strength, and she would need to figure out a way to achieve more lasting effects before it would be ready to use at the police station—but still, she had done it. The door had been locked and bolted, and she had been the one to open it a crack, enough to let an inch of light in.

She was drunk on glee, so exhilarated that she pulled out her phone to text Rawlins then and there: Very, very excited to see you tonight xxx

Three dots appeared, indicating that he was typing. And then they disappeared, with no reply.

THE RESTAURANT ELLSBETH AND RAWLINS were meeting at on Saturday was a long walk from Ellsbeth's apartment, but she was still buoyed by the morning. And so Ellsbeth trekked across campus and up the small hill, enjoying the feeling of moving her body despite the surprisingly bracing chill that came at an instant when the sun went down.

Her face was flushed when she arrived at Abyssinia, the blast of stale indoor heat and the strong smell of Ethiopian cooking hitting her at once as she walked inside. She unwound her scarf and gave the hostess Rawlins's name; she led Ellsbeth upstairs without a word.

He was already there even though Ellsbeth was five minutes early, sitting at a corner table with a cup of water in front of him. He hadn't replied to her text, and a part of her was almost surprised that he had still come. But here he was, and Ellsbeth smiled as she approached him, instinctively going for a hug. But though he rose to greet her, Ellsbeth knew in an instant that something had changed: He was stiff, maintaining a few inches of distance between their bodies during the hug and releasing her a fraction of a second sooner than felt natural.

The glowing pride at what she had accomplished, her eagerness to share it with him, was immediately replaced with shame. *Is it possible that he's reading my mind? Does he already know what I've done?* She balled her hands into fists. She had washed them a thousand times, scrubbed at the red residue left by the compounding clay, but maybe he had seen the pinkish stain on her skin. *Maybe he knows how careless I've been. Maybe he finally understands what sort of person I really am.*

Rawlins pulled out her chair for her, but he didn't make eye contact. The chair was lower to the ground than she had expected and it took Ellsbeth a moment to catch her balance. "I like that you're always on time," Ellsbeth said, trying to keep her voice light.

"One of those habits I find difficult to break."

"Me too. A symptom of perennial impatience. I hate waiting and so I never make anyone wait for me. Except, I guess, you in this case, since you got here even earlier than I did. But really, that's on you. I was also early."

She could feel herself talking too much, trying to fill in the space he was leaving, where just days before there was none. She told herself to pull back and say less. The upstairs area of the restaurant was empty, but she could make out the hum of chatter and clinking glasses downstairs. There had been music playing when she walked in, but there wasn't any up here.

"So," he said finally, "how was your week of classes?"

She had skipped the research-and-methods lecture that was required for all first-year graduate students that entire week to continue focusing on her obscuration ritual, barely eating and thinking of almost nothing else. "Well," Ellsbeth said, "to be honest, I've spent most of my time focusing on the obscuration ritual." She waited for him to say something. He didn't. "Did you get my email? I sent it to you."

Rawlins adjusted slightly in his seat. He was wearing a brown tweed blazer that was a little too warm for the aggressive heating system of the restaurant, but he didn't take it off. "I did. It was—" He paused. "—interesting."

"*Just* interesting?" Ellsbeth noticed the way Rawlins's brows pressed together slightly. He had sat up straighter, pulling farther away from her. They were still alone in the upstairs section of the restaurant, but he was acting like someone was watching them.

"It was a good start. I can tell a lot of thought went into it."

Ellsbeth wanted to laugh in his face. "You actually read it, right?"

Rawlins leaned back in his seat and closed his eyes. His shoulders slumped. "Ellsbeth," he said, and then he sighed.

"What?"

Rawlins lolled his head around and brought his attention to the napkin he was fidgeting with in his lap. He scratched his graying beard with a curled hand. "What are we doing here?"

"We're having dinner," Ellsbeth said, leaning closer into the table and trying to hold his eyes, forcing herself to smile. "We were supposed to see if I could impress you." Her flirting felt oddly off-key, as if she were reciting lines that someone else had written.

"No," Rawlins said, looking at his napkin. "I meant here. You and me."

"What do you mean?" Ellsbeth was careful to keep her voice calm and level. She felt something that might be the start of hot tears in the base of her throat and swallowed it away. The music in the restaurant was too quiet, a murmur that she could barely make out, a prickling at the back of her brain.

"I'm twice your age. I'm your adviser. There's . . . There's no future here."

Was it a speech he had prepared? Had he walked from his front door to the restaurant rehearsing the words he would say in his head? A breakup speech before they had even properly gotten together?

"Well, you're not twice my age. You're—" She did the quick addition in her head. "—twenty-one years older than me, which isn't *ideal* but isn't enough to get people really scandalized these days. And you are my adviser, but I'm a graduate student. It's not like I'm some teenage undergrad. I checked the Newlyn rules, and there's actually nothing against what we're doing, technically. I'm sure it would be *frowned upon,* but—" She stopped talking when she saw that he was still looking at the napkin in his lap. "I'm sorry. I'm not trying to talk you into dating me. I'm not that pathetic."

"Ellsbeth." He finally looked at her then. "The last thing in the world you are is pathetic. I'm just—" Just then, the server returned and asked if they were ready to order.

Ellsbeth hadn't looked at the menu, and so she deferred to Rawlins, who ordered them a gomen and a doro wot to be shared on the spongy, sour injera. If he had planned on breaking up with her this entire time, they had chosen the wrong restaurant—this was a place where they would be using their fingers to scoop up their entrées from a shared flatbread. It was only a degree less intimate than practicing writ magic together. "And a green salad," Rawlins added.

When the server had left, Rawlins cleared his throat and continued speaking. "It's kind of a miracle I haven't been fired already, given everything we've done."

"I thought being tenured meant you never had to worry about things like that."

He smiled a little at that, but he didn't show his teeth.

The heating in the restaurant had caused Ellsbeth's underarms to become sticky with sweat. She gripped the small water glass and felt the condensation cool her palm. Rawlins was still talking, had gone into professorial mode and continued his lecture on why the two of them couldn't be together.

"It's only going to lead to problems," he said. "Not just for me, but for you, too. For your reputation as a scholar. For the wonderful career I know you're going to have. It's only a matter of time before people in the department begin talking . . ."

"It's not like I've told anyone," Ellsbeth snapped. "If you were worried about that. About us. Or about . . . what we were working on."

"I wasn't," Rawlins said. "Worried, I mean. I just know how these things go."

"Okay, fine," Ellsbeth said. "Great. You're breaking up with me. I mean, not that you can even break up with me given that we're not actually together, but it's fine. I get it."

"It really is for the best," Rawlins said, pat and dismissive and self-satisfied in a way that made Ellsbeth want to slap him. She hated the sound of his nails stretching his beard, the small smack of his lips when he took a sip of water and swallowed. "If you're comfortable, I would love to continue working with you as your adviser, but I understand if—"

"—if what? I'm going to ask Professor Tran or Gallway to supervise a thesis on writ magic?"

"No, I just—"

"—No, it's fine. Yeah. I'll think about it. Maybe writ magic was a stupid idea to begin with." She took a sip of water and looked away from him and forced herself through sheer force of will not to cry.

Their food arrived, and when their knuckles accidentally touched as they ripped the injera, Rawlins apologized.

"Here's another life lesson that you probably should know by your age," Ellsbeth said. "When you go out to dinner to break up with a girl, don't do it *before* the food comes. It's right up there with 'send a message the morning after rough sex.' I should write an advice pamphlet or something for middle-aged men."

Rawlins laughed, the first genuine laugh of the evening, and she hated it. She hated that he thought she was able to make jokes because she was okay, and not because it hurt too badly to admit that she wasn't.

What had caused the sudden, seismic change in him—this new guilt because she was his student and fear they would be found out? Ellsbeth couldn't figure it out. She had been careful not to make her closeness with Rawlins obvious to the cohort, but was it possible that someone had seen the way her gaze lingered? Had someone noticed the brief electric jolt that flashed between them in class when they made eye contact?

Or maybe it was something else entirely. Ellsbeth remembered the delirious sense of helplessness when she had been bound to his bed, and the distinct moment when it became apparent to both of them that he *liked* it. Liked tying her up, controlling her. Maybe he was ashamed at the realization that he was someone who wanted to dominate a woman in bed.

Ellsbeth wished she had the right words to explain that *she liked it, too.* It was something she still had trouble articulating to herself. It felt *good* to submit, to stop *thinking and planning* and let her brain turn off, to feel herself sink into someone else's control like it was a warm bath. And not just *someone*—someone brilliant, with taut arms and a smile that still made her stomach involuntarily clench. Someone who seemed to want her with the same illogical animal passion with which she wanted him. She wanted them to become depraved together. She wanted to descend into ruin with him and then emerge with their limbs entangled, smiling at each other from across bedsheets.

But that was all over now.

"Your ritual really was extraordinary," Rawlins said after the meal as they were walking to the door. He had loosened up over the course of dinner when it became apparent that Ellsbeth was not going to cry, or scream, or throw a drink in his face. Not going to email Dean Lennox or publicly ruin his reputation or perform any of the many acts of retribution that were technically now available to her as a woman scorned. "It's a shame it's illegal to perform it. Because I think it might actually work."

"It does," Ellsbeth said before she could stop herself.

Rawlins paused, his hand still on the handle of the door, and turned back to her. "What do you mean?"

Ellsbeth scrambled. "I mean, I *think* it does. You get that sense when you write a ritual, you know? I can just tell."

Rawlins swallowed hard and pushed out into the cold night air. "Yes," he muttered. "Of course. You would never actually perform obscuration on someone."

"No," Ellsbeth said quickly. "Of course not."

Rawlins blinked, seemingly mollified. He stepped forward, seemingly to hug Ellsbeth, but then extended his hand at the final moment. She shook it awkwardly. "Well, Miss Storer. Have a lovely evening," he said. She mumbled something incoherent back at him and set off walking back to her apartment.

She missed the Rawlins who still wanted her, who cooked her dinner and licked his way down her thighs and sighed into kisses with her that made her head spin. She missed the Rawlins who would have spent that entire dinner talking through every step of the ritual she had sent him, who would have been as astonished and excited as her by what she had managed to put together. They should have spent the night discussing Poirier and debating the criminalization of rituals, making each other laugh and letting their feet touch under the table. They should have ended dinner by slipping around the side of the building and finding a shadowed door stoop to kiss against.

Instead, Ellsbeth was walking down the narrow, darkened streets alone. Rawlins had ended their relationship, and all she could think about was how badly she wished she had been able to change his mind.

RAWLINS

Rawlins had hoped that ending things with Ellsbeth would put his mind at ease. He had anticipated a persistent sense of relief, falling asleep easier every night with the need for fewer drinks, thoughts freed up from rumination to give back to his work. But in the week that followed dinner at Abyssinia, those hopes were dashed one by one as she continued to consume his thoughts. His obsession was like a rat let loose in his mind; driven from the attic, it was now loose in the walls, gnawing at the wires of his subconscious.

He felt guilty for having hurt her. No matter how much he believed that this was for her protection in the long run, he could not forget the sight of her across the table, fighting back tears while attempting to project strength. Every instinct compelled him to comfort her, but he knew trying to do so would only push her further away.

Her behavior toward him did not help. In class, Ellsbeth acted unfazed, as though the incident, and their entire relationship, had been erased from her mind. Rawlins didn't *want* her to be sad and sulky, but at least then he would know what was going on with her, rather than be left guessing at the meaning of her inscrutable expressions.

When he retrieved his mail from the faculty lounge one afternoon, he crossed paths with Gallway, who asked him with affected casualness, "Say Tad, about the Storer girl . . . I heard she's been having some trouble with her thesis and might be looking for a new adviser?"

Rawlins froze up; the question caught him off guard, and questions ricocheted through his mind. Was this rumor driven by Ellsbeth inquiring after a change? Or was it simply the result of Lennox grumbling about the lack of a précis? Part of him thought he should seize on this possibility and encourage it, to push her further out of his life; perhaps then he could get his mind back and untangle the web of complicated feelings. But some strangely possessive instinct reared its head; he could not bear the thought of any other professor being the recipient of her startlingly brilliant thoughts.

So he brushed off Gallway's question dismissively. "Oh, we'll see . . . She's just having trouble locking onto a topic, but I think we'll get there."

Gallway nodded, apparently agreeing to leave it at that.

By Thursday night, Rawlins had convinced himself that the reason Ellsbeth wouldn't leave his mind was not anything to do with his feelings, or the breakup, or the persistent sexual fantasies. It was her obscuration ritual.

He was trying to grade papers but kept clicking back over to her PDF, saved on his desktop. He had read through it a dozen times. He needed to know if it could actually *work*. And since ending things between them romantically had caused her to pull away, he would have to find out on his own.

He reviewed the list of elementals required for the ritual Ellsbeth had written; none were especially rare, but he didn't have everything in his personal collection. The smart course of action would've been to wait until he could stop by the Practicum and get what he required without logging an after-hours visit. But he was buzzing with excitement, itching to get started. So he drove down to campus, briefly parking in a fire lane with his hazards blinking while he hastily retrieved the substances he needed.

Back at home, he assembled his materials on the dining room table and again considered Ellsbeth's written ritual. If it was successful, the effect would be held latent in a clay compound, then activated upon contact with its subject; it was calculated for a ten-second duration, but Rawlins edited Ellsbeth's quantities to increase it to thirty seconds. He needed to be able to actually *use* the ritual, and while the duration was easy to scale, he could see a different problem. If the target was affected the moment the compound made contact, that might raise suspicions; it would not be terribly difficult for any onlooking strangers to connect the *touch* with the *effect.* So Rawlins added an additional step, infusing the clay compound with a quantity of elderwort to build in a ten-second delay.

Rawlins conducted the ritual in his study; the desk rolled aside easily, and a ritual circle was engraved on the floor. The mathematics were complicated, and it was nearly midnight by the time he was able to begin, but the ritual itself did not take long (though the smell of sizzling metal clung to the inside of his nostrils and his curtains). Half an hour later, he retrieved the clay compound from the center of the ritual circle. He could not be confident of success until he had a subject on whom to test the effect. But he thought he could sense a crackle of energy within.

Unfortunately, given the late hour and the fact that the shops were all closed, there was no one to test it on. Rawlins had no choice but to try to get some sleep, knowing well that it would be a battle. He was constantly aware of the clay compound in the next room—the danger it posed, as if it were a loaded gun. He quieted his mind with whiskey until he was at last able to fall asleep.

In the morning, he woke with his mouth sticky and dry, feeling hung over but buzzing with anxious energy. He brought the clay compound with him wrapped in a handkerchief, sweating as he walked around campus, trying to appear casual when he greeted students and colleagues despite carrying in his possession an arcane-influenced substance that was, if effective, extremely illegal.

Rawlins made his way across the quad toward the student union. Dense crowds were streaming in and out of the building, students talking and eating breakfast on the way to class. A gangly undergraduate in short sleeves was unlocking his bike out front. Perfect. Rawlins walked behind him, pretended to trip, and grabbed the boy's arm—pressing the clay compound into the skin of his forearm.

"Pardon me," Rawlins said. The boy gave a curt *no problem* nod and went back to unlocking his bike while Rawlins kept walking, slowing down, checking his watch, counting down the ten-second delay.

The boy was about to climb onto his bike when suddenly, he froze. He stared straight ahead, eyes glassy, expression blank.

It worked.

Rawlins was momentarily petrified by his own success—and the terror of being found out.

But he needed to test the effect. He walked briskly back over to the boy and spoke quickly. "Touch your nose." The boy complied immediately, seemingly without even questioning why he was doing so. Rawlins nearly laughed in astonishment.

Now it was time for the real test. "You should go get a sandwich," Rawlins said, pointing toward the student union. "You need a sandwich." The boy immediately seemed to agree and abandoned his bike, leaving it unlocked on the rack. He walked up the wide steps without even looking back. Rawlins watched him, glancing at his watch, as the thirty-second duration came to a close moments before the boy reached the entrance—and stopped in his tracks.

The boy glanced around, apparently confused, second-guessing the impulse that had led him up there. When he looked back with a befuddled expression, Rawlins turned away and fled toward his office, glancing over his shoulder briefly to confirm that the boy was indeed returning to his bicycle.

That told him everything he needed to know. The ritual was effective, producing the intended effect of suggestibility and compliance. But the effects did not last beyond the prescribed duration. They didn't penetrate deep enough into the mind to affect someone's decisions on any timeline beyond the immediate. And that's what Rawlins *actually* needed to do. Change someone's mind. It was possible.

Rawlins retreated to his office, reeling from his own success. He desperately wanted to tell all of this to someone. Not just *someone,* of course. The only person who could possibly understand. He wanted to bring her in and shut the door and tell her she was brilliant and unburden himself of it all. Not only what he had *done,* but how it felt. The rush of excitement, but more than that, another layer to his response—one he dimly recalled from his earliest days experimenting with arcane mechanicals in his childhood bedroom. It was the pleasure of *power.* Of opening new horizons of what might be possible, exerting his will upon the universe in exciting new ways.

But the return of that pleasure was overshadowed by another feeling: *guilt.* He recalled the boy's docile expression, the vacancy in his eyes, the confusion that had followed the expiration of the effect.

Harmless as the short-lived magic might be, Rawlins knew it was unfair and potentially traumatic to meddle with the mind and will of another like that.

It was strange to feel the guilt and exhilaration live side by side, and he wanted to share it all. He felt certain she would understand. She may have even gotten it working herself. But at dinner she had said that she would never do such a thing. Which was either *true,* in which case he couldn't tell her about his own use of the ritual, because she would think him a monster . . . or it was a lie, in which case he could *never* tell her because she was deceiving him, which meant he couldn't trust her with his secret.

Rawlins looked at his calendar. Five weeks until Max's parole hearing. The clock was counting down. He needed to act.

But he wasn't ready yet. The arcane influence he would need to enact was something more lasting and subtle than the superficial control he had exerted over the boy with the bike. Rawlins needed to build on Ellsbeth's work, take it to another level. But as he considered the complexity of her ritual . . . Rawlins didn't have a clue where to begin. He had to talk this out with her, to enlist her mind to help him solve the problem. He needed to find a way to reopen dialogue between them . . . when he had just pushed her away.

KNOWING HIS OFFICE WAS NO longer neutral ground, Rawlins instead proposed that they meet in the statuary garden behind the Hays Library. He hoped that the familiarity of a text would help defuse the tension growing between them, but her reply of a thumbs-up kept things feeling strained.

He sat at a picnic bench, attempting to grade papers so he'd look busy when she arrived. Clouds hung in the sky, and the chilly air meant that it was barely warm enough to reasonably sit outside. Rawlins sipped tea from a thermos to keep from shivering. The weather, he told himself, was entirely to blame, not any sort of nervous anticipation.

Rawlins felt uneasy. He rationalized that he shouldn't feel guilty about ending things—that still seemed like the right and responsible thing to do—but the way things had shifted cast a shadow over his feelings about the entire relationship.

When Ellsbeth walked up, bag slung over her shoulder, she wore a gray wool peacoat he'd never seen, cinched neatly at her waist. She looked fantastic. As the semester unfolded, there had been a subtle shift in her wardrobe, her posture, even the way she wore her hair, as though she was coming into her own and finding her confidence.

"Nice coat," he said as she stepped up next to the table, hoping to warm her with a compliment. "Is that new?"

Ellsbeth fingered the coat's hem. "I figured it was time I began dressing like a proper academic. Or at least not an underemployed undergrad who mostly shops at thrift stores."

He was momentarily tongue-tied, not sure if he should compliment her attractiveness or aim for more professional distance, and settled on a change of subject. "I wanted to talk about your work," he said, indicating the bench across from him; she sat, the wooden picnic table between them. "I feel like our conversation last time might have been a little . . . compromised."

"When you broke up with me?" she said dryly. "It's fine. We were never . . . What did you want to tell me about the ritual?"

"Well, even if we'll never be able to test it . . . let us suppose, hypothetically, that it *did* work," he said cautiously. "I was thinking that would open up the possibility, in theory, of a deeper level of obscuration."

"What do you mean by 'a deeper level'?" she asked.

Rawlins frowned. Her question was not coming from genuine curiosity; he had seen her when she was curious, and it was gorgeously wide-eyed and sincere. This was a ploy to make him say aloud what she was already thinking, and gave him no choice but to do so. "I mean the very thing *you* talked about when you brought up obscuration to me. Making the subject not only suggestible, but . . . changing someone's mind. Altering their beliefs. So you could affect long-term future behavior, without them ever realizing they had been manipulated."

Ellsbeth nodded thoughtfully, as though the idea had not been hers in the first place. "That's interesting. So you're asking me to go further with this research, even though it's purely theoretical, and I won't be able to include any of it in my thesis?"

"I'm encouraging you. In the direction *you* wanted to go."

"How thoughtful," she said, crossing her legs. "I'll consider it. Is that all?"

The wind picked up, rustling leaves in the garden, and they both huddled into their coats. Rawlins felt like he was running up against an impenetrable wall. "No, it's not . . . Listen. I can understand that you might feel angry with me."

"I'm not angry," she replied, her voice cold as marble.

He lowered his voice as a group of students passed nearby. "I actually . . . I wanted to tell you something, that I should've told you before, when I was . . ."

"Breaking up with me?" she filled in.

He sighed. "This isn't easy for me. Because the thing is . . . I've been in your position before."

She squinted, waiting for him to go on.

Rawlins exhaled. "When I was an undergrad, I had . . . a *thing* with a teacher. And it didn't feel like there was a power differential when it was fun and exciting. But there was. There absolutely *was.* And when it ended . . . it affected me much more than it affected her." He studied her expression, which remained pinched as she watched him closely, and he continued, emotion catching in his throat. "Ellsbeth, look at my life. Why do you think I've been alone this whole time? I don't want that for you."

Ellsbeth's expression softened. "You were in love?"

"I was," he said, conscious that this might hurt her to hear, but convinced that that pain would be best for both of them. "Very much so."

"I'm sure that was hard," Ellsbeth said, and he wished at that moment that she looked less beautiful. "But the thing is . . . I'm not in love." She said the words kindly, as though she were now trying to be careful with *his* feelings, but even so, Rawlins's stomach dropped. He stared at her as she continued, her tone matter-of-fact. "I like you, obviously. But I know that there's a clock winding down for us. I want a career as a scholar, which will almost certainly take me away from here. And no matter what else happens, I don't want the rest of the world to think I only accomplished what I did because I happened to be in a relationship with the famous Thaddeus Rawlins. There's no future here. So . . . I was never about to let myself fall in love."

"Of course," Rawlins said, blinking. "I didn't mean to presume, I just . . . wanted to be open with you."

"I appreciate it," Ellsbeth said. "But I'm not going to get my heart broken here. I just thought we could have fun. Both of us."

Rawlins's cheeks burned with embarrassment. Had he overestimated their connection when Ellsbeth was doing no such thing? Had he pushed her away unnecessarily? Part of him wanted to tell her the entire story of his own past heartbreak, to try to explain himself, but he feared that he would just appear pathetic and manipulative.

Before he could settle on how to proceed, Ellsbeth leaned forward, elbows on the picnic table, and continued, "The thing is, I'm an adult. I know what I want in bed. And I can't get it from any of the boys I've dated around here. Believe me, I've tried." His stomach twisted with a surprising twinge of jealousy. "I need someone smart. Someone I actually *respect.*" She looked up at him. "And I like older men."

Her directness disarmed him. He had ended things between them, fearing romantic entanglement could get too messy—but now that seemed like it had been an embarrassing overreaction. He floundered, swallowed hard, searching for firm ground. "Still. There's a . . . *power dynamic* here . . ." He wasn't quite certain how he was planning on finishing the sentence.

"Yeah, so?" Ellsbeth snapped back, "I shouldn't need to turn in my feminist card for saying that maybe I have a professor fantasy. I don't think that being interested in being dominated in bed means there's something wrong with me. I'm not Catholic. Actually, on second thought, the whole pain-and-punishment-submission thing *is* pretty Catholic. You don't happen to have one of those collars, do you?" The corner of Rawlins's mouth twitched. Not quite a smile, but close. Ellsbeth matched it, and the ice between them thawed slightly. Then she repeated, more forcefully this time, "I'm an *adult* . . . And I'm not looking for some fairy-tale romance."

"And what are you . . . looking for?" he asked.

"Honestly, this doesn't have to be emotional at all," she said. "It was nice to spend time with you, getting dinner and whatever, because you're smart and I like talking to you and we clearly work well together, but if that's a problem, we don't have to do that part. That's not what I need."

"I see," Rawlins said, trying to maintain what he hoped was an impassive face while shifting as his cock hardened in his pants, hoping his movement was covered by the picnic table.

"What I *need* . . . is someone who can take control," Ellsbeth said. "Who can tell me what to do. And fuck me the way I like. And I think you want that, too."

His tongue felt heavy in his mouth, his neck felt hot despite the chill in the air, and he thought, uncomfortably, of the boy with the bike, numbly compliant, which made Rawlins feel once again the *exhilaration* of that power. Then the image intertwined, strangely, with the sight of Ellsbeth on his office chair, thighs parted. A twisted marriage of two memories, creating a Gordian knot of feelings—desire and guilt and curiosity and anger and excitement—all overlapping and inextricable.

Ellsbeth leaned in, waiting for his reaction, and when it became apparent he didn't have a clue what to say, she broke the silence. "But hey, if you're not interested . . ." She shrugged and stood up, pulling her coat tight against the wind. "I'll find someone else who is."

From: Rawlins.T.M.
To: Storer.Ellsbeth
Subject: Our Conversation Yesterday

Ellsbeth,

After giving the matter some thought, I agree that it might be possible for us to enjoy our complementary proclivities without any emotional entanglement. But to make that work, I will need you to be . . . cooperative. As a scholar, you are served by your willfulness and your impatience and your pride. But those traits make me wonder if you can really let someone control you in the way you say you want.

So first I would require a demonstration of your willingness. When you come to class tomorrow, I want you to wear a top that is low-cut enough to be revealing, and a skirt that is short enough to draw attention, with nothing underneath. Given the weather, a coat or sweater is permitted, so long as it is removed when you take your seat. And since you are so proud of your punctuality, I want you to come five minutes late, and make a convincing apology to me and the entire class.

You will sit in the front row and take notes diligently. When I look at you, you will part your thighs and show me that you have cooperated fully with my instruction. Nothing underneath.

I think I have been clear, and there should be no need to write back until your demonstration of willingness is complete.

Rawlins

From: Rawlins.T.M.
To: Storer.Ellsbeth
Subject: Re: Our Conversation Yesterday

Ellsbeth,

Good girl.

I'm sure you were eager for an evaluation of your performance, and it's rare that I have a chance to give a student evaluation in such blunt terms. Sartorially, impeccable choices. I noticed that Curt was quite taken with your new look, and he did not have nearly the view that I did. Which, I must say, was exquisite.

I am impressed enough to proceed, but as your instructor, I think it's important for us to work on your patience. So I'd like you to stop by during my office hours today. No need to say a word, simply step over and take off the black leather belt I am wearing. But nothing more after that. I want you to go home, put it on your desk, and leave it there for me.

This time, we'll meet at your place. Send me your address and I'll come over. Before I arrive, take a hot bath. I want you not only clean, but relaxed. Wear a pair of white underwear and nothing else.

When I get there, have a bottle of decent red wine open to breathe on the table, with a proper glass, and my belt beside it. Leave the door open and unlocked at 8 p.m.; I will come sometime after that, but I won't say how long. Whether it's a minute or an hour, I will endeavor to make it worth the wait.

Rawlins

ELLSBETH

Ellsbeth had a routine she tended to abide by after Rawlins's lectures. The class let out at noon, and Ellsbeth would walk across the small grassy quad on the western side of campus to the student center, where she could purchase a sandwich and a self-serve cardboard cup of black coffee without needing to actually interact with another human being beyond a nod of acknowledgment to the sleepy undergraduate cashier who swiped her student ID.

She'd bring her lunch into the graduate center library, where one of the wooden study carrels carved with decades of initials and bad doodles was always free underneath the stained-glass windows. Normally, the time passed so quickly that Ellsbeth wouldn't even realize it was evening until the lamp at her desk automatically clicked on, set to a timer like the cabin of an airplane. But her thesis proposal, not due for months, was all but written, and she had already finished Rawlins's deathly boring assigned reading (*A Metaphysical Understanding of the Arcane as a Reflection of Victorian-Era Paranoia*).

And so Ellsbeth opened her computer, refreshed her email twice, went to the homepage of *The New York Times,* and counted down the minutes until Rawlins's office hours.

The hours until three o'clock were like a massive block of ice in front of her; she was forced to stare at it, bored and unmoving, until it melted. She had no motivation to accomplish anything productive until then. All that was to be done was to keep checking the clock in the corner of her laptop screen and hope that more than two minutes had passed between each glance.

Ellsbeth despised afternoons like this, lazy uninspired stretches that she spent wishing away time, the one precious recourse of existence. She scrolled through a celebrity gossip site, and then the *New England Journal of Mechanicals.* She recognized a byline: Curt Ladove. His article was rudimentary and proved a self-evident point—an explanation of a study he had done on whether the amount of smoke produced in a diagnostic ritual correlated with the accuracy of the results. Curt's conclusion: It did not. Still, just being published as a graduate student in one of the most prestigious journals in the field would no doubt give Curt a leg up when it came to applying for the all-too-few remaining tenure-track positions that existed in their field. (Ellsbeth comforted herself with the knowledge that as soon as he had his degree, Curt would almost certainly be the type to abscond from the pilled-sweater-and-warm-wine-in-plastic-cups world of academia and make six figures consulting for a pharmaceutical company or an investment bank.)

Ellsbeth refreshed her email again. It was the *waiting* that she hated, the feeling that there was a new, thrilling development in her life just around the corner but there was nothing she could do to speed its advance. No emails promising glamorous internships or buzzy fellowships appeared in her inbox. Nothing new from Rawlins. On the third refresh, there was an invitation from the College of the Arcane Arts to a wine-and-cheese mixer after a lecture from Dean Lennox on the "possibility and promise of perpetual motion" before the winter holidays.

It would take all of five minutes to walk across campus to reach Rawlins's office, but Ellsbeth left the library at two thirty, walking slowly, only to find with a shock of disappointment that she arrived at the arcane mechanicals department building at two thirty-four. She sat in the courtyard across from the statue of Gregory Hale on a freezing-cold stone bench, where she tried to read the novel she had been keeping in her backpack for weeks. In actuality, she was just staring at the pages, taking in the prose with all of the nuance and analytical ability of a security camera. At two fifty-one, she allowed herself to pack the book away and go into the building itself.

His door was closed and locked, but she knocked. There was a strange buzzing in one of her ears. She could hear him shuffling around his office, standing and walking toward the door and then finally unlocking it.

"Miss Storer," he said. "Early."

Ellsbeth didn't respond. She walked into the office behind him (grateful, too grateful that no other students were waiting for his office hours. Would they have been able to see how flushed she was? How she had to adjust herself with a squirming shimmy to keep her jeans from pressing into her? Would someone be able to know how turned on she was after just three words from Rawlins's mouth? Would he?).

Rawlins walked back toward his desk, but he didn't sit down. Ellsbeth shut the door behind her and pressed the knob on the handle to lock it. She inhaled and walked to him. Neither of them spoke. Ellsbeth could hear his breath quicken, and she smelled his cologne.

She lowered herself onto her knees and pressed her palms against his jeans, dark and stiff.

She ran her hands up his thigh, listening for his sharp inhale when she grazed the place that his cock was pressing against the denim, but she didn't let her fingers linger. She undid his belt buckle and, in a single motion, pulled it through his belt loops. It whistled against the fabric, and then it was there, in her hand. Ellsbeth rose without a word.

They stood almost face-to-face, with Rawlins leaning into her, and Ellsbeth pressing forward on her tiptoes. She leaned in, just a little, just enough to see him lean in back with his lips parting—and then she turned around and left his office. The dull, flat expanse of sluggish procrastination that had eaten the previous few hours was replaced by sharpness and adrenaline. Her brain raced, the electrical impulses firing quickly and forcefully. Her sophomore year, a boy named Jono at a house party had offered them all bumps of cocaine off his student ID. Her senior year before their dissertations were due, her roommate Roxana had pressed a trio of Adderall pills into her palm with a wink. Neither high had felt as good as this: as clear or as exhilarating. Ellsbeth wanted to sprint home, to read a book, to *write* a book. And her feet were moving faster than her brain. She walked past the grad center library, through the main quad, and the several blocks down to the wine shop on Wickenden without touching the ground. An image was burning itself into her brain: the look on Rawlins's face when she rose. He was impressed with her, and a little surprised, but more than that: It had been a look of naked desire. Despite his earlier misgivings, his half-hearted, self-righteous guilt, Ellsbeth knew at that moment without a doubt just how badly he wanted her.

WHEN ELLSBETH MADE IT BACK to her apartment, a forty-dollar bottle of wine tucked under her arm (a previously unthinkably extravagant expense, but she was buoyed by the fizzy awareness of Rawlins's belt rolled up in her backpack), she found a package leaning against her front door. It was wrapped in brown paper, not quite like a gift, but certainly a step above the industrial plain cardboard most items shipped in. Her name and address were written in neat script. There was no return address, and no stamps.

The package contained a robe. A white robe lined with acid-green piping at the collar and wrists, and made of the thickest, softest material Ellsbeth had ever felt. It was the type of robe that hung in five-star European hotels, and Ellsbeth ran her fingers across the plush fabric almost reverently. It had come with just a stationery card embossed with the initials TMR. And in the dark ink that spilled from a fountain pen, just a few lines:

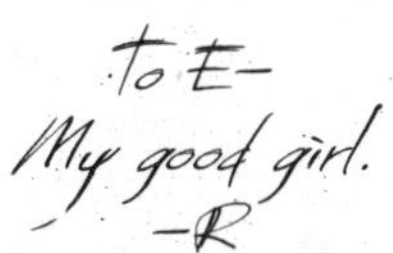

She took a bath and used the *good* bath salt, the tiny jar that smelled like honey and lavender. She had bought it years ago from a fancy department store in London, and it was still half full because she only doled it out to herself on special occasions. She wrapped herself in the robe when it was over, feeling like someone more glamorous than herself, like she shouldn't be living in an apartment with dust collecting at the corner of the moldings and thick layers of paint on all of the light switches.

It was still half an hour until Rawlins said to be ready, and who knew how long he would make her wait until he actually arrived. Ellsbeth opened the wine and poured herself a generous glass, leaving the rest of the bottle open to breathe on the kitchen table. Banestooth was having a party—she could hear boys' voices arguing whether they should put a recently delivered ice luge in the front room or the kitchen. There had been no shortage of drinking during her time as an undergraduate at St. Andrews, but fraternity culture seemed to be a distinctly American phenomenon. Of course, Banestooth Club promoted itself as a *society*, with a purposefully obscure process for invitation to entry, and Ellsbeth had no doubt that a small but fair number of congressmen and Fortune 500 CEOs emerged from its ranks, from the rarefied world of privilege and old-boys connections. Still, despite all the cloak-and-dagger and self-serious branding (those brass wolf buttons they all wore!), Ellsbeth could look out her window and see that, at the end of the day, it was a fraternity. A place for twenty-year-old boys to drink themselves silly on kegs of beer and let piles of dishes gather mold in the sink. All college students imagine themselves to be impossibly important and grown-up. Ellsbeth certainly had—she cringed remembering nights she spent sitting on the floor of a party, swirling a cup of warm rum and Coke, and talking (too loudly, probably) about Hegel or Marx or Hale.

It only takes a few years' removal from the coddling womb of being an undergraduate to realize that the world is far more indifferent to you than you would have ever believed.

Ellsbeth was still wearing the white robe when Rawlins knocked gently on the door at 8:12 p.m. He had barely made her wait at all. Maybe he was as impatient as she was.

"Come in," she said. And then she added, "Sorry, the place is a little messy," even though she had spent the last hour tidying up and it had only looked neater the day she moved in.

Rawlins was in jeans and a dark-green T-shirt that clung to his flat stomach. Ellsbeth exhaled as she took in every detail of him: the faint smell of the cologne he wore, the small curl of chest hair that escaped his collar, the stiffness in his posture.

She turned to pour him a glass of wine (her own glass, half empty after being refilled, was already sitting on the table). As she walked away from the door, she let the robe fall to the floor. She was naked, as Rawlins had requested, with nothing on but a white lace thong. “Fuck,” she heard him mutter.

She kept her shoulders back purposefully as she returned with both glasses, and handed him his. “Cheers,” she said, and took a long sip.

“My belt is—”

“On the desk, like you told me.”

“What a good student you are.” His words caused something to twist and snare inside her, and she suppressed a shiver. “Into the bedroom now, and kneel on the bed, facing away from me.”

She did.

She couldn’t see what he was doing, but she could hear it: the snap of the belt as he picked it up, the gentle clang of the buckle hitting itself, his fingers running across the leather. And then, before she was ready, she felt Rawlins take both of her wrists in his hand. In one fluid motion, he looped the belt around her wrists and pulled it tight enough to cause Ellsbeth to gasp. Rawlins did not bind her as a loose suggestion, playacting at domination. She knew that even if she struggled, she wouldn’t be able to pull her wrists apart.

“How do you feel?” Rawlins murmured, his lips so close that she could feel his breath in her ear.

“More turned on than I want to admit,” Ellsbeth said. She couldn’t see him smile, but she could sense it. And then she felt a finger trace its way beneath the lace of her panties. “Do you remember the safe word?” Ellsbeth nodded, and Rawlins’s finger continued, pressing into the wetness between her legs, then withdrawing the moment Ellsbeth tried to press back into him. “Impatient, though. Always impatient. I think a spanking is in order.”

He sat on the bed and pulled Ellsbeth stomach-down onto his lap as if she weighed nothing. She couldn’t see him; she was facing away, toward the wall, her hands still tied behind her back. At first, Rawlins gently slid his palm across her exposed ass; and then came a sudden *smack*, more painful than Ellsbeth had expected. The stinging lingered.

"Say, 'Thank you, sir,'" Rawlins said, and he spanked her again, harder.

"Thank you, sir."

Ellsbeth counted in her head, reaching fifteen and thanking him after each one. He ran his hand along her ass again, and she could feel the warmth radiating from her red and swollen skin. She imagined the outline of his fingers leaving marks.

It felt like swimming in the ocean, that moment you go out far enough that your toes no longer touch the sand, and you float, taken by the current, just working hard enough to keep your head above water. That was what it was like for Ellsbeth to relax into Rawlins's orders. To obey him. But the ocean was unfeeling and indifferent: Rawlins wanted *her* specifically. She was on his lap, her ass in the air and her hands tied behind her back, and knowing how much he wanted her, she felt more powerful than she had ever felt in her life.

"You've had your punishment," Rawlins said. "But by the looks of it, I think you might have enjoyed it." Ellsbeth had the presence of mind not to respond.

He undid the belt from her wrists. "Thank you, sir," she said, and smiled back at him.

"Oh, no," he said, "Don't thank me yet. The binding is going to stay on. I just wanted to make sure you could get in the right position. Kneel on the bed. Facing away from me."

She obeyed, and felt the belt cinch itself around her wrists again. And then a shove forward from which she couldn't catch herself, and she landed with her cheek down on her duvet. Behind her, she sensed Rawlins pull off his T-shirt and unbutton his jeans. The foil of a condom ripping.

"Tell me what you want, Ellsbeth," he said.

"I want you to fuck me."

"I just spanked your ass raw and tied your hands behind your back. You want me to fuck you?"

"Yes. God. Please. More than anything."

He teased her then, the tip of his cock barely touching her. And then all at once he was inside of her and the rest of the world disappeared. There was just the sensation of him filling her up completely, the lingering stinging of her ass, and the feeling of him being close to her. She pressed in against him. She wanted more. Deeper. She wanted it to hurt. Rawlins seemed to read her mind; he reached out with one hand and twisted it into her hair, pulling just enough to make Ellsbeth catch her breath. She could feel the orgasm rising in her, but before she could come, he pulled his cock out and flipped her over, her back pressing into the bedspread. She looked up at him, hallowed by the faint glow of a streetlight from outside the window.

"You're so impossibly fucking beautiful," he said, drinking her with his eyes. And then he was inside her again, and now that he was close she could see his face, see his thick hair falling onto his forehead, the tendons in his forearms straining while his hands squeezed their way down her body. The crest was rising in her again.

"I'm going to come," she said. "I'm going to—"

"Ask permission."

"Please, sir, let me come."

"Beg."

"Please. Please. *Please.*"

He waited just a single, torturous breath before he replied. "Good girl. Come for me."

She did, and at that same moment Rawlins shut his eyes and shuddered and came, too.

Ellsbeth could see the young man in his face then, the boy he must have been at twenty, an undergraduate, already tall but not yet filled out. Cocky and too sure of his own brilliance and inevitable success. Fucking a teacher, too.

Rawlins collapsed onto the bed beside her. "Here, let me." He undid the belt, and rubbed at the red marks it had left in Ellsbeth's wrists. "You have distinctly perfect wrists," Rawlins said, kissing each one. "I didn't know until this very moment that someone could have *wrists* that turn me on."

Ellsbeth just lolled her head over and breathed in the smell of him. She wanted to bottle this moment, the perfect pain and pleasure of it, the way she had given Rawlins complete control and had only wanted him to go further.

She kissed him deeply, and he kissed her back, and she wasn't sure if that was breaking the deal they had made to avoid feelings, but she couldn't stop herself. She wanted to *disappear* into him.

It was another half an hour lying beside each other in bed before they were both stable enough on their feet to get dressed and return to the living room to finish their barely sipped glasses of wine. It felt surreal and a little absurd to see Rawlins in her tiny apartment, in an expensive shirt half buttoned, perched on the couch she had picked up used for fifty dollars.

"I understand what people say about arcane mechanicals being a useless Ivory Tower discipline," Ellsbeth said, tucking her legs beneath her on the couch. "Because you could have spent forty minutes preparing to bind me with writ magic, when a belt saved us both a lot of time and trouble."

"Precious metals get expensive."

"And it's so hard to get the smell of burning out of upholstery. But alas. The pursuit of scholarship is about ideas, and not practicality."

"Just don't mention that to any fellowship committees," Rawlins said. "Try: *A new study that will change the face of the world as we know it.* Although—" He took a sip of his wine. "—ironically, your obscuration ritual *could* actually change the world. It was brilliant. The most innovative ritual I've read in fifteen years, and it came from a graduate student. And no one will ever be able to see it."

"But I impressed you," Ellsbeth said.

"You did impress me. But that shouldn't be enough."

Ellsbeth put her wineglass down. "Oh? A ritual for a form of arcane mechanicals that until this point had existed as an urban legend? In *less than a semester*? That's not enough?"

Rawlins sipped deeply from his wine, and then held it up to the light, watching the blood-red legs of the liquid slide down the glass. "Well, *promising* as your ritual is, its effect is very limited in practice. It would work only as long as the compounding clay is actually touching the target. After that . . ."

Ellsbeth answered fast. "You could put the ritual on a delay. Thirty seconds. Adding cadmium. Although—" She shifted her weight and moved her legs under her. "Then there's another problem. The ritual itself lasts so long. If you suggest something to someone under obscuration, they'll *do* it, but only until the ritual wears off. How do you change someone's mind over a longer period of time? So that you can tell someone to do something, and they'll still feel the impulse to do it over the next few days or weeks?" Her mind felt as fizzy as a shaken can of sparkling seltzer. She tried to visualize the ritual in her head, hoping the final piece would appear behind her closed eyes.

"Hmmm," Rawlins said. "It's an interesting problem. Lingering mental effects. Not that it even matters, of course. Because this is all academic."

And then the answer came to her. Simple as if she had been squinting through a dirty window, and she finally realized she could open it.

"Time dilation," she said.

Rawlins didn't respond. He kept his eyes closed for so long that Ellsbeth worried for a moment that he had fallen asleep. "How would slowing down time—"

"Not for the person, for the ritual itself," Ellsbeth said quickly. "Give the magic a . . . slow release. Like a cold medicine pill."

Rawlins blinked. "It's compounding a ritual onto another ritual, using magic *on* magic."

"Very meta," Ellsbeth said. "I don't know how you'd actually go about *doing* it, but—"

Rawlins sat forward, getting excited. "Do you have a pencil?" he asked.

Ellsbeth brought back a pen and a pad of paper, and Rawlins began writing quickly. "It could work," he said. "And in theory, the effects could linger for . . . weeks, at least, if you set the metrics slow enough. Obviously, the mathematics would be incredibly complicated—"

Ellsbeth was reading over his shoulder while he wrote.

"—but it would definitely be possible."

Rawlins scribbled for ten minutes straight, Ellsbeth watching him in silence, and when he finished, he collapsed back onto the couch. Ellsbeth continued staring at what he had written.

"I feel like I need a cigarette," Rawlins said. "I haven't thought about mechanicals this way since *I* was a grad student."

"You need a cigarette after *that*?"

"You're right. I deserve two cigarettes." He pulled her in by the waist and kissed her. "You're very, very pretty. Did you know that?"

"I think you're biased because this robe hanging open gives you a very good view of my tits."

"I'm an arcane mechanist. Very empirical. Absolutely no bias. And I say, with all of the authority of my *numerous* academic accomplishments: You're stunning."

Ellsbeth ran her hand through his hair and pressed her face into his neck. "I like you," she said, hoping that his skin would swallow her words before he could hear them. He wrapped an arm around her, and she got a fresh smell of his cologne. She burrowed deeper inside the crook of his elbow. She still wasn't sure if he had heard her or not.

He finally got dressed to leave at one in the morning. "I would invite you to stay the night," Ellsbeth said, "But I'm afraid that would cross the line when it came to the this-is-just-sex thing."

Rawlins straightened the sleeve of his T-shirt where the hem had folded up. "You have a seminar at nine in the morning. I consider it a good deed to leave now and let you get all of the sleep you can manage. Because if I stayed, you would be getting very, very little sleep." He kissed her again, on the lips, and then his eyes caught the paper he'd written his new formula on. "I should take that. Don't want to leave any evidence lying around that could get you hauled in front of an academic tribunal. Or the police." He stuffed the paper into his pocket.

"God knows the legal system would love another juicy case of arcane mechanicals gone bad—corruption and disgrace among the God-hating liberal academic elite who twist nature to their will. It's been, what, ten years since the tabloids got to sink their teeth into the Maxwell Keene case?"

"Seven years," Rawlins said stiffly. "Since the trial."

"Oh," Ellsbeth said. "Sure, yeah."

His demeanor changed; his posture straightened, and he pulled open the door to let himself out. "Thank you for a lovely and inspiring evening."

"Good night," Ellsbeth said.

As soon as the door shut, Ellsbeth returned to the pad of paper on the table and replicated what Rawlins had written. It didn't matter that he had taken his work with him—she had memorized it in an instant.

RAWLINS

When Rawlins got home, he put the note he had made at Ellsbeth's apartment on the corner of his desk. It was not enough to completely unlock the ritual he would need to complete, but it was enough to give him hope, to convince him that what he had in mind was *possible.*

So in the morning, he called the office of Alan Greywall, the chair of the parole board who would decide Max's fate, and left a message. His call was returned just as he was about to launch into his lecture for his undergraduate course, and he signaled to one of his TAs to vamp for a couple minutes while he answered his phone in the hallway.

It was not Greywall himself, but an assistant on the phone. Rawlins got quickly to the point. "I'd like to set up a meeting with Mr. Greywall, regarding the case of Maxwell Keene. Sometime before his parole hearing next month."

"What for?" she asked sharply.

"It's a high-profile case," Rawlins said. "And as a prominent scholar in the field of arcane mechanicals, I think my perspective on clemency should be heard."

"Mr. Greywall is very busy," said the clipped voice on the other end of the phone. "And he doesn't take meetings regarding parole hearings. If you're interested in writing an amicus letter, he will be happy to consider your perspective."

Rawlins had been prepared for this, and had a strategy—but his heart started pounding as he launched into the lie. "I understand the standard procedure, but here's what I'd like you to communicate to Mr. Greywall. I've been talking with a few newspaper editors about publishing a larger editorial piece. To articulate my thoughts on this case, and how Mr. Greywall has historically handled parole for such offenders."

There was a pause, silence on the other end of the phone.

Rawlins hated lying, not so much for the ethical quandary as for the way it made him nervous; he was used to speaking the truth with ease, but now he could feel himself breaking out in a sweat, and fought to keep his tone level. "If Mr. Greywall will hear me out in person, I'd appreciate it. And I promise, I'll refrain from making my case more publicly."

There was another beat before the assistant replied coldly: "I will pass that along."

All day, Rawlins kept refreshing his email, hoping for a response, distracted in his office and unable to focus on any of his work. But before the email came, Lennox arrived unannounced at his door. She didn't knock, just strode into his office with her arms folded over her chest, making no effort to hide her displeasure. "I just got off the phone with Max's lawyer, who tells me that you're trying to get a meeting, in person, with Greywall. After *threatening* him?"

"It wasn't a threat," Rawlins said. "I gave him an option."

Lennox stared at him with a mix of anger and bewilderment. "I don't understand what you're doing. You know this won't help."

"I can be very persuasive," he said casually. "Some consider me charming. A minor celebrity, even."

He had expected Lennox to laugh. She did not. "Sure. Within the narrow confines of an academic world that Greywall utterly deplores."

"All the more reason to change his mind. And what is there to lose at this point?"

"How about the reputation of our field?" Lennox shot back. "Your job? The college's funding? The lawyer asked me to get you to back off."

"Tell her she should thank me for doing her job," Rawlins said. Then he softened. "Just trust me on this, Maggie. I really think it could work."

Lennox shook her head, irritated, and left his office without closing the door.

The email from Greywall's office came an hour later. Terse as he expected, but delivering the news that he had secured a thirty-minute meeting with Greywall, three weeks from now.

Three weeks, then. To take a rudimentary obscuration ritual to the next level. To achieve a deeper effect than, as far as he knew, had ever been attempted. To create a ritual that could truly change someone's mind.

It was possible. It would have to be.

OVER THE FOLLOWING WEEKS, THE problem of the obscuration ritual took up more and more of Rawlins's mental bandwidth. He attended to his own work in the most cursory manner. His lesson planning was rote; his grading was lax. He gave up making progress on the book that was due, informing his editor it would have to wait until next semester.

But his mind was continually pulled from the singular focus of the work by Ellsbeth. He had hoped that having his carnal appetites sated would liberate his thinking, that the moratorium on emotional attachment would compartmentalize the whole thing, but it continued to expand its footprint on his mind. And while her mature, matter-of-fact attitude had mostly placated his guilt about having a relationship with his student, he now wondered if he should feel guilty about *using* her—both sexually and intellectually.

He told himself to enjoy this more and think about it less. Since he met Ellsbeth, their relationship had been fraught with second-guessing, contemplating consequences, carefully making sure not to hurt her or create a mess of drama. Now she had given him permission to ignore the problem of emotional entanglement, so he could finally indulge his desire in the most simple, selfish way possible. He was like the driver of a sports car who had finally left behind the stop-and-go of city traffic and opened up onto the highway. Every debased thought and impulse he had only seemed to please her more—which prompted him to try to come up with more perverse pleasures (and ways of inflicting pain). His mind drifted in faculty meetings and while undergrads droned on during their class presentations. His cock hardened in the library, as though he were seventeen years old again and the thought of sex was omnipresent.

The difference was that it wasn't just a *thought* now. A text or an email could lead to Ellsbeth half naked on the floor of his office an hour later. Then she'd be tugging up her jeans and heading off to class, leaving him at his desk, pleasantly confused by his own good fortune.

It was perfect. It was the thing he'd wanted his whole adult life—sexual gratification, without the challenges and vulnerabilities of a relationship. And Ellsbeth was fully on board with this arrangement; it had been her idea in the first place, and he knew that her pride, her fierce independence, and her relentless ambition all meant that she would protect their secret.

So why did he still feel a twinge of dissatisfaction?

He tried to chalk up his misgivings to something fundamentally wrong with him, a perpetual inability to feel *content,* and he resolved to enjoy what was, on its face, an unimprovable situation.

TWO DAYS BEFORE HIS MEETING with Greywall, Rawlins sat in his study in the waning light of late afternoon, rereading the ritual he had been agonizing over for weeks.

He felt stuck. The ritual had grown shockingly complex, a delicate balance of variables. There was the primary effect, which would render the subject compliant and susceptible, but it now needed to be modified with both a delay mechanism and, even more difficult, a time dilation. The mathematics required multivariable calculus to determine the interplay of effects, and it wasn't apparent to him in what *order* the different components of the ritual should be conducted. The natural solution would be to *test* the ritual, to put it into practice, study the effects, and revise if necessary. But something this dangerous, this wildly illegal, could not be field-tested. He had to get it perfect on the basis of theory alone.

On his own, he knew he could only do so much. Every scholar had blind spots; Rawlins needed someone to bounce his ideas off, someone who could offer a fresh perspective, and there was only one person he could possibly go to. But he needed to maintain the façade that this was entirely an academic exercise, so he could not reasonably summon her over for that purpose alone. It needed to feel more casual, an afterthought.

Fortunately, his mind had no difficulty cooking up a reason to invite her over. He sent her a message instructing her to stop by a sex shop after class and purchase a new vibrator.

An hour later, Ellsbeth was naked and tied to a chair in his study. He took his time teasing her with the toy. They had been together enough that he knew her cues well—the way she gasped when he surprised her, bit her lip impatiently when he backed off, and shivered when she got close. He felt like a conductor and her body was his orchestra; the music of her pleasure swelled at his command when he slid the pulsating toy up her thigh and pressed it against her clit, only to then move it off, creating one mini-crescendo and decrescendo after another. She writhed and whimpered and groaned, loving and infuriated by his teasing in equal measure—until at last he pulled her forward to the edge of the chair and entered her so that he could feel her climax and join her in the release they both needed.

Afterward, he untied the ropes, letting his fingers linger on the red lines they had left on her wrists and thighs as she squirmed against them. "I like it," she said as he kissed the marks.

"Why don't you stay for dinner?" he asked offhandedly. "I'm making risotto with mushrooms and peas, and there will be plenty to share."

"Oh, thanks, but I should get home," Ellsbeth said, reaching for her underwear. "I've got the reading you assigned. And a paper due for Sapersky's seminar."

Rawlins glanced at his phone. It was only four o'clock. "Well, you could get to work here while I start cooking," he said, gesturing toward the desk. "We'll eat, talk about what we're working on . . ."

"I appreciate that, but I think here I might be a bit distracted," she told him, standing up and brushing past him.

"I'm sure we could offset the distraction," he said, intercepting her with a hand on her waist. "If you had a brilliant professor helping you with your work, I bet it would go much faster."

"You don't make it easy, but I really should go." She smiled, but he sensed a tightness around her eyes. What had felt like flirtation a second ago suddenly seemed to him like wheedling. Ellsbeth had been letting him down nicely.

Part of him wanted to adopt a tone of authoritative command, to tell her to stay in the confidently direct way he knew that she enjoyed. But to do so now felt ugly and even desperate, and he worried it would ruin the playful dynamic.

Another part of him wanted to tell her the truth: That he needed her help. That he was actually planning to use obscuration, and he needed it to work. But that was too risky. It raised too many questions he didn't want to answer. And he worried that needing her would somehow crack the illusion of the roles they had agreed to take on.

So instead he retreated, stepping away from her and trying to keep his voice light. "Yes, you should get back home, before I come up with another punishment." He left the room while Ellsbeth put her clothes back on, busying himself in the kitchen; when she emerged, they said a goodbye that was friendly but perfunctory.

Ellsbeth did not exactly *slam* the door behind her, but pulled it shut with a thunderous finality. The sound echoed through the house, making Rawlins more acutely aware of the size—and emptiness—of his home. He glanced toward the front room as though he might catch her departing and see the expression on her face—anger? Irritation? Sadness?—but she was gone and there was nothing to see but the sculpture in the foyer, wobbling on its pedestal.

In Ellsbeth's absence, the house felt oddly like a museum without visitors; he could see the rows of books in his study, the ceremonial masks hung in the dining room. All those items he had filled the house with, to imbue it with the joy of his travels and his learning, now seemed cold and dead.

He grabbed his phone to put on music and fill the silence while he cooked, and could not help but wonder what Ellsbeth listened to. Did she like jazz? He imagined trying to explain to her the spontaneous complexities of Charlie Parker, the history of bebop that informed mid-century jazz experimentation. He wanted to let her choose what would come next, to feign horror at whatever song she might select.

He craved the sort of teasing, bantering debate he knew they could have. About music. About anything.

Those conversations were for couples. For the interpersonal dance of discovering each other's minds and tastes and habits. And that was not what they had agreed to.

He tried to appreciate the fact that he could listen to whatever he damn well pleased. But as he scrolled through playlists, nothing struck his fancy. No longer in the mood to cook, he ordered takeout that he would eat alone while reviewing the ritual.

Tonight was the night. He had not gotten to ask for Ellsbeth's input after all, but he would have to make do without it. The most difficult, high-stakes ritual of his life, and he was on his own.

ELLSBETH

On the walk over to the police station, Ellsbeth had worried about how she was going to find an excuse to touch the compounding clay to Officer Marcos's skin. But as soon as she entered the dingy back office—water-stained on the ceiling and stuffed wall-to-wall with filing cabinets—he extended his hand in greeting. A polite habit, even when faced with someone like Ellsbeth who had been nothing but a hassle for him. She was an item on his to-deal-with list that kept reappearing, the specter that wouldn't go away.

Officer Marcos seemingly hadn't noticed the small pat of red compounding clay that she had stuck on the inside of her palm. If Ellsbeth had prepared the ritual correctly, the time dilation would obviously mean a slight delay in how long it would take for the obscuration to take effect.

And so she waited.

"Miss Storer," he said, pushing the sleeves up on his rumpled button-down shirt. There was uneven stubble on his cheeks. He didn't offer her coffee or a seat. He was meeting with her only because she had promised the receptionist that this would be the last time she came to the precinct and asked about her sister's death. If everything went according to plan, it would be.

Officer Marcos sighed and sucked at his teeth when Ellsbeth didn't begin speaking. "How can I help you?" he asked finally, with no question in his voice. Ellsbeth's vision narrowed, blinking white at the edges. This had to work. It *had* to work. Otherwise, what was all of it for?

"Um," she said. How long could she stall for? How long could she keep Officer Marcos in this room? "I still have some questions about my sister's death. Roberta Storer."

"I am aware," Marcos said, pinching the bridge of his nose, "that you think there are unanswered questions." He sniffed, as if he were getting a cold. "I have shared all of the information on the case available to the public. If you continue to harass officers—"

Ellsbeth would never find out the consequences he was promising in his threat. At that moment, his eyes clouded gray and filmy, and the muscles in his face relaxed.

"Officer Marcos," she said with as much confidence as she could muster, "I want every file available on Roberta Storer. Every *classified* file." Ellsbeth pulled a Post-it note from the table and a pen from her purse, and wrote her email address in clear and careful block letters. "Email the scanned files here. Do you understand me?"

"Yes." His voice sounded far away.

Ellsbeth's heart was still pounding. "Are there classified files? Is there more to the case than you've shown me?"

"Yes."

Ellsbeth's skin tingled and vibrated. It felt like she was watching the proceedings from somewhere above her body.

She had been right.

It wasn't grief, or insanity, or self-importance. *She was right.*

"Okay," Ellsbeth said. "Okay, okay. Once you send the files to me, delete the record of the sent email, and you'll forget this entire interaction. If I ever ask you anything else about Roberta Storer, or this case, you'll be completely honest with me."

Officer Marcos gave a slack nod, and a strange feeling of disquiet settled in Ellsbeth's stomach. There was something ghoulish about seeing someone like this, almost real but slightly hollowed. Like Officer Marcos had become a wax figure of himself.

"Thank you," Ellsbeth said. He didn't reply.

She let herself out of the back room. As soon as she left the station, she started walking up the block, taking long, fast strides, as if the distance would dislodge the memory of Officer Marcos's blank face from her memory. It would be worth it, she told herself, if it would lead her to the truth about Bertie's death. It was all worth it. But as she felt the moisture from the snow on the grass creep up through the thin soles of her shoes, Ellsbeth knew that all sorts of people told themselves things like that all the time.

THE FIRST PAGE OF THE file was so heavily redacted that bile rose into Ellsbeth's throat. What if this was what it all was for? A blurry scan of a page filled with black ink. But the file Marcos had sent was thirty-eight pages, all stamped CONFIDENTIAL, and Ellsbeth exhaled when she scrolled through quickly, feeling her eyes catch on specific phrases—"moved after death," "blunt force trauma," "blood loss."

And then there were the photos. Ellsbeth turned away from the laptop when she realized that pictures of the bathroom where Bertie's body was found were included in the file.

Thankfully they were grainy from the scan, and in black and white, but Ellsbeth still retched, feeling the saliva in her mouth go thin and sour. She vomited twice into the small wastebasket underneath her desk, a yellow bile the texture of wallpaper paste. Her eyes watered from the force of it, and then the tears started, hot and stinging. They were messy, cruel, heaving sobs, the sort that started deep in her chest, like each retch was trying to exorcise something permanently lodged inside her. It became hard to breathe.

Before she knew what she was doing, her fingers were fumbling for her cellphone, and she scrolled numbly until she found Rawlins's number. She didn't know what she would say when he picked up—maybe she just wanted someone to hear that she was crying, someone to know that she felt alone and scared even if she didn't have the words to tell them.

The phone rang and then went to voicemail.

Ellsbeth hung up without leaving a message. She somehow felt calmer, as if even making an overture toward the outside world had tethered her back to reality, anchored her free-floating grief and hopelessness. She forced herself to drink a glass of room-temperature water from the sink before she returned to her laptop screen.

Bertie was discovered in the bathroom of her freshman dormitory at 6:21 a.m., though the police report indicated that she died several hours earlier, likely around 2 a.m. The immediate cause of death was blood loss, though there were lacerations and evidence of blunt force trauma on her body.

The police officers had interviewed several students in Bertie's dormitory. Her roommate was a pre-med student who also rowed crew—she left the room before dawn and was often studying late. She just said that her roommate had seemed like a really nice person. "She didn't seem depressed or anything, but I guess I didn't really know her that well, to be honest." A girl across the hall told the police officer that Bertie had recently begun talking about a boyfriend. The officer asked if the boyfriend treated her badly, or if he had broken up with her. "No," the girl replied in the transcript. "She said things were going really well. I remember that. It was only a few weeks or so, but she was excited about him. I think he was a senior. Chem major, I think. Banestooth, maybe."

Ellsbeth's heart sank. Bertie hadn't told her that she had been seeing a boy.

When Ellsbeth played back the memories she had of her and Bertie together, they were moments of closeness, of laughter and a natural ease they had every time they were in the same vicinity no matter how much time had passed. It took reading those words on a page, from a girl who lived across the hall from Bertie for a semester whose name Ellsbeth had never heard, for the sinking shame to metastasize inside her body. Maybe she and Bertie had not been as close as she told herself they were. They were four years apart in age; Ellsbeth had chosen to get her undergraduate degree a seven-hour plane ride away. Ellsbeth hadn't texted as often as she could have. She checked in occasionally, but it hadn't been enough. There were things that Bertie chose not to share with her, and all Ellsbeth longed for in that moment was one more chance with her little sister, an opportunity to hold her tight to her chest, to be the one who made phone calls, who sent random text messages in the middle of the day, who asked how things were and had the patience to always listen to the answer. If Ellsbeth had one more chance, she would be the big sister that Bertie deserved. But there were no more chances. The finality of Bertie's death crushed her like an ocean's worth of water pressing down onto her body. It suffocated her in regret.

Ellsbeth looked at the photographs again. They were no worse than the nightmares. Than the memories. They were exactly what she had seen in the scrying ritual. Even the fuzziness of the scanned images reminded her of the way the surface of the water in the ritual had rippled the scene. She wasn't crazy. She had been right.

Bertie was bloodied and beaten.

There were cuts up both of her arms, but there were also three deep parallel cuts across her chest, near her clavicle.

"Coroner report: suicide. At the request of the university, no autopsy was performed."

No autopsy was performed.

Ellsbeth read those words over and over, until they dissolved into their individual syllables and stopped making sense. Her body had injuries and lacerations! No autopsy was performed. Did the university have that much power? To stymie a police investigation, brush something grotesque under the rug with the most palatable explanation and hope that most people wouldn't look too closely?

Apparently, it did.

Ellsbeth studied the photographs for so long that she stopped registering the subject as a person, as a bathtub, as a room. It became shapes, geometry. She traced the blood splatter as if she were capable of deciphering what that might mean. There was clothing on the bathroom floor, sopping wet. A button or a pin had popped off Bertie's blouse, and Ellsbeth stared at it. It was brass, carved with some sort of animal. Ellsbeth had never seen Bertie wear it. Yet another reminder that her little sister might have become a stranger to her.

Rawlins had texted her. Is everything okay? Suddenly, Ellsbeth's entire body was heavy. The thought of responding to him felt daunting and impossible. She saw Rawlins's call, and watched it go straight to voicemail. Ellsbeth put her phone into DO NOT DISTURB mode and crawled underneath her duvet without taking her clothes off.

She had been right. Bertie's death had been boxed up and tidied to keep the university from facing the scandal of possible murder. A headache hammered behind her eyes. She had the file, but what could she do with that? She wasn't some Sherlock Holmes who could figure anything out from a few black-and-white photographs on a computer screen.

Ellsbeth considered sending the file to her parents, *proving* that Bertie's death *had* been suspicious, that she had been right, but what would that do? Rip open wounds that her mother and father had spent months trying to heal? Bertie was still dead, and nothing would change that. Even the darkest corners of arcane mechanicals theory hadn't figured out how to bring someone back from the dead.

Sleep came fitfully. Ellsbeth's dreams echoed with drawers left slightly open, staircases with missing steps, the sense that there was something that she couldn't quite find, and that she would never find.

When Ellsbeth woke, her mouth was dry and thick with white scum. Rawlins had called twice in the night, and texted once more, but Ellsbeth plugged in her phone without responding.

There was too much to explain. Her relationship with Rawlins was supposed to be fun and casual. An escape from the real world. She didn't have it in her this morning to be the girl he expected her to be—shiny and independent, vivacious. She would become that girl again eventually, and then she would be able to see Rawlins.

The shower was a hissing animal. Phantom blood appeared on the linoleum with every blink. Ellsbeth left the mirror foggy. She and Bertie had always looked alike from certain angles, and when Ellsbeth looked at her distorted reflection, she imagined her sister staring back at her. Bertie was a ghost, and Ellsbeth stood there, watching her in the mirror until the condensation rolled down the glass and she was looking back at her own face, blotchy and gray.

RAWLINS

Rawlins gave himself two hours for the drive to Greywall's office in Montpelier, but it took less than an hour and a half. The roads had been cleared, and this early in the season there was no accumulation of ice. Gray clouds hung low in every direction, casting diffuse light over the entire landscape, which had a flattening effect; one could not have guessed the time with any degree of accuracy.

As Rawlins parked a few blocks from the low concrete building, he checked his phone again, disappointed to see that Ellsbeth still had not responded. He bristled with irritation; she had called *him* in the first place, and left no message or text—and now, despite numerous attempts to call her back, she was ignoring him. He vacillated between concern for her well-being and wondering if this was merely a game she was playing, demonstrating that in their new arrangement she was not beholden to him. He decided not to press the issue.

The state parole board's offices were among a collection of government buildings in the city center. Rawlins crossed an open mall, the lawn wet with snowmelt. He was as conscious of the clay compound in his pocket as though it were a loaded gun. When he entered the justice administration building and passed through the metal detector, he was halfway afraid it would trigger an alarm and he'd be surrounded by guards with guns drawn. But the security guard merely gave him a friendly nod and handed over the tray with his keys.

The building was bureaucratic to its bones—a relic of the 1960s, with green and white tile, fluorescent lighting, and radiators that rattled in the hallways. An ancient elevator delivered Rawlins to the fourth floor, where he found the door stenciled ALAN GREYWALL, DIRECTOR OF THE STATE PAROLE BOARD.

Rawlins was twenty minutes early for their meeting but nonetheless checked in with the receptionist, who informed him that Greywall was still at lunch and would see Rawlins as soon as he was back. The waiting area was tiny, and his knees nearly touched the receptionist's desk; the room felt unreasonably stuffy, the heat cranked up and stifling in the cramped space. Rawlins took off his jacket, feeling himself starting to perspire.

Rawlins's plan was simple: to apply the compound when he shook the man's hand. That meant he needed to be ready to deliver it when they met. So he kept slipping a hand into his coat pocket, making sure he could readily palm it. But he was afraid to keep it against his skin, worried that his sweat might adulterate the mixture.

At quarter past two, the door Rawlins had come in through opened, and Greywall appeared—an aggressively bald man in his sixties with a thin tie. He carried his suit coat in one hand, while the other pressed his cellphone to his ear; he was mid-conversation, speaking with loud confidence. "Yes, and we won't review them until next quarter, so there's no use in posting their appeals now . . ."

Greywall went to the receptionist's desk, continuing his conversation, as she handed him two notes on Post-its, which he read, nodding, and then headed through the door into his office.

Rawlins felt certain he hadn't even been noticed, but Greywall paused at the threshold, still on the phone, and beckoned him to follow.

Rawlins did, stepping into the office. It was carpeted and poorly lit; legal texts overflowed the bookshelves, and Greywall's desk was piled with stacks of mail and manila case folders. He sat behind it and gestured for Rawlins to take a seat in one of two identical chairs, holding up a finger to indicate *just a second.* Rawlins sat, waiting as Greywall wrapped up his call—"Yes, yes, I'll talk to you then . . ."—and then looked at Rawlins with a theatrical exhale. "I appreciate your patience. One of those days. Now, you are . . ." He scanned the indecipherable assortment of notes on the desk in front of him, apparently finding the one he was looking for. ". . . Right. The author guy. Wanting to talk about the Keene case."

He looked at Rawlins and gave a subtle head-nod, the least-inviting invitation to state his business imaginable, making little effort to hide his *let's get this over with* attitude.

Rawlins swallowed hard, gripped with panic. He had not gotten the handshake he needed.

Without it, this entire visit was a waste of time. He had to force it, one way or another. So he stood up awkwardly. "That's right, I'm Thaddeus Rawlins. Pleased to meet you."

He extended his right hand across the desk. The clay compound was pressed into his palm, angled down so that Greywall would not see it—but that meant it was sticking to Rawlins's perspiration-wet skin, and he worried it would fall off at any moment.

Greywall stared at Rawlins's hand, clearly conscious of the strained effort at an introduction. But eventually he reached out and took it, shaking in return. Rawlins made sure to push his palm into the other man's, needing to be confident that the clay compound made contact, but at the same time fearful at any moment that it would be noticed by Greywall.

He pulled away and sat back down. He wasn't yet sure if it had worked, since he had built a one-minute delay into the effect; until that minute passed, he was merely vamping, since nothing he said would make much of an impact. "Max was a student of mine," Rawlins said. "Prior to his . . . incident."

"Oh, yes, I know," Greywall said. "And if it was up to me, you would've been tried, too."

Not a promising start to the conversation. Nonetheless, Rawlins pressed on. "I certainly acknowledge my own part in the tragedy that took place. And it's undeniable that a crime was committed. But it was a crime of negligence, not ill intent."

"Look. The study of arcane mechanicals is just inherently dangerous to the community," Greywall replied. "It's like teaching a class on how to build nuclear weapons, and hoping no one actually does."

"I think the comparison is apt, but I would reframe it with a meaningful distinction," Rawlins replied. "It's more akin to teaching physics. There's the potential that certain particulars of the study could give students tools to make powerful weapons—but we protect that *specific* knowledge, and we restrict the availability of materials that would make it possible. By all means, we should do the same for arcane mechanicals. But to stop teaching physics entirely would cut off hundreds of vital applications of that knowledge. And it would vastly limit our understanding of the world and how it works."

Greywall's face remained impassive. He ran a hand across his shiny scalp. "Physics didn't kill anyone at Newlyn, as far as I know."

Rawlins glanced at his watch. More than a minute had passed . . . yet Greywall showed no sign of the ritual's effect taking hold. *Shit.*

Rawlins continued the conversation, stalling for time and attempting to lay out his arguments in a logical manner. But he was nervous and overly attentive to Greywall's disposition, pausing every few seconds to try to read any shift that might indicate the obscuration was taking hold. Greywall was irritated by these pauses, feeling that his time was being wasted.

Fifteen minutes passed, and it became apparent to Rawlins that he had failed. He considered trying again—some desperate move would be required to touch the man's skin. But no . . . he was certain that the clay compound had made contact, which meant that there must have been a mistake or something defective with the ritual. He was now merely lobbing pebbles against a brick wall in the hope it would come down. He pressed on, more out of a social need to justify his appearance here, but he could feel the meeting winding down to its necessary conclusion.

As Rawlins wrapped up a point about the pro-social potential for arcane mechanical research, Greywall steepled his fingers and leaned forward. "Interesting. You've given me a lot to think about as we consider Max's case. I thank you for your time." He stood up, clearly signaling an end to their conversation, and Rawlins had no choice but to do the same.

But then Greywall paused, standing behind his desk, as if he had forgotten what he was doing. Rawlins was puzzled, expecting to be escorted to the door, but then he saw on Greywall's face an expression of blank openness. His eyes, which had been pinched with skepticism a moment earlier, were wide and glassy. He did not speak.

It worked. Somehow the effect had taken hold on a significantly greater delay than he had intended. Perhaps a significant miscalculation? How could he be off by an order of magnitude?

Time dilation. The mechanism he had built into the ritual, which would (hopefully) prolong its impact, must also be having a meta-effect on the elements of the ritual itself: The delay he'd calculated had been dilated and significantly extended. It was a painful oversight—one that Ellsbeth might have helped him anticipate, if they could have worked on it together. But at the moment, it didn't matter. His window of opportunity was narrow.

"Let's sit back down and continue our conversation," Rawlins said. Greywall did so immediately. His irascibility had evaporated.

Rawlins cut straight to the point. "Maxwell Keene deserves to be paroled." Greywall nodded, offering no disagreement, and Rawlins went on. "Paroling Maxwell Keene will help send the right message to the community. You will grant Maxwell Keene his parole, and it will be seen as a sign of your wisdom and lenience."

Greywall gave a vague *hmmm,* taking this in. "You will grant parole to Maxwell Keene," Rawlins said firmly, needing to leave no room for uncertainty. "Now tell me what you think about Keene's case, in your own words."

"Seems like Keene is a good candidate for parole," Greywall said, sounding like an intelligent but slightly absentminded man putting the thought together at that moment, one word at a time, like railroad tracks being laid out.

"That's right," Rawlins said. "And I'm not influencing your decision on this. You've decided, on your own, to parole Maxwell Keene."

"Yes, I think so," Greywall said. He fell silent for a moment, then blinked rapidly as the effect of the ritual wore off.

"Are you all right?" Rawlins asked. "You look like you got a little lightheaded when you stood up."

"I think I did," Greywall murmured, the edge of certainty gone from his voice.

"Thank you for your time," Rawlins said, and headed out the door.

As he strode back to the car, Rawlins felt the buzz of exhilaration, making his ears hot despite the chill in the air. But it was not the clear-headed rush of triumph; even though his spell had worked, it was unclear if the period of susceptibility he had created was sufficient for his ideas to infiltrate. And the time-dilation slow release was totally untested; it had impacted the delay mechanism, but that was a mistake, and he had no clue if it was influencing the primary obscuration. Now he would have to wait a full week to learn the outcome of the parole hearing.

The more troubling question: Was it possible that Greywall might suspect him? The man was innately suspicious of arcane mechanicals, and was aware that Rawlins had come here to influence his decision. Could he put it together? The awkward handshake, the strange conversation, the (probable) gap in his memory. Rawlins imagined arriving home to find the police searching his house, tossing his papers; for god's sake, they wouldn't even need to search, the written ritual and materials to do it were right out in the open in his study.

He was exploding with the need to talk to someone, to try to sort out whether his anxieties were legitimate fears or not. But there was only one person he conceivably *could* talk to. One person who would understand the arcane mechanicals involved, of course. One person who might understand *him,* and his reasons for doing so.

But when he glanced at his phone, considering sending a text to ask if she could talk, he was reminded that she was already ignoring him. And he realized that even if Ellsbeth had once been someone he could be honest with, she wasn't anymore. She was keeping things from him, which meant he had no choice but to keep things from her. And it wasn't only that he couldn't trust her; he couldn't trust *himself* when he was around her. Desire clouded his decision making; he wouldn't know where to draw the line. If he told her anything, he'd have to tell her *everything.* And that was not only unwise, it was impossible, and unfair to ask her to take that on.

This was his secret, and his burden to bear alone.

ELLSBETH

She hadn't planned on going to the wine-and-cheese lecture at the graduate department, but then she looked at her phone and saw that it was four o'clock in the afternoon, and Ellsbeth realized that she hadn't brushed her teeth that morning or showered in two days. If she went any longer without forcing herself to interact with the outside world, it might become altogether impossible.

She examined herself in the mirror before she got into the shower. Her eyes were watery and small in her swollen face. Her skin was sallow and pale, with recently discovered divots of cellulite clinging to her upper thighs. Her hair hung lank, several months past when it needed to be cut.

She had been tempted to text Rawlins, or better yet just show up at his house. It was almost a physical impulse, to get away from her computer screen and dank apartment, from the take-out containers building into a precarious tower in her small trash can, away from thoughts of obscuration and from scanned photos that had long since blurred in her mind into meaningless strips of light and darkness. She wanted physical exertion. She wanted a hand around her throat, a palm leaving the skin of her ass tingling and red. She wanted to leave her body completely, to disappear into the control of someone else. She wanted Rawlins.

But she didn't want him to see her like this. Studying herself in the bathroom mirror, Ellsbeth tried to imagine the dazzling girl Rawlins might have seen in her, the flirtatious *ingénue* quick with repartee and shiny with confidence. She had been able to trick him for a time, masking her ordinariness with youth and cleverness and the novelty of something new, but as she looked at her naked form in the stark overhead lighting, she knew it was only a matter of time before his attitude toward her evolved into indifference or, worse, pity.

THE SECOND FLOOR OF THE arcane graduate department was where the school's endowment became visible. The carpet was clean and plush, the bookshelves lining the lecture hall were thick cherrywood, and the hors d'oeuvres were being passed by university employees in pressed white linen uniforms. The lecture was taking place in the room they called the Library, although the leather-bound volumes lining every wall seemed to have never been touched.

Several rows of chairs were already set up, but Lennox hadn't arrived. Neither had Rawlins, and Ellsbeth realized it was possible he might not come at all, a thought that shocked her with a sting of disappointment. She hadn't known until then how much her motivation to come to this lecture had been to see him, to make eye contact with him across a crowded room.

Ellsbeth took the glossy program she was handed when she walked into the Library mostly so she would have something to do with her hands; by the time she was settled into an aisle seat, the program was already mangled and folded a dozen different ways. Margaret Lennox (Harvard BS, Oxford MA, DAS) is the dean of the College of the Arcane Arts at Newlyn University. Prior to her position at Newlyn, she was the youngest-ever tenured professor in the arcane mechanicals department at Yale University. Selected publications: ***Perpetual Motion*** (Oxford University Press), "Conjuration Rituals as Means of Survival" (***New England Journal of Mechanicals***), "The Economic Impact of Arcane Conjuration" (***NEJoAA***), "Metallurgy as a Means of Standardizing Ritualistic Strength" (***California Review***). Rhodes Scholar, Percy Fellow, Taskosis Fellow, American League of the Arcane Gold Medal, President's Council on Higher Education.

"The real question is what he's going to do now."

A few other members of the cohort were gathered near the bay window to Ellsbeth's left, standing with their heads huddled together. Gracie, Rachel, and Mary-Abigail. "I mean, it's not like he's ever going to get a job. He *killed* people," Mary-Abigail said.

"Well, come on," Gracie said, "It was an accident. It wasn't like *murder*-murder. And you're pretending they didn't convict him in the first place because there was a witch hunt happening against arcane stuff in general. It's not like that was Max's fault. It was part of the zeitgeist. Magic maligned. He was a scapegoat."

"No, no, no," Mary-Abigail said, backtracking immediately when faced with Gracie's challenge. "I mean, I think it's a good thing he was paroled. I'm just wondering what he's, like, going to do."

"He can probably just get a normal job," Gracie said, looking at her nails. "The academic job market is shit even for people who actually *completed* their DAAs. Like, good luck to any of us trying to find tenure-track positions somewhere other than Bumfuck, Nowhere."

"And I actually heard Bumfuck no longer offers tenure." It was Valentine. Ellsbeth hadn't seen him standing behind the girls. They all laughed.

"But isn't Maxwell, like, still a felon?" Rachel asked. "I know he got parole, but you still can't get a *normal* job or whatever when you have a record."

"Personally," Valentine said, "I'm shocked they gave him parole at all. Have you seen photos of him? He looks like a creep."

"Classic school-shooter vibes," Gracie agreed.

Rachel was the fastest to pull out her phone. "Ohmygod, you're so right," she said. She flashed her screen toward the rest of the group, and Ellsbeth caught a glimpse of the photo. It was a mugshot of a teenage boy with dark stringy hair and familiar eyes.

"I'm just hoping he doesn't show up here today," Valentine said.

Rachel gave a mock-squeal and slapped his arm. "Why would he be *here*?"

"To see his mom, obviously! Of course Lennox is just doing this lecture like business as usual today. Ice-cold, that woman."

"Did you know Rawlins was his adviser when Max was at Newlyn?" Gracie said. "They were apparently super close. I think Rawlins took a sabbatical after it all happened."

"Well, yeah," Valentine said. "So would I. If my student murdered someone."

Ellsbeth stood. "I'm sorry," she said. "Are you talking about Maxwell Keene?"

They all turned to look at her.

"Yeah," Gracie said. "He just got paroled, apparently."

"Are you *okay*?" Rachel said. "I mean, no one has seen you outside of class for, like, weeks."

"Oh." Ellsbeth tried to hide the crumpled program and her quick-bitten nails. "I've just been working on my thesis. It's been kicking my ass. And you know, winter."

"Seasonal affective disorder," Rachel said, nodding sympathetically. "What? It's real!"

"Do you think Lennox will bring it up?" Valentine said.

"SAD?" said Rachel.

"No—her son," said Gracie. "And not a chance. I don't even know if she publicly talks about having a kid at all. Even if he weren't a felon, it's not like Lennox gives *Leave It to Beaver* vibes."

"What about the dad?" asked Ellsbeth.

"Oh, he's a nobody," said Valentine. "Something Keene. Bradley or Ben or something. You can google him. He wrote one book twenty years ago, about owls or falcons or something nobody gives a shit about. Lennox has his balls in a jar on her desk."

An imperceptible shift in the energy in the room alerted people to the fact that it was time for people to take their seats. Ellsbeth scooted down the row to make room for the rest of the group.

Lennox approached the podium, her shoulders pulled back and a soft practiced smile on her face. Her hair was enviably thick, dyed an expensive chestnut brown. Even in her mid-sixties, fine lines tracing the corners of her eyes, she conveyed a sense of professional glamour that Ellsbeth had imagined was impossible outside of movie stars and French women. She was stunning in a perfectly tailored navy dress. Ellsbeth could only imagine how beautiful she had been in her youth, as a wunderkind professor at Yale. Rawlins had been at Yale as an undergraduate, hadn't he? A nagging memory of an email Rawlins had once sent tugged at Ellsbeth's fingers, and she tried to pull out her phone as subtly as she could while Lennox began her introductory remarks. (Valentine was right: There was no mention of Maxwell Keene or the parole, just polite greetings and a segue into the recent promising developments in the field of perpetual motion.)

She searched in her email account. There were months of correspondence for her to scroll through between her and Rawlins, mostly about her thesis, but also emails that had been so intimate, so explicit that even just seeing familiar subject lines made her cross her legs. She tilted her screen to make sure no one nearby could see what she was doing, and scrolled all the way back to September. And then there it was.

When I studied under Dr. Lennox, she gave me an analogy that I have embraced: an adviser is a student's opponent more than her ally.

Rawlins had studied under Lennox, possibly when he was an undergraduate. Ellsbeth's face began to tingle strangely. Lennox continued talking, but nothing she was saying seemed to make any sense; the words simply did not connect to one another anymore. The letters on Ellsbeth's phone inflated and blurred. She closed one eye, and then the other. Rawlins had studied under Lennox. He'd had an affair with a professor when he was an undergraduate. She had been a professor at Yale. Rawlins had gone to Yale.

And Maxwell Keene's eyes looked very familiar.

"Sorry," Ellsbeth whispered, standing. "I just—bathroom."

Rawlins had come to the lecture after all. He had arrived late and was standing at the back of the room with an untouched cup of white wine balanced in his hand. Graying bags sagged beneath his eyes. His lips were colorless. Even his hair looked fairer, as if some vital life had been drained from him.

She stared as she made her way out the back of the lecture hall, trying to catch his eye. When he finally looked at her, it was a blank expression, flat and listless as a lake on a windless day. Still, when Ellsbeth made it into the hallway, Rawlins followed her out of the Library, holding the door as it closed to soften the sound.

"You studied under Lennox," Ellsbeth said.

Rawlins's mouth opened and then shut again. "We should talk in my office," he said.

They walked there in silence, steps softly echoing on the carpeted floor.

"So. You studied under Lennox," Ellsbeth repeated when they were inside.

"I did."

"And you had an affair with her. When you were an undergraduate."

Rawlins blinked. He ran one hand through his hair and put the other in his pocket before he thought better and withdrew it. He looked at Ellsbeth as if he was waiting for her to say something else, but she didn't. "Yes," Rawlins said finally.

"You didn't tell me."

"Why would I tell you that?" he said, and a stone settled deep inside Ellsbeth's chest. She felt hot tears tingling her sinuses, even though she wasn't entirely sure why she would be crying.

"Maxwell Keene was paroled, did you hear?" she said.

"I did." Rawlins looked behind her at the door, and tried to move past her. Ellsbeth tried to close the space between them. "Excuse me," he said. Rawlins's eyes became vacant. He looked right through her. Ellsbeth took a step closer.

"He's your son, isn't he?" Ellsbeth said. "Tell me. *He's your son.* I can see it. He looks like you."

"Of course not," he hissed. "What a ridiculous thing to say."

Rawlins's face flushed, and he turned to Ellsbeth with a shocking flash of rage that she glimpsed for only a moment before his face became a blank, waxen mask again. "I think we should go back to the lecture."

"Does *he* know?" Ellsbeth said.

Rawlins walked past her, leaving his office door ajar and leaving Ellsbeth standing dumbfounded and alone.

She didn't go back to the lecture. She walked down the stairs of the department building, out through the double doors, and into the chilly blast of December air. The grass of the courtyard was stiff with frost and crunched under Ellsbeth's shoes with a satisfying squeak.

Of course Rawlins didn't owe her anything. He didn't need to tell her about his past. He didn't need to reveal any of his secrets. She was the one who had told him that all she wanted was sex. But maybe she hadn't quite believed that herself. Because now, as she warmed her hands in the pockets of her too-thin coat, passing students with their faces hidden in oversized scarves, she realized it was entirely possible that Rawlins was a stranger.

RAWLINS

The first time Rawlins set eyes on Margaret Lennox, he was nineteen years old, overdressed even among his Yale classmates, with a leather satchel slung across his torso; with his weighty mechanicals textbooks, the bag was uncomfortable to carry, but he treasured the way it set him apart from his fellow undergraduates with their ergonomically superior backpacks.

Lennox was drawing a ritual circle on a whiteboard while her students filed into class. His eyes remained glued to her as he walked up the steps of the aisle and slid into a desk in the third row. When she turned around, Rawlins felt like he had been struck a physical blow. Her beauty was not conventionally feminine; it was severe and austere, like he imagined a Nordic goddess might look, descending from the icy steppe.

Rawlins hung on every word of her lecture, and when she briefly fixed him with her gaze, he went dizzy with exhilaration. He was so enraptured by the poise with which she spoke that at the end of class, he looked down at his notebook and discovered that he hadn't made a single note.

He stopped by her office hours the first week, eager to show off his mastery of the material and his hunger for additional reading. She watched him across her desk, fingers steepled, laughing generously at his attempts at wit. She probed him for gaps in his knowledge, and then for personal information, testing his willingness to open up to her while giving away nothing of herself. They talked for an hour and Rawlins considered, on his walk home, that it might have been the most enjoyable hour of his life.

The affair took some time to materialize, but in hindsight, Rawlins could see that it was on both their minds the entire time; he made no secret of his desire, and Lennox only slow-played the development as she assessed his ability to be discreet. From office-hours conversations, they moved up to late-night drinks at a bar a few miles from campus. He kept pace with her through two martinis, conscious of flirting, but unsure how far they were from escalating things—until she rather abruptly signaled for the check and told him there was a decent hotel at the end of the block.

In the bedroom, Lennox took charge of teaching Rawlins to take charge. She was uninterested in a single night of passion; she was cultivating a lover, making a project of him. She instructed him in what to do, not shying away from giving detailed instruction on how she liked to be undressed, touched, licked, fucked, and spoken to afterward. He was an eager pupil, soaking up every command, fixated on her completely. They met weekly; she initiated every encounter and kept control of their schedule.

Rawlins knew she was married, of course, and wondered about Lennox's life with her husband. It was not guilt that he felt, he was simply *curious*—about her domestic life, and how she rationalized and compartmentalized their affair. But she remained steadfast in her refusal to divulge any details about her marriage; there was no hint that it was abusive, or neglectful, or lacking in any way that would typically suggest a need for something on the side. The one time Rawlins met the man, at a holiday party hosted by the department, he seemed perfectly nice, albeit boring.

Lennox kept careful control of the entire affair. Around anyone else, she was disciplined in her refusal to even meet his gaze. There were no sudden, passionate hookups in empty classrooms or offices; every meeting was prearranged, always at the same hotel, and they would arrive and leave separately. Lennox paid for the rooms but put them under Rawlins's name, and she always encouraged him to stay the night while she headed home. He often did, savoring a bed far more luxurious than the one in his dormitory, though her departures left him lonely and seething with a sense of jealousy, which revealed that he was not nearly as content with the arrangement as he let on.

In the cocoon of post-coital bliss, Rawlins sometimes became talkative, expansively revealing himself while Lennox listened, touching his arm or his hair, occasionally offering wise perspective on his stories, his memories of his family, his dreams and insecurities. She seemed to genuinely enjoy his thoughts on arcane mechanicals, and delighted in his unchecked ambition.

But she rarely shared much of her own life, and the few times his feelings bubbled up, she was indulgent but dismissive. When he told her at one point, "I *really* like you"—avoiding but clearly intending the word *love*—she merely gave a wistful smile and replied, "I like you, too, Tad, but let's not get carried away." He tried to content himself with the belief that her amorous feelings echoed his, but they were merely being sophisticated and adult by holding back from speaking the truth.

It always seemed like Lennox had thought of everything, as if the entire affair was perfectly in her control. When he offered to put on a condom, she told him breezily not to worry about it, to simply pull out when he was ready to finish, which he attempted to do—though over time, he may not have always been as prompt as he should have. He reasoned that she was married and ambitious and intelligent; surely that meant she was on birth control, or otherwise unable to conceive.

He was surprised when she invited him for coffee; it felt like an oddly formal venue for conversation, given the weekly intimacy that was available in the hotel. As soon as he sat down, she told him matter-of-factly that she was pregnant, and based on the timing, she was confident that it was his. He was stunned into silence as she laid out her plans to keep the baby and present it to her husband as his. Rawlins was physically similar enough that it was unlikely any telltale physical trait would give away the truth of the child's parentage. Rawlins did not protest, nor was he given a chance to do so. The affair ended overnight—as did nearly any acknowledgment from Lennox that it had ever happened.

In the aftermath, Rawlins spun out. He tried to tell himself that he was fortunate, that their secret would be kept, that he would be spared life-altering consequences and could focus on his work and never worry about it again. But he was obsessed. He tried repeatedly to contact Lennox, and her brief replies were all to the effect of *we have nothing more to discuss.* Once, he showed up at her office hours, attempting to force a conversation, and she politely closed the door and let him speak his piece, let him confess his love and offer the possibility of the life they might have if she left her husband for him. She nodded, then told him none of that was going to happen, and it was time for him to act like an adult and forget about it entirely.

He tried. He threw himself into his work with a zeal that paid off. Years later, he looked back and wondered if the breakup was responsible for *The Arcane and the Ordinary;* wondered if he ever could have completed such a book, devoted himself so completely to his work at such a young age, if he were not actively running from the prospect of any human relationship . . . and if he were not hoping, in some secret corner of his mind, that Lennox would see the book, witness his success, and realize she had made a terrible mistake.

If she did, she did not let on. After the book had reached stratospheric levels of popularity and he appeared on a popular talk show, she sent him a tersely worded email of congratulations. Rawlins tried to ignore the sting of it as he lost himself in the pleasures of his newfound celebrity, hopping from one glamorous guest-teaching stint to another, from one brief relationship to the next. He delighted in the beauty and status of those he was able to date and bed, but the pleasures were hollow. He could not heal the wound Lennox had left; he could merely harden it into a scar such that he no longer craved her, nor even hoped to experience the love he had once felt for her with anyone else.

Years passed. Rawlins's fame dimmed slightly, and the time came to settle at a university where he could teach and settle into tenure. Many were surprised that he opted for Newlyn. Lennox must have known that he'd passed up bigger offers from schools in far more glamorous locations; surely, she was aware of the reason he chose hers. But they never spoke about the matter; she greeted him cordially when he arrived for orientation.

By the time Rawlins started teaching, Max was entering high school. The first time he glimpsed his son in person, it was in passing at a café near the university, where the boy was doing his homework. Time stopped. Rawlins could not help but stare. It was not at all like looking in a mirror—thankfully, Max resembled his mother most—but there were subtle details that even pictures online had not prepared Rawlins for. The boy's eyes. The shape of his ears. The way his brow furrowed as he bent over his studies, and the way he waggled his pen as he thought. Rawlins felt an ache, but left the café before it might compel him to do something rash.

When Max started attending Newlyn, Rawlins felt like fate had contrived a way to bring his son into his life. In truth, it was a prosaic train of causation; he had come to teach at Newlyn because of Max, and Max had enrolled there because he lacked the high school grades to get into an elite, competitive school, except for the one where his mother's position ensured his admission. Back then, Rawlins had taught an introductory class required for every freshman majoring in arcane arts, and it was not out of the ordinary for a prodigiously intelligent young pupil to feel unsatisfied with the conservative curriculum, and seek him out in search of further reading.

Lennox spoke with Rawlins about Max exactly once, when she pulled him aside after a faculty meeting. She did not even explicitly acknowledge Max's parentage. She merely warned Rawlins that Max was impressionable, and he ought to exercise caution. "Of course," he replied, even though his bag contained a pair of forbidden books he intended to give the boy in their weekly tutoring session later that day.

Had Rawlins shown him special attention? Certainly. Had he encouraged his pupil to expand his studies beyond the curriculum? Without a doubt. Had he laid the groundwork for the boy to spiral into an unhealthy obsession with pushing the limits of what could be done? Yes, undeniably; it never would have happened without Rawlins's intellectual encouragement.

But was he *responsible* for the crime? Was he every bit as negligent as Max? Should he have wound up in jail alongside his son? Should he have confessed, at some point during the investigation and trial, that he was the boy's father?

Those were the questions that still kept him up at night.

∞

THE MEMORIES PLAYED OUT IN Rawlins's mind like a degraded old film—the colors saturated, the details grainy.

He sat on the back deck, shivering in the early-evening chill as he stubbed out a cigarette.

It had been years since he had indulged his smoking habit beyond an occasional late-night cigarette, but he was making his way through a pack with abandon.

Barely past six o'clock, the sun had already set, plunging the valley into cold darkness.

Headlights were visible on the roads down below as the streets filled with students heading home from class. This time of year, the onset of evening always felt abrupt and violent, as though the daylight were being choked out prematurely.

A glass of scotch sat on the table, one large ice cube softening at the edges. Rawlins had poured the drink with celebratory intentions. His impossible plan had worked. News of Max's parole had reached him earlier that day, shortly after arriving at his office. Yet he could not bring himself to take a drink, instead ramping up his anxiety with nicotine as if to punish himself.

For years, guilt over Max's imprisonment had been like shackles that he dragged along—slowing his progress, stifling his joy, spoiling every holiday and success. An incessant voice that whispered into every pleasurable silence, *You don't deserve this.*

He had hoped Max's parole would bring him some measure of triumph. But it was only met with a knot of dread in his stomach. A panicky stomach-dropping sense of vertigo. He hoped it was merely shock, perhaps amplified by fear that his crimes would be discovered and both he and Max would be unceremoniously carted off to prison. He expected the panic to pass quickly, replaced with a longed-for sense of relief. But as the day progressed, his breathing remained shallow, his chest remained tight, and he couldn't shake the sense of impending disaster.

Rawlins had grown accustomed to the low-grade, seething loneliness of having no one with whom he could talk about this. Max's parole was supposed to be the milestone that freed him from that need. Instead, it had only grown.

Lennox, of course, was the one person who knew the whole history. But he was terrified that she would figure out he had used obscuration, or at least suspect. Based on her unflappable behavior at the lecture, he was also confident she had no interest in discussing the matter, certainly not with him.

There was only one person he could actually talk to. He picked up his phone and texted simply, Need to see you. Come over tonight?

When Ellsbeth stepped into his foyer an hour and a half later, she was more cagey than usual; even as she slipped off her coat and hung it up, revealing a plunging top underneath, her body language was closed off, and a tone of challenge entered her voice as she asked, "So, what did you have in mind? You want to punish me?"

Rawlins shifted uneasily. "Look, I didn't invite you over for . . . *that,*" he said. "I was thinking . . . Can we just have dinner? I'm making chicken cacciatore."

Her brow furrowed as she looked toward the kitchen, smelling the tomato sauce simmering on the stove for the first time. "I'm okay for now, thanks."

"Okay, well, how about a glass of wine?" he asked. "After everything today, it would be nice. To talk to someone."

"Talk to someone . . ." she repeated slowly, then snorted out a bitter laugh. "I'm sorry, but you're the one who put an end to things like *dinner.* We agreed to keep it just physical."

"Look, I was caught off guard earlier," Rawlins said. "And there are certain things, for your own good, that I can't tell you, but—"

"You can't do that," she cut in, with an edge of anger he had not heard before in her voice. "It's not fair. To ask to talk, and then set the terms."

"Have you been completely honest with *me*?" he asked. "About everything?"

She looked away, avoiding his gaze. But her jaw hardened and she turned back to him. "Is Max your son? With Lennox?"

Rawlins took a deep breath, then nodded slowly. "Come have a seat, and I'll tell you everything." Ellsbeth wavered and he tried again, a tremulous crack entering his voice. "Ellsbeth, I've never told any of this to anybody. And I don't just need to talk to *someone.* I want to talk to *you.*"

ELLSBETH

She listened on the couch, her legs tucked beneath her, as Rawlins told the story of his undergraduate affair, of the decades of watching his son grow up anonymously, of finally becoming his mentor when Maxwell arrived at Newlyn. The only time Rawlins looked away from Ellsbeth, bringing his eyes down to the ring of red wine staining the bottom of his wineglass, was when he alluded to Max's horrible mistake. A ritual that Max never would have attempted if Rawlins hadn't encouraged him, hadn't given him books and individual attention. "It was my fault those students died," Rawlins said. "That their parents never saw them again. Never got to say goodbye. Their entire lives, their futures—gone in an instant. And it was my fault Max went to prison."

"No," Ellsbeth said, finding her voice for the first time all night. "Stop, no. That's not true. You can't think like that."

He offered her a sad smile. "I pushed him. I gave him access to magic far beyond his capabilities. If I hadn't encouraged him . . ."

"No," Ellsbeth said. "That's not how things work. You can't go back and rewrite history. You have no idea how cause and effect might have played out. If you hadn't been encouraging him, maybe he would have tried even *more* dangerous rituals to try to impress you, to get your attention. Maybe he wasn't even trying to impress you! He could have been trying to get into a society or, I don't know, to impress a cute girl down the hall. Maybe he was trying to get his mom's attention. You just can't know."

"I suppose that's reasonable," Rawlins said, but he didn't seem convinced. He stood. "May I?" He took his and Ellsbeth's empty wineglasses back to the kitchen, a retreat from his vulnerability, which hung in the air like fog. He returned with two glasses of water.

"Does he know that you're his father?" Ellsbeth asked.

Rawlins shook his head. "It's possible he has some idea, but no. Now that he's out, I think it's time to tell him the truth."

"Really?"

Rawlins just kept staring at the small fire burning itself down in his grate. He hadn't taken a sip from his water, but he gripped the glass tightly in his hand.

"It must have been lonely for you," Ellsbeth continued. "Not telling anyone all of that. For so long."

"It didn't seem lonely. It seemed like—" He paused. "—the way grown-ups are supposed to live. Holding on to things, hiding parts of yourself away in back closets, painting over the doors so that if you ever have company over, nobody is put off."

She had taken his hand as he was speaking, running her fingertips over the rough skin of his knuckles, down his long, calloused fingers. And then, on instinct, she brought his hand to her mouth and kissed it. "I like your hidden parts," she said. "And I like that you can tell me about them."

"I'm not trying to make things more difficult for us, Ellsbeth. I know there's no future here, for good reason, and that we had made an arrangement to keep things . . . simple."

He was wearing a faded Yale T-shirt and no shoes. It was the most casual Ellsbeth had ever seen him dressed, and the hint of chest hair peeking out of his T-shirt's stretched neckline made her heart race.

"Is it bad if I want to kiss you right now?" she said.

In answer, he pulled her against him and pressed his mouth to hers like a drowning man searching for air. His hands found the back of her head, her neck, her shoulders, and then she was pressing into him, too, shocked at how immediate and right it felt to fall into his arms.

AFTER THE INITIAL RUSH TO get their clothes off, their hands became slow and lazy. Rawlins lay facing Ellsbeth on the narrow couch, running a finger down the curve of her side. The finger left a trail of goosebumps on her flesh—her ribs, her waist, her hips. "I can't believe you look like this," he said.

"It's because I'm twenty-four," Ellsbeth said, trying to make her voice sound light.

"No," Rawlins said. "It's not. It's you. It's the impossible curve of you, the tiny hairs that stand up on your skin, the way you look right now. The way you look at me. It's *you.*"

The image popped into her head unbidden. A small elopement, seeing his face beaming at her as she walked down an aisle in a white dress that he would pull up when they finally reached a honeymoon suite, too impatient to deal with the tiny buttons running down the back.

A lifetime of tangling in white sheets together, of ordering room service somewhere on a honeymoon and feeding each other french fries in bed while bad television played in the background. She saw herself moving into his house, fucking on the floor, in every room, waking up next to him, feeling the warmth of his sleeping body and kissing his eyelids until he woke up and smiled at her.

There would be pancakes, and singing in the kitchen while dinner cooked, and individual preferences for their favorite coffee mugs. There would be essays of each other's to proofread, half-formed ideas to solicit advice on, and debates about mechanicals over bottles of wine that would descend into furious make-out sessions, lips stained burgundy. There would be dinner parties where she could touch his thigh under the table, see him glancing over at her slyly, secret codes of communication only the two of them knew.

There would be more nights together than they could count. Nights he could bind her with rope or writ magic, or play with new magic that hadn't been invented yet, that they could invent together. Nights to spank her and make her beg, to leave her raw and needy in a way that she had never been with anyone before. And then mornings where he would kiss her and hold her and whisper words in her ear so soft and so kind that she would have to turn away from him so that he wouldn't see her tear up.

But the longer Ellsbeth imagined that life, the more it began to hurt somewhere in the middle of her chest. It was like waking up from a dream where you had won the lottery, and being forced to reckon with the fact that you now had to live in the real world. There was no version of their story where their romance wouldn't be tawdry gossip. She might get kicked out of the program. He might lose his job. Both of them would lose their reputations.

And then there was the simple fact that he didn't actually know her. He wanted her, sure, for now, because she was young, and pretty enough, and smart. Because he had seen the version of herself she had shown him.

He didn't know that she was a liar, that she could lie like breathing. He didn't know that she had used obscuration.

He hadn't seen the way Officer Marcos's eyes had gone flat and empty. That life, of pancakes and soft kisses in the morning, would only ever be a façade, because the moment she showed Rawlins the truth at the heart of her, he wouldn't want her anymore.

Rawlins had been able to show her his true self, to untwist the calcified knot he had kept in a clenched fist, and as she ran her hand up his neck and into his thick hair, she realized that she loved him for it. But she would never be able to show herself to him.

"I love you," she said before she realized the words were coming out of her mouth and not just echoing in her head. "Please don't say anything back. Please. I didn't even mean—I just . . ." She turned her body away from his so that they were both lying on the couch facing the same direction. "I just want you to hold me. I didn't mean it."

I love you, too. He breathed the words so faintly that Ellsbeth wasn't certain whether he said them at all, or whether she had imagined them. She didn't ask, she just let him hold her for long enough that the candle he had burning on his mantelpiece sputtered out.

By the time they were eating chicken cacciatore, the food was cold and it had begun snowing outside. Rawlins popped her plate in the microwave and delivered it to her at the table. "It's better when it's fresh," he said.

"It beats cereal, which had been my dinner plan for the evening."

Rawlins smiled and brought his own plate to the table, taking the seat next to her. "Bon appétit," he said, his accent halfway between joking and pretentious.

Ellsbeth lifted her fork with a bite of chicken on it, but she let it drop before it reached her mouth. "I have something to say that I fully realize will sound insane, but: I'm jealous of Dean Lennox," she said. "Just from hearing that story."

"It was decades ago."

"I know!" Ellsbeth said. "It's not *rational.* I know that. And for the record, she took advantage of you." Rawlins opened his mouth to protest, but Ellsbeth didn't let him. "I'm just jealous! I'm jealous of every other woman you've ever touched. Let alone *loved.* I can imagine you, in that hotel room. Her: so smart, so *important.* How impressed you must have been. I don't like the thought of you impressed with anyone except me." She had drunk more wine than she had thought, and was talking too much and slightly too loud. "I'm sorry, forget I said anything. We should go back to the fun part of this. No neediness, no feelings."

Rawlins wiped his top lip with a curled finger. "I don't know where you got this idea in your head that you can't need anything from anyone else, but it's not true. You're allowed to need other people. And you really should eat. You're looking pale." Ellsbeth took a large bite and lifted her eyebrows as she swallowed. *Happy?*

"*Needing* other people just isn't something I'm interested in," she said. "You need someone, and then what? When you don't have them anymore, you're helpless."

"I doubt there is anyone on earth who would ever call you helpless."

"Maybe because I never need anything from anyone!"

Rawlins laughed at that, his tongue pressed against the bottom of his dog teeth, and Ellsbeth thought it again—*I love you*—but this time she managed not to say it out loud. Instead: "What's that?"

She gestured toward a photo framed on the kitchen shelf that was taken by the Newlyn gates. She stood to examine it.

It must have been from a decade or so earlier, a group of people with their arms around one another. Ellsbeth found Rawlins, his face slightly rounder, his sideburns longer, smiling with his mouth closed. Dean Lennox stood at the far end of the group.

"Oh," Rawlins said. "New faculty orientation. My first day here at Newlyn."

Ellsbeth scanned the photo. "Lennox, obviously. There's Professor Gaines—she was blond! And . . . Professor Gallway."

"Paul, yeah. We started at the same time." They were the only two men in the group.

"He's *barely* aged. It's weird!"

"Good genes, I suppose," Rawlins said.

"Or a vanity ritual," Ellsbeth said, and Rawlins snorted. Vanity rituals were largely a joke in the world of arcane mechanicals—expensive, impractical, and only ever temporary, sold to the desperate by arcanist hacks and has-beens. Vanity rituals were the type of thing you saw poorly designed ads for as you scrolled on social media, or advertised in bad neighborhoods on billboards promising low prices for whiter teeth and fewer wrinkles.

Ellsbeth stared at the photo, trying to imagine what Rawlins was thinking as it was taken.

He was the most famous person in the group at the time, riding the success of *The Arcane and the Ordinary.* Was he still in love with Lennox then, trying to stand up straight to impress her? Was he cocky in the way that twenty-something prodigies must be, certain that their continued success was inevitable and upward progress the only plausible future? She couldn't read anything in his tight face. Paul Gallway, on the other hand, was grinning madly, his arm thrust jocularly around Rawlins and his blazer flapping open in an invisible breeze. There was a pin in his blazer, right on his lapel.

Rawlins had risen to stand behind Ellsbeth, his hand hovering over the small of her back as if he wasn't certain whether or not he was supposed to put it there.

"What's that?" Ellsbeth asked. "The pin or button or whatever Professor Gallway is wearing? Do you recognize it?"

Rawlins picked up the photograph to get a closer look. "He attended Newlyn as an undergraduate. I think that's from one of the societies. Banestooth."

It was a pin featuring a wolf with teeth exposed, a smile and an attack at the same time.

Paul Gallway was wearing the same button as the one that Ellsbeth had seen in the photographs of Bertie's bathroom floor.

From: Storer.Ellsbeth
To: Rawlins.T.M.
Subject: (no subject)

Let me know how your talk with Max goes. However he reacts, I think he's lucky to have someone like you in his life.

And, unrelated, when I said "I love you," it was in that post-orgasm haze when my brain is still coming online, and words aren't actually attached to their actual linguistic meaning. I'm sure you had already forgotten it but I just wanted to be on the record, just in case. And if it doesn't violate wherever we are in our non-relationship agreement, one of these days I'd like to cook you dinner. Fair warning, it might be on a hot plate, but I WILL try to do better than cereal.

x
Ellsbeth

From: Rawlins.T.M.
To: Storer.Ellsbeth
Subject: Re: (no subject)

Ellsbeth,

Thank you for listening. For a long time, I thought that I could never say any of that aloud. That anyone who heard the story and knew what I had done would never speak to me again. Much less invite me over for dinner, which I gladly accept (hot plate or not, it's the thought that counts).

Any post-orgasmic mutterings that you need to have stricken from the record, I understand. No one can be expected to think straight in the aftermath of such pleasure. But I am currently sitting in my office, in the bright light of day, with no such excuse, and guess what?

I love you.

Rawlins

RAWLINS

Rawlins's scalp tingled pleasantly as he left his office. The email to Ellsbeth had been sent hastily, and as he hoisted on his coat while walking down the hallway, he wondered if he ought to have given it more thought. Voices of sensible reason drifted in the distant background of his mind—he knew *why* they should not say such things, knew that it would make any sort of an ending harder. But at present, the fact of his love for Ellsbeth was such a simple reality that it seemed disingenuous to pretend otherwise.

The feeling had crept up for a long time, layers accumulating with every new aspect of her that he saw, eliciting respect, affection, admiration, and—most jarringly and ceaselessly—desire. Those threads had braided together into a rope long ago, and he only now had the good sense to call the whole thing by its proper name.

The turning point had not simply been her saying it first; really, it happened when he told her the truth and she didn't run away. After living with so much shame for so long, his worst fears had become unchallenged facts—namely, that if anyone knew the whole story, he would be exposed, abandoned, destroyed in every sense. He had not even told the truth to his therapist during the brief time he'd had one. Worried that she would judge him, and even more afraid she would try to convince him to forgive himself when it felt like the guilt was all he had to hold on to.

But his assumptions had been challenged, and his fears, if not obliterated, at least mitigated. He had confessed his secret and Ellsbeth responded by embracing him, both literally and figuratively. If she could meet the truth with such warmth, perhaps Max eventually might do the same. The prospect of telling his son the truth of his parentage had long seemed impossible, and only grew more so with each passing year as the accumulation of time increased the weight of the betrayal. But perhaps his fears had been exaggerated by his guilt—and while he was nervous about Max's reaction, he had, for the first time in a long while, *hope.*

His perspective colored his perception of the snow drifting down on the campus, giving it a festive feeling, a foretaste of the upcoming holiday break. The chilly air invigorated him as he pulled his coat tighter, stepping over the trickling river of snowmelt in the gutter to cross Stuyvesant at the edge of campus.

The Callistoga Café, where he and Max had agreed to meet, was situated just across the street from the university, which made it popular with students and faculty. Rawlins never went there to work; the atmosphere was too distracting and dense with familiar faces for him to focus. Inevitably, he would run into a student begging him for an extension, or another professor asking him to substitute for them on a committee. But he occasionally stopped in for a midday Americano if he needed a jolt of caffeine to make it through the afternoon, as had been the case over a decade earlier when he first saw Max. Rawlins hadn't said anything to his son that day; the shock of seeing him in the flesh was too great. He had just stood watching the boy for a beat too long. Max had never looked up. It felt fitting to now meet up with his son at the same location where he had first laid eyes on him, though of course he neglected to mention that coincidence in his email invitation. Perhaps Rawlins would tell him someday.

In his desire to ensure he didn't arrive late, Rawlins wound up fifteen minutes early. He got in line and ordered a tea, which he took to an open table in the corner. It wobbled badly, its legs uneven, revealing why it was the only seat available. But for Rawlins's purposes it was perfect, providing a view of the door and enough separation to have a private conversation.

Rawlins kept checking his phone as the time crawled. Five minutes past, then ten, and he started to wonder if he was being stood up; Max very well might have forgotten, or decided at the last minute not to come. Rawlins opened his email to see if a message to that effect had arrived, and when he looked up—there he was.

It felt surreal, seeing Max out in the world once again. The boy had obviously not refreshed his wardrobe since before he was sent away; his dark jeans were tight at the ankle, long since out of style. But despite his sallow skin and long hair, he looked good, even intimidating; his skinny build had filled out during his time in prison, and the calf-length coat he wore took on an imposing silhouette with his new dimensions.

Rawlins stood and waved to get Max's attention, and he came over with a loping gait, sliding between the other customers with a look of displeasure.

"Can I buy you a coffee or anything? They have good pastries, too."

Max shook his head. "I'm fine."

"Sandwiches, if you're hungry for a real lunch," Rawlins offered, surprised at his own nervousness. "I've had the tuna before, which was decent, and . . ." He trailed off, conscious that he was filling silence awkwardly, while Max had long since made up his mind not to get anything.

Rawlins sat back down, and Max slid in across from him. But with his back to the rest of the café, Max was twitchy and nervous, looking over his shoulder, his gaze following anyone who walked through his periphery. "Would you rather switch?" Rawlins stood up, vacating his seat, and Max wordlessly swapped with him. "Probably hard to get used to being out in public, isn't it?"

Max shrugged, eyes darting from one customer to another. "Can't believe I used to do my homework here. Even back when I was in high school."

The mention of it brought Rawlins back to the first moment he saw his son in person.

They were only a few feet away from the table where the boy had been sitting. His face, even at fifteen years old, had been serious and withdrawn—but there had been a light in his eyes then, a gleam of excitement and curiosity.

The memory made Rawlins realize he'd been hoping that youthful light would return to Max's eyes once he was out of prison. Perhaps eventually it would; the boy had only been out for a couple weeks, and no doubt it took time for the mind to readjust. But at present, the eyes across the table were like smoldering embers, dark and simmering with rage.

"How are you adapting so far?" Rawlins asked.

Max gave a heavy sigh. "Fine, I suppose. Nice to wake up when I feel like it. Eat some real food for a change."

"Have you been back to Paratha yet?" Rawlins asked, referencing a nearby Indian restaurant they had both loved. When Max would linger after office hours, Rawlins often ordered it in for the two of them. They ate at his desk, dissecting Max's essays together line by line.

Max brightened slightly, and the ghost of a smile danced at the edge of his lip. "First meal home, I got takeout. But my tolerance for spice is gone completely."

"You'll have to work your way back up," Rawlins told him. "That vindaloo doesn't mess around." It was too jovial; he felt it as soon as the words left his mouth.

Max fixed him with an incisive gaze, suspicion clouding his expression. "Why did you want to see me?"

"Well . . . I've missed you," Rawlins answered, afraid to jump directly to the heart of the conversation. "I'm glad you're out, and now that you've been granted parole, I just thought you might . . ."

"What—resume my education?"

Rawlins looked away; he knew that Max's parole terms included a prohibition on practicing arcane mechanicals in any form. "What am I supposed to do now anyway?" Max continued. "You think anyone wants to hire me? You think anyone wants to be my friend, or have anything to do with me at all?"

"I do," Rawlins said softly. "I care about you. Really."

Max shook his head, clearly unwilling to believe this. "I hear you had a word with Greywall."

Rawlins tilted his head evasively. "I'm not sure I made much of a difference. Just tried to remind him of the context around the case. The fact that you never had a fair shot to begin with." Max rolled his eyes at that, and Rawlins added, "Hopefully there's a shift under way in terms of how people view arcane mechanicals. You might've been sentenced at peak witch hunt, and now attitudes are softening a bit."

Max leaned in, elbows resting on the table, causing it to wobble. "But why do *you* care so much about my case? Is that some validation for you? A benefit to your reputation, if I'm not seen as such a monster anymore?" He gestured toward Rawlins in his well-fitted jacket, and the cozy campus surrounding them. "You seem to be doing fine."

Rawlins swallowed hard. If he was ever going to tell the truth, this was the moment. He had an impulse to reach across the table and take the boy's hand when he delivered the news, but knew that Max would recoil. So he merely matched the boy's posture, leaning forward as he searched for the words. "Listen, there's something that I want to tell you. That will be strange to hear, but . . . I hope that you'll understand." Max's gaze tightened, as if bracing for impact. "Max, I'm actually . . . I'm your father."

The boy's expression betrayed nothing. He leaned back, creating some distance, and shook his head slowly in disbelief.

Rawlins barreled on, attempting to convey the whole story as succinctly as possible. The affair. The pregnancy. The secret. Years and years of keeping the secret.

When he was finished, Max's mouth formed an O as he let out a long exhale, his expression still betraying no clear emotion. "So . . . let me make sure I've got it. You slept with my mother twenty-six years ago."

"Yes."

"And you two let me believe, for my entire life, that my dad . . . that *Ben* was my real father," Max said matter-of-factly.

"I had no choice," Rawlins insisted. "Your mother was explicit."

"And you kept this secret. For *decades.*" Max's volume remained even, but anger crept into the low register of his voice. "Even when you met me. Even when we spent hours together, day after day. When you became my fucking *mentor*, you didn't think to tell me then?"

"I wanted to," Rawlins said, emotion starting to crack in his throat. "Every one of those lessons we had, those conversations that went on for hours . . . it was on the tip of my tongue. But I convinced myself that the only relationship I could have with you was as your teacher. That that was the closest I'd ever get to being a father. I tried to give you what I could. Encouragement. Education. Maybe even a little . . . wisdom?"

Max let out a bark of laughter at that, and Rawlins chuckled at himself, trying to lighten the mood as he conceded, "Okay, maybe I didn't have much of that to offer, but . . . I tried."

"You *tried* . . ." Max said, holding the word on his tongue like a bitter berry.

"I wanted to tell you," Rawlins said. "But Maggie—your mother—she was adamant that it would only make things worse. For you. For everyone."

"Oh, of course," Max said. "Interesting, isn't it? How the thing that was best for me . . . was the one that meant no consequences for you."

Rawlins felt a knot forming in the pit of his stomach; he was losing control of the conversation. "Max, there *were* consequences for me. The guilt I've lived with. The sleep I've lost. The . . ." He shook his head and lowered his voice. "I don't expect your sympathy, I just need you to know, this has been the most difficult thing in my life."

"Well, how nice that you can let it go now that I'm out," Max said. "You've unburdened your conscience. You're free."

"I'm not doing this for me. I'm doing it for *you,*" Rawlins said. "You deserve to know the truth. And I figured it might . . . help make sense of certain things, at least."

Max pursed his lips, his gaze burrowing into Rawlins with a cruel gleam as he said, "You know . . . it does, actually. Because I always looked at my dad and thought: How does someone as awful as me come from someone as nice as him?" Rawlins tensed up, seeing Max building a head of steam and wanting to stop him, but afraid to interrupt. "I knew that my mom was cold, but I figured, a *little* of my dad should've rubbed off on me. A bit of decency. But now it makes sense. I'm the offspring of an ice queen . . . and a narcissist."

"Max . . ." Rawlins didn't have a complete thought; he said the boy's name as a plea, hoping he would stop.

"It makes sense why you'd tell me now," Max continued. "Because now, you're realizing you're actually irrelevant. Your whole rockstar-professor thing isn't what it used to be. The cult of personality has dimmed. You need someone new to look up to you."

"That's not what's happening," Rawlins protested. "This isn't about me. You deserve to know the truth."

"But I didn't back then?" Max asked, his anger rising. "When it might've actually been useful? When it might've made me understand why you were giving me your time, your attention, your forbidden books. I thought I was *special.*"

"You were!" Rawlins insisted.

Max shook his head. "You were just trying to spend time with the kid you abandoned. And look how that worked out. Look what your 'love' led to. *You ruined my life.*"

Rawlins swallowed hard; this had gotten away from him. "I would give anything to go back and change it. But I can't. And you're right . . . I should've told you."

"I liked not knowing just fine," Max said. "I liked having no relationship with you whatsoever. But neither of those are really an option for me now, are they?"

"I'm sorry." Rawlins fought to keep his gaze locked on Max despite the burning recrimination in the boy's eyes. "I just . . . had to tell you."

Max smirked without a trace of genuine amusement. "You don't know the meaning of 'had to.' You don't understand what your choices are until they're taken away. And *this* . . ." He pointed at the air between them, as though the conversation were a corporeal thing that could be seen. "*This* was a choice. And I promise you, it's one you'll regret."

Max's eye twitched with what could've been rage, or holding back tears, or both. But before either feeling could escalate enough to reveal itself, he stood up, his dark jacket sweeping behind him, and marched toward the door.

Rawlins wanted to go after him, to try to apologize, to make this right, but he had no idea what to say or where to begin.

And it was not only uncertainty that kept him glued to his seat, watching his son exit the café without looking back. It was *fear.* Rooted in the realization that he had barely known his son to begin with, and the intervening years of incarceration had hardened him into someone unrecognizable, perhaps even incomprehensible, to Rawlins.

Max's last words before he stormed out were not only a prediction (an accurate one, since Rawlins already *did* regret telling him the news). They were a threat. And Rawlins was afraid.

ELLSBETH

Winter break gave the Newlyn campus the feeling of a dollhouse inverted and shaken empty. Ellsbeth could walk the entire campus and only run into one or two other students, all made anonymous by their scarves pulled up across their faces. The normally bustling cafeteria was reduced to a single sleepy buffet line manned by one employee. Ellsbeth could not recall if there was usually ambient music playing that she never paid attention to beneath the cacophony of hundreds of students eating and talking, but if there was, whoever was responsible for selecting and playing it had gone home for Christmas; Ellsbeth poured and chewed her cereal in the mornings in echoing silence.

Still, she found she settled nicely into the solitude, perfectly at peace to spend the majority of her day without saying a single word to another human being aside from her coffee order to the barista at The Puddle Jumper, where she was able to easily claim her favorite corner table by the window and settle into its plush armchair.

Without making official plans, she and Rawlins had fallen into a comforting domestic routine, spending every evening together. The Puddle Jumper closed at 5 p.m., and she would trek across the South Quad toward his Victorian home to find him in the kitchen cooking for both of them.

Her promise to cook him dinner had fallen by the wayside; she began to let herself in past his unlocked front door and kick off her shoes and be greeted by the smell of coq au vin, or roasted chicken thighs nestled into buttery rice, or sizzling guanciale from the local specialty store that caused Ellsbeth to gasp when she saw the price on its casing in the trash can. Once, Rawlins made something he charmingly called lasagna soup, a warming pot of noodles and cheese that needed to be eaten with a knife and fork.

"Please, let me help!" Ellsbeth protested as Rawlins poured her a glass of wine while keeping an eye on a pan of caramelizing shallots.

"Absolutely not," he replied. "And do let that wine breathe, it's a good one." He seemed to glow with the pleasure of being a host, of cooking for her and insisting on cleaning up afterward.

And so, while Ellsbeth occasionally brought over French bread or focaccia or worse wine than Rawlins would have wanted to drink, just as often she showed up empty-handed, forcing herself to quiet the screaming voice in the back of her head telling her to make herself useful. It was a strange and new experience for a girl who had always prided herself on her ironclad independence: being taken care of.

Rawlins's records were eclectic and charmingly dorky. Though he often chose jazz records while he cooked, he also played Gilbert and Sullivan and Sondheim. While she was going through his books in his study, she overheard him singing along to the *West Side Story* soundtrack with a voice so shockingly tone-deaf she knew that he must have forgotten the possibility that another person could hear him.

They did not say they loved each other again. But she heard it every time he scooped up her plate to put it in the dishwasher before she could get up, in the way he pulled her legs onto his lap when they were reading together on his overstuffed leather couch, in the expression in his eyes when she straddled him and pulled off her shirt.

The Vermont snow felt like insulation. They almost never left his house together; a playing house made permissible by the liminal quality of winter break, the long stretches without work or class when the campus was only half alive.

Rawlins mentioned his conversation with Max only briefly, and only after Ellsbeth had noticed him staring off into the distance, blinking and withdrawn. "It was a start," Ellsbeth told him. "It's a big shock, and a big transition. Give him a minute." Rawlins had nodded, taking her hand and kissing every one of her fingers.

They spent hours naked, long after the needle ran out on whatever record had been playing, running fingertips over any errant centimeters of skin that hadn't been touched yet. Ellsbeth told Rawlins about her lonely childhood, how her parents had been polite but cold and she had felt like an adult long before she should have. With his hand running down her torso, she confessed the unflattering extent of her ambition, how she saw a future in which she became *important* as the lifeboat away from a life that was dull and ordinary. "I know this is the wrong thing to say, but I really do believe I would rather be impressive than happy," she told him.

"What does 'impressive' mean to you? Because when you get to my age, I hope it's a comfort to know, you will begin caring less about what other people think."

Ellsbeth flipped her hair in a way she hoped would read as sexy and French. "I suppose I mean, making people jealous of me." Rawlins cocked an eyebrow, and Ellsbeth continued, "It's not the jealousy *necessarily* that I want. It's that if people are jealous of me, it means they aren't pitying me. I want enough money, or power, or fame, or *importance,* or *whatever* so that I never become an object of pity. Someone helpless. Someone who *needs* the goodwill of someone else to preserve my basic dignity."

Rawlins didn't laugh at her, or argue. He just kissed her again and then trailed his lips down her neck and her collarbone. "I can't imagine anyone ever pitying you, Ellsbeth Storer," he said.

Rawlins told her about the years he spent as an outsider at boarding school, and the thrilling rush of becoming a literary wunderkind after the success of *The Arcane and the Ordinary.* He had achieved exactly the type of success Ellsbeth fantasized about: feted at dinners and parties, respected by both academics and the general public. "But I don't know if I was actually *happy* during any of that time," he said. "The money was nice. But most of those galas were nightmarishly boring. And they would always seat me next to some donor who secretly believed he would be a genius at mechanicals."

"Still," Ellsbeth said. "It's *power.* The money, yes, but also the recognition. Plus, there must have been women throwing themselves at you."

He ran his hand down her calf and lolled his head toward her. "I'm not sure that's the type of thing you want to hear about."

"It makes me *furious,* to be completely honest. Women touching you before I even met you."

"Before you were born!"

"I was *born*!"

"Still."

"You're right," Ellsbeth said. "I hate hearing about it. You, the young genius, surrounded by *models* and *actresses* probably, all hoping that your genius would rub off on them. The Arthur Miller to their Marilyns."

"There were some girls, yes," Rawlins said. And even though she had asked for it, the sting was intense and venomous. Ellsbeth pressed herself upright and pulled Rawlins into a kiss, snaking her tongue into his mouth. She smiled when she pulled away. "I want you to use writ magic on me tonight."

Rawlins raised an eyebrow. "Oh, do you?"

"Yes. I want to feel like I belong to you."

He kissed her then hard, and she clasped her hands behind his neck, gasping in surprise when he rose, lifting her, and carried her to the bedroom.

THEIR LIMBS WERE STILL TANGLED when Ellsbeth rose early on a Saturday morning. Rawlins came to as she was returning from the bathroom, his hair shaggy and mussed from sleep. "Morning," he said, smiling at her. "Can I make you breakfast?"

Ellsbeth pulled on the pair of jeans that had been disposed of beneath the bed the night before. "I want to get an early start. Finishing an article I'll hopefully submit to the journals in the spring." She kissed him and felt the way he pressed toward her, making the kiss linger. "Not everyone gets to become a tenured professor on good looks alone."

"Hopefully this is at least *somewhat* relevant to your thesis? Or something you'll be able to submit to the department?" Rawlins propped himself up by the elbows, and Ellsbeth's breath caught at the glimpse of chest hair running down his stomach. "Lennox is asking me about your topic. And the longer we delay, the more she'll scrutinize it."

"I'll have something for my thesis the first week of classes, I promise. This is just something I'm working on for me. Very early stages. I'd be embarrassed to have you read anything this rudimentary." The lie had come out more easily than she had imagined.

"If you're writing an article for publication about writ magic—"

"God, no. I'm not. Just a few thoughts on reversing magnetic fields. I read Jonathan Cartwright's new book about magnetism and it gave me some ideas. I feel like I should at least be doing *some* work while classes are out."

"Oh," Rawlins said, lowering himself back down. "Sure, of course. Well, send it to me when you feel it's ready."

Ellsbeth pulled her hair into a messy ponytail. Another benefit of an empty campus—no one to see her returning home with her teeth unbrushed and wearing last night's underwear turned inside out. "Absolutely."

It was a shockingly bright morning, the sun reflecting off the thin sheen of frost that had encased the grass like a carapace in the night. The only life Ellsbeth saw as she walked to the library were a few dull-brown sparrows undaunted by the cold, pecking half-heartedly at the hardened earth.

Ellsbeth had expected to feel guilty about returning to obscuration. The incantation and runes, which had seemed so daunting the first time, now were almost comforting in their familiarity. It took her only half an hour to complete the entire ritual in her apartment, complete with the time-dilation component Rawlins had inadvertently suggested.

The online archive of the school library that was available to anyone on the Newlyn network only contained newspaper articles back to the 1980s, but the neo-Brutalist building had a basement of yellowing computers with a much longer memory, and a microfiche collection with a longer memory than that.

The whoosh of warm circulated air hit her as she strode through the automatic doors. There was only one student-employee working behind the library desk, and he didn't look up from his manga when Ellsbeth swiped her ID to get past the mechanized gates.

"Is the archive library—"

"Closed for break," he said, still not looking up. "Second and third floors are still open."

"Oh," Ellsbeth said. She thumbed at the compounding clay in her palm, feeling it absorb her warmth. "Is there . . . any way you could make an exception? I have a . . . paper due."

The Manga Boy sighed and closed his book. "Yeah, okay. They pay me jack shit here. I don't give a fuck."

She almost burst out laughing. Illegal magic was staining the palm of her left hand red, and she was being let into the library she needed just because she asked, and someone didn't really care.

The lights in the archive library required Ellsbeth to wave her hands wildly a few times before they acknowledged her presence and popped on. The computers hummed pleasantly in a row, and she slid into the chair at the first one and began her search. There was no way she would be able to find the name of the boy her sister had possibly been dating, and she couldn't search "why was a Banestooth pin in my sister's bathroom when she died." And so instead she just searched "Banestooth" and scrolled as far as the scanned newspapers allowed her.

Maybe Bertie had been dating someone trying to pledge Banestooth. Maybe he had come with her into the bathroom that night, looking for a private corner away from a shared dorm with a roommate. Maybe something had happened—maybe even an accident—and he had covered it up. Maybe he had gotten away with it. Maybe Banestooth had helped.

As soon as the theory sprouted in Ellsbeth's mind, she could see it so clearly. Of course, no one would want to ask too many questions; prevent a scandal, that was all that Newlyn sought to do. And after the massive, public scandal of Maxwell Keene, another accidental murder of a fellow student would have been a disaster. Dean Lennox had personally requested that the police not perform an autopsy: She more than anyone would have understood how calamitous another accidental murder would have been for Newlyn's reputation.

Ellsbeth groaned when the search loaded: There were thousands of results in the archive for Banestooth. There was an article on the front page of the *Newlyn Courier* from 1951 about the commemoration of Banestooth's centennial celebration. The accompanying photo featured three rows of stern-faced men in suits standing in front of the same house Banestooth still occupied, only here strung with a banner proclaiming ONE HUNDRED YEARS! Ellsbeth scanned the article: It was fawning, congratulating the "fine men of Banestooth" on their collective excellence in "academia and sport!" Ellsbeth kept scrolling through the online newspaper scans: There was an article about a new chairman of the federal reserve who had been a Newlyn alumnus and a member of Banestooth. Another Banestooth member won the Pulitzer Prize in journalism. Ellsbeth scrolled past three Rhodes Scholars and a handful of Fulbright awardees.

The only vaguely interesting thing Ellsbeth found was a poorly scanned blueprint of the building itself from the 1970s, hidden in an uploaded packet of all of the housing options on campus. She zoomed in on the fuzzy image: The first floor had a large foyer, a dining room, a kitchen, and a handful of double rooms. The second floor had more bedrooms—mostly singles—and something labeled the club room. The third floor had a game room and the largest bedrooms of all, mostly suites. There was no basement.

She printed out the blueprint, just in case, wincing at the whirring of the industrial library printer as it chugged to life, even though she was completely alone on the floor.

The problem was, she wasn't finding anything *nefarious.* The club itself had never been investigated for any wrongdoings. There were no cheating scandals, no allegations of sexual assault or harassment. For something akin to a fraternity, Banestooth had a shockingly chaste reputation, at least in the public record.

Ellsbeth searched "Banestooth + suicide" and was disappointed to find it yielded only two results: a glowing review of a 1991 campus production of *'night, Mother* starring a Banestooth boy, and a mental-health advocacy program led by the Banestooth class of 2009.

Trying to find records of all of the suicides at Newlyn was even more unhelpful. Several years ago, there was a student petition to put up a suicide net below the top floors of the science library to prevent possible jumpers (it never happened). There were scattered obituaries, and though the obituaries themselves never mentioned the cause of death, there was always the telltale punctuation at the bottom of the article: *If you or someone you know is at risk of suicide or self-harm, please call . . .*

Newlyn was a small enough school that there was never anything like an epidemic, not nearly enough suicides that Ellsbeth could pin red string on a corkboard and gasp at the discovery of a mass murderer. Just one, it seemed, every few years, usually a bright-eyed young girl who crumbled under the pressure of life away from home for the first time. Nearly five years ago, there had been a girl named Catherine Teale who had jumped from an open window on the eleventh floor of the science library. Her obituary was equal parts glowing and vague—Catherine was a brilliant girl, with a bright future, et cetera. Only one aspect of the article caught Ellsbeth's eye. It was a quote from one of Catherine's friends: *"I'm still in shock. I just never thought Catherine would ever do something like this. Friday night, we went out together to a party on Governor Street. Saturday morning, she was dead."*

Ellsbeth lived on Governor. About half of the street was graduate student housing. The other half was dotted with aging Victorian homes occupied by locals or junior professors. It was not a street any undergraduate would ever trek to in order to attend a party. Unless they were going to a party at Banestooth.

There were frustratingly few articles about Catherine Teale in the archives. Her obituary had just two photos of her—what appeared to be a senior class picture, and a photo of Catherine in a tank top, her hair in a braid, sitting on a rock and grinning, face flushed having reached a mountain peak after a hike.

Ellsbeth needed more. She needed the police report. She needed photographs of the scene. The compounding clay seemed to vibrate in her pocket. She began making mental plans to go back to the police station, but as it turned out she didn't need to.

While she scrolled, she found a link to a forum she didn't recognize.

> i was there the day catherine teale died. i was fucking there.

>> You saw her fall?

> no, but i saw her body at the bottom of the library. fucking gnarly.

> Pics or it didn't happen.
>
> She was in my freshman dorm. She was nice. RIP. don't ask for pics of a fucking dead girl!!!!!
>
> :'((((((pics.

The last comment was a hyperlink. Ellsbeth held her breath and clicked. The photos were taken on a cellphone, through police tape. Catherine Teale's body was bloodied and twisted like a circus performer on dark pavement slick with blood and blackened snow. Her dark braid covered her face, but still, Ellsbeth had to turn away from the photos several times before her stomach settled enough to let her look in earnest.

There were cuts across her bare arms, and a sickening pool of blood so dark on the concrete that it looked brown, soaking into her jeans. But there, in the third picture, she could see it—three cuts across her chest, deep and already scabbing over. Three parallel cuts on a diagonal, from the clavicle to the breast.

The same cuts that Bertie had.

The buzzing sensation started again in Ellsbeth's head, the feeling she got when she was about to complete a ritual correctly or solve a difficult problem.

Ellsbeth went back through the obituaries in the archives, looking for connective threads. She looked for girls, for freshmen, deaths that involved blood.

There was Bertie last winter. And Catherine Teale four years before that.

But four years before Catherine Teale, there was a young woman named Emily Kirkman who jumped in front of a train. And there was Paula Rodriguez who leapt from the top of the library four years before Emily. Ellsbeth couldn't find a suicide four years before Paula, but there was a girl named Constance who was hit by a car while walking home from a friend's house at midnight. Every death was in the winter, at the top of the second semester.

Ellsbeth didn't know exactly what connected the deaths, but she printed out all the obituaries anyway. Maybe it was just a coincidence.

But if Banestooth was involved, she would find out how, and she would get proof.

As Ellsbeth returned to her computer station carrying pages still warm from the printer, she stopped in her tracks, a wave of shock flooding through her. Sitting at the next station over, evidently waiting for her, was a dark-haired young man with hollow cheekbones she recognized in an instant. *Maxwell Keene.*

It felt strange seeing him in person, after having glimpsed his face in so many news articles and imagined him so vividly in the story Rawlins recently unfolded to her. It was like meeting a celebrity—or even more, like a fictional character stepping into the real world.

Max sat in a swivel chair, rotating idly back and forth, and gave a tight grin as she approached. "Ellsbeth, right?"

She nodded and swallowed hard, trying not to show her fear. "And . . . you're Max."

"I'm Max," he agreed. "Sorry if I startled you, I just saw you over here, and . . . since we have something in common, or *someone,* really . . . I thought I'd come say hi."

"You were . . . here, in the archive?" she said, glancing around. The large space now felt ominously vacant; she wished there was *anyone* else in sight.

"That's not a crime, is it?" he replied, then looked back in the direction of the entrance—far enough away that Ellsbeth wasn't even sure she'd be heard if she shouted for help. "They're certainly not very rigorous about security." He eyed the printed pages she carried. "What's he got you researching?"

"Oh, this is . . . just a personal project, actually," Ellsbeth said.

She took a breath and studied Max; seeing the similarity to Rawlins in his features, the nose and eyes of the man she loved, softened her toward him. He frightened her, but she could also see the pain under the surface, and a wave of compassion rose up. "You know, Max . . . I can't imagine how hard it was, what you went through, but . . . your dad really does care about you. A lot."

The remark was intended to disarm him, but it was instantly clear it had the opposite effect. Max's features darkened. "So . . . he told *you*? Wow. You two must be *very close.*"

Ellsbeth's skin prickled at the insinuation in his voice, but she decided to ignore his contempt and try to get through to him sincerely. "I just think you should give him a chance," she said. "He's made mistakes, like anyone, but he's . . . a good person."

Max's lip curled into a mirthless smirk. "That's what you think, because you're still *in it.* I feel bad for you, really. I know how it feels, when his light shines on you. You feel like the most brilliant person in the world, I bet. Like you can do *anything*."

Ellsbeth said nothing. His words rang a bell of truth inside her.

"It's funny," Max went on, looking away as he lost himself in memory. "When he was working with me, it felt like I actually *got* the father I'd always wanted. But . . ." He shook his head, fury showing through the pain, then locked his gaze on Ellsbeth. "Whatever you think he's giving you . . . it's a lie. All he does is *take.* So . . . fair warning: Get away while you still can."

With that, Max stood up, pulling on his coat, and headed off. Ellsbeth remained frozen in place for a long time, only realizing after he'd left that her fingernails were digging into her palms so hard they had left marks.

Though it was only late afternoon, the sky had darkened by the time Ellsbeth left the library. She could see the spire of Rawlins's Victorian house from the hill where the library was perched. He was probably cooking dinner at that very moment. But instead of walking south, she turned back toward her own apartment.

Part of her wanted to go tell Rawlins about the encounter with Max—to unload her anxieties and put her fears to rest, to be reassured that he wouldn't actually *do* anything. But she didn't want Rawlins to worry about her. She didn't want to torture him further with more evidence of his son's contempt. The kindest thing here, she rationalized, was to keep this to herself.

Besides, she still needed to shower, and to think more about how she would prepare to interrogate the brothers of Banestooth without raising suspicions. She needed to be alone, because if she curled up on Rawlins's couch next to him that night, she knew she would want to tell him the truth about her investigation, and that was impossible.

The blue safety lights that dotted campus caused the bare trees lining the footpath to throw long and sinister shadows.

More than once, Ellsbeth felt a prickle on the back of her neck and heard the sound of footsteps behind her, but every time she turned, no one was there. She kept her numbing fingers on her phone just in case, but the campus was empty. Everyone else had gone to warm family homes to celebrate Christmas, and Ellsbeth was here, walking alone with only her theories and her ghosts.

RAWLINS

Spending the winter break with Ellsbeth was like living in a dream, and the rules of reality bent accordingly. Time moved strangely; their moments together felt dense and expansive. Rawlins would blink and find that hours had passed. The distance between his home and the campus seemed to extend, isolating them from its concerns.

But eventually, Rawlins had to go into his office to post his grades, collect his mail, and fill out requisition paperwork for the Practicum. Newlyn looked like a wasteland, nearly dark in midafternoon, with wind whipping the snow. The lights were on and the heat was going in the office, but aside from a department secretary filling out a sudoku puzzle, Rawlins thought he might be the only faculty member present—until Lennox intercepted him in the hallway, as he was getting out his keys to unlock his office. "Tad," she said dryly. "Can I have a word?"

"Hi, Maggie," he said as he opened the door, indicating for her to step inside ahead of him. He dropped his bag on the desk and took a seat.

Lennox remained standing. Her gaze was stony as she closed the door. "What did you tell him?" she said.

Rawlins did not answer immediately. Uncertain yet what she knew, he decided the best course of action was to play dumb. "What do you mean?"

"Max won't come out and say it, but he's been . . . *insinuating* things."

"I'm sorry, Maggie . . . I'm sure it's a tough transition," Rawlins offered blandly.

Lennox laughed bitterly, sinking into the chair and staring through the floor with a haunted look in her eyes. "Honestly . . . it's a *nightmare.* I feel horrible for thinking it, but . . . it was easier before he got out. Not just for me, I think . . . for *him.*"

Rawlins's insides twisted with guilt. If his intervention hadn't made things better, what had it all been for? "I'm sure it just takes time to readjust. For everyone."

Lennox shook her head. "I don't know . . . When he's home, he barely comes out of his room. Like a teenager, he won't let me in there. Won't come sit with us for meals, just takes his plate off the table and goes upstairs. Ben and I sit there and I try not to cry. And then Max will come down and leave sometimes for ten, twelve hours at a time, without telling me where he's going. And if I ask, he absolutely *explodes.* He was always an angry kid, but there's something else there now . . . *hatred.*"

"He's traumatized," Rawlins said. "I tried to talk to him, but—"

"Did you *tell him*?" Lennox interrupted, and when Rawlins hesitated, she turned away, seething. "How *could* you? Without talking to me first?"

"He deserves to know the truth," Rawlins said, attempting to keep his tone even. "He deserved to know a long time ago." Rawlins expected a sharp retort, but Lennox's eyes glistened, her unflappable stoicism failing her. She looked weakened, like she had borne a heavy burden for years and was finally starting to buckle under its weight.

Rawlins was struck with an impulse to console her, but before he could find the words, her vulnerability vanished, replaced with cold fury. "You always thought you knew best," she spat at him. "You thought I was a bad mother. But I wasn't. There's just . . . a *darkness* in him. And now . . ." She shook her head and stood up, heading for the door but pausing at the threshold. "I don't know how you thought this would go. But I promise you, it's going to end badly."

Then she was gone, and a knot of dread settled into the pit of Rawlins's stomach.

THAT EVENING, WHEN HE RETURNED to his home, Rawlins considered telling Ellsbeth about his conversation with Lennox, but ultimately he decided to keep it to himself. There was nothing to *do* for now. Best to give the matter some time, let Max calm down, and try to enjoy the present.

The moments Rawlins shared with Ellsbeth felt both mundane and precious. The domesticity of their routine did nothing to dampen their erotic enthusiasm. Rawlins knew that the excitement he felt every time he caught a glimpse of her exposed skin could not survive indefinitely, but so far his lust had not abated—primarily because their imaginations kept yielding novel possibilities. Their sex life was playful; he was able to confess to her fantasies that might have seemed too embarrassing to admit to himself. And dabbling with writ magic opened up new horizons entirely; he bound her body in a delicious variety of ways, in every room of the house (and once, both painfully and pleasurably, on the stairs).

One night, she brought up the possibility of taking their experimentation to the next level. "Do you ever think obscuration could be . . . I dunno, kinda sexy?"

He looked at her, a mixture of curiosity and nervousness twisting his stomach. "How do you mean?"

"It's such an incredible power," she said. "The thought of somebody using it . . . especially *on me* . . . it's hot. And for me, the idea of submitting to *that* level of control, over my *mind* . . ." She trailed off, clearly turned on by the prospect.

Rawlins had to admit, he was intrigued by the possibility; the taboo around the practice had softened slightly in his mind, no doubt both from secretly trying it out on his own, as well as from trying so many things already with Ellsbeth. But he couldn't tell how serious she was about actually *doing* it. "It's definitely . . . an interesting fantasy," he said, noncommittal.

"Oh come on," she said teasingly, sliding closer. "Are you telling me that you don't like the thought of having *some* control over my mind?"

He cocked his head, playing the possibilities through in his mind. "Not if you were . . . *unconscious* in any way."

"No—I wouldn't want that, either," she said. "I'd want to feel it all. And remember the whole thing. But there are lots of possibilities. I read an account in one of the books . . . maybe the Sayoto? About a ritual for implanting trigger words in the subject's mind. I bet that would be possible."

Rawlins nodded absently. "I recall something like that. Never substantiated, though, was it?"

"The reports are all anecdotal," she said. "Some of them seem a little ridiculous. But others track, at least in terms of what I'd expect to be logical and effective."

He squinted at her. "Are you seriously considering . . . ?"

"I don't see why not," Ellsbeth said with a shrug, clearly trying to seem casual about it. "It's not like it's that much *more* illegal than writ magic. In for a penny."

"But it is more dangerous," Rawlins replied. "Meddling with someone's mind, using untested mechanicals . . . I like your brain too much to take any chances with it."

"I'd trust you," she said. "And even more—I would trust *us*. If we designed the ritual together, I'm sure we'd see any potential pitfalls and avoid them."

"We do work well together," Rawlins agreed. "You're sure about this?"

"I am," Ellsbeth said. "It's exciting. And with *you* involved, I'm confident it will be safe."

Rawlins could not deny the primal thrill it gave him to be trusted by her, and he felt his defenses softening. He *had* gotten obscuration to work on his own, after all, with no apparent side effects, using the ritual Ellsbeth had designed.

"So . . . trigger words?" He cocked an eyebrow.

Ellsbeth beamed, seizing on his apparent agreement. "Yes, exactly," she said. "The Sayoto ritual proposes that you can induce a stimulus response. An action, or a physical reaction, elicited by hearing the trigger. Which could be a spoken word or phrase, or even a specific sound."

"Very Pavlovian," Rawlins said. "But is that really *obscuration*? Aren't you describing more of a . . . physical body effect? A reflex?"

"Classical conditioning happens in the brain," Ellsbeth said. "Definitely obscuration. I mean it's not as deep as some other effects that might be possible, but I don't want to be *brainwashed.* I just want to give you a little conduit directly into my head." She took his hand and put his finger against her temple.

He weighed this, trying not to let on how much the possibility excited him. "Could be fun . . . but I haven't had much difficulty getting you to do whatever I told you to, without any need for magic. Turns out, some people like being told what to do."

"That's true," Ellsbeth said, smiling up at him. "But it could elicit an action. Or, you know . . . a very specific physical response."

"Ahhhh." Rawlins grinned and rolled on top of her, pinning her wrists down. "I like the way you think."

Crafting the ritual was a project they undertook together, filling a few long afternoons in his study. The ritual Ellsbeth had sent Rawlins weeks earlier served as a jumping-off point, providing a structure from which to build something new. It was an intriguing intellectual puzzle—how to cause an involuntary physical response—and also slightly ridiculous; the whiteboard overflowed with theories and calculations, advanced work that looked deadly serious, when in fact they were crafting a method for magically inducing an orgasm.

They worked together as equals, Ellsbeth sitting at his desk with her laptop open while he pored over volumes. Sometimes they laughed, then fell into silence for extended periods as they both churned over a problem in their minds, only to erupt into newfound excitement when they made a new flurry of progress. "You have to read this!" Ellsbeth would exclaim every few hours, forcing the screen of her laptop toward him with a pertinent paragraph highlighted, and every time, he couldn't help but smile at her unfiltered enthusiasm.

When they ran up against a challenge, they talked it out in tandem. "We need to isolate the subject of the ritual so that only the target is affected by the trigger word," Rawlins mused aloud. "A metallic elemental would be good for the targeting. The tricky part is, all the metals have secondary effects, which could complicate the efficacy."

Ellsbeth interrupted quickly, when he had only barely finished his sentence. "What about silver iodide? I feel like that would work."

Rawlins was surprised by how fast the answer came to her, out of dozens of different possibilities. It was a brilliant idea—not intuitive, but quite possibly perfect. For a moment, he wondered if she had al ready thought this through, and was only pretending to figure it out now for his benefit. Or was her knowledge of metallic elementals and their various effects so comprehensive that she could recall such a thing in an instant?

He tried to set aside his momentary suspicion and focus on the task at hand. "Yes . . . silver iodide might work . . . but it has a time-dilation effect," Rawlins said. "It could extend or contract the duration."

"It *would* work. And we could easily just factor the dilation effect into our calculations," Ellsbeth said. "There are timetables about the effect of silver iodide on rituals. The math might get complicated, but we should still be able to calculate it predictably."

"It could be used as the basis for setting the duration of the entire ritual . . ." Rawlins murmured, picking up on her point, as a grin spread over his face. "You're brilliant," he said, kissing her neck while she typed the latest addition to their recipe.

As they neared completion, Rawlins could not help but wish they could publish their results; it was an elegant, interesting piece of work. Even more, the thought of publishing a paper with his name and Ellsbeth's sharing a byline brought him a surprising rush of joy. It was the prospect of winning *together,* and having someone to celebrate with.

Of course, the illegal (and tawdry) subject matter of their investigation precluded it from ever being shared with the world. It would need to be their secret, just like their entire relationship. And while the secrecy had been exciting before—the sneaking around, the stolen glances—he found himself wishing, on some level, that what they had could be shown off in public.

The weekend before the semester was about to start, they could both feel reality coming back toward them, like a train whistling in the distance. They decided to test the ritual on a Saturday afternoon, creating a circle on the floor in Rawlins's study, with Ellsbeth, the subject, at the center. Her eyes stayed on him as he spoke the Latin of the ritual, and then he said the word that would become the trigger; to her amusement, he chose *licorice.*

Afterward, she fidgeted, nervous. It was unclear if the ritual had worked. "Aren't you going to test it?" she asked, crossing and uncrossing her legs on the couch, both eager and slightly fearful at what it would be like, if it was successful, to have an orgasm with no buildup at all.

"I'm confident in our work," he said, and made a show of looking at his watch. "I calculated the duration for eight hours, so we've got plenty of time. You should get home and change."

"Change . . . for what?"

He feigned surprise at her question, holding back a smile. "For the ballet. I got us tickets for tonight."

AN HOUR AND A HALF later, they were crossing the snowplowed highway toward their destination, a theater in Bennington. Ellsbeth sat in the passenger seat in a dark-blue dress, her hair pinned up. Rawlins worked hard to keep his eyes on the road while her face hovered in his periphery, drawing his gaze with a pull like gravity. Spending so much time with her lately and studying every inch of her skin for hours in bed had somehow only deepened his attraction; he felt like a scholar whose entire field of expertise was a single person. As passing headlights framed the delicate curve of her cheek and slid away, two thoughts came to him at once, paired in a way that delivered a shiver of pleasure.

She's perfect, and she's mine.

But to speak such thoughts aloud seemed excessive, bordering on psychotic, so he told her simply, "You look beautiful."

"And you clean up nice," she replied, reaching across to smooth his tie, fingers drifting down to his waist. It took all his focus to keep his eyes on the road. "So are you going to test it out in the car or make me wait even longer?"

He grinned without turning his head. "I've told you before, you need to learn patience."

Being out in the world together, all dressed up, felt like they were getting away with something. They hurried through the cold into the theater and found their seats moments before the performance began, a modern staging of *Romeo and Juliet;* Rawlins had always enjoyed the Prokofiev score and had been eyeing the performance for months.

Sitting in the dark beside Ellsbeth, Rawlins was struck by the sense of *belonging* that filled his entire being. They were anonymous as ever, unlikely to encounter anyone from Newlyn so far from campus and while classes weren't in session. The self-consciousness of their first dinner date was a distant memory; even if they could not be a couple in any traditional sense, it seemed so natural now to be out in the world with her at his side.

She leaned into him, wrapping her arm around his and leaning her head lightly on his shoulder while the bombast of the music began below. His hand settled onto her knee, pulling the fabric of her dress up just enough for his fingers to rest on her skin, lightly tracing her flesh. They both gazed at the stage, but his attention was as attuned to her as he knew hers was to him, their bodies subtly straining toward each other in a shared bubble of quiet affection.

He waited long enough that he hoped she would forget the ritual entirely. Twenty minutes into the show, when he was confident she was caught up in the performance, the music swelled, and Rawlins leaned in and whispered into Ellsbeth's ear, "Licorice."

If he had any doubt the ritual had worked, it was dispelled instantly; he heard her sharp inhale, and the faint catch of a stifled moan in her throat; her entire body tensed and she squirmed in her seat. Her arm tightened around his. She stifled her response enough to avoid drawing attention, but he was thrilled with the rush of power over her pleasure.

"You're terrible," she whispered to him in the darkness, and her hand drifted up his thigh, tracing his cock hardening through his slacks.

He did it once more during the show, and again at the final curtain call, forcing her to stay seated a moment longer when everyone else stood to applaud. He glanced back at her as though chastising her refusal to stand, and she bit her lip, shaking her head at his mischief.

He had forgotten how fun it was—or perhaps he had never known—to *play* like this. To amuse each other. To live with a shared joke, the premise of which was the absurd excess of their mutual desire.

After the performance, they filtered out into the lobby, borne along with the river of spectators headed for the exits, when a voice interrupted. "Ellsbeth?"

Rawlins turned along with her to see a handsome man in an ill-fitting suit.

"Oscar," Ellsbeth said, clearly taken aback, and then self-consciously looked at him, unprepared to make an introduction smoothly. "This is, uh, my friend . . ."

"Thaddeus Rawlins." He offered the young man a handshake, feeling the gaze appraising him as Oscar tried to suss out whether or not this was a date. "Nice to meet you. The . . . runner?"

"Yes, that's me," he said, visibly confused that Rawlins had heard about him at all. He looked to Ellsbeth. "So, uh . . . how have you been?"

"I'm good!" she said, nervousness making her overly effusive. "Just really busy. During the semester, I mean. Now, it's nice to have some downtime, right? I like the winter."

"That's great," he said. "I'm more of a summer guy. If I can't get outside, I go stir-crazy."

Rawlins watched the way Oscar's eyes scanned Ellsbeth. He could see that Oscar's interest in her had never completely waned; he was testing the waters, uncertain if there might be something to rekindle. It gave Rawlins a twisting sensation in his gut—not wholly unpleasant, but primal. Jealousy, he realized. The recognition of a rival.

"You might have seasonal affective disorder," Rawlins said, keeping his tone friendly. "Weeks without seeing the sun takes a toll." He shot Ellsbeth a sideways glance. "You should get a blue-light lamp. Perk yourself up with a piece of fruit or candy. Personally, I'm fond of licorice."

The word had its intended effect. Ellsbeth closed her eyes briefly and swallowed hard, her body responding to the shock of the sudden orgasm while she did her best to hide it.

"Yeah, maybe," Oscar said, puzzled by Rawlins's suggestion and sensing a shift in Ellsbeth, though he seemed to have no idea what was happening.

"Well, it was great running into you," Ellsbeth choked out, giving a friendly wave in an evident effort to avoid a hug before breaking off. Rawlins nodded a farewell to Oscar and followed her into the crowd.

"*Terrible*," she said once they made it outside, but he could see she was barely suppressing a smile.

He shrugged. "If we run into one of my exes, you are welcome to do the same."

"He's not an ex. We went on, like, two dates," she replied. "Which only made me realize how much I wanted you. And for the record, *your* ex is running the department. You really want me to humiliate you in front of her?"

He raised his hands in a mea culpa. "I'm sorry if I embarrassed you."

She looked at him incisively. "It's okay. I like seeing your possessive side."

"I am definitely not *possessive,*" he replied. But it was undeniable at that moment that he wanted her to belong to him completely—and he felt both the joy, and the fear, that came along with that realization.

ELLSBETH

Rawlins's sheets were deliciously cool, and Ellsbeth found that she preferred spending lazy mornings working from his bed, with her books and papers spread across his duvet. Rawlins deposited a mug of green tea on the bedside table and kissed her on the head. He read over her shoulder: "Orpheum rituals?" For centuries, theaters had employed arcanists capable of casting rituals for vocal amplification to ensure their actors' lines would be audible to the last row. Microphones made the tedious and difficult ritual obsolete.

"Just trying to practice my ancient Greek."

"Remind me to tell you about the summer I spent on Naxos. The heat from my sunburn could have powered the entire island."

"Why are Orpheum rituals so *hard*?" Ellsbeth said, snapping her laptop shut. "They were doing them back in Shakespeare's time!"

"Well," Rawlins said, "they're easier when you find the rhythm of them. They were originally songs. Hence Orpheum, after Orpheus—the singer, son of the muse Calliope."

"I *know* who Orpheus is," Ellsbeth said, grinning up at Rawlins.

"Sorry, I got into professor mode."

"Can I just say," Ellsbeth said, taking a sip of her tea, "I always thought Orpheus was kind of an idiot. So he goes down to the underworld to save his wife, right? And then they specifically tell him, *Don't look back at her until you're at the surface.* That's all he needs to do!

Just don't look back until you're home and the love of your life is alive again. Simple directions!"

"You've *always* thought this?" Rawlins sat on the edge of the bed beside her and nuzzled into her hair.

Ellsbeth wriggled away. "Yes. I have. If I was Orpheus, I would have saved Eurydice, easily."

Rawlins laughed then. "See, that's where you're wrong."

"I'm not usually wrong," Ellsbeth said.

"That's true," Rawlins murmured. He took her mug and placed it back on the bedside table and then slid into bed beside her. "But if you were Orpheus, you absolutely would have looked back because you would love Eurydice the way he does. That's the whole tragedy. He loves her so deeply that when he stops hearing her footsteps, he doesn't have a choice. He needs to make sure the woman he loves is still walking behind him."

They were lying next to each other. Ellsbeth pressed herself onto her side, her face just inches away from his. His eyes were blue, but up close Ellsbeth realized his irises contained golden flecks. The sun coming through the window lightened his hair, and Ellsbeth could see the boyishness in his face. She wanted to run her finger across every one of his planes and surfaces, across his brow, down his cheek, over his lips. But instead, she just kept looking at him, willing herself to preserve that moment in her mind, of the two of them in bed, surrounded by papers and the motes of dust suspended and sparkling in the sunlight.

"No," Ellsbeth said. "That's the thing. If I were Orpheus, I would have trusted her."

AFTER LUNCH, RAWLINS WENT BACK to his office to finish a few undergraduate essays he still had overdue, and Ellsbeth returned to her own apartment to do laundry and shower in her own space after two straight days at Rawlins's house. She sang as the hot water came down and she washed her hair, almost embarrassed at the tactile pleasure of using her nails to scrub her scalp. She felt present in her body in a way she hadn't since Bertie's death; it was as if her life had been on tape delay, her consciousness moving through the world half a second slower than the world had been moving. Now everything was immediate. Ellsbeth was acutely aware of the sensation of the spray of the shower hitting her, of the slick conditioner dripping down her back, of the steam filling the small bathroom and making the almond-y scent of her body wash hang in the air.

It had been only a few hours since she had last seen Rawlins, and she already wanted to be next to him again. She checked her phone as she was wrapping her hair in a towel: Reading through these essays and I'm almost embarrassed to say I miss you already. So let's pretend I texted you to say something else. Like . . . did no one teach college students the difference between "effect" and "affect" and "elicit" and "illicit"?

Ellsbeth texted back: You elicit illicit thoughts in me. The effect is clear. I guess you just affect me.

God that turns me on. Good girl

They were both pedantic, cerebral, self-isolating, ambitious, academic. They were both lonely. And they had somehow found each other.

The first time Ellsbeth had brought a hot beverage to Rawlins on campus, she had brought him two teas to choose between. In the months since, she had learned that he preferred coffee. And so Ellsbeth used her ID card to buzz herself in to the arcane mechanicals department building while balancing an Americano for him and jasmine tea for her.

Because it was winter break, the hallway was eerily underlit, shadowed strangely from the windows. She felt herself speed up as she got closer to his office, the light visible under his door an island on the well-worn carpeting. It was only the hot drinks in her hands that kept her from a full run.

She pushed the door open with her shoulder without knocking. He was looking down, red pen in hand, his hair mussed and sticking up at odd angles.

"Surprise," she said. "Thought you might need an afternoon pick-me-up." There was half a second where Ellsbeth worried she had overstepped, that he would be angry or annoyed that she had interrupted when he'd told her that he was going to be working, but then the pen dropped and he beamed up at her with such genuine delight that her fear drained away in an instant like water from a tub.

Ellsbeth kicked the door closed behind her. "How are the essays?"

"Awful. Thankfully I'm almost done. And desperate for a distraction."

Ellsbeth perched at the edge of his desk and handed him his coffee. "Black, like you like it." He took a long sip and Ellsbeth reached over to take a handful of black licorice from his dish.

"Have you even had to refill this once over the course of the semester?" Ellsbeth said. "Or does no one except me actually like this stuff?"

"You," Rawlins said, "have very particular tastes. Luckily for me." He took a piece of licorice and examined it in his hands. "Do you think the ritual still works? *Licorice.*"

"Mmmm, nope," Ellsbeth said. "Unfortunately. But the good news is, I don't think you need it."

In another breath, Rawlins was kissing Ellsbeth while she was still sitting on his desk. In another breath, they were both standing, and they were kissing up against his bookshelf. Ellsbeth wrapped one leg around him and pulled him closer, then spun the two of them so that he was against the bookshelves. She took his wrists in her hands.

"What if *I* controlled you?" she mused. He playfully struggled against her (admittedly weak) grip. "Have you ever wanted to be dominated?"

Rawlins ran his lips down her neck and across her collarbone. "Actually, no," he said. "But I'd try anything with you." They kept kissing, the taste of black licorice astringent and tannic on their tongues, and the world disappeared in a blur the way it always did when she was with Rawlins.

Until she heard a creak. Ellsbeth had been carrying two drinks, and she hadn't locked the door to the office.

"I'm so sorry," said a small, squeaking voice. "I'll just . . . come back later."

The adrenaline flooded Ellsbeth's body. Her hairline became icy with cold sweat and her throat suddenly felt swollen. It was hard to breathe. Her vision spun and narrowed.

Mary-Abigail Pinkney was standing in the doorway, half covering her eyes with her hand. But there was no mistaking that she had seen exactly what Ellsbeth and Rawlins had been doing.

RAWLINS

Rawlins's mouth went dry with panic. He froze, searching for words, but before he could find any, Mary-Abigail was gone, pulling the door shut behind her. He considered chasing after the girl, but running her down might only make things worse.

He looked up at Ellsbeth standing by the bookshelf, just as frozen as he was. The look that passed between them was strangely one of *mourning*. The brittle lock on their hermetically sealed secret was broken. The only question was how far the damage would spread.

"Fuck," he muttered. "So, so stupid . . ." Then he saw the hurt look on Ellsbeth's face, and amended, "I mean . . . not you. Me. I should have made sure the door was locked . . ."

Ellsbeth paced, restless and anxious. "What was she even doing here on campus? In the middle of fucking winter break." Her cursing was uncharacteristic; he could tell that her anxiety was coming out as anger.

Rawlins took a deep breath, trying to be rational. "I should go talk to her. Maybe I can explain that this was . . . *my fault*, at the very least."

"No, let me," she replied, grabbing her coat. "I can try talking to her, sort of . . . woman-to-woman. Maybe she won't feel the need to tell anyone. If I beg."

"Ellsbeth, no, I'm the one who's been irresponsible here." He reached out to touch her shoulder, hoping to get her to pause, but she shrugged off his hand.

"*Please.* I can handle this."

"Ellsbeth . . . you shouldn't have to—"

"Do you trust me?" she interrupted him pointedly. It was not merely a question, he saw in her expression; it was a challenge.

"I do . . ." he said cautiously, and he mostly meant it, though he wasn't sure if he *should.*

"Then let me take care of this," she said. She slung her backpack over her shoulder and headed out the door.

After she left, Rawlins was a bundle of nerves. He stayed in his office for a while, trying to pretend everything was normal, and not to think about the fact that he may have just torpedoed the rest of his career, and Ellsbeth's with it. The romantic ruminations of the last few weeks suddenly felt hopelessly naïve. How had he ever imagined that he and Ellsbeth could have a future? That he would get away with all this, that there would be no consequences?

Once it became clear that he wasn't going to get anything done in his office, he pulled on his coat and started walking home. The sun set so early these days, most of his walk was in shadow; he slid on the ice, distracted, and bowed his head against the bone-penetrating wind.

He watched his entire downfall unfold as a movie projected in his mind. He could see Mary-Abigail telling the story of what she had seen to Lennox, whom he knew would fire him immediately. He imagined his colleagues, sharing the news in gossipy huddles around the office. He could already picture Gallway's smug delight, with the rest of the faculty lining up like vultures to poach his classes and be first in line to get his office. He could see Ellsbeth trying to continue, thinking she was immune to the whispers behind her back, but she wouldn't last more than a semester; maybe she'd try to transfer somewhere far away, in the hope rumors wouldn't follow her, but this might derail her career permanently.

And Max. Still seething with anger at the revelation that Rawlins was his father, this public humiliation would only confirm the boy's suspicions that Rawlins was some sort of monster who preyed on his students. Any hope of his son speaking to him again had just been obliterated.

These thoughts and more followed him all the way home, through the first drink he downed hastily before his coat was even off, and the second one that he sipped, allowing the whiskey to burn on his tongue with every drop.

He was just starting to feel its warmth melting the edge of his anxiety when Ellsbeth sent a text: Talked to her . . . we don't have anything to worry about. Promise. Rawlins stared at the message, feeling the knot of tension loosen in his chest but uncertain if he could dare believe his good fortune, when she sent another message: I'll come over later?

In his kitchen that night, Rawlins was eager to hear Ellsbeth recount the incident. "Tell me everything," he said as he poured her a glass of wine. "I want to know everything."

"It wasn't too bad," Ellsbeth said, taking a sip; there was a peculiar vacancy to her expression, as though she were still in shock. "I just sort of said it was my fault, and that . . . it wasn't what she thought it was. And she seemed fine to just forget about it, and not make a big deal."

"That's . . . not entirely reassuring," Rawlins said. "It sounds like she just wanted to get out of the conversation. But that doesn't mean she won't tell anyone."

Ellsbeth looked away, bit her lip, then let out a dramatic exhale. "Okay, look. The truth is, I told her I've had a crush on you for a long time. And that I basically *threw myself* at you. And you were actually in the middle of rejecting me, and I was practically begging you to hook up with me . . ."

Rawlins studied her expression, not sure how to react to this. "Really? And . . . she believed that?"

"She did," Ellsbeth said. "I'm a terrible liar, normally. But when I was telling her about you rejecting me, I thought about what it would be like if you *had* rejected me, and . . ." Ellsbeth sniffed and looked up at him from beneath her eyelashes. "I cried, okay?"

He pulled her into a hug. "I'm sorry . . . I'm sure that wasn't easy." He stroked her hair. "I know you hate the thought of being pitied."

She sniffled against his chest and laughed at herself. "I promise, it's taken care of. I won't let anything . . ." She didn't finish the thought.

Rawlins kissed the top of her head, then pulled away. "It was a smart idea, but . . . Maybe I should still have a word with her, too. Just to . . . you know, shore up any uncertainty."

Ellsbeth stared at him intently. "Don't you trust me?" It was the second time that day she had asked him, and while the intended effect of the question was undoubtedly reassurance, this time it felt defensive.

"I do," he said hollowly, and gave her a thin smile. "You're right, I'm sure it's fine . . . we'll just have to be extra careful for a while."

"Of course," she said. "Back off a little. No more office fucking . . . for a while, at least." She gave him a wounded smile, and he nodded. Then disappointment entered her expression. "Sorry, are you asking me . . . to leave?"

Part of him *did* want her to go; getting caught had made him feel prickly and paranoid. But the hurt already coloring her face was plain, despite her effort to hide it, and he told himself to man up and not make this any worse on her. He shook his head. "No, of course not. Just . . . once the semester resumes, we'll have to be . . ."

"Very careful," she said. "Of course."

The rest of the night was more strained than any they'd had since before the winter break began. Rawlins tried to relax during dinner, but he couldn't stop thinking about how adamant she had been that he not follow up with Mary-Abigail. It bothered him. But maybe that was just Ellsbeth's independent streak—the girl who hated the prospect of being taken care of, insisting on being the one to clean up their mess.

They both worked for a while after they ate, and slipped into bed at ten o'clock like an old married couple, reading side by side. She smiled at him before she turned off the light on her side, and gave him a kiss that was unmistakably an invitation to more. But he met her lips with a perfunctory peck and continued reading, while she rolled over on her side.

Rawlins tried to focus on his book but found himself increasingly restless, while Ellsbeth dozed peacefully beside him. He was familiar enough with the rhythms of his insomnia to know that staying in bed at this point was useless; he'd have to get up and try again later.

Downstairs, he got himself another drink and took it to the study, which had still not been cleaned up entirely from the obscuration ritual he and Ellsbeth had conducted the day of the ballet. Pleased to have a worthwhile but mindless task, he started putting away the elementals that had been left out, pushing drawers shut softly so the sound would not carry upstairs and wake Ellsbeth.

As he filed away the vial of yellowish silver iodide powder, he smiled at the memory of Ellsbeth's brilliant idea, which had indeed worked out perfectly. But as he recalled the very ease with which it had come to her, he paused. Troubled. Literature on obscuration was all ancient and obtuse, with nothing about specific elementals. So how could she have known with such confidence that it would work in exactly the way she anticipated?

There was only one way: If she had already tried obscuration herself.

Rawlins looked around the study, remembering the afternoon he and Ellsbeth had done the obscuration ritual together here—her excitement to try it, her eagerness to see if it worked, the effortless intimacy between them that had lasted all night . . . and suddenly, he felt very much like a fool. Had she been pretending that whole time? When really, she had used obscuration before and knew perfectly well that it would work. The thrill of shared discovery had been a lie, a performance; he bristled at being so utterly condescended to.

Of course, the fact that Ellsbeth was already using obscuration should not have been shocking, considering that *he* had used it as well, and kept that fact secret from her. But he had a very specific purpose that justified what he did. A worthwhile *reason.* What could she possibly be using it for? Was she really just testing it out on a whim?

No, he realized with a certainty that hit him like a swallowed brick. She had wanted to pursue this line of inquiry since the beginning of the semester; it had been an outgrowth of her studies into writ magic. She had brought up the idea of studying obscuration so casually, but now he felt certain that it had always been her plan.

What could she have wanted that required obscuration, bending someone else's mind to her will? He played through the timeline in his mind, trying to understand.

Ellsbeth had begun studying obscuration around November—the same time he had tried to put an end to their affair. They had agreed to "no feelings," but then it had slid into . . . not just feelings but professions of love. And the night of the ballet . . . that was not just an illicit sexual game, but an outing, a proper *date,* and afterward he was left wondering if they could actually be together, have a relationship publicly.

He had changed his mind about her in a way that surprised even him—at the exact same time she was studying the magical manipulation of the human mind.

Were his thoughts about her really his own? Were the *feelings* that caused them even real? Or were they the result of an obscuration ritual, implanting ideas and emotions into his brain so deeply that he would never suspect?

Suddenly every romantic thought he'd had for the last few weeks felt suspect. The way this felt so different, so unique, so *unlike him.* Was she *playing* him? How could he ever possibly know?

His mind dove back in time to the one occasion he had been in love before—with Lennox. If he was honest with himself, it had never been truly reciprocal. She had always had all the power, a fact that was only revealed when the proverbial shit hit the fan, and he was left devastated and damaged while she sailed on smoothly with her life.

With Ellsbeth, it felt different. He was the older one, in the ostensible position of power. She *liked* being in the submissive role. And yet, despite that, their relationship felt uniquely egalitarian. In the last few weeks, as they had opened up to each other, it all felt so *real.* But that was the horrible beauty of obscuration—if it was artfully practiced, the subject might never know they had been manipulated.

Rawlins walked out of the study. His breathing had become shallow as spiraling thoughts spiked his anxiety. He saw Ellsbeth's backpack, discarded on the floor by the kitchen island. He could not help himself; he paused and knelt, tentatively probing a finger around inside it. He knew it was a violation of privacy, and hoped that he was just being paranoid—but he froze when he noticed, at the bottom, a rolled-up cloth handkerchief.

Tentatively he took it out and opened it, as though pulling the petals from a flower, dread building in his chest as he revealed the secret at its center: a lump of compounding clay. Exactly like the one he had used on Greywall.

Heat flooded his body—a mix of fear that his worst suspicions might be true and anger, already building, at the very possibility that they were. The fact that she was using obscuration on her own was undeniable. The questions that assaulted his mind now were about whom she had used it on, and when, and how. Had she used it on *him*? It was hard to believe she had not, and his stomach twisted with the sickening discovery that he could no longer trust her, or his own mind, at all.

He wrapped the compounding clay back into the handkerchief and returned it to her backpack, certain that he would not be sleeping tonight, and doubtful that he could ever share a bed with Ellsbeth again.

ELLSBETH

It had become a habit, glancing over at her phone as soon as her alarm went off and seeing a message from Rawlins. Usually it was just a simple good morning, but occasionally it was an article he knew she would like, or a very specific memory from the previous night he told her he'd relived in a dream. Ellsbeth was only slightly dismayed when she woke up that day to find nothing from him.

The morning after the Mary-Abigail incident, he had been cold and distracted, kissing her on the cheek before she left and mumbling something about a conference he needed to prepare for. That had been several days ago, and they hadn't made any plans since. "I'm going to be tied up with this lecture," Rawlins had said, not meeting her gaze. Ellsbeth had responded to his stiffness with stiffness in kind, refusing to be the one to initiate communication with him again.

On some level, she couldn't blame him for pulling away after the disaster back in his office. It was a miracle, really, that she had still had the compounding clay in her backpack. She had frozen the moment she saw Mary-Abigail pale as a ghost in the doorway, but when the wash of adrenaline allowed her to move again, she had sprung into action.

"Mary-Abigail! Wait!" Ellsbeth called to her back.

Mary-Abigail didn't stop walking. In fact, she slightly hastened her pace.

"Wait," Ellsbeth called again. "Please. I just need to explain."

Mercifully, she stopped, and Ellsbeth managed to cross the space between them. She caught her breath while unzipping her backpack. "Here," she said. "Let me just show you something." And then she had forced the compounding clay against the exposed inside of Mary-Abigail's arm. The obscuration took effect like a shade being drawn over Mary-Abigail's face. She told her to forget what she had seen, to go home, to forget that she had planned on seeing Professor Rawlins at all.

And then Ellsbeth had followed her out of the department building, and sat on a stone bench turned to ice in the December cold, and tried to remember to breathe.

When she had seen Mary-Abigail, instinct had taken over; she hadn't even thought about what she was doing—her vision had narrowed, she had become an animal, clawing with whatever power she had to save herself, to save Rawlins. Ellsbeth looked at her chapped hands, cuticles pulled and raw. She had been squeezing the compounding clay; the undersides of her nails were bright red. Objectively, she knew what she had done was unforgivable. She had manipulated a girl's brain, wiped out a piece of her memory.

But even worse than what Ellsbeth had done, there was a single terrible truth that settled in her brain like mold. It had been easy for her to use obscuration on Mary-Abigail. The truth was, it hadn't felt like anything at all.

THE END OF WINTER BREAK arrived like a river cracking through ice. Overnight, the paths around campus were flooded with grinning strangers in peacoats and knit hats, arm in arm with friends. The coffee shop Ellsbeth had gotten used to walking into now had a line reaching the door.

For the College of the Arcane Arts graduate cohort, the spring semester was purposefully light so that they would have time to finalize their thesis proposals before presenting them to the board for approval. Ellsbeth was enrolled in a research seminar led by Paul Gallway, and an optional advanced runic studies class taught by Professor Langdon. Professor Rawlins taught no graduate classes during the second semester, but in theory Ellsbeth would continue meeting with him to finalize her thesis plans. The truth was, her thesis proposal had been more or less complete since October, so if Rawlins was pulling away, there would be almost no academic reasons to serve as excuses to see him.

With nothing pressing academically, she could focus all of her attention on investigating Banestooth, something that had the added benefit of distracting her from Rawlins.

After Langdon's class, Ellsbeth caught up with Curt Ladove in the hallway. "Hey!" she said. He turned and looked at her, eyebrows raised. This might have been the first time she had ever initiated a conversation with him. His hair, blond, was thick with a product so stiff she could see comb lines tracing through it. Ellsbeth had watched him during the seminar, drumming his fingers against the tiny desk attached to their chairs instead of taking notes, a gold Banestooth ring clinking against the desk's wooden surface.

"Do you want to grab coffee?" Ellsbeth asked. When Curt's face melted into an insufferably smug smile, she quickly added: "I have a few questions about Banestooth Club. I know you were a member when you were an undergrad here."

"I *am* a member. It's one of those for-life things."

"Sure."

"And yeah," Curt said. "I don't see why not. I'm not meeting with Gallway about my thesis until three."

Curt walked fast. Ellsbeth followed close as he led the two of them across campus to an espresso bar that Ellsbeth expressly avoided because they charged eight dollars for a latte that tasted like stomach acid, and their only pastries were expired-looking gluten-free muffins sitting behind smudged glass. Curt ordered a double shot. Ellsbeth ordered a single and paid for both of them.

"Congrats on winning the Taylor Prize, by the way," she said as they sat down.

"Oh," he said. "Yeah, that. The money is nice but getting the prize itself feels like luck of the draw. You know how those things are."

"I doubt that," Ellsbeth said. "Your energy amplification stuff is supposed to be amazing."

Curt brushed her off with his hand and took another sip of espresso. "So," he said, "why the interest in Banestooth?"

"Well, my apartment is also on Governor, down the street," Ellsbeth said. Curt's eyes drifted behind her, and she scrambled to find a halfway-convincing lie. "And I was thinking of trying to write an article about the benefits of community when it comes to the mental health of young adults. Is there any chance I could . . . tour the place? Talk to some current or former members?"

Curt took a slurping sip of his espresso. "Oh that's going to be a no-go unfortunately."

"I really do just want to talk. It can be off the record, or—"

"Sorry, Ellie." No one called her Ellie. Ever. "The whole point of Banestooth is that it's a secret society. No guests, no visitors, *definitely* no interviews."

"No *visitors*? I see people having parties there all the time."

"Only in the foyer. First floor. Rest of the house is strictly forbidden for non-members. Including bedrooms, which, trust me, causes some distress among the new Initiates. Every class has *one* dude who thinks he can get away with it. Takes a girl upstairs after a party, and then gets kicked out."

"The *girl* gets kicked out?" Ellsbeth asked.

"No, the guy. Of Banestooth."

"That's how strict you are?"

"Oh yeah. Part of the whole cloak-and-dagger thing. It's how we maintain an air of secrecy and discipline. There's, like, a classic story they tell incoming freshmen about a new Initiate trying to impress a girl by bringing her down to the basement. They say he got them down three stairs before he was caught and kicked out and his former peers made his life so miserable that he dropped out of Newlyn altogether and transferred to a state school."

"Jesus."

"Yeah."

"Did you like being a part of it when you were an undergrad?" Ellsbeth asked.

Curt smiled and waggled his finger. "Oh, are you trying to interview me now? Yes, I liked it. Met some of my best friends. Great social connections. All that classic junk."

"But you're not telling me anything else."

"To be honest, there's not much else to tell. It's probably pretty close to whatever you're imagining. But no. I'm not." He ran his hand through his hair with absentminded confidence. "So this mental-health thing you're doing . . . it's because of your sister, right?"

"Oh," Ellsbeth said, a little taken aback by his abruptness. "Yeah. Sort of."

"A journal will love that. Add a little addendum to the front with a bit about how your sister killed herself and so this is *so personal to you* or whatever, and you'll be able to publish it wherever you want," Curt continued, seemingly enjoying giving Ellsbeth professional advice. "People love tragedy porn. Just find something to make it personal. Like, talking about Banestooth is fine, but she was a girl so she was never going to be a member. You should find some way to make it about her."

"Well, I'm not sure Newlyn has a Nora Ephron Club, but if they do, I'm sure she was a member there."

Curt clapped his hands once and laughed. "Oh, shit, right. She was obsessed with *When Harry Met Sally.* She tried to get me to watch it, like, five different times."

Ellsbeth sat up straighter. "Wait. You knew her?"

The music in the coffee shop hung between them for a beat while Curt blinked. "Oh, yeah. I met her a few times. She was sweet. Funny."

"You said you didn't know her. At Gracie's party." Ellsbeth could hear all of the warmth draining out of her voice, her tone becoming icy and robotic.

Curt didn't seem to notice. He shrugged. "I forgot the name. And then by the time I realized who it was—well, I wasn't just going to come up to you and be like, *Hey, turns out I did hang out with your dead sister once or twice.*"

Ellsbeth shifted her weight in her seat. The coffee had left an unpleasant film on her tongue. That *Curt* had known her sister, this boy in front of her, that he had met her, felt impossibly strange. Like a dream in which your second-grade teacher meets Celine Dion. Had Curt lied to her? Or had Bertie just been one of a number of interchangeable freshman girls to him, bright-eyed girls who showed up to Banestooth parties wearing tiny dresses and borrowed shoes, hoping to find someone to make them feel special?

"So how's your thesis going?" Curt said. "Rawlins is your adviser, right?"

At the sound of Rawlins's name, Ellsbeth felt the immediate and unexpected sensation of a splinter being lodged in her chest. He still hadn't texted her, which she justified to herself as his independent streak reasserting itself as he busied himself getting ready for a conference. But there had been something strange in his manner the last time she saw him, a hardness that she hadn't recognized before. If she didn't know better, she would have thought he was angry with her, even though the change had occurred sometime overnight while she was asleep.

"Yeah," Ellsbeth said, trying to keep her voice light. "Although I actually should get back to work on it. You're outdoing everyone else in the department—we have to try to keep up!"

Curt gave her a little salute and turned his attention toward the attractive barista with a nose piercing and thick winged eyeliner.

If she took the most effective route from the coffee shop back to her apartment, she would crest a hill where Rawlins's home would be visible. But Ellsbeth stuffed her hat onto her head and instead turned back toward campus, taking a slightly longer, meandering path. She told herself she needed time to think.

She hadn't expected Curt to be forthcoming with any of Banestooth's secrets, but he had revealed something essential despite himself.

He had told her that Banestooth had a basement.

She had seen the blueprint of the building in the school's library archive search: *no basement.* They had hidden their true floor plan from the university, which meant there was something they were hiding. Now she just needed to get in and find whatever it was.

She had considered that she might just obscurate Curt and get him to escort her inside, but if all guests were forbidden, she would inevitably run into problems. It's not as if she could obscurate a whole house—there was no way to obscurate beyond touching one individual at any one time. But even if she could, the fundamental principles of what obscuration accomplished would begin to fray the more people were involved.

The brain was an incredible object, capable of filling in blank spaces in order to stitch the world into logical sense. After an obscuration ritual, the object should never have known they were manipulated; they should believe that *they* made the choices they were compelled to make, and their mind would either justify it or skim over thinking about it like a deliveryman skipping a door. But multiple people being obscurated at once could talk to one another. Their brains would each have found a unique way of processing what happened. And if the rule against visitors at Banestooth was that well established, Ellsbeth couldn't imagine a scenario in which a dozen or so Banestooth members would be unable to figure out that something had happened to them if they all had the hazy memory of a girl being permitted to wander their upper floors.

Obscurating a large group might be an interesting intellectual challenge (could the ritual be transmitted through the air? Or through sound instead of touch?), but it wouldn't help her get inside Banestooth.

She walked past the faculty center and instinctively turned to see if Rawlins was visible inside through the window. He wasn't. She wished he had texted, just so that she would have been able to text him about her idea for the academic possibility of group obscuration. It was exactly the type of esoteric, ultimately meaningless conversation he would have loved, and she could imagine talking about it with him, half naked, her hand roaming through his hair so vividly it was almost a memory. He would get excited at some point and jump up, wearing just his boxer-briefs, to write a formula on the pad of paper he kept by his bedside or to pull a book from high on a shelf somewhere, exposing the hair under his arms as he reached.

She checked her phone again, for the third time in as many minutes. No messages.

Maybe the simplest answer was the truest one: He had always wanted the two of them to be no-commitment, just sex and work. He had told her explicitly he didn't want them to be in a relationship. She had promised him she wouldn't fall in love. She had been the one to convince him to be with her in the first place, by making that promise. It was no wonder he was distant and pulling away. She had lured him in and then broken her word. Any text she sent to him now would be further reinforcing that she was needy, that she was desperate, that she loved him when she'd said all she wanted was for the two of them to get into bed.

She could suppress these feelings, she thought, as she walked past the red-brick administration building, too impatient to stay on the proper walking path and letting her footsteps fall heavy in the snow-covered grass instead. She could box them up neatly and put them away. She could turn Rawlins into an anecdote, a life story to make her more interesting and glamorous at book clubs in her thirties—the professor she had once had kinky sex with, a narrative that made her more worldly and him vaguely pathetic in equal measure. In the story she would tell about it later, love had never been a consideration.

Ellsbeth distracted herself by making a plan to infiltrate Banestooth. Obscuration wouldn't work, but it also wouldn't be necessary. Not every problem required complicated and illegal arcane mechanicals; she had been so impressed with pulling it off in the first place, her instinct had been like using a power drill when a tiny screwdriver would do. What she needed was fairly straightforward: an invisibility ritual, and probably a ward in case they had any protective magic on the house. Invisibility spells were easy, the type of thing professors did on the first day of undergraduate lectures in order to impress impressionable eighteen-year-olds. Making the invisibility last longer than thirty seconds was slightly trickier, but not impossible, as was creating a ritual strong enough so that the invisibility would still be reflected in photos and video recordings.

Even as Ellsbeth built the invisibility ritual and a plan to infiltrate Banestooth in her mind, she couldn't quiet the nagging part of her brain that still wanted to find an excuse to talk to Rawlins. Maybe she would try to figure out a way to size up obscuration after all. Something clever and impressive she could email; after all, he was still her adviser. If she had an academic inquiry tangentially related to her thesis, there was no reason she shouldn't be able to reach out. A small part of her burned with pride at the thought that she could send him a completed ritual and force him to reckon with what she was able to accomplish without him involved.

She picked up everything she needed from the mini-mart near her apartment. She already had a small store of arcane elementals, but for the invisibility, she needed sodium borate and glucose. She picked up a small, leaking box of borax from the narrow aisle containing laundry detergents, and grabbed a large bag of stale gummy bears on the way to the cashier.

"Big night?" the cashier asked, not looking up.

"Mmmm," Ellsbeth replied.

The invisibility ritual was prepared within twenty minutes on her kitchen floor—melting the gummy bears into the final formula would increase its strength, strong enough to defy even a motion detector, and a tablespoon of borax would extend the ritual's duration. She calculated that she would have about a full hour—any longer and the invisibility itself would be unstable, cycling in and out of focus. Easy.

But Rawlins still hadn't texted, and so Ellsbeth began working on her idea for a new obscuration ritual alone.

Technically, a mass obscuration ritual was useless; she already knew that the second the group woke up, if they spoke to one another, it would be immediately obvious there was magic used. But it was still an impressive feat of mechanicals, and Ellsbeth spent the next hour writing and rewriting a formula just to prove to herself she could do it. Her moment of brilliance came when she realized that the ritual didn't need to be transmitted by touch or through the air: It could be initiated with a trigger word. She and Rawlins had already figured out how to do it.

From that point, the work was fairly straightforward. She eyed the mostly full box of borax and realized she could contain the ritual within a salt circle. That way, if something went wrong, she could say the trigger word and obscurate everyone who had been in the house when she laid the salt out. Mass obscuration wouldn't offer a safe lasting effect, but it would probably be enough to get her out of Banestooth if she needed an escape route.

She still had the printed blueprint of the house from the library; she used it to make the calculations for the radius of the circle.

When she finished, she typed up the entire ritual to send to Rawlins, but when she glanced back down at her phone and saw that he still hadn't texted her, she deleted the email. It was a pathetic and obvious bid for affection, a dog begging for a treat. She would do this on her own. She didn't need anything from him.

RAWLINS

The sidewalks were perilously slick with ice as Rawlins walked down the hill to The Parlor. It was rare for him to go out to a bar, especially on a Friday night; he preferred the comfort of his own home, with his own well-stocked liquor cabinet and his own music. But his house felt haunted by Ellsbeth's absence, and he found himself claustrophobically trapped with his thoughts of her.

The first week of the semester had been grueling. He usually enjoyed returning after the holiday break—the rush of energy from new students, new schedules, new possibilities, hurrying in from the cold. But he was anxious and continuously troubled by his thoughts of Ellsbeth, which had reached a fever pitch earlier that day.

He had been walking to his office to prepare for his freshman lecture when the front doors of the department building opened and two figures emerged: Ellsbeth and Curt Ladove. Rawlins froze in his tracks and watched them from fifty yards back; he even melted off to the side so as not to draw attention. He could not be sure at that distance if Ellsbeth was *flirting,* but it was clear that she was watching Curt closely, hanging on every word. They turned right at the bottom of the stairs, going away from him, and wherever they were headed, they were clearly going *together.*

Rawlins's insides curled with anger. It was not only the jealous fear that Ellsbeth was *involved* with Curt, though that now seemed bafflingly possible. He suddenly felt like he didn't know her at all. She had never been particularly close with any of her cohort members—a distance that Rawlins understood, since she was smarter than all of them, yet also less worldly, less attuned to the politics of the academic world. But even among that group, she had professed a particular distaste for Curt, who was the epitome of everything she despised: smug, privileged, overconfident, unfairly rewarded by life. But watching their backs recede, he could tell from Ellsbeth's posture that she was eagerly attuned to him. Had she only pretended to dislike him because she knew Rawlins did? And if he had been wrong about that, was his entire sense of her completely off base?

It only seemed to confirm his fears from the previous weekend. Ever since the night he found the compounding clay, he had pulled away from her—and while he told himself he was merely trying to get some needed perspective, he was also, he realized, testing her. Perhaps that wasn't particularly fair, but if she truly cared about him, she would reach out, she would tell him that she was hurt by his distance. She would be willing to be *vulnerable,* as he had become so openly vulnerable to her.

But instead, she retreated in sync. She didn't seek him out at school, she didn't text him at night. Which might mean she *was* guilty of using obscuration on him, and suspected he was onto her, and was keeping her distance to avoid his suspicion. Or it might mean that she had merely gotten what she wanted, the love of her professor and the power that came with it—and moved on.

He couldn't square these possibilities with the Ellsbeth he had come to know. But he also couldn't trust his own mind. The sense of deep familiarity he'd felt with her could be nothing but an obscuration-induced deception.

He considered confronting her, pulling her aside to ask, point-blank . . . what exactly? *Do I think I'm in love with you because you manipulated me with magic?* In a way, that was the most logical approach: to catch her off guard when he could see her reaction, before she had time to formulate a reply. But he couldn't even trust himself. If she *had* performed obscuration on him, he might be compelled by whatever influence was acting inside his mind to believe whatever she said.

Rawlins pulled out his phone as he walked. It would be patently stupid to come right out and ask over text if she had manipulated him with magic, but he considered sending something passive-aggressive and oblique like, *Hope you're having a nice time with Curt.* But that wasn't his style; even that evinced caring more than he was willing to show at this point. He reread their last exchange, days earlier, as he considered other possibilities for what he might say—but with his eyes focused on the phone's bright light, he slipped on the ice and nearly lost his balance. He put his phone away before it cost him a broken bone.

He reached The Parlor and went inside, grateful for the warmth and the noise; even if the raucous undergrads surrounding the dartboards were obnoxious, he appreciated the distraction of their jovial din. He took a stool at the far end of the bar, ordered a beer and a whiskey neat, and took out one of the books he had brought. He had reading to do on obscuration. Not because he was trying to figure out how to use it this time, but because he needed to figure out if, and how, he had been so spectacularly *used.*

ELLSBETH

There hadn't been a party at Banestooth on Friday night, so Ellsbeth hoped that early Saturday morning would be quiet. She knew if she made her way to the house's basement, she would find *something* there. She was sure of it. Societies like that had libraries with meticulous, self-congratulatory records. If they were involved in covering up girls' deaths, there would be correspondence with the college. There would have been depositions, testimony—there would be *something.* Otherwise, why all the secrecy?

And, as Ellsbeth had been preparing her trigger-word obscuration, another idea occurred to her: Maybe their secrecy was because they were doing arcane mechanicals outside of the Practicum. Maybe the basement of their house was their own ritual room. If she could prove that the club was doing unauthorized arcane mechanicals, she could force the college to investigate them in earnest.

Still, for all of her willingness to engage in illegal magic with Rawlins, as she applied the invisibility ritual to herself that morning in her apartment (stepping through the cherry-gummy-bear-scented distilled ether that she misted through a spray bottle), she admitted to herself that she was *scared.* Her hands shook disconcertingly as she put the spray bottle back onto her desk. If she was caught, she would almost certainly be expelled. There would be no more graduate school, no more Newlyn. No degree. No bright or brilliant future. No more Rawlins.

And that was if Banestooth didn't decide to do worse to her.

But something had happened to Bertie. Her little sister had come to college, and died alone and scared, and that thought was a shard of glass in Ellsbeth's stomach every single day. She needed to do this. She needed to find out the truth, for Bertie.

And then there was another small nagging voice at the back of her head, a tiny thought that only made itself known in the brief seconds while Ellsbeth wasn't working: Once this was all over, once she learned the truth about Bertie and she could put all of this in the past, she wouldn't have to lie anymore. Wouldn't have to use obscuration. She could step forward, away from the selfish, dishonest person she had been, like a snake shedding its papery skin, and become a new person. A person Rawlins might even be able to truly love.

JUST AS ELLSBETH SUSPECTED, AT seven in the morning, Banestooth Club was entirely quiet. Birds chirped faintly on her walk down her street, their hearts not entirely in it. Thankfully, there had been no snow overnight—she wouldn't leave footprints.

The house itself was a three-story, square brick building with a large porch, and a lawn so neatly trimmed it revealed their dues were significant enough to pay for an independent landscaper. Ellsbeth, already invisible, took a lap around the house, dropping handfuls of powder behind her from a loosely clenched fist at her side as she went. Performing the invisibility ritual early had been a precaution so no one would notice her slowly trawling around the house, but it turned out it was an unnecessary one. The shades on the windows were drawn, and she walked around the entire house without seeing a single soul.

The problem with an invisibility ritual was that nothing *felt* any different to her. Her hands remained stubbornly visible in front of her face. And so, before Ellsbeth approached the house in earnest, she pulled her phone from her pocket and pressed the button to turn the screen into a forward-facing camera to double-check her work. She was gone. A vampire. The camera image showed the bare trees and plowed street behind her.

She would have approximately one hour of invisibility since she initiated the ritual back in her apartment, but the exact timing was affected by atmospheric pressure and temperature. It would be nearly impossible to calculate precisely how much time she'd get, so Ellsbeth wanted to plan conservatively; she figured she was down to about fifty minutes.

Ellsbeth lingered by the door, waiting for someone to leave the house. The door was heavy and formal, carved wood with a brass wolf's head knocker in the dead center. After about twenty seconds, a boy wearing basketball shorts swung the door open and hopped down the stairs, passing Ellsbeth without a glance. She managed to slip in through the door before it closed behind him with a *thunk*.

The foyer was astonishing; it was frankly no wonder this one room was all they needed in order to properly entertain. It was two stories tall, with an ornate stained-glass window high on the southern wall that Ellsbeth had never noticed from the outside. The ceiling was painted with scenes from Greek mythology: Hercules wearing the skin of the Nemean lion; golden apples growing in the Garden of the Hesperides; Argus Panoptes as a giant, and as a peacock. If it weren't so beautifully done, Ellsbeth would have almost scoffed at their grandiosity—they thought of themselves as heroes out of mythology.

Every piece of furniture—straight-backed chairs, a tufted couch, a grand piano with ivory keys—looked as though it weighed a thousand pounds and had a provenance that could be traced back to the *Mayflower*. Even a wooden door laid out horizontally for beer pong was oak and six inches thick, with carved grapevines along its sides.

But she wouldn't find anything she needed on the main floor. She could hear the shuffle of footsteps from somewhere on a higher floor, farther back in the house, and low muffled voices. Bedrooms. As quietly as she could, Ellsbeth slunk through the house, walking gingerly—first her heel, then rounding the side of her foot, before putting her weight into the step. No matter how strong her invisibility ritual was, it wouldn't do anything to mask her sound.

The moment she passed through the foyer into the main house, the air became several degrees cooler. Dust particles hung suspended in the kaleidoscope-colored light coming through the stained glass.

Beyond the foyer was a long hallway of closed doors. The walls were lined on either side first with portraits and then, the farther

Ellsbeth walked, with photographs. Each had a small plaque beneath it. Most of the faces and names were unfamiliar. Ellsbeth passed THOMAS NEWCASTLE III, SECRETARY OF STATE, and JONATHAN R. MARROW-TICK, CHIEF OF SURGERY AT MASSACHUSETTS GENERAL, before spotting a tasteful black-and-white photo of a movie star also known for his Shakespeare performances on Broadway and for dating pop stars.

It was a hall of distinguished alumni, and the men of Banestooth were even more distinguished than Ellsbeth had previously understood. In addition to the movie star, there were several billionaires whose names she recognized from buildings on campus, more congressmen than she could count, two Supreme Court judges, a Pulitzer Prize–winning playwright, Olympians, a famous violinist, and a newspaper magnate. Their dark eyes gazed impassively from their ornate frames, amused and sure. It was almost dizzying, the sheer volume of success of the men who walked these very hardwood floors, which she was, at the present moment, hoping didn't creak.

Was this the secret of success? Joining a fraternity at an elite college filled with rich boys who pulled one another up like a human ladder? The farther Ellsbeth walked down the hallway, the more disgusted and dejected she became. The gentle smiles on the faces became mocking. *Do your best,* they all seemed to say. *The system has been rigged the entire time.*

She was distracted when a door behind her opened. A tall boy with a towel around his waist exited, whistling quietly to himself. Ellsbeth pressed herself against the wall, and the boy passed so close that the breeze of his stride caused the hair on her arms to stand on edge. She gave a small, involuntary hiccup of fear, and the redhead turned slightly, but mercifully, he continued on his way to the shower without taking half a step to his left.

Every other door Ellsbeth passed in the hallway remained closed. Behind some, Ellsbeth could hear the low sounds of ordinary morning routines—gentle snoring, drawers opening, a television on low, someone singing a country song quietly to himself.

There was a staircase at the end of the hallway, with a plush runner and a gleaming wooden banister burnished the glossy walnut of an Upper East Side woman's hair. But it only went up.

It took her fifteen anxious minutes of listening at doors and winding through the deceptively large house before she found it: a staircase behind a thin wooden door not fitted quite right against its frame, a door with cracked and peeling paint. The door was so inconspicuous that Ellsbeth had almost walked past it. Thirty minutes left, she thought. If that.

This staircase was narrow and modest. It led down into darkness. She held her breath, prayed for stairs less creaky than they looked, and started down.

When she gently closed the door behind her, the darkness became all-encompassing. Ellsbeth kept her steps small and hesitant; if she fell and crashed down the stairs, half the house would come to investigate.

After what seemed like a century, her left foot landed on concrete. She could feel the chill even through her shoe. Ellsbeth contemplated the danger in attempting to turn on the lights—the light might seep under the doorframe, and someone on his way to breakfast might know that something was amiss. So instead of flipping the switch she found by groping blindly at the wall, Ellsbeth pulled out her phone and thumbed on its flashlight.

She gasped.

Banestooth's basement was a cross between a gothic cathedral and a Roman pantheon. The floor wasn't concrete; it was black and smooth as marble, reflecting the light of her phone like a still pond. Pillars surrounded a mosaic ritual circle on the floor, inlaid with depictions of the constellations, with each node marked with a white stone that seemed to glow in the reflected light from Ellsbeth's phone. A Fibonacci spiral swirled out from the center of the room.

They were doing rituals here—and, if the size of the ritual circle was any indication, incredibly powerful ones. Ellsbeth took a picture, and then another, and then another, trying to capture the room from every angle, despite the fact that the lack of light left the images blurry and nondescript. Only when she reached the far side of the room did she realize that that entire wall was a bookshelf. She held her phone up to try to read the titles. They were arcane mechanicals books, with titles promising dark magic and blood rituals. *Magickal Influence upon Cognition and Behavior. Arcanus Rictus.* The entire collection of books by Rudolf Wentz. *Diviner's Touch.* There were banned titles and books that were thought to have been lost for centuries. Titles that Rawlins had recommended she study, that she hadn't been able to find in any public university library. Ellsbeth ran her fingers along the spines. Most books were bound in leather; one was bound in something that looked hauntingly like human skin. The farther Ellsbeth walked, the older the books became, until the labels were so faded and peeled she could barely read them.

This was it. This was the proof she needed that Banestooth was, if nothing else, engaging in unauthorized magic. And probably far worse. Could she take one of the books out of the house without being noticed? She was vaguely aware of the possibility of magical security, but there was also the problem with her invisibility ritual: She couldn't remember whether picking up a book and hiding it, say, under her shirt would also render it invisible or whether she would be attempting to parade a floating leather tome down the street for anyone to see. She closed her eyes to try to picture the correct paragraph of Calliope D. Arthur's text on the functionality of invisibility in contact with tertiary objects. That was when she heard it: footsteps.

There were voices at the top of the stairs. Just as Ellsbeth heard the creak of the door opening, she remembered to extinguish her phone's flashlight. There would be no way to get out now. She prayed her invisibility was still holding strong and ducked behind a pillar as the footsteps made their way down the stairs. She tried to quickly calculate how much more time she had in her invisibility. Twenty minutes. Probably less.

The lights flicked on, and Ellsbeth blinked. The room was even more dazzling when lit, light reflecting off the marble and making the mosaics dance with color. Ellsbeth was so distracted admiring the room that she almost didn't recognize the two figures who had made their way into the ritual circle: Professor Gallway and a boy with dark, stringy hair and a hunched posture. When the boy turned, Ellsbeth saw the eyes so familiar it made her breath catch in her chest.

It was Maxwell Keene.

"—thank you for making an exception for me," Maxwell said, his voice strangely reedy.

His neck extended forward from his body like a kitten being held by the skin of its nape.

"There are certain perks to being the Magister," Gallway replied evenly. "And given the . . . seriousness of what you're alleging, it seemed . . . prudent to allow you to *borrow* our copy of *Arcanus Rictus.*"

"I'm not *alleging* anything. Don't play dumb with me, Gallway. We both know what sort of thing happens here—there's no use now playing coy."

"I'm not sure what you're implying."

"Of course you are."

"Enlighten me, then," Gallway said. "What do you *think* you know?"

Maxwell took a deep breath, and a flush extended up his cheeks. "The ritual."

"A ritual," Gallway repeated.

"Not *a* ritual," Max said. "*The* ritual. *Fortunatis Favori.*"

"A legend." Gallway's nostrils flared. "A story to tell naughty children before bed. You're smarter than to believe in something like that, Maxwell."

"It's not a legend," Max said. "I know it's not. It's the ritual that's turned the mediocre boys of Banestooth Club into masters of the universe for the last two centuries. Luck and charm, foresight and talent. A ritual for *success.* Nearly impossible, incredibly dangerous. A ritual that requires . . . you know."

Gallway breathed through his nose. Behind her column, Ellsbeth was close enough to see his chest rise and fall. "I assume you think you have proof?"

Now Max laughed, a high-pitched honking laugh that became a cough halfway through. "My mother might be content to turn the other way and ignore anything that happens here because of how *generously* Banestooth alumni donate to the school, but that doesn't mean the proof isn't there. And if someone had access to the dean's computer, and her internal files—"

"What do you want, Keene?" Gallway interrupted. Gone was the placating, condescending politeness. His voice was sharp as a poison-tipped dagger. "Because I assume you aren't attempting to blackmail me to borrow a book."

Maxwell squared his shoulders and made eye contact with Gallway.

To Ellsbeth, he looked impossibly young, like a child. "I want the same thing I wanted eight years ago. I want *in.*"

Gallway snorted. "If the ritual you're alluding to is real—and I'm not saying it is—you would be aware that it's only performed once every four years. If it is real, it would have already been performed just last winter for the *members of Banestooth.* A group, I regret to inform you, to which you do not belong."

"But I could've!" Max raised his voice, which warbled slightly. He tried to calm himself. "I was trying to impress *you all* with that thaumaturgy ritual! *You said* if I could do something extraordinary I could—"

"—and you could've. But you didn't do anything extraordinary. You killed three innocent students and got yourself sent to prison."

"It was an *accident*! I didn't kill anyone on purpose! *You don't think I—*" His voice sputtered and he took a breath, trying to control himself. "And how are *you* going to try to take the moral high ground here? I know what the *Fortunatis* takes! You *kill a girl* every four years! You pick one and make one of your frat-boy cronies *date* her and then you kill her. Murder! I'm right, aren't I? Tell me I'm right!"

Ellsbeth had to clamp her hand over her mouth to stop herself from crying out. The skin on her face was hot and tight, tingling like it was crawling with insects.

Gallway didn't reply to Max, and the boy continued. "All I want," he said, "is the thing I was promised eight years ago. I want the ritual. I want a *life* again. A successful fucking life. I'm good enough to be in Banestooth. We both know it. I'd be the best fucking mechanist you've had in decades. I *should* be one of you."

"We only do the ritual every four years."

"Make a fucking exception."

Gallway paused. He adjusted his cuff links. Ellsbeth considered whether she could sprint past them both and make it up the narrow staircase without them hearing her footsteps on the marble or the stairs. No, they would hear the door open. All she could do was wait, hiding behind the pillar and mentally counting down the minutes until her invisibility would wear off and leave her completely without armor.

"I'm afraid that's impossible, Maxwell."

Max looked away from Gallway, first toward his shoes, and then to the far wall of bookshelves, and then, unsettlingly, what seemed to be directly at Ellsbeth. It hadn't been an hour yet; she should still be invisible. But still, he was *staring* at her.

Ellsbeth felt sweat prickling at her underarms. *How is he looking at me?* She could try to use the trigger word; try to keep the two men in place until she could escape. But it would require speaking, and giving up her position, and there was no guarantee that the ritual would work.

Ellsbeth built her courage, letting the word hover in the space between her brain and her tongue. But then Maxwell looked away from her.

"What if I prove myself? What if I do something extraordinary again? I've researched—you offer honorary memberships for 'exceptional services to the club and its members,' don't you?"

Gallway sighed. "Yes, in theory, we do."

Time was running out. Ellsbeth knew she had ten minutes—probably fewer—before she would become visible again. Her brain was a bleating siren. She forgot about taking one of the leather-bound books as proof; all that mattered was getting out. She would need to make a break for it, sprint up the stairs, as fast and quiet as she could.

Maxwell nodded his head aggressively. "Okay. Okay."

Ellsbeth gave herself a countdown, motivating her frozen limbs to come back to life. *You have to do this. Three, two, one.*

"If that's all," Gallway said, turning away from Maxwell and toward the stairs, "I think it's time you leave the house."

Fuck.

The two of them walked together up the staircase and Ellsbeth held her breath as she forced herself to follow, three steps beneath them.

When Maxwell reached the basement door, he turned back again, staring at what should to him just appear as empty space. Ellsbeth stopped, and felt her heartbeat in her ears. But then Max turned and slammed the door behind him, leaving Ellsbeth alone on the pitch-black staircase.

She waited ten seconds, hopefully long enough for Gallway and Maxwell to have gone far enough down the hall that they wouldn't notice a door opening. And then she was gone: out of the basement, down the hallway, dodging the few stirring students pouring themselves cereal and hoisting backpacks onto their shoulders. She *flew*, oblivious to the sound of her footsteps, carried by adrenaline and by a single thought: *I need to talk to Rawlins.*

She didn't bother to wait for someone else to open the front door so she could slide out behind him. She opened the door and sped across the patio, down the steps, and past her salt circle. The ground had become frosty while she was inside; she was leaving footprints now, but she didn't care. She felt her body become visible again with every step, a sensation like blood flooding into a numbed limb. And as she walked, she pulled out her phone and texted: I need to see you now. It's important.

They were doing rituals. They were killing girls. *They were the ones who killed Bertie. Curt knew Bertie—he might have even dated her. He was probably the one that killed her.*

Ellsbeth's mind whirred with a plan being formulated in real time. She could use obscuration on Curt, on Paul Gallway, on any of them. She could get them to confess. But that wasn't enough. It wouldn't work. Courts wouldn't accept a confession given under the power of illegal mind-control magic. She needed to do *something*.

She was three houses away from her apartment now, delirious with adrenaline and rage. Maybe she could use obscuration, force them to collect evidence of their own misdeeds. Her phone chirped—a reply from Rawlins—but before she could unlock her phone, a hand from behind pressed itself over her mouth. Bitter skin, salty with sweat.

And then an arm was across her neck. Ellsbeth struggled, a terrible gargle escaping her throat. Her brain flooded with panic and the white-hot pain of not enough oxygen. She flailed her elbows but caught only air. She was alone. She was helpless.

And then the world went spotted and brown, and the last thing Ellsbeth saw was the frost on the grass, the way it clung to each blade like spun sugar, before the world disappeared completely.

RAWLINS

I need to see you now. It's important.

Rawlins looked at Ellsbeth's text again, shaking his head with irritation. It was Saturday morning, and he was at his kitchen table, treating himself to his usual weekend breakfast—but his cappuccino had gone cold and his eggs Benedict was barely nibbled, since he'd lost his appetite entirely.

After days of radio silence, this was the message Ellsbeth had sent, offering no context whatsoever. He had replied quickly—I'm home, come over and we can talk—aiming to sound casual, even aloof. In truth, he was nervous to see her, uncertain what to expect.

Enough time had passed without contact between them that it plainly needed to be addressed. Something, undeniably, had changed. He knew exactly what it was on his end, and the past week of cold silence had only hardened his conviction that she had used obscuration on him. His suspicion now needed to be discussed explicitly, even if he wasn't sure if he could trust her reply—much less his own mind. He had been reading about obscuration throughout the last week, trying to figure out if there was precedent for the sort of manipulation he suspected. But the literature was remarkably unhelpful. There were stories of "love rituals" going back hundreds of years, but with little reliable evidence, since the modern scientific approach to arcane mechanicals was roughly coincident with the banning of obscuration. It was nearly impossible to find anything reliable about the duration of effects, or what to expect.

He needed to understand what Ellsbeth had done. And *why*. Was it only to get him to help her with her illicit studies, so that their romance had merely been in service of that goal? Or had romantically claiming him been what she *really* wanted all along?

It was clear now that the only way to get the answers he wanted was from her. And it was possible that if he confronted her directly and appealed to her rationally, she might confess the truth to him.

Perhaps, but not likely. As he waited for her to arrive, he went up to his study and retrieved from the bottom drawer an object he had been keeping there in case of emergency: a ball of compounding clay, still charged with the power of obscuration. He wasn't sure if he would really use it on her, but if she continued to deny that she had manipulated him, it might be the only way to get the truth. He tucked it into his pocket, wrapped in a handkerchief, like a loaded weapon, and felt a wave of shame at considering using it—but what alternative did he have?

He checked his texts again; his reply had been sent at 8:14 a.m., and it was now past 9, but Ellsbeth still had not answered. He understood what was happening. She had reached out to him with a sense of urgency, and when he replied casually, she had retreated. It was a reassertion of power; the only thing more aloof than a casual response was none at all.

So he sent her another message: Must not have been that important. He hoped that might jar her to her senses and speed her over, or at least get her to say *something*—but after five more minutes waiting for his phone to buzz, he felt disgusted with himself and decided on principle to leave the house; he would not sit around when she couldn't even be bothered to text him back.

He drove down the hill to the farmers market, trying to distract himself. The local co-op stubbornly continued operating it year-round, weather permitting, though at only half the size in winter. Customers with steaming coffees filtered through two blocks of booths, filling their baskets with root vegetables and baked goods.

Rawlins parked a few blocks away and tried to lose himself in the usually pleasant activity, but his mind was elsewhere, keenly attuned to the phone in his pocket, and he kept having the phantom sensation of a vibration. He pulled it out again and again, checking the screen to find no new message—and his annoyance gave way to genuine concern.

He sent another text to Ellsbeth, dropping any pretense of indifference. Just want to make sure, you all right? After that he kept the phone in his hand, and by the time he finished his round of the booths at the market, he still had not received a reply.

A sense of creeping dread grew in his belly. If Ellsbeth was deliberately ignoring his messages, she was more callous than he had suspected. Perhaps he hadn't known her as well as he thought, and now, feeling scorned, she was revealing her true character. He tried to convince himself that this was the case, even though it stung to consider how foolish it would make him; but if she had used obscuration on him, he couldn't really blame himself.

His mind turned on itself, an ouroboros, self-devouring, as he oscillated between mistrust and escalating fear that something consequential was happening. As he headed back to his car, he passed a police officer, directing traffic at a shut-down intersection; he nodded to her, and his blood ran cold as he was struck by a thought, the only possibility that made sense . . .

Ellsbeth had been arrested.

She must have texted him when she realized she was in trouble, the target of suspicion and investigation—but soon thereafter was taken into custody, unable to answer her phone. Her use of illegal rituals had been discovered. Whether it was writ magic or obscuration hardly mattered; either was a crime that could land her in jail. It could land *him* in jail as well, as the teacher who provided her with the means and collaborated with her on writing the rituals.

But the danger to himself hardly even registered; despite the fact that he had recently become convinced she was manipulating him, he was only concerned for her. His mind flashed to images of Ellsbeth in handcuffs, in a holding cell, in a courtroom—being publicly humiliated and shipped off to prison. Just like Max. Her sentence would not be as severe, but it would wreck any possibility of an academic career for her. It would ruin her life. And it would be his fault.

He tried calling her; the phone rang through and went to voicemail. There was no sense leaving a message. Texting her again wouldn't do any good, and only risked incriminating them both further.

He hurried back to the car, tossed his impulsive farmers market purchases in the passenger seat haphazardly, and started driving straight to her apartment, his car sliding through the ice of the turns as he hurried to get there. He prayed that he would find her at home reading, or perhaps asleep—having inconsiderately silenced her phone after texting him. But he knew it was unlikely.

He parked a few houses down the street from her building, staying in his front seat to look for police cars out front. He didn't see any; he was no expert, but he tried to guess if any of the nondescript sedans might be unmarked detectives' vehicles. Impossible to say. He got out and proceeded up to the entrance, attempting to look as casual as he could.

He knew her building code from when she had invited him over, and proceeded up to her hallway on the second floor. He felt his heart beat rapidly, not sure what he might be walking into. He paused and listened outside her door but heard nothing, so he knocked. No response. He considered texting her one more time, but it seemed stupid. If she was there, she would have heard him.

He needed to get inside—so he went down to the end of the hall, where she kept a spare key hidden beneath a potted plant, and retrieved it. She might be angry with him later, but he didn't care; his anxiety was mounting and he could not imagine walking away now.

If she had been arrested, as he feared, then this was the best opportunity to help by removing any incriminating evidence from her apartment.

Rawlins moved quickly, conscious that police officers could swarm in to search the premises at any moment.

As soon as he came through the door, he was struck by the sprawling mess of notes, books, and printouts that covered every horizontal surface. Ellsbeth's place had been tidy when he visited before, and while he was sure she had cleaned up to impress him, he knew that she was not prone to living in this level of disarray.

He went to the kitchen table, looking for evidence of any rituals she had been working on. But he paused when he recognized the smiling face of a young woman at the top of a printed article, about the tragic death last year of freshman student Roberta Storer. Ellsbeth's sister Bertie. Rawlins's heart sank as he imagined her, caught in the whirlpool of grief, poring over the dry, lifeless words of the newspaper.

Beside the article, pages slightly overlapping, was a similar news story from a few years back, about the tragic death of another young woman: Catherine Teale—a freshman as well. Why was Ellsbeth interested in *that* particular tragedy? Was she hoping it would help her understand what had motivated Bertie to take her own life?

Those two were only the tip of the iceberg. Over a dozen similar stories were laid out on the table—some news articles, some merely obituaries. Many were suicides, along with several accidents: alcohol poisoning, drug overdose, a drowning, a car crash, at least one girl who had gone missing and never been found.

Ellsbeth had placed them chronologically into a timeline, with dates circled, charting a grisly pattern: the death of a young woman at Newlyn, usually a student, every four years, in the spring semester, with nearly mathematical precision. Going back decades . . . almost a *century*.

Rawlins's blood curdled. The coincidence was impossible to ignore. He gathered up the papers, keeping them in order, and put them in a shopping bag, then turned his attention to Ellsbeth's desk.

At the center: a building permit with blueprints for a massive house. He googled the address on the top left of the form, which brought up a street-view image of the building's façade, and he instantly recognized the massive wooden door with a wolf's head knocker. It was down the street from where Ellsbeth lived.

What was she doing with drawings of the Banestooth house? He studied the blueprints and saw, in the margin, underlined and circled in Ellsbeth's starkly neat handwriting: No basement.

Rawlins puzzled over what possible significance that might have as he scrutinized the plans further, noting thick ink lines where Ellsbeth had made measurements on top of the architectural drawings, calculating distances using a key in the corner. She had found the farthest point from a corner of the house to its geographic center.

It was a radius, and he knew instantly what it was for: a ritual circle. One that circumscribed the entirety of the house. One that could be used to enact a large-scale magical effect upon the inhabitants therein.

To what end, he could not guess, but he was certain it was connected to the string of deaths she had uncovered.

She was planning something big. Something dangerous. But he had no idea if she had already completed her plan . . . or, it seemed more likely, if she had gone there, and tried, and never gotten the chance.

Rawlins's throat constricted, as he was consumed by fear so acute that he felt like the blood was draining from his entire body.

He was not one to pray for anything, yet he found himself suddenly, desperately pleading with the universe. That the woman he still loved was still alive. He would do anything to keep her safe—even if it meant walking down into the underworld and bringing her back himself.

ELLSBETH

A piece of her skull had been removed, and it was being used to scoop out the exposed part of her brain. That was the only possible explanation for the searing pain in the back of her head. The pain pulsed with every heartbeat. The inside of her eyelids flashed with a hot, fleshy red color, but her eyes remained shut.

She knew she wasn't home, but for a moment, some confused part of Ellsbeth believed that she was still asleep in Rawlins's bed. She was cold because they had sweated through his crisp percale sheets in the night, but if she reached over, she would find his warm arms and be able to wriggle herself close against him, pressing as much of her body against his as was physically possible, a perfect tessellation of their skin. She kept her eyes closed. Any second, she would feel his breath in her hair. His hand would wind under her waist and pull her toward him. He would murmur *My Ellsbeth* in her ear and the two of them would fall back asleep until the sun through the curtains put up too big of a fight and he would make coffee in the French press and the pain in her head would be gone.

"She needs to be awake."

Ellsbeth moaned. It was a man's voice but it wasn't Rawlins's. "She will be."

Gradually, the physical world came into focus around Ellsbeth the way blood returns to a numbed limb. She was sitting in a chair, but she couldn't move her wrists or ankles. *Writ magic,* came the irrational thought, a nagging voice insisting that she shouldn't have let Rawlins do writ magic on her so late at night because it still hadn't worn off. But no. It wasn't writ magic: She was in cuffs and tied to the chair with rough rope. A thin cotton rag was gagging her—it pressed her tongue deep into the back of her mouth and pulled at the dry corners of her lips.

Ellsbeth blinked her eyes open. The light caused the pain in the back of her head to sear white-hot and she cried out, the sound almost entirely disappearing into the fabric of the gag.

She wasn't in Rawlins's bed. She was back at Banestooth, in the columned basement.

And she was at the center of the Fibonacci spiral of their mosaic ritual circle.

A figure lowered his head until their faces were even, but she couldn't make out the face beneath his hood; his features remained in shadow, his silhouette backlit by torchlight. He held something in front of her face. A phone. *Her* phone. It lit up with recognition, its sensors perceptive enough even with a gag in her mouth, and clicked open.

"Did she call anyone for help?" asked a man somewhere behind Ellsbeth.

"No," said the figure in front of her. "One vague text, but nothing we need to worry about." He scrolled through the blurry photos she had taken of the Banestooth basement that morning and deleted them one by one. "There we go." Ellsbeth's eyes adjusted to the torchlight and glimpsed blond hair under the hood. His voice was familiar but she couldn't quite place it.

"I admit, Maxwell," said a second voice behind Ellsbeth, "I didn't expect you to be of service to Banestooth quite so quickly."

"Yes," said the blond man in front of her. "Where did you find her? And how are you sure you weren't seen?"

"It was an invisibility ritual," said a third voice. *Maxwell Keene.* "She had performed an invisibility ritual so she could snoop around this place. I thought I heard her. And then I saw the footprints in the frost outside. She wasn't paying any attention. I managed to get a hand around her throat and—"

"*Why?* Why was she snooping around in the first place?"

"You killed her sister," Maxwell said. He spoke fast, eager to please.

"Last year. And she found proof, too. I followed her at the library and saw what she was doing. She was looking into you right in the open. Roberta Storer, that was her sister. It's her last name, too. Obviously."

At the sound of Bertie's name, Ellsbeth came to life, struggling against her bindings.

Maybe the salt circle was still holding. She needed to say the trigger word and she could get out of here. But the gag kept her tongue stubbornly in place. She could barely breathe. A few boys chuckled at her effort: The room was full of people wearing cloaks and hoods, surrounding her in a circle.

Ellsbeth couldn't be sure how much time had passed since the last time she had been in the Banestooth basement. Was it that morning, or had days gone by? Someone had taken off her shirt and jeans; she was wearing just a bra and underwear, the chill of the air prickling at the small hairs on her skin and causing her arms to goosepimple. If this headache would go away, she could think more clearly, she could come up with a way out of this.

"If I hadn't come along, you all would've been waking up tomorrow morning to feds banging on your door. You owe me this ritual and more," Maxwell said.

The soft voice behind her spoke again. "The fact that her sister committed suicide here will make a cover-up easy. Bereft, and suicidal herself."

"And she was fucking her professor," Maxwell said. "Rawlins."

The blond figure lowered down again, his face inches from Ellsbeth's. She could hear the smile in his voice even though his face remained in shadow. "Oh, *really*? Storer, you are just full of surprises. A torrid affair gone wrong—this really *is* a gift." *It was Curt.* Curt was the blond man in front of her. Fucking Curt, and she forced herself to contort against her ropes, but they were too tight. The rope bit into her skin, and the gag in her mouth seemed to tighten of its own accord. "Easy, girl," Curt said.

"I still don't understand why we're doing this," someone else said from somewhere in the darkness. "The ritual isn't going to do anything for us again. We already did it. And he isn't even an Initiate."

"We reward those who provide the club exceptional services. And that is exactly what's been done here. We'll perform the ritual again for

Mr. Maxwell Keene," said the voice behind her, and Ellsbeth recognized it then: Paul Gallway. "A rare and deserved honor."

"Poor lonely Rawlins," Curt said. "Finally finds a student to fuck, and she has to die tragically."

Max stiffened his neck, and Gallway came into Ellsbeth's eyeline. He was wearing a white mask. "Your dagger," he said, handing Max a blade. Max was the only one in the room not wearing a black cloak. "You secured her for us, so it only seems fair that when the time comes, you'll be the first to make her bleed."

At the sight of the knife, the fog around Ellsbeth's head cleared in an instant. Bitter adrenaline pounded through her body, and Ellsbeth fought as hard as she could against the bindings. *They're going to kill me.* The only way she would get out of here alive was if she could say the obscuration trigger word, and even then she wasn't sure it would work. Still, it was a *hope,* the only one she had right now. She chewed and spat at the gag until drool rolled down her chin.

"Whoa, there." A stranger approached then, a tall gangly boy with a voice Ellsbeth didn't recognize. He put a piece of masking tape over her mouth, securing the gag in place.

"Will this work?" Maxwell asked, his voice low and steady. "Even though you just did the ritual last spring?"

"It won't do anything for the rest of the Initiates," Gallway said. "Doing the ritual multiple times doesn't increase one's luck or fortune. But it will work for you. And it will have the added benefit of getting rid of this one. It really is a pity. She was doing so well in my class."

The tape partially covered Ellsbeth's nostrils; it was becoming harder to breathe now.

Someone had done something to make the room warm and smoke-filled; Ellsbeth smelled incense. Myrrh.

Someone behind Ellsbeth jerked painfully at her cuffs, untying her from the chair and binding her wrists to her ankles. She was pushed onto the mosaic floor, contorted painfully. Movement whirled around her: arcane gold ingots being placed at even, precise distances. Her eyelids felt heavy. An unpleasant ache crawled its way around her neck, and the hard bone of her shoulder was grinding against the floor.

And then, at once, every cell of her body screamed in dizzying terror when she realized what was happening.

She was going to die.

She was going to die the way Bertie had died, scared and naked in a basement, flayed by knives with no one to tell the truth about what happened to her. Rawlins would believe that it was a suicide; that she was a sad and broken bird he couldn't fix. Her parents would shrink even further into themselves in their grief. Ellsbeth's entire life would become a perfunctory obituary in the student newspaper. They would probably say something awful. *She lit up the room. She had so much promise.* Would Rawlins mourn her? Or would a part of him be relieved that their affair had ended without any trouble for him?

"Ex infortunio, potenter benedic nobis."

The voices around her began to chant, low enough that she felt the vibrations in her stomach. Her cheeks were wet; she had begun to cry.

"Ex infortunio, potenter benedic nobis."

Maybe she could just close her eyes. Maybe at the moment the knives entered her body and life left her, she could will herself back to Rawlins's bed, and let that be her final thought.

RAWLINS

When Rawlins strode up to the door of the Banestooth house and reached out to take the wolf's head knocker, his hand was shaking. An electric current of anxiety ran through his body and frayed his nerves.

The first knock brought no immediate response; he tried the door, in case it might be unlocked, but no such luck.

His plan was half formed and probably foolish. All he knew was that he needed to get inside immediately. If his worst fears were correct, Ellsbeth was here and in danger. If he was wrong—well, he might embarrass himself, ruffle some feathers, and piss off Ellsbeth when she found out what he had undertaken. But he would be more than happy to find himself cleaning up that mess.

He had considered calling the police, insisting this was a matter of grave danger, but that seemed unlikely to work; Ellsbeth's evidence was limited and circumstantial, certainly not sufficient to summon a door-busting assault. He had to do this alone, with only one weapon available to him—the ball of compounding clay, charged with the power of obscuration and wrapped in a handkerchief. He had put it into his pocket intending to use it on Ellsbeth, if he needed to, and now it was the only thing that might help him save her.

Rawlins knocked again, then took a step back, eyeing the windows facing the street, wondering if there was another way inside. A metal gate to the side was too high to scale, but if it was unlocked he might be able to go around back. Before he could commit to that course of action, the door creaked open. An imposing young man, most likely an undergraduate member of the club, peered out the narrow gap, irritated. "Can I help you?"

"Good morning," Rawlins said, palming the compounding clay in his pocket as he strode back toward the door. "I'm Professor Thaddeus Rawlins." He extended his arm, offering a handshake.

"Okay . . . I'm Percy," the young man said, then shook his head, declining the handshake as though wary of a solicitor. "Sorry, we're not having any guests right now. Private event." Percy started to close the door. Rawlins could see his chances slipping away. He wedged his foot in the gap, stopping it. "Hey!" the boy said. "What're you—"

Rawlins's hand shot through the narrow opening and grabbed the boy by the arm, pressing the compounding clay against bare skin—and immediately, Percy fell silent, his demeanor changed. He looked at Rawlins's hand on his arm, dazed, and stopped his efforts to slam shut the door.

"Percy, you good?" someone called out from deeper in the house.

"Tell him everything is fine," Rawlins said quickly and quietly.

"Everything's fine!" Percy shouted back, his tone hollowed by the effect of the obscuration.

There was a moment of silence, followed by a door closing that reverberated through the foyer, and Rawlins stepped inside. He'd never been inside the Banestooth house before, more on principle than anything else, and quickly adjusted to the grand scale of the entry hall. The place appeared to be deserted, or close to it, though he knew it was home to twenty or more of the club's members.

"Tell me where everyone is right now," Rawlins said.

"They're down in the basement."

"Tell me what they're *doing*," he hissed.

"The ritual," Percy said vacantly. "*Fortunatis.*"

The words struck Rawlins like a physical blow, and he was silent for a moment as it all came together. The *Fortunatis Favori* ritual was a legend; its practice had been banned for centuries, but most modern scholars doubted it was *ever* real, considering it more likely to be a fabrication invoked at various historical moments to paint the study of arcane mechanicals in an extreme light—either positively or negatively, depending on how and why it was mentioned.

To Rawlins, it had always seemed far-fetched—the notion that one person's good fortune in life could be taken and passed along by the consumption of their blood. But since he had learned, only an hour earlier, of a quadrennial murder spree targeting Newlyn women, the notion of a ritual requiring human sacrifice seemed all too plausible. And now . . . Ellsbeth was missing.

"Take me to the basement," he told Percy. "*Now.*"

The young man nodded dumbly and led the way.

Rawlins's heart pounded as he followed Percy down a hallway, their steps echoing on the wood floor. The house felt eerily quiet, but as they progressed deeper inside, he could faintly make out voices, coming from somewhere he could not place, like whispers melting out of the walls.

They reached a door in the middle of a hall. Percy knocked on it twice sharply, waited a beat, and knocked once more, then said into the wood, "It's Percy."

Rawlins heard a lock turning, then the door opening, revealing a massively thickset undergraduate standing sentry on the other side of the door. He peered out at Percy and Rawlins, his eyes narrowing.

Past him, Rawlins could faintly make out a stairwell plunging into darkness, with the flickering glow of candlelight visible down below—and for a moment, the voices became clearer, chanting Latin in unison. But they fell silent as the door opened above and they all realized their ritual had been interrupted.

"Percy. The fuck are you doing?" said the sentry.

"Taking him to the basement," Percy said flatly.

The sentry's eyes narrowed on Rawlins, and Rawlins attempted to seize his chance at surprise. He reached out for the sentry's bare hand, hoping to press the compounding clay into his flesh, to use obscuration to claim at least one more target. But the sentry jerked his hand back. "Don't touch me."

Then he went on the offensive and grabbed Rawlins by the front of the shirt, forcing him backward, out of the doorframe, aiming to pin him against the opposite wall. Rawlins stepped back, grappling with him; the sentry was stronger, but Rawlins was able to twist out of his grasp, slipping past the young man's momentum, and attempting to rush down the stairs.

But his kamikaze plan backfired disastrously when the sentry recovered quicker than anticipated. As soon as Rawlins began running down the steps, he felt a boot between his shoulder blades as he was kicked from behind. He launched forward, and the world became a tumbling whirlwind of darkness and pain as he somersaulted down the steps.

On the way down his lip split open, his head cracked on wood, his right wrist rolled hard, his ribs audibly cracked. He came to a rest belly-down, on marble so cold it felt like relief from the fiery pain that was already blazing everywhere in his body.

He opened his eyes—or rather, his left eye, finding his right one already swelling shut—and his vision swam, struggling to focus, as he blinked away the blood that streamed down from his scalp. He opened his mouth, feeling a tooth that had loosened on the bottom, and spat blood onto the floor as he pushed himself up to his hands and knees.

Robed figures swarmed around him, their silhouettes ominously dark in the flickering glow of the candlelight, faces difficult to make out beneath hoods that left their faces in shadow. He heard various voices, murmuring with surprise as they approached, puzzled by his disastrously violent entrance. The voices were unfamiliar, except for one that spoke from directly in front of him: "You just couldn't stay away."

It belonged to his son.

As Rawlins painfully tilted his head upward, he saw that Max was gripping a curved knife, which gleamed in the flickering torchlight.

And beyond him—at the center of a ritual circle, surrounded by burning incense and glowing metal ingots—was an even more disturbing sight, one far more painful than any of the injuries Rawlins had just sustained.

Ellsbeth. Stripped to her underwear, hands and feet bound, with a gag taped over her mouth—in a pose of such helplessness that his insides convulsed with disgust. The most awful detail of all was the look in her eyes, where he saw the all-consuming fear of someone who knew they were about to die.

"How *perfect,*" said another voice, vaguely familiar—this one belonging to a man in a white mask wearing the only red robe in the room, marking him as the ostensible leader. "The secret affair was just revealed, and the aggrieved lover comes crashing in moments later to try to save her."

"Gallway . . ." Rawlins said, making the connection in his mind.

"It's quite fortunate," Gallway said. "We were wondering how much she might have told you about her suspicions. And now we don't need to worry."

Rawlins's mind raced, attempting to calculate a way through this. Pleading for mercy was pointless. He needed leverage; power was the only language they would understand.

"I have evidence," Rawlins said, trying to sound confident. "An email that will go out tonight, if I don't cancel it. Laying out your connection to murders going back *years.*" He looked around, trying to see if this was working. "But if you just let her go, I'll delete it. All of it. She won't say anything, and you can have me instead."

There was silence for a moment, then Gallway chuckled. "What do you think, Max? Did your old professor have the foresight to prepare an elaborate unsent email before rushing over here?"

"He never thought much of anyone else's intelligence," said Max. "But I never imagined he'd take me for *that* stupid."

Rawlins swallowed hard, his throat dry, mind reaching for any other stratagem. "Sorry, Tad," Gallway said. "Whatever you know—and whatever secrets you two kept—will be buried right here in this room."

Gallway gestured proudly to their surroundings, and Rawlins looked around, taking in the grandiosity of the Banestooth Club's secret ritual chamber. *No basement* indeed, he thought, remembering the words Ellsbeth had written beside the architectural drawings . . .

And with the recollection of her note came another image: the measurements she had made on the blueprints. The *radius* she had drawn. For a ritual circle of her own.

He wasn't sure what the ritual was that she had planned—or if she had gotten a chance to enact it. He looked at Ellsbeth again. Her painfully restrained body looked helpless, yes, and there was terror in her eyes—but that was not all. A ferocity was there, too. She had not given up. And he wouldn't, either.

"Would you like to do the honors, Max?" said Gallway.

Rawlins thought that he saw a moment's hesitation in his son, but Max hid it quickly behind bravado. "My pleasure." He advanced on Rawlins, knife flashing in the candlelight.

Rawlins pushed himself up to his knees, holding out his hands. "Max, wait . . ."

But his son was undeterred, hand tightening on his weapon. "You deserve this."

"I know I do, but . . . it's better if it's slower." Rawlins looked at Gallway. "Isn't that right? The ritual works more effectively if you draw it out. Make it hurt. Make her suffer, emotionally."

Gallway nodded, puzzled by this response. "It's true. Which is why it's fortunate that you showed up. So she can watch you die."

"Let me ask her something first," Rawlins pleaded. "I just want to ask one question."

Max darkened. "You're about to die . . . and the only thing you want . . . is to ask *her* a question?"

Rawlins nodded. Bitter rage clouded Max's features, and he pulled the weapon back, readying to slash it across his father's throat, and Rawlins quickly spoke again: "Are you really that scared to hear what I'll say?" Max hesitated, and Rawlins pressed him further. "You *know* the ritual works better if you make it last . . . but you're so wounded, so *afraid* . . . you can't bring yourself to do it."

Max lowered the weapon, his pride wounded, and spat the words, "Fine. Ask your question."

Rawlins looked at Ellsbeth, locking his gaze onto her across the room. "I just need to know . . . was it real?"

Max smirked. "That's it? The last seconds of your life . . . and you want to know if your little girlfriend really loved you?"

"That's all," Rawlins said. "You need her to be in pain for the ritual, right? Suffering? Well, let her tell me if she loves me or not . . . and let her say goodbye."

Ellsbeth moaned through the gag. Max looked her way, hatred burning in his eyes. "Let's hear it, then."

One of the Initiates ripped the tape off Ellsbeth's mouth and pulled out the gag. She spat on the floor, working her tongue, and Rawlins could have sworn that he saw the faintest hint of a smile tug at her lips before a single ragged word spilled from her mouth:

"Licorice."

ELLSBETH

A few of the blades slipped to the floor with a metallic clang, but some of them just hung limply in the hands of the boys standing around the circle, who had all gone limp as ragdolls.

Paul Gallway's eyes behind the white mask were hazy and unfocused.

"It worked," Ellsbeth muttered to herself. She looked at Rawlins. "Mass obscuration . . . a trigger word . . . a borax salt circle. I didn't know if it would work."

"I knew it would," Rawlins said. "It was a ritual you wrote."

Relief flooded through her body then like the antidote to a poison. Rawlins approached and untied her wrists from her ankles. "I don't know where your clothes are," he said apologetically. "Here." He pulled his jacket off and wrapped it around her shoulders.

Ellsbeth scrambled to her feet on unsteady limbs still twinging with pain from the contortion they had her in. "I don't care about my clothes. All I care about now is *them.* These fucking killers. How many girls do you think they've murdered over the years? How many Berties?" She turned to one of the slack-jawed boys in a cloak. "Do you remember her? *Do you remember Roberta Storer?*"

She found Curt's face among the group, and the realization spread through her body like she had swallowed ice water. "Did you know my sister? *Did you kill her? You dated her, didn't you? Tell me the truth.*"

"Yes," came his reply, half gurgled and dreamy.

"You killed her," Ellsbeth choked.

"Yes," he said again, every muscle in his face slack.

She felt frantic then, electricity flooding her system. Her muscles felt strange and alive, making erratic, jerking motions. She whipped her head around the room, looking at the blank, doughy faces of the boys of Banestooth.

"Lift your knives up," Ellsbeth said, and fifteen boys and Paul Gallway obeyed with disconcertingly puppetlike movements.

And that was when she saw him. Maxwell. His eyes were still alert and active, and fixed on Ellsbeth. He had backed out of the circle, hiding himself partially behind one of the columns. The obscuration trigger word hadn't worked on him. He must have been outside the salt circle when she cast the ritual. "Don't come near me," she said. "I can make them hurt you."

Max lifted both of his hands, a defensive, apologetic gesture, but he stayed silent. He finally looked away from Ellsbeth and over to Rawlins.

"How could you do this, Max?" Rawlins said. Ellsbeth had never heard his voice like that before, quiet and vulnerable. Heartbroken.

Maxwell glanced over at Ellsbeth, eyebrows raised, as if asking for her permission to speak. She shrugged, and Max took a step closer to his father. "I deserved a life, too," Max said softly. "I deserved a future."

Ellsbeth's eyes kept coming back to the blank faces of the Banestooth members under their robes. There had been no remorse or hesitation when they had been gathered around her. They had been ready to kill her, make her feel pain and fear, to make their own lives easier. As she stared, she saw one of them flutter his arm under a robe. It was a jerky, tight motion, a half-clenched fist coming to life.

"Ellsbeth," Rawlins said. "Potency is diminished by the number of targets. The obscuration isn't going to last long."

"Tick-tock," said Maxwell quietly.

Rawlins took a step toward Ellsbeth. "You need to—do something. We should call—"

Ellsbeth's mind flipped through the options fast as a carousel photo reel. "Do we have proof? If we call the police, they'll know I did illegal magic."

"But *they're* the ones doing illegal magic," Rawlins said. "I'm a witness, I can tell the police—"

"They're protected," Ellsbeth said. "By *Fortunatis.* Who knows if they even *would* get in trouble. Maybe the power of the ritual from last spring means they'd just get a slap on the wrist. And then they all go on to their good jobs and good lives. And wives, and kids, and houses and—" She was crying then. Hot, furious tears. The rage was the only thing inside her. She saw flashes of Bertie's body mangled in her bathtub. And then she saw the faces of the men in the hallway, the distinguished alumni grinning proudly from their gilded frames, celebrated and successful. Ellsbeth wondered how often they had nightmares of girls crying in darkened basements, of blood and knives. Maybe never. Maybe they convinced themselves that it never happened at all, happily allowing themselves to forget.

The boys beneath their robes began to wriggle slowly. Gallway's face was slowly contorting behind his mask. "Ellsbeth," Rawlins said, panic creeping into his voice. "Do something quickly."

"What can she do?" Max said, taking a step forward. His face was gaunt and gray. "No matter what she does, everyone is going to find out your little girlfriend was doing illegal magic. Another disastrous protégée for the brilliant Professor Thaddeus Rawlins." His fingers twitched and he coughed, the sound of it echoing in the cavernous room. "And the worst part is, nothing's going to happen to Banestooth. She's right. They're all covered under the *Fortunatis.* What'll happen? A slap on the wrists before they go on to their shining futures. I'm already fucked, it doesn't make a difference what happens to me." Cold panic crept into his cracking voice. "But at least it's some comfort to know that *she's* fucked, too, now. How does it feel, Dad? To know that you've ruined both of our lives?"

The color had gone from Rawlins's face. His unblinking eyes darted from Maxwell to Ellsbeth and back. "Ellsbeth," Rawlins said finally, in a low guttural voice that frightened her. "You can run. You should go. I can—"

The Banestooth boys were stirring in earnest now.

"The obscuration will last another minute," Ellsbeth said. "They're still in my control."

"There's nothing you can do," Rawlins said.

"Yes there is." Ellsbeth looked around the room. "Raise your knives," she said to the boys of Banestooth. The boys of privilege and potential. America's finest, its future. Its unrepentant monsters who murdered girls without a second thought to ensure their own lives would be blissfully free of friction or concern. "And stab yourselves in the heart."

RAWLINS

"And then what happened?"

"Then . . . they did," Rawlins replied simply. "As instructed, they stabbed themselves in the heart."

His description was a pale shadow of the reality—sixteen men, in perfect sync, plunging knives into their chests. Sixteen simultaneous eruptions of blood. Sixteen bodies collapsing to the tile floor, with sixteen growing crimson pools filling the underground air with the metallic odor of their exsanguination. Cries of pain and rasping final breaths echoed through the marble chamber but soon gave way to eerie silence.

Those details were seared into his brain. Along with the even more troubling image that followed: Ellsbeth's face as she witnessed the result of her words. Gripped with horror at what she had done. Traumatized by the violence she had just wrought . . . yet her expression did not betray a shred of regret.

It was the third time in as many days that Rawlins was recounting the events that took place in the Banestooth basement, this time for a pair of police officers: a detective named Marcos, as well as the chief of the Newlyn Police Department, Tanya Blakely, a petite, fiery woman in her mid-forties with short black hair.

"So if I understand correctly," Officer Marcos said, "they did exactly as they were told, because they were . . . what? Brainwashed?"

"The best way to describe the effect is a state of intense suggestibility," Rawlins explained. "It renders the subject incapable of resisting any instruction given by the person who cast the ritual."

"And that person was . . . ?"

"Maxwell," Rawlins said, repeating his well-rehearsed lie. "Maxwell Keene performed the ritual before he entered the house—so it affected all of the Banestooth members. But it didn't affect me or Ellsbeth, since we weren't there yet."

The police nodded, and Officer Marcos wrote something illegible on a notepad. This was the story Rawlins had been telling for three days now, the one he had quickly gotten Ellsbeth on board with, that they had both agreed to stick to. The one that would, if it worked, keep her out of prison.

Chief Blakely leaned back and folded her arms, looking thoughtful. "So Maxwell kidnapped Ellsbeth in order to bring her to Banestooth and get the club to do the fortune ritual . . ."

"*Fortunatis Favori*," Rawlins provided.

"Right. But then they refused to do it . . . So he did this *other* magic to take control and kill them all. As some sort of revenge." Rawlins nodded in confirmation, and the chief pursed her lips. "Okay, here's the thing that bothers me. If Max could control people, and he was trying to get them to do this *other* ritual . . . why didn't he just make them do *that*?"

"He tried," Rawlins said. "But the *Fortunatis* ritual requires intense mental focus. Once the Banestooth members were under the influence of obscuration, they were like automata. Following his commands, but unable to enact a sophisticated piece of magic."

Chief Blakely and Officer Marcos shared a look, but Rawlins couldn't tell if it was genuine skepticism or merely bafflement at the complexity of arcane mechanicals. He knew this part of the story was a bit flimsy, and he hoped that Ellsbeth, in her telling of events, was vamping through it in a way similar enough to him.

Blakely shrugged imperceptibly, and Officer Marcos moved on, consulting his notes. "So after Max made all these people kill themselves, he fled on foot?"

Rawlins nodded. "He demanded my car keys, and my wallet, and just . . . took off." This was Rawlins's other significant omission.

After the twitching of the bodies of the Banestooth members had finally stopped, Rawlins had seen his son backing away from the corpses, moving toward the stairs, preparing to flee.

"*Wait,*" Rawlins had said. Max had frozen in place, his face betraying abject terror at the prospect of going back to prison, and Rawlins had gone to his son and handed over his car keys and wallet, and given him rapid, breathless instructions: to take the car, pull out money from an ATM, quickly get as far from Newlyn as he possibly could, lay low, and disguise himself with a *persona* ritual until he could get across a border and flee the country. Rawlins did not say, *I'm sorry.* Or *I wish I could do more.* Or even *goodbye.* He said none of many things he needed to say to get to something remotely resembling closure, though that was most likely the last time he would ever see his son.

"It's interesting that Max didn't attack *you,*" Officer Marcos said. "He had just murdered sixteen people, and he leaves two surviving witnesses?"

"We posed no threat to him," Rawlins said. "And it would've been a very different sort of violence. Picking up a knife and stabbing someone is a world apart from killing with words." Again, the police officers exchanged a look, apparently seeing some validity to this point, and Rawlins added, "Besides—I believe that Max still has a certain affection for me. Even if I did interrupt his plan, he knows that I supported his release from prison."

"Bet you're not feeling so great about that now," Blakely said dryly.

"Of course." In truth, the guilt Rawlins felt at helping secure Max's release was complicated. He had drastically miscalculated the boy's anger and the danger it posed, and Ellsbeth had nearly paid an unthinkable price for his error. But Rawlins was unable to imagine *not* taking the action he did, given the harm he had caused to Max's life.

As for the results . . . Well, it was hard to call sixteen dead a *good* outcome, but he could think of few people more deserving of death. Without his intervention, it was unlikely that Ellsbeth ever would have revealed Banestooth's century of crimes; her evidence had all been circumstantial, and the club was well connected and deep-pocketed enough to fight a lengthy legal battle and keep their secrets hidden. But now the police were combing through the secret ritual chamber and years of records; the club's culpability in the murder of two dozen young women would be impossible to hide.

"Did you try to detain Max at all?" Officer Marcos asked.

Rawlins shook his head. "He was armed with a knife, and had just killed sixteen men. I was terrified and in shock. I handed over my car keys, and as soon as he was gone, I called the police."

Chief Blakely tapped a pen on the table as she studied him. "You were once Maxwell Keene's adviser, right? I'm no expert on arcane mechanicals, but as I understand it, the ritual Max performed . . . that was highly advanced, highly *illegal* magic. Where do you suppose he learned that?"

Rawlins was prepared for this; he knew there was no way to fully protect Ellsbeth's innocence without compromising his own. "You mean . . . Did I point him in the direction of certain books that I shouldn't have? Did I answer his questions, without considering the danger he might pose?" He let out a theatrical sigh. "I did. If you think that's a crime, go ahead and charge me. It wouldn't be as bad as the guilt I have to live with."

Blakely continued to eye Rawlins suspiciously. "Just keep in mind, Professor . . . We *will* catch him. Whatever story he has to tell, we're going to hear it soon enough. So if there's anything you want to add . . ." She opened her hands, inviting him to go on.

"I think I've told you all of it." Rawlins was acutely aware that Max might be caught; his son was a fugitive now, the target of a massive manhunt, with no friends and little money. But he was also very smart, very resourceful, and very motivated.

"Thank you for your time, Professor," Blakely said, as it became clear the interrogation would not yield any further information. "We'll be in touch if we have any other questions."

RAWLINS LEFT THE POLICE DEPARTMENT and stepped into the blistering cold. Half a dozen news vans were camped out front, and reporters rushed toward him as he emerged.

The Banestooth story was a sensation, and it only got juicier with each new detail that came to light. Sixteen dead. Dark rituals. Allegations of decades of murder, an elaborate cover-up. A recently released convict who was now a fugitive on the run.

When the news broke, one of the most crowd-pleasing parts of the story was how a teacher, concerned about his student after getting a worrisome text message, had gone to check on her well-being and ended up saving her from ritualistic murder. Rawlins had briefly been hailed as a hero . . . but the narrative changed the very next day, as soon as his relationship to Max came to light. The fact that he had been Max's teacher years before—and even worse, that he had spoken up on behalf of Max's parole—quickly changed the dominant perception of him from savior of a helpless student to champion of a mass murderer. As the story shifted, everyone started to believe that Rawlins had personally taught Maxwell Keene the obscuration ritual he had used to kill.

Rawlins waved off reporters as he hustled across the snowy parking lot to his rental car, which he detested. But he was holding out on buying a new one, since he was confident the police would soon find his beloved old BMW abandoned somewhere, and once the investigation had processed it, he was counting on having it back. Hopefully in one piece.

Rawlins blew in his hands to warm them while the heat kicked in. It was three in the afternoon and he was eager to get home—to a cup of tea, while the sun was still up, and the night's first whiskey, as soon as it dipped below the horizon. But he had another stop to make.

The campus was quiet but had not shut down entirely; classes in the arcane mechanicals department were canceled for the week, and students were being encouraged to make appointments with counselors. But the department building still showed signs of activity; students and teachers came and went, huddled against the flurrying snow.

As Rawlins headed in, he looked under every hat and hood, hoping to catch sight of Ellsbeth's face. It had been three days since they had spoken, in the charged moments before the police arrived at the Banestooth house, when they had hastily agreed on a story to tell, and on what they would keep secret—their research on writ magic and obscuration, their entire romantic and sexual relationship. Rawlins knew they would both be scrutinized closely for the foreseeable future, and if they were going to maintain the lie, they needed to act as if they had no connection beyond being student and teacher. He had deleted all their previous correspondence and refrained from texting or calling, since any communication could be monitored or subpoenaed. But if he were to run into her, purely by chance, surely it would not be suspicious for them to converse briefly in public.

He caught the eye of a dozen students, all of whom stared at him with a mixture of awe and fear while giving him a wide berth. He had been a recognizable figure on campus for his whole career, but this was different; he could feel the nebulous horror that his presence evoked. Even if he was not being accused of any crime, his proximity to such violence had lent him an aura of darkness, and people retreated from him as though it might be contagious.

Rawlins entered the arcane mechanicals building and headed straight up to Lennox's office; her assistant had him wait while she finished up a call. A minute later Lennox beckoned him inside, closing the door and gesturing for him to sit. "How are you holding up, Tad?"

He ignored the question and the offer, preferring to stand for what he needed to say. "First, I just have to know . . ." He leaned in, watching her reaction, as he asked, "Did you *know*?"

Lennox shook her head indignantly. "About the murders? Of course not. You really think I was aware they were killing girls, six blocks from here? Although . . ." Her voice became small, and she looked at the floor. "I wish I'd asked more questions."

"When Bertie died," Rawlins prompted her. "The autopsy . . . ?"

Lennox sighed, and when she looked back up at him, she appeared exhausted. "I was trying to protect the school. After everything with Max—the last thing we needed was another scandal, do you understand?" She used the heel of her hand to rub at her temple. "It was Paul, actually. Gallway came to me, offering friendly advice. It's just a tragedy, he said. And he was right. It was. He said that there was no use in stirring up trouble, bringing in the media, hurting the family." Her lip curled and she made a hard little sound halfway between a laugh and a sob. "If I had known what was happening, I would have killed him myself."

Rawlins knew Lennox well enough that he did not doubt her sincerity. He took a seat, a gesture of peace. "I'm sorry. It's been a tough few days."

"I can imagine," she said. "What a nightmare."

He leaned forward and got to the point. "I'm here to tender my resignation. Effective immediately. I can get it to you in writing, but . . . I wanted to let you know in person."

"I see . . ." Lennox pursed her lips, looking as if she were not entirely surprised but also calculating how to proceed.

"It's the best thing for the university," he went on. "My connection to what happened . . . it will overshadow any teaching I do for years to come. The college has to move on."

"Are you sure you don't want to take a sabbatical?" Lennox asked. "Go away, finish your book, come back in the fall?"

"No . . . I'm done here. It's not just the distraction my presence would create, it's . . ."

He looked out the window at the bare trees collecting snow on their branches as he searched for words. "It would hurt too much. Being in a classroom. Talking about mechanicals, when I know . . . where it can lead."

Lennox sighed. "You will certainly be missed. We'll draft a statement to share tomorrow, and I'll figure out who can take over your classes."

"Thank you," he said. "I'll send all my lecture notes and syllabi, which should make it pretty easy."

"Much obliged," Lennox said, pushing back from the desk, assuming their meeting was over. "And if there's anything else you need, just let me know."

"There is, actually," he said delicately, remaining in his seat. "A favor to ask, regarding . . . Ellsbeth."

"Right, the girl," Lennox said, with a pitying shake of her head. "Quite an ordeal. I'll suggest a semester off, keep her funding in place, and hope she comes back in the fall."

"She won't want the time off," Rawlins said. "She'll prefer to keep working. I just . . . need you to look out for her." Lennox frowned, not sure what he meant, and Rawlins continued, "Make sure she gets a good adviser. I know it can be hard to convince anyone to take on a new student midway through the year, but she needs someone who can challenge her intellectually—maybe Koenig or Sapersky."

"I'll try to help," Lennox said. "If she's as bright as you say, it shouldn't be that difficult."

"It might, actually. Because the thesis she's doing . . . it's on writ magic."

Lennox's eyebrows shot up, and Rawlins continued, "It's purely theoretical, of course, but—it's important, rigorous, *interesting* work. So you need to convince someone to let her continue those studies. And when it comes time to publish, I need you to back her. The work will be strong, I promise, but she needs access, and someone with credibility to stick their neck out and vouch for her. Now that I'm gone, there's no one better positioned to help her with that than you."

Lennox steepled her fingers, tapping her nose. "Tad . . . with the controversy I'm dealing with already—these murders, and *Max* . . . you want me to defend this girl's investigations of illegal magic? Even academically—"

"It will be a couple years before she's ready to publish," he said. "And I wouldn't ask if I didn't think she was a uniquely capable student. Who will someday be a great teacher and, even more important . . . a researcher and a writer. The originality of the rituals she's designed . . . Honestly, I believe Ellsbeth could do more for our field than either you or I ever did."

"You must think she's very special, then?" Lennox eyed him knowingly.

Rawlins tried to keep his voice impassive. "She's brilliant, and talented, and ambitious. Just like you were. I'm only asking you to make sure she gets the same chance at realizing her potential that you did."

Lennox considered him, folding her hands on her desk. "Does she know about Max?"

Rawlins sucked his teeth for a moment as he considered lying, but he saw no benefit in it. "She's the only person I've told in twenty-six years."

Lennox looked away and sighed in exasperation, thinking for a moment. "You were close with her . . . like you and I were close?"

Again, Rawlins considered a lie but saw no point. "We were close."

"Jesus, Tad . . ." She exhaled heavily.

"You owe me this, Maggie," he said. "After the way things ended between us . . . this is your chance to make it right."

Lennox rubbed her temples for a while, until—apparently failing to come up with another excuse—she finally conceded. "I'll do what I can."

Rawlins smiled. "Thank you, Maggie. That's all I'm asking. And I promise: She'll make you and Newlyn look good."

THE JANUARY DAYS WERE SO short that by four, the sun was already starting to dip as Rawlins began packing up his things to leave Newlyn for the last time. He moved quickly to complete the task before darkness fell.

From Lennox's office, he'd gone straight back to his own. He could have the department get a mover to pack up and deliver his books, but he needed to clear out his personal effects. He took diplomas and commendations off the walls now, stacking them in a box, then went through the drawers of his desk, finding it remarkably easy to toss almost everything in the trash. The accumulated memorabilia of an illustrious career—and it all felt like junk.

As he prepared to leave, his gaze settled on his dish of black licorice candies—paired now, eternally, with the only student he ever had who seemed to like them. He saw her so clearly, taking one the first day she had come to his office, with that curious mix of nervousness and bravado on her face. The memory aroused the particular strain of desire in him only she could ever evoke—but now it was undercut with an ache of emptiness, an unfillable hunger. He popped a candy into his mouth on the way out, savoring the bitterness, letting it get caught in his teeth.

Rawlins kept moving, trying to escape the specter, but found that the entire campus was haunted now, her ghostly presence grazing every place he looked.

He passed through the garden where she had first asked him to be her adviser, and could see it through hazy double vision; in the present, blanketed with snow, spindly tree branches reaching into the gray sky . . . and at the same time in the past, just as vivid, with flowers in bloom, and Ellsbeth beside him on the bench, trying to control her emotion as she told him about her sister. His chest burned with the thought of how callous he had been to her then.

He stopped by the Practicum to return his logs of elementals for whoever was assigned to take over his role. With the lights low, he could almost *see* Ellsbeth, standing at the center of the ritual circle. Vulnerable and trusting. He stepped into the space, closed his eyes, and could feel the weight of her bound hands resting on his shoulders the first time they almost kissed.

Last, he visited the auditorium where he taught his freshman lecture, retrieving the dog-eared copy of *The Arcane and the Ordinary* that he kept under the lectern for giving assigned readings. He stood there for a moment and his eyes moved to the place where he had first seen Ellsbeth, wearing that unfortunate red sweater. When she was only a girl in a crowd, looking both wide-eyed with curiosity and more mature than the students around her. Before he could have possibly imagined her talent and potential—much less that she would tear his heart open and change his life forever.

He carried his possessions back to the car, the load growing heavy, and left the Newlyn campus for the last time, turning on his headlights in the half-light of early dusk. His hands felt stiff and icy on the steering wheel, and he decided to stop at The Puddle Jumper to get a hot tea on his way home.

Some corner of his mind may have also seen it as the final stop on his tour of all the places that Ellsbeth's memory haunted. He paused at the glass door, looking into the cozy well-lit café at the table they had once shared. The one where she had pressed her leg against his and started all this in motion.

Then his breath caught in his throat. She was there. Not only in memory but in bodily presence, undeniable. The gray peacoat she'd acquired as part of her project of dressing like a "proper academic" was draped on the back of her chair, and she wore a cream-colored sweater rolled up to her elbows. She leaned over a table cluttered with notes, focused and diligent, hair tucked behind her ear.

He smiled; he knew the expression on her face well. The way she looked when she was deep in thought, lightly nibbling her bottom lip, practically begging to be interrupted with a kiss. Her mouth moved wordlessly; she was reading something she had written aloud to herself.

This was his chance. A run-in at a shared public place. Perhaps not *entirely* coincidental, since she would not have come here and sat at that table if she were not hoping he might find her. And he had.

Yet he hesitated out in the cold. There were a million things he wanted to say to her . . . but where to begin?

He could at least ask her the question that had plagued him for a week before her kidnapping: Did she use obscuration on him? Had his emotions been puppeted by a ritual? But as he looked in at her, he realized he already knew the answer. Desire like this was not the product of any ritual. As inconvenient and unreasonable as it may be, his love for Ellsbeth was the most real thing he had ever felt.

He could talk to her about the future, he supposed. Or really, their respective *futures,* since they would not be shared. He had set his course already, and he would be leaving Newlyn the next day; he had to go his own way and she had to go hers. Immediate legal threats surrounding the investigation demanded they steer clear of each other—but even beyond that, he could not be part of her life. He was disgraced—and if they were together, his reputation would follow her everywhere. With every paper submitted for publication and every interview for a teaching post, no one would *mention* their connection, but everyone would silently assess: Do we want to link our institution with all that ugliness?

Even if he explained all of that to Ellsbeth, she would not *accept* it; she would tell him it was unfair, and she would not base her life decisions around gossip. But he knew the way the academic world worked better than she did. He would not allow himself to limit her potential, and he could not possibly ask her to wait for him.

Which meant there was nothing to say but goodbye. And in truth, their goodbye had been said already, in the Banestooth basement. Amid the scene of unspeakable violence, when Ellsbeth, her skin sticky with evaporating sweat and shivering under the jacket he put on her, had collapsed against him, burying her head in his chest and surrendering to her sobs. When he held her close and whispered into her hair, "You're all right . . . I've got you . . ."

He did, at that moment. He had her. But he knew that he could not any longer. As the sirens approached, he knew he needed to let go. She was no longer *his,* in any sense.

So he stood a moment longer at the window of the café where his life had teetered on a precipice, and he had felt himself begin to fall—and despite all the chaos and pain that had followed, he could not possibly find it in himself to regret it. He could never regret *her.*

Then he turned away, shivering in the cold, and headed back to his car alone. Hoping that she would be all right, and that somehow, someday, he would see her again.

EPILOGUE

SEVEN YEARS LATER

As the auditorium for the Boston Cultural Society filled, the high ceiling created a cavernous echo of chatter and the sound of programs being folded and rifled through. The room fit three hundred, and as the sign on the door announced to the audience entering, it was sold out. Each member of the audience clutched their hardcover copy of *The Mechanical Mind.* They were told that Ellsbeth Storer would be doing a signing after the interview event had ended.

It was the type of turnout any publicist would dream of for an author, but Brianna was still on edge. This was the final stop of Ellsbeth's book tour, and Brianna wanted to send it off on a high note. But the moderator for tonight's event was a wild card, and Brianna did not like having any variables outside her control.

Sitting in the front row, she reviewed the evening's program, which featured a small black-and-white photograph of Ellsbeth in a turtleneck, not quite smiling and not looking toward the camera. She was only thirty-one years old, but her résumé was already staggering. Brianna had written the short bio herself: Dr. Ellsbeth Storer (BA, DAA, PhD) is the author of the number one bestselling book *The Mechanical Mind*, which has been praised as "the singular work of literature, psychology, and science that will come to define arcane mechanicals for the 21st century." It has been translated into twenty-five languages and sold more than a million copies around the world. Storer received her doctorate of arcane arts from Newlyn University, and her PhD from Oxford.

where she was also a visiting lecturer. She recently served on the White House Committee for Arcane Oversight. Storer divides her time between New York City and London. She lives with her black cat, Juliet. The final sentence had been Brianna's suggestion to help humanize Ellsbeth, a concession her client had made only begrudgingly.

In the eight months since the book's release, Ellsbeth had appeared on late-night talk shows and popular podcasts, in the process becoming that rarest animal: a genuine academic celebrity, who had written a book that dazzled both critics and readers, and who attracted crowds of hundreds in every city she visited.

Boston was strange, though. At every other event, the moderator interviewing Ellsbeth onstage was a celebrity or massive cultural figure. In Chicago, it had been a former First Lady; in Los Angeles, the movie star who had read the *The Mechanical Mind* audiobook. But most people in the audience that day in Boston had never heard of the man who would be appearing alongside Ellsbeth. The name of his book, maybe, sounded familiar, but the man himself was, to put it politely, a footnote. His biography in the program was just a few sentences long: T. M. Rawlins is the author of *The Arcane and the Ordinary*. He is a former lecturer at Cambridge University and Newlyn University. Currently, he teaches at Coleridge School in Boston.

Brianna had been skeptical when Ellsbeth insisted that she invite Thaddeus Rawlins to be the moderator for the event. I haven't talked to him in years, and I think I would be a little embarrassed to reach out myself. Do you think you could get in touch with him? Ellsbeth had asked over email.

Are you sure? Brianna had emailed back. I don't want to use the phrase "has-been," but I think we could easily find someone higher profile for such a prestigious event. The new dean of arcane mechanicals at Harvard already inquired to get a copy of the book, and we have an in with Helena Thompson (!) who's teaching at Tufts now. Obviously I also loved *The Arcane and the Ordinary* back when it came out, but Thaddeus Rawlins is sort of under the radar these days. Obviously, still happy to reach out if you want!

Ellsbeth affirmed that yes, she did want, and Brianna made it happen, because that was her job.

The lights in the auditorium dimmed and the crowd burst into applause when Ellsbeth appeared onstage, wearing a designer dress and black boots with a long, pointed heel. Brianna was impressed. Ellsbeth always looked impeccably put together, unimpeachably professional, but tonight was something else. A dress that was cut a little lower. A bolder red lipstick. And Brianna could swear she must have gotten a haircut that day.

In stark contrast, the event's moderator, T. M. Rawlins, wore a blazer pilling at the sleeves. The gray in his hair had begun an aggressive occupying offensive across his head, and his stubble, though well trimmed, was almost entirely gray as well. He settled into the chair opposite Ellsbeth, and Brianna felt herself relax slightly; even though he wasn't *famous,* Rawlins was clearly comfortable in front of a crowd. He had a nice, deep voice, and his questions were thoughtful and intelligent. More than once, Ellsbeth began what had become a pat answer before she stopped herself, paused, and answered with new candor and insight.

Brianna had to admit, Ellsbeth was right; inviting Rawlins had been a good move. Over the past few weeks, Ellsbeth's onstage answers to questions had become flat and rote; she repeated the same few talking points and winning lines that she knew would lead to an audience's applause. But something about Rawlins was bringing Ellsbeth back to life. She was lively and engaged, leaning forward and looking over at Rawlins as she spoke to him, almost as if she was unaware she was performing for a room of hundreds.

"I wanted to make sure this book was something I was proud of," Ellsbeth said. "I knew I could've put something out sooner, but it would've felt like a momentary cash grab, after . . . you know, everything that had happened with Banestooth Club." There were a few sympathetic murmurs from the audience, and upon hearing them, Ellsbeth turned toward the crowd and pointed at Rawlins. "In case anyone doesn't remember, he's the professor who saved my life." This was met with a chorus of applause, which Rawlins waved off, embarrassed.

Ellsbeth continued, "I knew my story was interesting and scandalous, and a publisher would have been happy enough to pump something out quickly that might have sold well enough before it was dispatched to bargain bins and oblivion. But I didn't want to be defined as the girl who survived what had happened."

"You've certainly proved to the world that you are much more than that," Rawlins said.

Ellsbeth took a breath, considering him. "Well, thank you. After it happened . . . I knew I had an opportunity to write something meaningful, and I didn't want to waste my chance, so . . . I spent years making it perfect. I blew past my first deadline—sorry, Deborah!—and my second deadline, making sure this book was everything I was capable of."

The audience applauded again, and Ellsbeth smiled out at them with professionally whitened teeth.

"A book is all-consuming . . . Did you find it hard to make time for a personal life?" Rawlins asked.

"I mean, I wasn't a *complete* hermit," Ellsbeth said, with a self-effacing laugh. Laughter from the audience. "But . . . Yes, I was consumed with my work. And the things I'd been through . . . there was no one around who had any idea what that was like. Maybe that was for the best, because the isolation *did* help me focus. But if I'm honest, it was a little lonely."

Brianna squinted, studying Ellsbeth closely. She had never seen such raw, transparent emotion on her client's face.

"I'm sorry you were lonely," Rawlins said quietly, with an empathy so genuine it felt almost *embarrassing,* as though everyone present were witnessing a moment far too intimate to happen onstage.

"What about you?" Ellsbeth said. "Have you had time to . . . socialize with your teaching schedule?"

"No," Rawlins said. "Not that I'm so busy, mind you, but I'm certain my best days of . . . socializing are behind me." To Brianna's relief, Rawlins then cleared his throat and turned outward, broadening the conversation to invite the crowd back in. "Well, your work is extraordinary—" Applause from the audience. "—and it's groundbreaking, the way you were able to marry ideas from the arcane arts with psychology. An understanding of the way the human mind and body interact."

"The original ideas—the linking of the body and the mind—actually all came from my thesis. I did my DAA dissertation on a controversial branch of arcane mechanicals called writ magic: the ability to control someone else physically.

"It was a struggle for a while—obviously, with such a potentially dangerous field, there were challenges, and some people didn't think I should be permitted to study it at all. Writ magic is illegal, and I want to be clear, I've worked very hard with the academic community and legal systems to ensure it's properly regulated. But fortunately, the dean at Newlyn, where I got my degree, was incredibly supportive of my work. Writing that thesis was one of the most challenging periods of my life. I had a few fellowships revoked when they found out what I was studying, and even though Dean Lennox supported me, not everyone at Newlyn did."

Rawlins's brow was furrowed. He looked at Ellsbeth appraisingly. "Your time at Newlyn . . . that was a challenging period?"

"Yes," Ellsbeth said. "It was. For a lot of different reasons. But I learned a lot. About arcane mechanicals and about myself."

Rawlins cleared his throat. "Knowing all of it then, everything that you went through . . . Would you do it again?"

"What do you mean?" Ellsbeth asked.

"Would you . . . do your thesis on writ magic again? When you could've chosen something easier. Less painful. Less lonely."

As Ellsbeth considered the question, she paused—for a beat longer than Brianna had *ever* seen her pause during an interview. But rather than leaning back as most people do when deep in thought, Ellsbeth leaned *forward,* coming a few inches closer to Rawlins, as she contemplated her answer.

"Yes," Ellsbeth said at last, looking directly into Rawlins's eyes. "I would have done it a hundred times."

Rawlins replied under his breath—too quietly for the microphone to pick up, but Brianna was watching with such rapt attention that she could make out the words from the shape of his lips: "Me too."

After the interview was over, Ellsbeth spent an hour signing hardcover copies of her book for audience members who lined up with their names printed neatly on Post-it notes so that she would spell them correctly. Brianna stayed at her side, helping briskly move the queue along.

When they were finished, Ellsbeth flexed her fingers and stood up from the table. "You," Brianna said, "are officially done promoting your book. Time to celebrate! I know a place nearby where we can get drinks, and Meredith Brauer, from Harvard? She couldn't come to the event but she wants to come meet you."

"I appreciate it, but I'm exhausted," Ellsbeth said. "I think I'll head back to the hotel."

"Come on, *one drink,*" said Brianna. "Meredith mentioned she's actively looking to fill a new research chair. It's an incredible position, and there's real money attached."

"I just can't tonight," Ellsbeth said. "But please, give her my regards. I'd love to meet her another time."

Ellsbeth slouched her expensive peacoat onto her shoulders and passed through the stage door, heading out to the street, and Brianna sighed. She exited the opposite way, passing through the auditorium to bid good night to the house manager before leaving.

The lobby was an airy space with windows facing three directions, dark now that the audience had left. As Brianna prepared to leave, she paused; through one of the east-facing arched windows, she saw the lanky figure of T. M. Rawlins, his collar pulled up against the night chill. Waiting.

Then Ellsbeth arrived, circling around from the back of the building to meet him. For a moment, Brianna felt mildly offended that Ellsbeth had clearly declined her invitation to instead meet with Rawlins. She could've invited him to come, too, if she wanted to see him so badly. But from the way they regarded each other, standing a few feet apart, it was clear that Ellsbeth did not want anyone else around.

Then Rawlins said something, inaudible from the other side of the glass, and Ellsbeth smiled. Brianna had known Ellsbeth for a few months, and traveled with her extensively; during that time, Ellsbeth had been unreservedly praised and applauded every night. Brianna had been with Ellsbeth when she got the call that she had won the Plaschke Prize, which included a two-hundred-thousand-dollar grant. She had watched, quite literally in the front row, as Ellsbeth's dreams came true. But she had not, in all that time, seen a smile like the one she gave Rawlins. It was a smile Brianna had not imagined her brilliant but emotionally reserved client was capable of. A smile of such naked, unreserved joy that there could be only one possible explanation for it. Rawlins cocked his elbow playfully, and Ellsbeth slipped her arm into his and leaned into him with unmistakable warmth and the two walked off, vanishing together into the night.

ACKNOWLEDGMENTS

This book exists thanks to the help and professionalism of several wonderful people. Thank you to Dan Mandel, the agent who saw this book's potential and has been a steady guiding hand for it from the very beginning; to Emily Archbold, for her keen editorial eye; to Paul Bogaards, for helping share it with the world; to Beowulf Sheehan, for making us look good; to Madi Margolis, for her careful and thoughtful behind-the-scenes work; to Caroline Schwartz and Sarah Schuessler, for being the first readers; to Ian and to Casey. Finally, thank you to Zoe Sandler and Chevalier's Books for bringing S. D. Coverly together.

ABOUT THE AUTHOR

S. D. Coverly is a pseudonym for the collaboration of Dana Schwartz and Dan Frey. Schwartz is the writer of the *New York Times* bestselling novels *Anatomy: A Love Story* and *Immortality: A Love Story*, and the host of the podcast *Noble Blood*. Frey is the author of the critically acclaimed novels *The Future Is Yours* and *Dreambound*. They both live in Los Angeles.

dana-schwartz.com
Instagram: @danaschwartzzz
TikTok: @danaschwartzzz

ABOUT THE TYPE

This book was set in Caledonia, a typeface designed in 1939 by W. A. Dwiggins (1880–1956) for the Merganthaler Linotype Company. Its name is the ancient Roman term for Scotland, because the face was intended to have a Scottish-Roman flavor. Caledonia is considered to be a well-proportioned, businesslike face with little contrast between its thick and thin lines.